SHADOW BLACK
TOM ARDEN

SHADOW BLACK
TOM ARDEN

Big Engine
PO Box 185
Abingdon
Oxon OX14 1GR
United Kingdom
www.bigengine.co.uk

Copyright © Tom Arden 2002

Typeset by Paul Brazier, www.brazier.mistral.co.uk

Cover artwork and Big Engine cover design concept by Deirdre Counihan

ISBN 1 903468 05 1

All rights reserved.

The right of Tom Arden to be identified as the author of this work has been asserted by him in accordance with the Copyright, Designs and Patents Act, 1988.

This book is sold subject to the condition that it shall not, by way of trade or otherwise be lent, resold, hired out, or otherwise circulated without the publisher's prior consent in any form of binding or cover other than that in which it is published and without a similar condition, including this condition, being imposed upon the subsequent purchaser.

CONTENTS

1	Ariette	3
2	The Pellucid Period	15
3	Pageant Faded	17
4	The Female Gulliver	25
5	The King and Queen	33
6	Vega, Arcturus	45
7	The West Tower	55
8	Scarlet and Indigo	61
9	The Line	73
10	A Positive Woman	81
11	The Negative Man	87
12	Hideous Thing	95
13	Fahrenheit 451	105
14	The Running-Back	109
15	The Weight of the Head	117
16	Punch and Judy	125
17	The Ice Bath	135
18	The Hidden Key	145
19	The Catcher in the Rye	161

20	Golden Band	165
21	Strange Heartbeat	169
22	The Sultan's Slave Boy	175
23	The Door to Dimension X	183
24	Galleons of Spain	193
25	The Charnel-House of Love	203
26	Travellin' Man	209
27	Prospero's Island	223
28	Crime and Punishment	233
29	Firmament	237
30	The Pleasure Faces	249
31	The Unveiling	265
32	Aftermath	281
	Appendix: The Films of Yardley Urban	295

To Antony Heaven

Shadow Black
July 14th, 1955

My dear Miss Locke,

This letter is an impertinence. Let me admit it at once – but declare too that I shall be unrepentant.

Mr Vardell has spoken of you so often that I cannot help but think of you as a friend. And it is because your name is so seldom from his lips that I feel I must implore you to join us at Shadow Black.

My reasons are wholly selfish. My husband is unwell, and his sittings for Mr Vardell certain to be his last. Of course my faith in Mr Vardell's talents is immense. But am I to believe he shall produce his best work – the masterpiece which shall stand as a monument to my husband – in the absence of his Intended (his Muse, I think I might say?)

I warn you, my dear, I shall accept no excuses. I know full well that your Aegean excursion has come to naught, and you are simply languishing in Highgate.

Wire me. Details of trains, &c., are enclosed.

I am, my dear,
Your sincere well-wisher,

Yardley

Lady Harrowblest

Tell Mr Vardell nothing of our plan – we shall give him the most tremendous surprise!

1
Ariette

The letter trembled in Harriet's hand. In the five days since receiving it she had read it perhaps a hundred times, always until now with a fascinated gratitude. Now it seemed almost to be a terrible mockery. Clumsily she bundled it back into her handbag.

She must not panic, she told herself again.

She stepped to the ticket window. Moments earlier she had seen a shadow, shifting about in the gloom within.

"Excuse me – "

There was no reply. Cautiously Harriet rapped at the glass.

"Excuse me – "

She felt her face beginning to colour. Was there no one there after all? Had the shadow been an illusion? Disconsolate, she turned from the murky window. Her hands felt sticky in her white cotton gloves and the brim of her hat, she was sure, had begun to droop.

The ticket hall pressed dismally around her, insistent in its decay. The tiles were discoloured and cracking. Tattered advertisements lined the walls, like litter plastered in place. Notices under glass announced ancient schedules of the Great Western Railway Company.

Harriet picked up her valise again, gripping the handle tightly. She had walked once already through the arch of the station entrance. The view from the steps was of an empty lane, narrow and shadowed by unstirring trees.

She passed back to the silent platform. The train, with a perfunctory whistle, had rumbled away minutes earlier and disappeared round a bend of line. No other passenger had alighted at this station. There was not even a porter.

She screwed up her eyes. In the afternoon heat the platform was divided, cut cleanly through, the zig-zag of the shelter etched hard against the tar. Across the tracks a chalky incline rose high above her, a blank but dazzling wall.

Panic, like a hand, gripped Harriet. Lightletter? It was some sort of resort town, wasn't it? She rushed back to the ticket office, rapping at the window.

"Excuse me! Excuse me!"

She pressed her face to the dirty glass. She *had* been right: a hunched silhouette was visible in the gloom. The figure stirred and lumbered forward. There was a sound like cracking, and the window-sash squealed up.

"Yuss?"

Harriet stepped back. The voice boomed alarmingly, issuing from a tangle of wiry whiskers, discoloured from white to a urinous yellow. Little eyes interrogated her through glassy half-moons of pince-nez, wedged atop the lumps of a tuberous nose.

Harriet cleared her throat. "This is Lightletter? I mean – "

"Oi am to take it, missy, you be a foreigner?"

Harriet, startled, said that she was not.

"Oi am to take it then, missy, you can read the Queen's English?"

Harriet said she could.

"Then good day to you, missy." The sash squealed down.

"Oh." Harriet flushed. She had been a fool. The guard had shouted out the name, she had heard it; the name was spelt above the platform, she had seen it: LIGHTLETTER. But could this really be the place? She rapped again at the window.

The sash slid up.

"*Yuss?*"

"This is *the* Lightletter? I mean, there isn't another, further down the line – ?"

Harriet wished that she had not asked this question. The old man swung away from the counter in disgust.

"Mother!"

"Please – " Harriet leaned into the window, her neck craning dangerously under the rickety sash. A sourness assailed her nostrils. In the gloom her eyes made out a mean apartment shrouded in cobwebs, choked with dust. On a desk, a thick ledger lay open like an exhibit. Behind the desk, yellowing papers were stuffed into a warren of pigeon holes or pinned, curling, to a crumbling board. A plump Queen Victoria presided above the mantelpiece and in a rocking-chair, unrocking by a low fire, a thin human form was propped like an understuffed Guy.

The Guy jerked up and shuffled to the window. A stick figure in a dirty shift, its face was seamed with vertical grooves.

"There is no Lightletter," the Guy spat. "There is no Lightletter but this." And its hand shot out like a lizard's tongue, snatching Harriet's hat.

Harriet started and knocked her head against the sash. She staggered back, hatless, as the window crashed shut.

She turned helplessly. A forlorn advertisement shimmered in her gaze. Blazoning faded seaside attractions, it depicted a boy in a bathing costume of the sort that covered his chest. Banded in blue and white stripes, looming above a sandcastle with a crazed grin, he stared at Harriet like a mocking malevolent imp.

Only as she turned again, in a second useless revolution, did Harriet see the new stranger who awaited her.

"My dear!"

The arms were outstretched.

Stretched, luxuriating, she murmured wordlessly.

His fingers traced the curves of her costume; ventured across the brown sleekness of her back. Stirring, she rolled her head. Her hair was a dark tumbling fire.

Shifting onto his haunches, he screwed off the cap from an upended bottle. Dark, pungent with coconut and spice, the liquid oozed into his hand. He spun back the cap onto the glass grooves; the bottle slipped from his fingers. His palms slimed together then slid, kneading, into the brown back.

She sighed, a high cheekbone pressing into her forearm. The sand's heat burned up through the towel. Between the parted fabric of her costume his hands moved caressingly. With curious detachment he studied the slithery flesh, the tiny wrinkles running in directions decided by his hands. Her skin had lost the immaculate texture he recalled it once to have had, perhaps in a sense expected it still to have. It was strange; each time he touched her there was a moment of surprise, her smooth-rough texture communicating a small shock, as on finding some seemingly silken garment to be in reality of a coarser cloth.

She rolled away from him, moaning. Her pungent back pressed stickily into the sand. Her fingertips ran through his forearm's bleaching hairs. He loomed over her, fascinated, in the blazing light. Her perfect face had cracked; the sun searched out each tiny line and sent running through it a rivulet of shadow.

He narrowed his eyes. Through eyes half-opened, like a camera-lens in gauze, he could smooth the cracked face into a blazing plane; he could drain away colour, he could alter light and shade. He could project the white plane back into the past, as if returning it to a flickering screen... Again the face was the tragic Madeleine's in *Boston Story* (Paramount, 1941); a white blur, the desperate Amanda's in *Damascus Road* (Warner Bros., 1938); darkening, the dark-eyed Emily's in *Mysteries of Udolpho* (MGM, 1935); lightening again, the ingénue Babydoll's, setting sail for happiness in *Showbiz Ahoy!* (MGM, 1930)...

It was all so long ago...

She reached up and drew down his dreamy face to hers. She sighed. The sun poured around them like oozing molasses.

He thought of the sea, the cliffs, the sun.

"Not to mention sexual intercourse."

"Pardon?"

"Sexual intercourse, Ariette."

"Oh."

"But of course, one hardly need be married for that! I myself have been married to – oh, a mere *seven* men, but I dare say I've been to bed with seven hundred."

"My goodness," Harriet said.

"In sixty-eight years, one may accomplish much."

The town of Lightletter flashed in and out of view around the twists of the hill road. They were discussing marriage, its advantages and disadvantages; or rather, Mrs Van Voyd was regaling Harriet with her views, delivered in braying patrician tones above the roar of a dilapidated Silver Ghost. Taking the sharp bends with alarming speed, the old woman accompanied her remarks with frequent wavings of an expressive hand, between two fingers of which she held a Dutch cigar.

Harriet's head ached. Sweatily rigid, with her left hand she gripped the passenger door; her right formed a restraining semicircle round a rather plump, rather smelly little ball of white fur which Mrs Van Voyd, in a loving coo, had introduced as 'Aldous'.

There were many questions Harriet might have asked: about Mark; about the town of Lightletter; about Shadow Black (why was it called that?). But Mrs Van Voyd steered the conversation, often as recklessly as she steered the Silver Ghost.

"Ever *had it*, my dear?" the old woman asked now. "Made *the beast with two backs*?"

"*Had* it?" Harriet faltered.

"Ah, the maidenly blush! *Marcus* not quite the thoroughgoing Bohemian, then? Well, I dare say we'll see you looking *enhanced* soon enough, hm?" Resting her cigar-hand lightly on the wheel, the old woman let her cigarless hand flutter to Harriet's thigh. She looked affectionately through her driving-goggles at Harriet, and Harriet looked uneasily at the liver-spotted hand. The long nails were painted silver, the fingers circled repeatedly with rings. "You must look upon yourself as a *postulant*, dear Ariette – myself as your Mother Superior."

Harriet cried:

"Watch out!"

Mrs Van Voyd pulled hard on the wheel, rounding a sharp corner with a squeal of tyres. She laughed, patting the dashboard of the decrepit motor-car. "Good old Ottoline. She won't let us down."

Harriet grimaced, holding the squirming lap-dog tightly. "Lightletter..." she attempted.

But Mrs Van Voyd was embarking eagerly on a narrative of her marriage, or perhaps it was her love affair, with a profligate Italian count. In any case it was an invaluable illustration of the ways of the male sex, or so the old woman insisted.

"Roberto was a deeply religious man," she shouted. "Whenever he seduced our chambermaids he refused to take precautions..."

Harriet drew a hand through the moist tangle of her hair. What was she to make of Mrs Van Voyd? From the moment she had been greeted by her new companion, she had felt herself torn between relief and alarm – relief, to be met at all; alarm, that Lady Harrowblest should send such an emissary. Dressed in a costume perhaps best described as a sari – appearing, as it did, to consist of successive layers of garish silk, wrapped round and round her considerable bulk – the old woman had at once seemed somewhat eccentric. A clashing shawl draped carelessly over her shoulders, patterned in what might have been an Aztec design; strings of bright beads swung from her neck after the manner of a Twenties flapper. Surmounting the whole was a slovenly turban, pinned above her forehead with a big flashing brooch.

Her face was as fantastic. Ruby-red lipstick rimmed her elderly mouth and the sagging skin above her eyes was coloured canary-yellow. From her earlobes hung twin miniature Grecian urns, jiggling in time with her turkey-gobble chins. She resembled, thought Harriet, no one so much as the fortune-teller into whose lair one of her brothers had made her venture, when she was a child, on the Palace Pier at Brighton. *Cross me parm wiv silva*, the fortune-teller had hissed, in broad Cockney, and Harriet, reaching for a sixpence, could not forbear from laughing.

She had felt no impulse to laugh at Mrs Van Voyd.

"My dear Ariette."

Kissed and crushed against the gaudy breast, Harriet had thought, rather, how strange it was that she could feel at once so unyielding, yet so passive.

"I may call you *Ariette*, mayn't I? You do remind me so much of my old friend, Ariette Comber... Do you know Baroness Comber, dear? – No, I suppose not... You may call me *Mrs Van Voyd*," the old woman added, and asked Harriet to excuse her *déshabillé*.

With that, Mrs Van Voyd had taken charge of the valise and led

Harriet down the station steps. It was not until they were winding through the Lightletter hills that Harriet remembered her box. It had been sent on ahead; she had meant – but she had forgotten – to ask for it at the station. Mrs Van Voyd dismissed the suggestion that they return. *Frederick* would be sent for it, she said with an airy wave, and promised to lend Harriet a *frightfully good book* on the subject of marital relations.

From the hill road the whitewashed town descended to the shore like a flight of steps, polished to a blinding glare. The sea beyond stretched supine, licking at the sand, a glassy cat curled about the curving bay. They could have been in Italy – Greece. With a pang, Harriet thought of the Aegean cruise she had planned with her schoolfriend, Mary Clevedon. Alas, Mary had contracted glandular fever just a week before they were due to sail. It was so typical of Mary, Harriet thought angrily. Mary had no spirit, none at all. And it was true what the other girls said – Mary's ankles were too thick. Really, they were elephantine.

At the next twist of the road Harriet saw the metallic dome, hovering unreally above the still sea.

"A pier!" she cried. "But it is a resort!"

And twisting back for a final glimpse she did not see the entrance to the tunnel. Ottoline plunged into blackness.

"My goodness!"

Mrs Van Voyd laughed and flipped on the headlamps. The yellow beams revealed a subterranean lane, curving into deeper darkness. In the tunnel Ottoline's violent shakings and the dogged grindings of her engine were amplified harshly, booming like discordant music.

"Shouldn't we slow down?" Harriet felt obliged to shout.

"Mm?"

There was a sudden screeching and a heavy object thudded past Harriet's face. She cried out, and Aldous began to bark.

"There are *birds* in here – "

"*Bats*, I should think, in these caves, Ariette!"

"Bats? Caves?" Harriet felt sick. Above them the moving glare of the headlamps disclosed a grotesque geography of rock – knotting, twisting, stabbing, jutting; swooping in smooth convexities, gaping in inverted chasms.

"These cliffs are filled with caves. A veritable honeycomb, as they say. This road was run right through them."

Ottoline rattled on through the strange tunnel. As they proceeded Harriet had the impression that they were climbing, first gently then sharply, much more sharply.

Mrs Van Voyd shifted gears, and declared that the Italian count, for all his charm, had squandered her entire income for the fiscal year of 1909–10.

"How?" Harriet dutifully enquired.

"Why?"

"Hm?"

"Why are you so moody?"

"Perhaps because I'm a fool. I thought it was real – "

"It is real – "

"I'm talking about the commission – "

"Not again, honey – "

"Yes, again! I've been here two weeks – "

"Not having a good time? Poor baby – "

"Oh yes. But – "

"You think I lied to you. Or is it that you *feel guilty*?"

"I'm certainly that!"

"Don't be a fool. You are kidding, I hope."

"Perhaps. Perhaps not."

"Not going to get all *dreary* about your little cousin again?"

"You have the strangest notions about Hattie – "

"I should think it's *you* who's got those! What the hell got into you?"

"I might have fallen in love – wanted to tie the old marital knot. I seem to remember a certain Miss Urban doing the same – "

"*Touché*? Is that what you want me to say?"

"You never told me why you married him."

"Pass me my cigarettes, honey, hey?"

"Why did you?"

"Can it, honey."

"*Tell* me – "

"*No*. Stop it, Mark. You're hurting."

"Oh. I'm sorry."

"You're not. You're laughing. I despise you – "

"You do not – "

"You're disgusting and crude. Sweeping that plain little schoolkid off her feet! Just how *loaded* is she, then?"

"Oh, very. Or will be – "

"I knew it… Say I gave you all the money you want – "

"You wouldn't. You just like to play with me – "

"Not a bad toy, if I may say – "

"*And* you don't take me seriously – "

"Poor baby – "

"Now is an example. Bitch – "

"Are you going to strangle me again? How romantic you are, honey!"

"Mark – "

"Hm?"

"Would you really go through with it?"

"I might have to. What would the Colonel say?"

"Your stupid old uncle!"

"You've never met him."

"Who'd want to? If there's one thing I hate, it's relations."

"I thought you rather enjoyed them."

"Oh, smart. I mean, like relatives."

"Your poor nephew."

"Poor nephew! I should have had him strangled at birth."

"Your sister wouldn't have been pleased."

"She was too stupid to be pleased or displeased about anything. Harder, honey."

"What do you mean, *might have to?*"

"Hm?"

"About your cousin. You haven't – "

"What a vulgar suggestion! Miss Locke and I have never attempted congress."

"Hm. Skirt pulled down and her legs crossed tight at all times, am I right? I just *loathe* her – "

"You loathe everyone – "

"I loathe *her* – "

"You haven't even met her – "

"Who needs to? I've seen your cute little photograph. What was that picture they did at Universal – *Freaks*?"

"Yarder, you are a bitch. Hattie is a very pretty girl – "

"If you like that brand of candy floss – Doris Day with a hockey stick, for crying out loud. *And* she's fat – "

"It's puppy fat! She's *eighteen* – "

"Shut *up*!... No, don't go like that. Mark, look – you're a successful painter. You've *stacks* of dough – "

"Hardly *stacks*. The last exhibition was a failure, had you forgotten?"

"That Pinker guy wrote the nicest notice – "

"Oh. Yes. Bertrand Pinker of the *Telescope*, of course."

"Come off it, honey. Do you think *I* could interfere with Eddie's papers?"

"I think you run his papers. You and that frightful old hag. She's your lover, isn't she?"

"Cora? You really *are* kidding – "

"She's your lover when I'm not here. Admit it – "

"I shan't. Get *off*."

"Tell me about 'Eddie'."

"I'd have thought you'd heard of him. Owns the Empire Press – "

"Funny. You know what I think? I think he doesn't exist at all. Just a delusion the world had. Or have you got him up in that tower, gibbering away in senile dementia?"

"Don't, Mark – "

"A 'sensitive spot'?"

"Let's not talk about Eddie."

"I never wanted to *talk* about him. I wanted to paint him. That's why I came."

"Oh, come on! Was that the only reason?"
"You've really got me where you want me, haven't you?"
"You make it sound like I seduced you."
"You have. You do. It's been going on for some time."
"I hope it goes on."
"You harlot. You beautiful harlot."
"You love me, don't you?"
"Perhaps. Perhaps not."
"Bastard! Oh – "

"Oh!"

The tunnel ended as suddenly as it had begun. A sharp curve in the cave walls led into a smooth, strangely glimmering passage. Then they were propelled into a flood of brightness, emerging onto a narrow acclivity of road cut into the side of a cliff. To their right a ragged chalky wall rose like a curtain billowing back, suspended eerily in the heat. To their left was a precipitous drop. The sea stretched below in a vast panorama, glowing silver-blue in the brilliant light. Gulls sailed high above, swooping and crying.

"My dear, you look positively unrelaxed!"

Harriet, struggling with the writhing Aldous, gripped him recklessly tight.

"Nervous, my dear, about our little surprise?"

Harriet said that she was not.

"Of course you must be."

"Oh yes," said Harriet.

"But you mustn't be, my dear."

"Oh no." Which was the correct answer? Harriet was confused. "In Her Ladyship's letter – " she attempted, not for the first time.

"*My* letter, really," said Mrs Van Voyd. "I do all the Yard's mail. She's practically illiterate," the old woman confided.

"Oh." The intelligence was strangely unsettling.

"He's been desperate for you, Ariette, of that you may be sure – positively pining for his fair inamorata. The Yard said to me, 'Cora, honey, we must have Miss Locke!' And here you are!"

And there they were. Ottoline tore round a last ascending bend. Harriet gasped. As if a curtain had been whisked away, the vast edifice was suddenly upon them. Concealed during their ascent by overhanging rock, the great house reared up from the clifftop like some monstrous creature, grimly scaling the empty sky. Black against the bright day, it seemed somehow to envelop into itself the vastness which surrounded it, draining away its blazing radiance.

Fascinated, Harriet barely noticed as Mrs Van Voyd's wrinkled hand alighted again on her thigh.

"Welcome, my dear. Welcome to Shadow Black."

2
The Pellucid Period

"Collidge – "

It was beginning again, the pellucid period. Collidge thought: *But of course.* Through the long years of his devotion, his tender watching, the signs had assumed for him a familiarity like his own heart's beating, like his own breathing.

The first stirrings had come that morning. There had been the twitchings, first in the index finger of the right hand, then in the thumb; then the pulse in the wrist was harder. There had been the new heaviness in the breathing… How many times had Collidge turned to the mask-like grotesque face, imagining about the mouth a ghost of movement?

But he had not imagined it.

Now came the voice: *Collidge.*

It was barely a human voice – marvellously, magnificently empty of expression. It pronounced his name as if his name were inconceivable, like an object utterly alien, retrieved from deepest space. If God could speak, thought Collidge, the voice of God would sound like this.

Collidge lowered his binoculars and moved back from the window. What thoughts he had indulged, only seconds before! Tracking the moving car, he had contemplated Van Voyd's expedition. Could this be the promised tutor for the boy? But the figure was female, surely. Now his puzzlement had vanished. It was meaningless. The world was contained in the West Tower. The loved, familiar tom-tom beat at his temple as he turned, gazing with secret rapture at the figure of his master.

Dispassionately the old man raised his good eye. Its depths returning, the eye seemed to absorb the light from the room like a black negative sun. It was as if a spotlight were shining on the face with a pitiless intensity that drew in tighter and tighter; to Collidge's fascinated vision the room around was vanishing, the starkness of the stone walls and the flooding bright sunlight fading to black. Shadow black.

"Soon I shall die."

"My lord," Collidge whispered, "it would be like God dying."

There was a heavy exhalation, a sigh. "But you shall never let her go."

"Oh no, my lord. Never."

"Her punishment shall never cease." The voice was becoming sharper, honed to a metallic edge.

Collidge knelt stiffly by the electronic chair. The buckled hand lay on the armrest like an injured ugly bird; the temptation to seize it was strong. Collidge looked up into the ruined face. The expression was still abstracted, wild. The pellucid period had not yet begun. Oh no. But it was coming.

"My lord, the portrait – "

"Tell me about the Empire."

Collidge bit his lip. He surrendered, of course, to the command.

3
Pageant Faded

"Tell me which."

"I don't know."

"Miss – "

"Milly?" Harriet did not turn.

"If these were my lovely blouses, I'd have a favourite I'm sure. Of course the pink's lovely too, miss." Milly's butter-yellow curls bobbed as she flitted ineptly about. "But you have some more lovely things, miss – surely?"

Harriet murmured something about her box.

"Ooh, miss! I do look forward to your box!"

Harriet did too.

"Now this is pretty." Milly held up a powder-blue evening gown which Harriet, at the last moment, had bundled into her valise. "I suppose all your clothes come from London. Or gay Paree?"

"Oh no." Harriet shifted on the window-seat. Through the open casement the sea stretched endlessly, glittering silver under the sunbleached sky. Pulsing at the window, the brilliant light contrasted starkly with the gloom of the interior – the ridged dark timbers panelling the walls, the stone-slabbed floor, the cold fireplace with its ashen sweepings. On the wall opposite the window hung an ancient tapestry; suspended above the mantelpiece was a large ugly mirror. The room swam backwards in its murky depths.

"I suppose you have an *exclusive couturier*. If I lived in London, I should have an *exclusive couturier*."

Harriet had to smile, against her will. If only Milly would leave! Yet it was impossible not to like the little maid, whose pert manner of speaking was curiously at odds with her nervous eyes and hands. She was a pretty girl, unfortunately disfigured by a hare lip.

"Her Ladyship has lovely things. Of course, your friend, Mrs Van Voyd – " Milly tut-tutted and rolled her eyes.

Harriet swivelled round. "Milly – " she began.

But Milly had changed to another train of thought. "Do you think Her Ladyship will ever go back?"

"Go back?"

"I'm sure I would. I should play a mature, but vibrant woman." And Milly held the powder-blue gown against her chest, strutting across the floor with an attempted elegance.

"Milly – "

"Her triumphant return to the silver screen!" Milly whisked the gown into the wardrobe and fluttered back to Harriet's valise. "I mean, if I were Her Ladyship," she murmured, colouring.

Harriet took advantage of the lull. "What did you mean about Mrs Van Voyd?"

"Miss?" Milly spirited the last of Harriet's possessions into the depths of an old oak chest.

"You said, *your friend, Mrs Van Voyd.*"

"Of course, miss! Mrs Van Voyd told me what great friends you are. Ooh, she has been looking forward to your visit!"

"Ah."

"You are funny, miss!" And the maid shyly brushed Harriet's shoulder.

"Have you been in service long, Milly?"

"A few years, miss. But of course it's not my real ambition."

"Oh." Harriet wasn't sure what reply she should make, so she said only, "Thank you, Milly. That will be all."

The door clicked after the little maid. Harriet sighed and turned back to the window, permitting her shoes to slip from her feet. Idly she hitched up her spotted frock, releasing a sticky stocking.

"Miss?"

Harriet started.

"I'm sure we'll be great friends too."

And the little maid was gone again as suddenly as she had returned. Breathing deeply, Harriet rested her head on her arm, staring out at the sea. A breeze was stirring and the open casement crack-cracked lightly. Dreamily, Harriet imagined she was looking from the cabin of a ship, becalmed in a vast ocean. From her lofty room the house appeared to be hanging over the sea. She closed her eyes.

Crack. Crack.

Harriet had been on a sea voyage only once in her life, when she was ten. The journey was from Bombay to Southampton, via Suez. India had become independent and the Colonel was retiring to England. The bright vistas of Harriet's childhood would be replaced now by grey London, and the tall forbidding house in Highgate. Pasty-faced maids replaced Ayah and the houseboys. The Colonel changed too, from the upright figure of Harriet's early years, resplendent in his uniform, into a dour man, suddenly old, shuttling restlessly back and forth between Highgate and his club.

When she thought of her father in these last years, Harriet saw him always in the one inevitable attitude: shielded behind his *Daily Telescope*, sucking on his pipe, mentally composing a letter to the editor. The letters were all on the same theme. As a sermon, whatever its text, deals at its heart with the love of God, so the Colonel, whatever item in the *Telescope* happened to prompt him, returned infallibly to his essential complaint: British civilisation was in decline. Chaps were letting the side down badly (this was his idiom). The letters were printed regularly, and the Colonel had become a minor celebrity. Harriet felt only a confused dismay.

From her earliest childhood, Harriet had been ill at ease in her family. Her mother had died when she was an infant, and her siblings consisted of six brothers, the youngest of whom was twelve years her senior. To the young Harriet they were remote incomprehensible beings, seldom seen, perpetually away at Charterhouse or in the Indian Army. When Walter and Rupert were killed in the war she could exhibit only the factitious sorrow one might display for the deaths of distant unknown cousins.

She had been a sickly child. In India the Colonel's friends, shaking their heads, had murmured that indeed she was, as they liked to put it, her poor mother's daughter.

Harriet knew her mother only from the photograph the Colonel now kept above the mantelpiece in his study. It was a very old photograph of a very young girl, dressed in the fashion of 1910. Miss Evelyn Vardell, as she had been then, had in her features none of the heaviness, the hint of plumpness, which Harriet had inherited from the Colonel: Miss Evelyn Vardell was beautiful. In 1910 she stared into the camera happily, a radiant girl on the brink of life. In the following year she would marry the Colonel. They met at a garden party in Highgate: on leave from the Indian Army, the handsome young officer was devoting his time in London to the finding of a wife. The beautiful young shipping heiress served his purpose admirably, or so he thought, and some months later, after a terse but ardent correspondence, she sailed to the subcontinent to join him. Her hopes were high, and highly romantic. They were not to be fulfilled. As Evelyn Locke she was to live for almost thirty years in Lucknow, Delhi and Lahore. From the first she pined for England, and from the first, she knew, she was something of a disappointment to her husband – never the formidable *memsahib* he had hoped she would become.

Years later, Harriet too would think of herself as a creature in exile, yearning in secret for her spiritual home. In England, she had imagined, she would become someone entirely different. Ceasing to be a sickly, shy, awkward girl, she would blossom into the gorgeous, sophisticated womanhood she knew in her heart to be her true destiny. It was not to be. She had been in England for eight years now, and the change had still to come.

She had thought that school might save her, but it had done nothing of the kind. In her five years at St Hell's she had failed to become the beloved school captain, hockey-field heroine, or even the schoolgirl detective she had dreamed she might be. It had been her own fault. Other girls had considerable handicaps, yet had achieved popularity: Mavis Blundell was spotty and fat; Etta Cranston was black; Sylvia Pym's father was a Labour politician. Harriet lacked some essential spark. Her first year slipped by in useless envy; her second she squandered on a half-hearted crush on her English mistress, Miss Padbury. By her third year, she was resigned to what she thought of as her fate. Her one friend, Mary Clevedon, was her true spiritual companion: a spiritless rich girl whose ankles were too thick. When Harriet left St Hell's a year ago it was not so much with relief as with dread of the life which stretched before her – a vista, it seemed, only of boredom and mediocrity.

There had been one escape, it was true, had she chosen to take it: Newnham College. But no. Impossible. It had been Miss Padbury's idea, and Harriet had known it was a bad one before she even applied. Why, the mere thought made her chest tighten with fear. Cambridge? A degree? Oh, Harriet enjoyed reading, but was she to be a bluestocking? Mary Clevedon had sniggered at the idea. The Colonel poohpoohed it in no uncertain terms. His daughter, straining her pretty little eyes? And Harriet, suppressing all misgivings, had to agree. She laughed with them both. No, Newnham College was no escape. If she had gone there, what then?

Why, she would never have met Mark Vardell!

Harriet opened her eyes, staring again at the glittering sea. Soon it would be time for dinner. Soon she would see Mark. She screwed her hands up tight, aware with sudden intensity of the golden band that gleamed on her engagement finger. She studied it proudly.

It was then that an extraordinary thing happened. From somewhere, from what direction she could not tell, Harriet heard a disembodied high-pitched voice, crying unmistakably *"No!"* The cry was repeated, then repeated again. At the third cry, a heavy object plummeted past the window.

It was a book.

The book had fallen with its covers open, and as it fell the leaves began to detach themselves, to flutter out effortlessly from the binding like birds released from a cage. For one suspended moment the pages were borne aloft, and Harriet, leaning from the casement, found herself surrounded by the billowing flock. She gasped with pleasure; at the last instant she grabbed, absurdly, at the air.

The page-birds were gone.

Turning from the window, Harriet felt a curious bereavement. Forlorn, she saw a single bird dashed against the floor. She picked it up. It was a small thin yellowed stained brittle rather wrinkled page of closely-printed text. Harriet read: *In a little time I observed the noise and flutter of wings to increase very fast.* She turned the page; on the verso was an engraving, depicting an eagle soaring high above the sea. Clasped in the eagle's beak was a ring, like the ring of a ring-bolt, from which swung, precariously, a curious cube-shaped object. In the sides of the object were rectangular openings, criss-crossed with lattice-work, and through the closest of these, scored across with lattices, was a tiny, stricken, human face.

Harriet smiled. The image came back to her of Miss Padbury's room at St Hell's, all faded chintz and musty books. It was winter, late in the afternoon, and Miss Padbury was reading. Six girls, hugging their knees on a Turkey carpet, clustered adoringly round the mistress's chair. Her voice was deep and rich, mingled in Harriet's memory with the redolence of her tobacco. The fire crackled in the grate; on a low table was the debris of a massive spread. Miss Padbury read, *In a little time I observed the noise and flutter of wings to increase very fast...* Ah, Miss Padbury! She drove her own motor-car, cut her hair short, and once she swore in class. Pressed close against the ankles of Mary Clevedon, Harriet gazed up marvelling, flooded with love for the tight tweedy suit, the moving jaw. Outside the snow fell softly; soon the curtains would be drawn.

Harriet thought of Newnham College.

How disappointed Miss Padbury had been!

Shaking herself, Harriet focused on the page. From where had the book come? Why had it been thrown? Slipping back into her shoes, she crossed quickly to the door, but it was stuck. Harriet tugged the handle. It was several seconds before she realised that the door was not stuck. It was locked.

"Milly! Milly!"

It was useless. The door was inches thick. Harriet pressed her hand to her temple.

The wall next to the door was covered entirely by the tapestry. Abstractedly Harriet reached for the ancient knottings. The texture was rough and damp and she drew her hand away. There was something terrible about the tapestry. Faded by time, its subject had long vanished into a grey-brown murk of fabric – she could make out only what appeared to be female figures clothed in classical robes, taking part in some confused, eventful pageant. Now the grey-brown murk looked ready to fall, a great tensile network held in suspension as if before the moment of collapse.

Harriet turned back to the cavernous room. Massive, indivisible, the bed stood by the window, a mysterious cave, a covetous blackness absorbing light. Gingerly she perched on the edge. How high the mattress was! Her feet did not touch the floor.

A languorous melancholy stole over Harriet. Already the house had cast a spell on her. She thought of it stretching mysteriously beyond her room, a dark convolution of decaying staircases and sinister, cool corridors. She crossed for a moment to the window, looking anxiously out; then, as if in surrender, she sank onto the bed. The discomfort was extraordinary. But her shoes dropped over the edge. She reached beneath her frock, peeling down her stockings. She breathed slowly, staring at the pendulous canopy.

4
The Female Gulliver

A story:

Once upon a time and a very good time it was there was a man called Theodore Lash. Lash was the youngest professor in the history of Harvard, and the youngest man ever to win the Nobel Prize. At the age of seventeen he had revolutionised human understanding of the cosmos, propounding the Curvo-Linear Theory of Time. When our story begins, Lash is thirty-seven and bent on breaking the time barrier.

Clifford and Hugo Wells had idolised Lash since grade school. The brothers yearned to study under Lash. In due course they did, but their talents were unequal. Clifford's were undoubted; effortlessly he acquired his doctorate and a place on the Lash research team. Hugo's grades were abysmal. He became a janitor in the university labs, looking on enviously as Clifford worked with their hero to build the Lash Curvo-Lineator, the world's first time machine.

It was after seeing Lash in a TV interview that Hugo had had the one great idea of his life. The interviewer had asked Lash to recall the moment when his great theory first occurred to him. "I know the day, the hour, the minute," said Lash. He had been working late in his Harvard office, jotting down figures, when suddenly the equation came to him which was to revolutionise modern science. "I leapt to my feet and cried 'Eureka!' It was 2.15 a.m., July 14th, 1931." Furiously Hugo scribbled down the date and time. Soon the prototype of the Curvo-Lineator would be ready. Hugo could hardly contain his excitement.

The time came at last. Late one night, Hugo emerged from his hiding place in the deserted lab and operated the time machine. Lights flashed. There was a maelstrom of colour. Hugo was snatched into a dizzying vortex.

Next thing he knew, he was standing in a dark corridor outside Lash's office. Through a glass panel in the door he saw a teenage Lash, head bent low over a sheaf of papers. On the wall, the glowing green of a clock-face showed the time – 2.15. Lash leapt to his feet and cried "Eureka!" Hugo burst through the door. In his hand was a cudgel. He dashed it against his hero's skull. The teenage professor crumpled to the floor. Hugo kicked the corpse aside and seized the sheaf of papers. The Curvo-Linear Theory! The Nobel Prize! It was his now, all his! He stuffed the papers into his jacket and sprinted from the office...

Continued on p. 76.

Toby flipped impatiently to the back of the magazine. 76, 76? He groaned aloud. Between pages 74 and 77 was only a jagged, torn edge. He threw the magazine across the floor and lay back, disgruntled, on his unmade bed. The late sun streamed into his attic room, glinting on the little silver-banded telescope that protruded through the open window.

The magazine had been Toby's last. In Exeter, where Mrs Van Voyd had stopped during the journey down to Shadow Black, Toby had found a second-hand bookstall which displayed, as in a vision, a huge pile of *Astronomical Stories*. He had read this magazine only once before, when the particular friend he knew as EEL had brought back a copy from his holiday in New York. Once was enough for Toby. Immediately, *Astronomical Stories* became his favourite thing. He had thought it impossible to find in England. And there, suddenly, were seventy, eighty, a hundred issues. He bought them all.

"Goodness me, Tobias," said Mrs Van Voyd, inspecting one of the more lurid covers. "They are *decent*, I hope?"

He had only winced.

That summer Toby Chance was fifteen years old, a slender, wiry boy with a tousled mass of straw-coloured hair and a large-eyed earnest face. In the evenings he made efforts – often regrettable – to dress for dinner; at present he still wore his daytime summer costume of crumpled khaki shorts and a dirty cricket shirt, not tucked in, the sleeves rolled loosely back.

He flopped an arm over the side of the bed, pawing the bare floor for his cigarettes and matches. Cigarettes made him mildly sick, but he was doing his best to conquer the aversion. Smoking was to be his holiday accomplishment. When he went back to school he would be a confirmed addict, compelled to keep supplies in innumerable secret places in order to relieve his relentless cravings. The risk of discovery would be constant, the threat of expulsion perpetual. Life would be a round of unending excitement.

He sat up, fearing a fit of coughing. With fleeting fastidiousness he inspected the squalid clutter of the attic: the piles of dirty shirts and underpants and smelly towels on the floor; the whorls of dust in the corners and the cobwebs on the walls; the ground-in cigarette ash on the room's solitary mat; the little mountain of butts by the bed. Some days after his arrival, Toby had found one of the maids touching his telescope, and told her he would clean his room himself.

He stubbed out his cigarette on the floor, swallowing back the sourness in his mouth. A strange anxiety throbbed in him.

"I wish I'd never come," Toby said aloud.

He had exhausted the amusements of Shadow Black. He had roamed through the dark ugly labyrinth of the house until its mysteries had begun to bore him; he had swum in the sea; he had scanned the stars at night; now he had finished his *Astronomical Stories*. None of these things, in any case, had taken away the gnawing restless feeling he did not quite recognise as loneliness.

He gathered up his espadrilles and one of the less dirty towels, and set out for the beach.

Mark Vardell splashed his face again. Straightening, he stepped back from the enamel bowl and pulled away the towel from around his waist. When he had dried himself he let the towel fall to the floor and stood for a minute, studying his naked form in the dressing-table mirror. There was no doubt that he was a handsome man – in the summer evening light, a handsome boy. He pushed back his lank dark hair from his forehead, admiring his angular features. Only the thought that he was now thirty disturbed his self-satisfaction. Thirty!

"I've laid out your things, sir."

Mark did not reply. He reached for a small glass bottle on the dressing-table, slapping his skin with a pungent cologne. Thirty. The thought was appalling. It was also difficult, Mark had found, to banish for any length of time. Until this year he had lived, it seemed to him now, in a willed unconsciousness, obliterating perpetually his awareness of time. In the Sixth, he had thought himself on the brink of life; he had retained this sense throughout the years that followed. Until now.

"Will that be all, sir?"

Mark, as if in acknowledgement, turned towards the bed. Thomas picked up the towel. *In a perfect world*, Thomas was thinking, *I would not be a servant. This is not my real existence.* He quietly removed the shaving-bowl, and left.

Mark dressed mechanically. He could have groaned with despair. That his position was intolerable was clear; that he would continue to tolerate it was equally clear. How eagerly he had fallen for the 'commission' story! He should have known it was absurd. But the last exhibition had left him devastated. Perhaps he had wanted to throw everything away.

He thought fleetingly of his cousin Hattie. His reformation had not lasted long... And yet he had been sincere in the beginning, he had!

Once upon a time and a very good time it was Harriet was invited to Vardell Grove in Wiltshire, the home of her Aunt Antonia. The old lady's husband had died some months before, and she hoped that her niece might make a suitable companion. The summer visit was designed to assess Harriet's suitability. As it happened, a few days were enough to convince Lady Antonia that Harriet was indeed, as she had hoped, *a sensible, plain creature, unlikely to make a good marriage.* She was ideal.

For some months Harriet lived contentedly at Vardell Grove, accompanying her aunt in a quiet routine of church-going, needlework, flower-arranging, visiting the poor, and reading aloud to the old lady from the novels of Edgar Wallace. If sometimes the young companion thought with a pang of Newnham College, she brushed the thought aside with a laugh. No, the Colonel had been right, and Aunt Antonia agreed. A bluestocking? The thought was absurd. Harriet was sorry, that was all, to have let down her old schoolmistress. Poor Miss Padbury! She meant well. But her expectations had always been too high.

It was that Christmas that Harriet first met her cousin Mark. The young man was visiting Vardell Grove – and his mother – for only the second time in almost thirteen years. The first had been earlier that year, after his father's death. That particular visit had been unfortunate, Harriet gathered, terminating abruptly on the afternoon of the will-reading, when Mark had learnt that his father had disinherited him.

On the afternoon before his arrival, Aunt Antonia recounted to Harriet something of his history.

"Oliver was so unbending," she sighed, "and Mark followed suit. Oliver expected Mark to join the business, like Vivian and William; Mark declared defiantly that he was going to be a painter. Mark was expelled from Charterhouse – a dreadful business; but dear Oliver did make things so much worse. The war was on by this time, and Mark simply disappeared into the army. He never wrote, never came home. After the war he remained as obstinate.

"I've followed his career with interest, of course," the old lady added, producing from the bottom of her work basket an article she had clipped from a magazine.

Harriet took it curiously. The story was from *Society Illustrated*, January 1954. Accompanying a monochrome reproduction of a rather alarming-looking painting, it was headed:

The Quintessence of Vardellism

Some say he's a genius [*it read*]. Some say he's a charlatan. But his name is on everyone's lips. He's Mark Vardell, guru-prophet of the most controversial new school of painting today.

Scion of a distinguished shipping family, English-born Vardell, 29, broke with family tradition to study art after the war. In Paris he sat at the feet of Henri du Garde, leader of the 'irrealist' school. But Vardell was soon disillusioned with du Garde's abstract style. "I wanted to be a portrait painter," Vardell explains. "But the conventional portrait is a limiting form. It shows only the surface of things. I want to get beneath that surface."

In 1948, Vardell left France for the United States. "The artist must respond to the world in which he lives," Vardell says today. "To understand our contemporary predicament, one must come to terms with America." It was in New York that Vardell embarked upon the 'commercial' work that has earned him the acrimony of some critics. The artist is unrepentant. "The images of advertising are the icons of the modern age. I wanted to understand that iconography."

It was also in New York that Vardell embarked upon the unusual series of portraits that was to earn him fame: the tableaux depicting Manhattan hostess Regina Drane, posed as heroines of history or myth, against backgrounds of dream-like distortion. The shock-waves rocked the art world. When *Virgin Queen in a Vat of Vomit* was exhibited in New York, outrage from morals groups combined with vehement critical debate to make Vardell the most talked-about young painter in America. Soon celebrities of all sorts were queuing to be depicted draped with melting clock-faces, semi-clad with dead donkeys, or wandering amongst forests of 'phallic' symbols. It was a style that critics were to dub 'Society Surrealism'.

Since 1952 Vardell has worked from a fashionable studio in London's West End. *Bordello Boadicea,* his recent portrait of Princess Margaret, provoked furious debate. "Vardell's skill as a draftsman is unrivalled," insists Bertrand Pinker, art critic of the *Daily Telescope.* "That is the quintessence of Vardellism. There's not a young painter in England – or America – who can match it." Brander Thornquist of the *Evening Watch* disagrees. "Vardell's work gives an illusion of being challenging," Thornquist argues. "But it is merely decorative. It lacks a compelling vision of life." The controversy continues.

"I'd heard of the Princess Margaret picture," Harriet murmured, "but I didn't realise – "

"No?" Aunt Antonia arched an eyebrow.

Harriet had realised nothing about her cousin. The prospect of his visit alarmed her. She expected, at the least, a bearded, foul-mouthed Bohemian. Her surprise was great when she was confronted instead with a smooth-shaven, handsome young man, dressed in the costume of a City gent. Only his hair, which was a little too long, suggested that her cousin had not joined the family firm. The quintessence of Vardellism? Indeed.

But the impression was false. When Vivian, William, their wives, and numerous children descended shortly afterwards on Vardell Grove, Harriet saw how much Mark differed from his family. The festivities were torture. Vivian and William separately were barely tolerable; together they were impossible. They were identical twins. Both were fat, forty, selfish, self-satisfied and given to declaiming business anecdotes in hee-hawing voices across the dinner table. Their wives were two interchangeable bitches, their children noisy ill-mannered brats. Aunt Antonia adored them all.

Frequently Harriet found herself thrown together with Mark. Huddled with him in a corner of the drawing room, she would watch, fascinated, as he caricatured with quick pencil strokes the stomping form of his most obnoxious nephew, or the porcine features of Vivian and William. In afternoon walks through the wintry grounds, Harriet would tell Mark about India, or St Hell's – but not, at that time, about Newnham College – and Mark would tell Harriet about Charterhouse, or the army, or his life as an artist. His stories about the silly people he had painted made her laugh aloud.

On New Year's Day Mark took Harriet skating on the frozen stream at the bottom of the estate. All the way, as they trudged through the snow, he reminisced about his childhood, and the skating excursions of twenty years before. When they went out onto the ice, Harriet fell. He rushed to assist her. When they returned to the house they were engaged.

Lady Vardell's response was unequivocal. At once, and with undifferentiated vehemence, she denounced her son and her niece alike.

Whether the son was a foul seducer, or the niece a designing harlot, it was clear that they both merited only condemnation. Vivian and William, outraged beyond reason, pitched furiously into the fray.

Next morning, when Mark left for London, Harriet left too, a failure as a companion after all.

Harriet had slipped into reverie; reverie slipped imperceptibly into dream.

She dreamt that she was leaning in an open casement, gazing at the sea unfurling far below. Thunder crashed above, but it was not thunder: it was the beating of massive wings. Her house lurched precariously as it was carried through the air. Then her house began to fall. It plummeted down and down, and as it plummeted it began to wheel round, at first slowly, then faster and faster. She did not cry out, she did not exclaim in terror, she seemed incapable of reacting at all. Transfixed, the female Gulliver watched the spinning ocean with a blank fascination, the whirlpool of the air whizzing past her window as she was borne inexorably down, down…

When her house crashed into the water there was a cataclysm of sound. The great wave broke crashing into the house, surging through the casement with an irresistible power. Only then did Harriet cry out. Desperately she clawed at the yawning casement, struggling to shut off the inundating tide…

Someone grabbed her arms.

"Miss! Miss!"

Harriet's arms were stretched above her head, her wrists imprisoned in Milly's firm grip.

"Milly! How long have I slept?"

"Long enough, miss. It's time to dress for dinner."

5
The King and Queen

The private beach at Shadow Black was truly, almost eerily, private: a rectangle of sand bounded on three sides by rising steep rock, on the fourth by the sea, it was reached first by a narrow cliff path that wound many yards beneath the level of the road, then by a long flight of steps cut in rock that descended the cliff-face in a steep diagonal.

Toby scrambled down the last of the steps and ran down the shelving sand. Eagerly he tugged his shirt over his head. In the daytime heat, the sand was a bland inscrutable brightness; now, in the evening, under the crimson sky, it took on an air of unearthly imminence. Kicking away his shorts, he plunged into the molten sea.

Behind him the blackening cliffs rose like guardians or massy, ineffable portents.

"And this, my dear – but surely you know?"

Harriet faltered. She had no idea.

"Travers, my dear – Mr Jellicoe Travers!" Mrs Van Voyd's eyes glittered mischievously.

"Of course," said Harriet. "Oh yes, of course." Instinct forced her to this feigned enlightenment. The little man, beaming, reached for her hand, pressing it to his lips with eager gratitude. His lips were clammily moist on her skin, and his plump fingers, holding hers, felt perhaps as sausages might, were one to handle them in a half-cooked state.

"Charmed, Miss Locke. Charmed and privileged." Mr Travers released her hand and resumed his seat at the piano. His sausage fingers pressed lightly on the keys.

The little party had gathered in what Mrs Van Voyd called the drawing room. It was an absurd name, in truth: the room was the Great Hall of an Elizabethan house. Above them the dark-beamed ceiling rose massively; beneath them the floor stretched, coolly sparse, between the French windows (added on the sea-facing side) and the minstrels' gallery, opposed at each end of the interminable chamber. Through the wide windows the light was brilliant, disclosing pitilessly the shabby furniture, the worn tiles of the floor, the mouldering stags' heads, heavy with antlers, suspended mournfully above the high wainscoting. At the far end of the room stood a large golden gong.

Harriet gazed about her with attempted insouciance.

"A sherry, Ariette." Mrs Van Voyd, bearing the offering, tottered towards the young guest on impossible heels. The old woman's cigar was clamped between her teeth and she clutched against her breast the reeking Aldous.

In the hours since Harriet's arrival Mrs Van Voyd had squeezed herself into a sparkling silver skin-tight dress. Replacing the turban was a flame-red wig, while around her considerable middle the old woman had tied a broad silken sash, matching exactly the shade of her wig, and looped into a massive bow. She bore some resemblance to a Christmas parcel, somewhat inexpertly wrapped.

"Thank you, Mrs Van Voyd."

Mrs Van Voyd smiled and said:

"Oh, but poor Aldous – "

And Harriet, receiving the glass in her hand, was startled when Mrs Van Voyd at once thrust the little creature's muzzle into the rim. "You're thirsty, aren't you, darling?" the old woman cooed. She stroked the little dog's furry white neck as he lapped greedily in the glass. The sticky liquid spilt over Harriet's fingers.

"Mrs Van Voyd, I must protest!"

It was not Harriet who spoke, but Mr Travers.

"About that animal you are *unconscionable*. Miss Locke, would you not say she was *unconscionable*?"

Harriet thought it best to be noncommittal.

"Ignore him, Ariette. Poor Aldous! Silly old Jelly has no finer feelings.

He can hardly comprehend the *profundities of the heart.*"

Mr Travers, affronted, said this was unkind, and as if to defend himself he broke into song:

> *Come into my arms*
> *With your tender charms,*
> *Let me feel the bliss*
> *Of your magic kiss,*

his high reedy voice warbled tunelessly.

"He imagines," Mrs Van Voyd murmured to Harriet, "that *that* proves he has a heart. Still, one may as well humour him – he's lost his inspiration. Hasn't written a thing since 1936."

Harriet applauded politely when the song was over. She had solved one mystery, at least. Jellicoe Travers: she had thought the name familiar. She recognised it now as belonging to one half of a once-successful team of musical comedy writers. Travers and Carp: Aunt Antonia had spoken of them fondly.

"You're to be married shortly, Miss Locke?" said the little composer.

"In the autumn," Harriet said shyly.

"What a lovely ring." Her hand rested on the ridge of the keyboard; he studied the golden band with admiration. "Ah, *love*. Perhaps you shall inspire me." He tinkled at the keys. "Was yours a whirlwind romance? Romeo and Juliet?"

"Not quite like them," laughed Harriet. "But Mark's my cousin, and – "

"Ah, so you played in childhood's Elysian fields!" Random notes began forming into chords. "A wild young Catherine and her wilder Heathcliff – "

"Mark's twelve years older than me – "

"An older cousin? Splendid! Fanny Price and Edmund Bertram!" Mr Travers essayed a change of key. Inhaling, he caterwauled experimentally:

> *Babe I shoulda known*
> *It was one o' those affairs,*
> *From the day I found you*
> *Cryin' on the stairs –*

"Oh Jelly, shut up!" said Mrs Van Voyd.

He broke off, with a discord. "Miss Locke," he said stiffly, "I suggest you spirit your *fiancé* away from here at once. This, as you see, is not a house in which *artistic genius* is nurtured."

"I was not aware that it was a house," murmured Mrs Van Voyd, "in which *artistic genius* was present. How hot it is," she added briskly, lighting a fresh cigar.

It was. The air was a heavy insinuating stillness. Standing by the fireplace, the old woman seemed to be studying the huge mantel. An edifice of carved infants and curving stalks, in the summer heat it was a mournful excrescence, framing an empty grate.

"Unconscionable," said Mr Travers, venturing some bars of Gershwin.

"My fourth husband," remarked Mrs Van Voyd, "used to refer to such weather as *wilting weather*. I dare say young *Marcus* wouldn't describe it as such – mm, Ariette?" She began to pace. "We used to take our summer holidays in Lapland, or the northernmost reaches of Siberia."

Mr Travers, with a delighted laugh, brushed his fingers up the keys:

> *I've been lappin' you up in*
> *Lap-Lap-Lapland*
> *Sighin' for you in*
> *Sigh-Si -*

"Oh stop it, Jelly!"

The entertainment ceased abruptly.

"I do beg your pardon," Mr Travers sniffed, muttering an *unconscionable* beneath his breath.

Mrs Van Voyd went to him. "I'm sorry, Jelly. I *am* sorry. But it's so… boring." Her wrinkled hand hovered above his bald shiny skull. Then, abruptly, she snatched it away. "Such a *sweaty* head you have, Jelly. Whatever happened to that nice toupee I bought for you?"

"You know what happened to it," he muttered, eyeing Aldous sullenly.

But Mrs Van Voyd was not listening. The door from the anteroom opened, and she swivelled towards it on dangerous heels. The words broke from her lips before the dinner-suited Mark was visible:

"Marcus, darling!"

Mark screwed up his eyes. A long spear of sunlight stabbed through the French windows, blinding him fleetingly.

"Marcus, she is an angel!" cried Mrs Van Voyd, enfolding Harriet in a rapt embrace. Harriet stiffened, aware of the cigar burning close to her neck. Mr Travers, as if on cue, launched into a lush romantic melody.

"Hattie!" cried Mark, astonished.

Mrs Van Voyd, releasing Harriet, propelled her towards him.

For an instant, as she stepped into the spearing sunlight, Harriet faltered. Since receiving the letter from Lady Harrowblest, she had wanted nothing but to see Mark again. Now a different desire swept through her, sudden and annihilating. She wondered why. Then she knew: it was the sense of herself as wrong, of the folly of her actions and the disaster they portended, that clutched at her heart with a cold horror.

Mark gathered her in his arms.

"Ah, love!" cried Mrs Van Voyd, and in time to Mr Travers' music she waltzed across the floor, circling an imaginary beau. Her cigar drew smoky circles in the air; Aldous gambolled at her feet.

Then came the crashing of the gong.

The moment was broken. Beneath the gallery at the far end of the room, the butler stood stiffly by the gleaming circle. Slowly the reverberations died. At the piano, Mr Travers launched abruptly into a different, stately melody. Harriet wondered what it might be. Later she would discover it was the theme from *Boston Story*.

It was her companions who made her direct her eyes upwards. Mark and Mrs Van Voyd were applauding politely and looking up to the gallery. Above the dark railings the white-gowned figure of a woman had appeared, her dark hair strangely gleaming. She gazed down at them, her face seeming to shine, smoke curling from a cigarette raised in an elegant hand. And Harriet seemed to have forgotten, or it was as if she had never known, and imperceptibly the awareness came to her: *this was Yardley Urban*.

Absurdly Harriet began clapping loudly, just as the applause of her companions died away.

The radiant figure withdrew. Then the vision had returned, suddenly humanised, swishing coolly through the dark double doors beneath the overhang of the minstrels' gallery.

"Yarders, meet our guest."

Harriet could not help but stare. She had seen perhaps thousands of photographs of the face which now confronted her. Nothing prepared her for Yardley in the flesh. Harriet had never seen so beautiful a human being.

"Miss Locke – well, well." Yardley's voice was soft. She reached for Harriet's hand.

"We certainly gave *Marcus* a surprise," Mrs Van Voyd said brightly.

"I'm sure you did." Yardley gave Harriet's hand a quick squeeze, and swished towards the drinks tray.

Harriet quavered, "Thank you – thank you so much for having me, Lady Harrowblest."

Yardley turned back with a benevolent smile. "The pleasure is all mine, honey, I assure you – all mine."

Toby's wiry arms cleaved the water expertly. He had swum along the line of the cliff that curved away to the east. He would go just a little further before turning back to the beach. He felt so remote, such a long way from everything. Shadow Black, to be sure, was far from Great Yarmouth!

That was where he had learned to swim, at his preparatory school on the coast. The sea, with its ripples and strange saltiness, had entranced Toby from the first. Even the humiliations of 'swimming days', presided over by a former drill sergeant, had not destroyed his ardour. Only once had he floundered, and had to be rescued by the irascible instructor.

Stupid boy. You stupid boy.

He had swum out of his depth when, quite unexpectedly, the thought had flashed into his mind that there, in the glaucous sea at Great Yarmouth, he was part of all the seas and all the oceans of the world. Immersed in one, he was immersed in them all. The thought was amazing, and he felt himself sinking.

It was three years now since he had been in the sea. Melton Overreach lay far inland, and in the summer Toby would swim instead in a willow-draped pond that lay in a wood beyond the far boundary of the school. A perfect circle, it held its still water like a vast chalice, buried mysteriously in the earth. Sometimes, before he dived from the bank, the stillness was so pure that it frightened him to violate it.

Now, Toby trod water and looked back behind him. He swept back his tangled hair from his eyes. He had swum around far enough for the beach to be concealed, hidden by the curve of the coast. The rocky vastness of the cliffs rose above him, a great arc stretching towards the promontory to the east. He propelled himself towards the cliff-face, stretching his hands towards slithery holds. His breath came in laboured gasps. He needed to rest.

It was not until he had clung to the rock for perhaps a minute that he registered the soft knockings which – so it seemed – came from within the cliff. He contemplated a jutting screen of rock which obscured the part of the cliff immediately to his right. Yes, the knocking came from behind the screen. Gently, Toby kicked away from the cliff-face. It was then that he discovered the extraordinary thing.

The cave was a dim watery hiding place under a rocky arch. It stretched back far into the cliff-face; and inside the cave, lashed to ring-bolts in the rock, rising and falling with the sluicing sea, was a little wooden landing-stage, and moored to the landing-stage, knocking at it gently, was a boat. Toby swum towards her, his exhaustion gone. She was a small but sturdy-looking lifeboat – the word came to him at once – painted a colour which Toby, in the strange cavelight, took at first to be a faded green. He soon realised that it was blue. In peeling white letters her prow bore the legend:

BLUEFINCH

Toby hauled himself up over her side. Inside the lifeboat were an old tarpaulin, a coil of rope, some rusted tools and a pair of oars. Yet *Bluefinch* was not a rowing-boat. The little tiller, Toby saw, directed the propulsion of a primitive outboard motor. Sitting cross-legged in the bottom of the boat, he pulled idly at the motor's starter. He expected the old cord to snap off in his hand. When the motor instead gave a peevish cough, Toby was astonished. He made a second attempt, and this time the motor spluttered into life. It was as he was shutting it off that he noticed the six tarnished metal fuel cans, lined up along the landing-stage. A strange excitement hammered at his heart.

"Cora, how could you?"

"It's true, Ariette, every word of it! There was the Yard, *genuflecting* to the royal box, and the wretched thing simply fell off! I heard that old Georgie's eyes nearly popped out of his head. It's a wonder the old bugger didn't have an apoplexy."

Yardley, grimacing, reached for a cigarette. "There was so little time for costume changes in that show."

"All your fault, Jelly!" Mrs Van Voyd waved her cigar in his direction.

"Oh no," said Mr Travers. He patted his small mouth with his napkin, which he had tucked in at his collar. "That was not Travers, Cora, that was Carp. Most definitely Carp."

"Travers," Mrs Van Voyd hissed, "blamed everything on Carp."

"This was your... *partner*, Mr Travers?" asked Harriet.

"My partner, my evil genius. Now alas deceased." The little man eyed his tonic water sadly.

Dinner was almost over. The dining room lay through the doors under the gallery. A cavernous dark apartment, heavy with unstirring heat, it was lit by vast silver-branched candelabra, spaced down the centre of a long polished table. Thick curtains blotted out the evening. At the head of the table, furthest from the doors, was a massive ornate chair, its back resplendent with golden scrolls. At the foot was a chair only slightly less elaborate: they suggested the thrones of a king and a queen. The queen's was taken by Yardley; the king's remained empty. Behind the door, barely visible in the candlelight, was a spiral wooden staircase, ascending to a curtained archway high in the panelling. It led, Harriet realised, onto the gallery in the Great Hall.

"If you are very good, Ariette, the Yard might tell you all about Mr 'Bret' Cable. And I mean all about, don't I, Yarders?"

Yardley blew out a long trail of smoke. "Cora is determined to undermine my dignity. When I know you better, honey" (She smiled benevolently at Harriet) "I shall tell you the truth about Cora. Cora is not what she seems."

Mrs Van Voyd let out a high braying laugh. She stroked Aldous affectionately. Sated, the little dog lay beside her on the tabletop. Beside him were the remains of a dish of mashed chicken, a dish of brandy pudding, and a dish of hock.

Harriet was feeling a little light-headed. She ventured, demurely:

"I'm sure Mrs Van Voyd has nothing to hide."

The old woman broke into delighted applause. "Oh, splendid! What a tonic this girl is! Would you not say she was a tonic, Marcus?"

"I'd say she was a bumper of champagne."

"An excellent idea! Staines, champagne. And more – yes, more *tonic* for Mr Travers."

The little man hunched morosely over his glass, his bald head gleaming.

"Say, where is the kid?" said Yardley, not for the first time.

"Tobias," Mrs Van Voyd whispered to Harriet, "is experiencing the *stirrings of adolescence*. I'm sure Marcus recalls them well."

Harriet smiled weakly.

"When is this tutor coming you've promised, Cora?" asked Yardley. "He seems more necessary every day."

"Soon, soon. One must assess the applicants."

"Cora's decided Toby needs to be *taken in hand*," Yardley explained to Harriet. "For one wild moment I thought *you* might have come to take on the *job*, honey," she laughed, then added, turning back to Mrs Van Voyd, "He doesn't *know* it yet, I take it?"

"Of course not, Yard. One mustn't excite the boy needlessly." The old woman sucked her cigar. "I do have one rather promising applicant," she mused. "The gentleman used to be a master at Tobias' *very own school.*"

"Aren't you worried why they sacked him?" asked Mark.

"Oh dear," said Mrs Van Voyd. "Do you think he could have been sacked?... Really, what would a schoolmaster have to *do* to be sacked?"

"Well..." Mark arched his eyebrows.

There was a ripple of laughter.

Harriet, meanwhile, was thinking that perhaps she should

contribute again to the conversation: her last effort, after all, had met with some success. She cleared her throat. "And how old is your son, Lady Harrowblest?" she offered.

There was an unexpected silence. Yardley's face assumed a strangely frozen look, and Mark seemed to be suppressing a spasm of coughing.

"Tobias," Mrs Van Voyd said gently, "could hardly be regarded as the Yarder's son – "

The arrival of the champagne was a great relief.

"To Ariette – may she always be a *tonic* for Marcus!"

But the toast was interrupted by a sound of sobbing. Mr Travers had burst into tears.

"Oh Jelly, stop it!" snapped Mrs Van Voyd. "He does get maudlin," she explained to Harriet. "It's the memory of poor David Carp's death."

Mark made a curious snorting noise, banging down his champagne flute. "Tell me," he said – as if expressing, at last, a long-held curiosity – "how *did* David Carp die?"

The question was addressed not to Mr Travers but to Mrs Van Voyd. The old woman leaned forward, cigar-smoke wreathing her flame-red wig. Her eyes travelling over the faces of her companions, she could have been a gambler, intent on a vital play.

"Crushed," she said simply.

"Crushed?"

"Beneath the wheels of an oncoming locomotive. It was in *Saskatchewan*, of all places. (The dominions, Ariette.) They still don't know if it was accident or suicide – I should think suicide, wouldn't you? I mean to say, my dears, one really could not find oneself beneath a train in Saskatchewan by accident, surely. They can hardly come *every five minutes* – "

The logic seemed compelling. Soon the company were noisily debating the desirability or otherwise of various methods of self-slaughter.

"Ugh! I just couldn't throw myself under a train," cried Yardley, as if other forms of transport might be considered more suitable. "Now *drowning...*" she mused.

"Yard, dear, that's the worst! You just see yourself as a dripping Ophelia – "

"What would you do, Cora? Stick your head in an oven, like a Midwest housewife – ?"

"It's a clean process – "

"Only if it's gas. I knew a woman in Beverly Hills – "

"Jelly would probably cut his wrists. No consideration for the staff."

The little man, who was still sobbing quietly, made no reply.

"I like the electric chair," the old woman went on.

"That's not suicide, that's execution."

"Oh Yarder, but think of the *thrill* – "

"What about – hm – driving over a cliff?" said Mark. "I like that idea. Hattie, which would you choose?"

Three faces turned eagerly towards hers. But it was just then that Mr Travers made an involuntary spasm, knocking over his tonic water.

"Millicent." Mrs Van Voyd clicked her fingers. "Yes, do tell, Ariette. Hanging? Sleeping pills? Exposure in the snow?"

Harriet bit her lip, her eyes cast down.

The door opened. A shaft of light fell across the room and Harriet exhaled deeply.

"Toby. Well, well. And you've dressed for dinner," Yardley said tartly.

"Yes, Aunt Eunice." The boy advanced sheepishly towards the table, slumping into the empty place opposite Harriet's. Yardley gazed at him, her brow furrowing. His hair was a wet tangle, towelled hastily.

"Sorry I'm late," he offered, after a moment.

There was no response.

Mrs Van Voyd nudged Harriet and hissed:

"*Stirrings of adolescence.*"

Harriet closed her eyes. The room seemed to be shifting. The floor was tilting at an ever higher angle and the walls and the ceiling were floating off into space.

When she opened her eyes she caught the little maid Milly studying her with a curious intentness. Quickly Milly averted her gaze, mopping inefficiently at the spilt tonic water. Harriet reached for her glass of champagne. Earlier that evening, as she was dressing for dinner, she had asked Milly about the locked door. The maid had laughed indulgently. "Ooh miss," she said, "it was all in your dream."

And the hare lip parted in a grotesque smile.

6
Vega, Arcturus

> Villa Santa Clara
> nr. Siena
> Fri. 15th Jul., 1955

Dearly beloved Chance,

  This WILL be short. As you may imagine your loving EEL can hardly BEAR to slither away from the splendours & ECSTASIES of the Villa Santa C. Picture it. The day begins. Early, early comes the lovely gold sun, tickling, teasing through the CRACKS in the shutters - but here in the SC we SLEEP & sleep... Only LATE do we LOLL from the sheets, dear M&H discoupling from their LAWFUL embrace, their darling EEL slipping from the arms of last night's LITHE olive-skinned MAIDEN (well she WAS - her gorgeous surrender dyes the big bed...). Berobed, stretching, the loving FAMILY converge on IL TERRAZZA, greeting (joyously) the pale-green HILLS that UNDULATE eternally under the brilliant sky. RAPTUROUSLY (EDENICALLY, indeed) we cast aside our robes, PLUNGING into the massive cool POOL before (our APPETITES ROUSED) the taking of a croissant and coffee (SCENE: again, il terrazza), the sun drawing up STEAM from our dripping tangled hair.

  The day SPREADS before us; we make our lazy plans. An EXPEDITION to Pisa or Siena or dear Firenze (D4

shall let EEL drive; MIRIAM shall come and go,
talking of Michelangelo)? Perhaps a little RAMBLE in
the history-rich HILLS? Perhaps we shall set out on
some EQUINE friends - a BROOD MARE for MIRIAM; for
DADDY 4 a STALLION; for LOMAX, EUGENE ERIC, a
Christ-style ASS? (Was it an ass? Poor EEL keeps his
hearing-holes shut VIRTUOUSLY tight against the
BUTTINGS of your Xn. stories in chapel - he SLEEPS.)

But enough: we are languorous, and our lovely
black-garbed Italian signora (she whose SIX VIRGIN
DAUGHTERS have in turn felt the SLITHERINGS of
euphoric EEL) has called us to a groaning board.
Olives, pasta, CHIANTI CHIANTI - & after the lavish
luncheon, SLEEP. When we wake, it is late
afternoon. Our eyes pleasantly bleary, we beguile
them with the pages of Mrs CHRISTIE or Miss SAYERS
in creaky (but WELL-cushioned) wicker chairs, till
day fades, & again we SIPHON up spaghetti through
kissy lips, GULP back chianti to the early hours.
For EEL a VIRGIN DAUGHTER waits; for his elders,
CONJUGAL joys. Tomorrow FIRENZE, SIENA, PISA: the
BROOD MARE, the STALLION, the ASS! (Ah, old EEL's
ears were PENETRATED after all: he knows we are a
HOLY TRINITY of love.)

No.

NO, dear Chance, it's NOT like that: naughty EEL
even invented the swimming pool. But he fears the
task of delineating the REALITY is one that defies
even HIS considerable powers. How to convey in its
gruesome INTRICACY the ever-astonishing VULGARITIES
& MEANNESSES of Hosepipe, the HARROWING details of
Miriam's CRAVEN marital whoredom? This morning poor
EEL entering downstairs bathroom, a LITTLE
incautiously - was confronted for perhaps THREE
stomach-churning seconds with the ABOMINATION FROM

BEYOND SPACE that is HOSEPIPE UNCLAD!!! - HOSEPIPE indeed (v. Cavalier). When Miriam lapsed, she lapsed. (HATE HATE HATE them both - they GRUNT through the wall at night - two PIGS.)
Enough.
EEL's rather WONDERING about you, little Chance. All this time you've had NO LIVING RELS (OH, what an object of the slithery EEL's envy!!) - THEN along comes AUNT CORA in her FLOWERPOT HAT (ACTUAL terracotta, ACTUAL gardenias) and DARK HORSE CHANCE is OFF for the summer. ARE you going to TELL ALL, D-H-C, or is there some SECRET you'd rather not reveal?... EEL should tell you that the odious CRAMBORNE has speculated that dear AUNTIE CORA is a FRAUD. The CRAB NEBULA noticed how AC was LOOKING at the CHAPS when she came for you and SUGGESTED - EEL curls with shame - that perhaps the dear lady's RELATIONS with Toe-by-Arse were NOT QUITE FAMILIAL... EEL of course told said CRAB to undertake the STIMULATION of his SMEGMA'D ORGAN in some location REMOTE from proximity to EEL's length - AND, of course, as EEL pointed out, a WOMAN in search of GIGOLOTIC JOYS would HARDLY light on our DEAR CHANCER for pref., wd. she?... EEL has DEFENDED yr. honour, so TELL ALL, Toe-by. Does Auntie Cora ALWAYS wear the flowerpot, & iznit FRIGHTFULLY heavy?

Yours with slithering SLOBBERY affect(at)ion,

How should he have replied?

Dinner was over, and Toby sat alone by the open window of his attic room. Glumly he slipped EEL's letter back into the envelope. The letter was his friend's first for the summer, and Toby had now read it seven times. Last Friday he had sent off his inadequate, stumbling reply; ever since, he had wished he could recall it. He grimaced in shame.

"The trouble is, I'm a liar," he said aloud.

The accusation floated onto the night air. Toby hadn't meant to lie. And EEL was the one person to whom he had almost told the truth. But Mr Collidge had advised him to say nothing, and Toby had agreed. There had been difficulties at his first school. At Melton Overreach his background was to be secret. The chaps would know vaguely that Chance's parents had been killed in an air raid, and that Chance had a guardian, an aunt he seldom saw. It was hardly as if both things were not true – ah, but what lies they were nonetheless!

Gently Toby spun his telescope on its stand. How he wished he had stayed at Melton Overreach! He thought longingly of the echoing dormitories, the deserted dining hall, the high windows of School House in the evening, flinging back the sun's rays like spears. On clear hot nights he would lie horizontal in the centre of the rugger field, his telescope panning slowly across the skies.

Your Aunt Eunice so longs to see you, Mrs Van Voyd had said.

But how could Toby believe that?

"*What have you done?*" Mark shouted, bursting into Yardley's bedchamber.

The goddess lay on her huge bed in a peignoir, her head propped on her hand, flipping idly through a copy of *Vogue*. She looked up at him coolly. It was past midnight. Hovering on the air was Mozart's Flute Quartet in D, K.285.

"I thought you weren't coming."

"How could you use *the signal* tonight?"

"You want to see me, don't you?"

"You know what I mean. Jesus Christ."

Yardley's brow furrowed. Each night she had a simple signal: if she left her curtains undrawn, letting her light fall across the courtyard, Mark was to come to her. If the curtains were drawn, he was not to come. They had started this game on the second night of his stay; since then, there had been no night when the curtains had been drawn. Seeing the light in the courtyard, Mark would return to the dining room. Stealthily he would climb the steps to the minstrels' gallery. In the wall at the end of the gallery a concealed door opened onto a narrow staircase, leading up into a dark passage.

"Jesus Christ," he muttered again, his knuckles white where he still gripped the door handle.

"You fool!" said Yardley. "It was Cora, can't you see?"

Mark looked at her sharply. He was trembling.

"It was Cora," Yardley said simply. "She wrote the letter; she used my name. It's what she does."

"What's the idea? Does she know about us? Is she – "

"Honey, Cora's crazy – flipped. She couldn't think of anything like that. She just did it for – well, what she said."

"*To bring the young lovers together?*" Mark moaned.

"It's your own fault. You told her how much you loved the little tramp – "

"Don't call her that – "

Yardley went to him. She squeezed his arm. "Honey, *honey* – hey. It makes no difference, does it?"

"You're unbelievable!" Mark broke away. "First this lie about the commission, now – "

"Mark – " Her nails clawed at him.

"You're hurting."

"*I did not lie about the commission.*"

He laughed aloud. "It's a joke – I have to wait. And what in hell am I waiting *for*? I'm sorry, it's all a bit too crazy for me, Yarder. I can just pack my suitcase *now*, I don't have to go through this – "

"Yes you do!"

"What?"

"You *do*. Because you're a great painter and you're going to paint a masterpiece. The commission is real, honey. But there are things you don't understand. We thought he'd be – *ready* by the time you arrived. He can't always see people, he goes through phases..."

"I don't believe a word of this."

"Mark, just stay. It must be nearly time – I'll talk to Collidge, *tonight* – "

"What *college?* What are you talking about?"

Yardley clutched him. "I said there were things you didn't understand..."

"You're right." Mark sighed deeply.

Yardley's hands massaged his chest. "Stay. Believe everything." Her fingers slithered through his long hair. She moaned, seeking his lips.

"No!" Mark twisted from her. "I'm sick of this, I'm sick of you! You're – "

"Go on, then. Hit me." She arched her eyebrows.

"Oh, you're poison!" He rushed from the room.

For an instant Yardley motioned to follow him. Then she dropped back. Left alone, she paced the wide carpet for several turns, her fingers raking distractedly through her hair.

"Damn," she said aloud. "Damn, damn." She rearranged her peignoir and crossed to the window, dragging shut the curtains. She stood for perhaps a minute, her hands crushing the expensive fabric, her face buried in the luxurious folds. Her body was like a taut wire; then her body relaxed.

When she turned back to the room she was smiling.

"It's down to three."

It had been a bright morning in spring when Mrs Van Voyd had mentioned the *artist issue* to Yardley.

"Who are the three?" asked Yardley, incurious. She had only come to show Cora the new gown she had received – Dior, from *next year's* collection...

"Bardinelli; Cratchit; some young chap... Vardell."

"Vardell?"

The scene had been laid in the large light room where Mrs Van Voyd would sequester herself to work through Yardley's mail. It was an impossible task. In bursting sacks the letters came, all these years after

Yardley had left the screen. *Dear Miss Urban, I must express my admiration... Yardley, your fans need you!! Please* please *PLEASE come back... Dear dear Yardley, I feel I know you, you've helped me to face life, now I don't know who to turn to but you... Urban YOU HOT BITCH you no what Id like to do with you... Deer Miz Yardly I write to propos marrij you be my best wife I liv in very good villij and am owning 32 goats...*

The sacks were heaped against the walls in teetering piles, like sandbags in wartime. Mrs Van Voyd would pick out letters at random, every so often presenting Yardley with a selection of favourite finds – the most sycophantic, the most pathetic, the most touching, the most obscene.

The correspondents so honoured received signed pictures of Yardley. Stacked in one window-seat Mrs Van Voyd kept a massive supply of black and white eight-by-tens of her friend, *circa* 1935. Every so often the old woman took up an armful of these pictures and carried them to the cluttered desk which stood in the middle of the room. Seating herself comfortably, she fixed a fresh nib into her pen, and scored across each picture the slashing *Y*, then the trailing squiggle, of her much-practised *Yardley* signature.

"Cratchit?" added Yardley after a moment. "Bardinelli?"

Mrs Van Voyd, trying not to wake the recumbent Aldous, extracted three foolscap files from beneath a mess of crumpled envelopes and eight-by-tens. Each file contained a series of cuttings about a particular artist, with comments by Bertrand Pinker, art critic of the *Telescope*. (Dear Bertie! Mrs Van Voyd had trusted his taste implicitly, ever since the holiday they had taken together in Morocco in 1938.)

"Eugenio Bardinelli." Mrs Van Voyd handed the top file to Yardley. "Italian fellow. Done a lot of last-of-the-royal-houses-of-Europe stuff, Bertie says. Branching out into communist dictators now."

"Don't like the look of the guy," said Yardley, extracting a photograph from the file. "Like a fat slug with a moustache, ugh!"

Mrs Van Voyd laughed, "It's not a beauty contest, Yarders!"

Yardley shrugged. "We'll have to look at the guy over the dinner table, won't we?"

"Cratchit."

Yardley scanned through the cuttings about Sir Silas Cratchit, R.A., *b.* 1868, who had rendered in oils Queen Victoria, Edward VII, George V, Edward VIII, George VI, and Elizabeth II, as well as Joseph Lister, Sir Henry Irving, Lloyd George, Neville Chamberlain, Florence Nightingale, Ellen Terry, Mrs Patrick Campbell and Lady Diana Cooper, among others.

"And Vardell?"

"Youngest of the three. Made his name with some very *avant-garde* work – "

"Say, the Princess Margaret guy!" Yardley snatched the file, swishing back and forth in the new Dior gown.

"He's *gone straight* since then," smiled Mrs Van Voyd. "Bertie says he's very promising – still, his last exhibition *was* rather a disaster…"

Yardley stopped at the window, casually fingering the eight-by-tens. Those on the tops of the piles quickly became faded, their edges curled and yellowed.

"Which do *you* think, then, Cora?"

Mrs Van Voyd, disturbing Aldous, searched for an ash tray. "Difficult," she admitted. "But I was rather thinking of Cratchit. Solid."

Yardley laughed lightly. "Oh Cora, you'd have cast Eddie Cantor in *Singin' in the Rain*!"

"Hm?"

"Cratchit? He's yesterday's man. Anyway, I'm sure he's a frightful old bore."

"Bardinelli, then?"

"Vardell."

"A wild card."

"Better than *solid*." Yardley, crossing back to the desk, draped an arm round her friend's shoulder. "You'd want to do your best for Eddie, wouldn't you, Cora?"

Mrs Van Voyd patted Yardley's hand. "Of course, Yard. Of course."

And Mark Vardell's face, in newsprint dots, slipped from the file in Yardley's hand.

It fluttered to the floor.

Toby cast himself down on the grassy clifftop. The night air pressed round him, still and hot. After half an hour of attempting to sleep he had abandoned the effort, throwing on his daytime clothes and wandering out into the darkness. In his hand, wrapped carefully in a dirty towel, was the little telescope he had removed from its stand.

Summer is thought to be the worst time for star-gazing. The period of darkness is short, and constellations such as Orion, so splendid in the winter, have fallen out of view. But the sky is often clear, and on hot nights one can lie outdoors, staring upwards for hours.

Toby once had a theory about the stars. The contrast between what the stars really are and how they appear to us, here on earth, had long been a source of fascination for him. Seen close, the stars would be immense flaming worlds; on earth, they are the merest pinpricks, consolatory scatterings in the darkness of night. They do not – any more than does the moon – diminish our sense that the universe is *black*. It was Toby's theory that this blackness was false, a delusion of the inhabitants of earth. Benighted, we could not see the real glory of the stars. In space they would be dazzling, extending lines of radiance so far as to make all the cosmos ablaze with light.

Nonsense, of course – the merest fancy.

But not everything in Toby's mind was nonsense. As he scanned the night sky, he could recite the names of the stars, and knew them all: Vega, Deneb, Cygnus, Altair, Arcturus, Capella, Antares...

It could have been a mantra.

7
The West Tower

The morning heat had begun already. On the landing it glowed at the window as Yardley, in her peignoir, slid noiselessly down the stairs. Carefully she made her way down the corridor to Mark's room, opening the door with an intruder's care.

He was sleeping on his back, his chest rising and falling under a single sheet, a bare arm flung out at his side. The room was dark but for the sun's thwarted rays, pushing at the edges of the drawn curtains. Yardley smiled to herself. In her hand she carried a small white envelope which she placed silently by Mark's head. Resisting the temptation to stroke his dark hair, she crossed to the window and drew back the curtains. Mark stirred. Yardley did not turn. She slipped back to the door and shut it softly behind her.

"Damn," said Mark, "damn."

Dazzling sunbeams speared through his eyelids. He rolled onto his stomach, burying his face in the pillow. It was only after some minutes that he felt the edge of the envelope, pricking at his sleep-numbed arm. He raised himself on his elbow, screwing up his eyes.

The envelope contained a small white card. It bore the following words, in Yardley's girlish curlicues: *He is ready. The West Tower.*

Suddenly Mark was entirely awake, dressing rapidly in last night's shirt and trousers, squashing his feet into a pair of espadrilles. Did he believe Yardley's note? He didn't know. But he was drawn into the game. Perhaps afterwards he would confront her, humiliated and angry. He imagined her, materialising in some gothic room in the tower, floating towards him in pale *déshabillé*. A trick? Yes, it could be.

He saw himself, her arms tangled round him, sinking unresisting onto a cold stone floor.

From his first day at Shadow Black, Mark had felt himself enmeshed in some perverse lie, some tortuous deceit exceeding by far the simple game of adultery he seemed called upon to play. He had allowed himself to be enmeshed. From their first night together he had felt Yardley's power, binding him inescapably to her will.

That had been in 1942, when Mark was seventeen. It was the month after his expulsion from Charterhouse. Fleeing his father's wrath, he had been lying low in London – in, as it happened, a luxurious flat in Bloomsbury – with a young man called Bertrand Pinker, future art critic of the *Daily Telescope*. Pinker Major – as Mark thought of him then – had left Charterhouse some years before, and after an uncompleted Cambridge career was engaged, on the face of it, in some dubiously 'administrative' form of war work. In truth he pursued a round of pleasures with as much ardour as the times allowed, and principal among these pleasures were those involving schoolboys. Then came painting. At times, he would see the prospects of his interests coinciding. This was such a time. For the young Mark Vardell, Major was quick to predict a glorious future.

Whether it was Major or one of his dubious friends whose idea it was to invade Yardley's party, Mark never knew. Probably it was Major; otherwise he would never have been so keen. To the accompaniment of massive publicity, Yardley had arrived in London to appear in a special wartime version of the celebrated Travers and Carp musical, *Showbiz Ahoy!* Financed by a Hollywood charity, the lavish production was offered as a morale-booster to beleaguered Londoners. The opening-night party at the Savoy was to be, it was said, the most thrilling social event in the capital since the outbreak of war. *Everyone* was talking about it, and this included Major; *everyone* had been invited, and this did not. His determination – like another part of him in the presence, say, of a uniformed Harrovian in the gentleman's lavatory at Piccadilly Circus tube station – grew hard as stone.

So it was that Mark, a forged invitation in his pocket, found himself amongst the milling celebrities, the clinking glasses, the muted swing wash of Antoine and His Orchestra. For the first half hour he frowned persistently, imagining that this made him look older: he did not much bother after that. Nor was he even amazed to see Yardley Urban in person, or Noël Coward, or Marlene Dietrich. They loomed at him like creatures in a bizarre dream. He became drunk quickly; the alcohol combined with the excitement, the churning smoke, and the white powder Major invited him to snuffle in a lavatory cubicle, to whirl his mind into a dangerous eddy. Earrings flashed like distant nebulae. Mellow light stroked him like hands; champagne glasses bloomed in hands like flowers. At the bandstand, Antoine and His Orchestra metamorphosed, shimmering, like figures in fairground mirrors. Above, the chandeliers were perpetually, slowly, falling.

When he woke he was naked, sprawled on stained sheets in an unfamiliar room.

It was only slowly that he became aware of the goddess, watching him wryly from an enveloping chair. Her long legs, crossed at the knees, thrust from the flaps of a silken robe. In his confusion the thought came to him that he had never slept with a woman: but that had been yesterday. She stubbed out her cigarette and moved towards him, shrugging back her shoulders to let the robe fall. Really, he had been a *very* handsome boy.

His affair with Yardley – if affair it could be called – was to last less than a month. Later the memories would stab back insistently, the rhythm of days shattered to splintered images. He saw the overheated hotel suite strewn with clothes; he saw their sweat running on the unmade bed; he saw Yardley's neck – its precise angle – arched back in a throaty laugh. Grey-blue smoke curled above the bed; a cigarette waved in her long, stained fingers. Outside, snow was falling. Her lips smeared redly over his. Cars passed in the street, far below.

One night she did not return from the theatre. An aching emptiness crept over him, terribly. He sent down to room service for three bottles of champagne and a bottle of scotch whisky. He drank the contents of all four bottles, then vomited.

Next day he walked up to Shaftesbury Avenue. It was the first time he had been outdoors for three weeks. Arriving just before the matinee, he said he had to see her. If they turned him away and laughed, it was not to be wondered at: his speech was slurred; he hadn't shaved; he stank of alcohol and there was vomit down his clothes.

When he returned to the hotel the doorman refused him entry. In Bloomsbury, Major was unwelcoming, surveying the young runaway with unveiled disgust.

Weeks passed.

It was at his father's house, chafing under his father's contempt, that Mark heard the news on the BBC. Surely it couldn't be true! He cycled recklessly into the village. It *was* true. There it was in the *Daily Telescope*, filling the front page, a massive announcement, proclaiming the marriage of its proprietor and the actress. In the musical, her understudy assumed her role; in a matter of weeks, the show would close.

Mark left home and enlisted in the ranks.

Grotesque. Really, it was grotesque.

Standing in the furthest of a network of courtyards, Mark looked upwards. The West Tower – so he had gathered – had been the folly of a seventeenth-century Harrowblest who had conceived a passion for astronomy. From the window of Mark's room the tower was distant, an ethereal fantasy. To stand at the base of it with one's head thrown back was to see it in all its monstrosity – a colossal cylinder of rising blank wall, teetering yet hideous in its thick solidity, thrusting up grotesquely at the sky. Ivy, like cancer, crawled across the stonework.

Doubtfully Mark advanced on the heavy oak door.

It swung open.

"Who's there? Is anyone there?"

He stood in a large gloomy hall. An enervated dim daylight trickled from a window, invisible round the curve of a stone staircase. The floor had been swept crudely clean. The ceiling was a circle of naked beams and planks. A curious apprehension gripped Mark. The thought that he was about to meet Yardley seemed suddenly, unaccountably foolish. That this was a game there could be no doubt. But suddenly

Mark knew it was a different game.

"Is anyone there? Who's there?"

The stairs, which rose on the left of the hall, did not wind around the tower in the spiral Mark had expected, but jutted up first in one direction, then the other, in a curving zig-zag. As he climbed higher, the light through the windows on the landings was brighter. On each landing was a heavy oak door. Mark tried the handle of each door as he reached it, and each door was locked. Behind the sixth door he thought he heard a sound. He pressed his ear close against the oak, but could hear the sound no more clearly. It seemed to be a low throbbing hum, as of machinery.

The seventh door opened.

"Ah, Mr Vardell."

The easel was ready.

8
Scarlet and Indigo

"The gentleman at the station misinformed you, Miss Locke. Indeed there is another Lightletter, though the railway does not extend to it. That's old Lightletter – "

"The empty part?"

"Not quite, my dear. Actually, not at all. Old Lightletter is an ancient fishing village; small but – ah – thriving, to this day. A simple rustic community. New Lightletter is the holiday town, built not much more than fifty years ago – the part you saw yesterday afternoon. The two towns face each other on opposite sides of the bay."

Harriet paused over her single sausage, her fat-trimmed bacon. She was thoughtful. Mr Travers faced her shyly across the table, his napkin drooping from his collar like a wilted petal, magnified massively. They were alone in the breakfast room.

"What happened to the holiday town, Mr Travers?"

"Ah, Miss Locke, now there is a tale." The little man seized his teacup with a flourish, spilling rather too much of the liquid on the tablecloth. "All the land round Lightletter Bay is owned by the Harrowblest family. But in 1900 Lord Stephen – he was the present Lord Harrowblest's older brother – Lord Stephen, shall we say, *lost* almost half of it.

"The new owner was a Mr George Captax – a most *progressive* gentleman. The imprint of his hand on many parts of our green and pleasant land is still deep today – oh, very deep indeed. Suffice to say that in the space of barely more than a year Mr Captax had transformed the western side of our bay – had flung up row after row of whitewashed houses, a long promenade, a great edifice along the seafront called the Paradise Hotel (now there's irony for you)... and to cap it all, a monstrous, silver-domed pier. At any moment the inundation of trippers was set to begin – in July of 1902, in fact. A grand opening was planned. Advertisements were plastered over every railway station in the country."

"But Mr Travers, what happened?"

"Hah!" The little man's eyes glittered. "Two circumstances, Miss Locke, combined to thwart this particular best-laid plan. First, Mr Captax had stretched his resources too far. In the April of 1902, he was bankrupted. Then, in the same month, Lord Stephen died. When Lord Edward – the present Lord Harrowblest – came into the title, his first act was to buy back the land his brother had lost – "

"Which now contained the holiday town – "

"Precisely, Miss Locke! Lord Edward intended to have it demolished, of course, but somehow it's never been done. There wasn't the money at first, not after the purchase, and Lord Edward was soon distracted by his publishing ventures... In any case our little corner of England was saved from the masses, and the holiday town remains as a talking point."

"Fascinating," said Harriet, and she was about to ask if anyone had ever lived in the empty town when the maid Milly, a little breathless, blundered into the room.

"Miss, here you are. Mrs Van Voyd wants you – in her sanctum."

"Sanctum?" Harriet glanced at Mr Travers.

"I think you are being *privileged*, my dear."

Setting aside her plate, Harriet gulped down the remainder of her tea. As she pushed back her chair Mr Travers, blundering up awkwardly, said:

"Miss Locke... perhaps, if you're not busy later, I could show you over the house – I've made something of a study of its history, and... perhaps after luncheon? I mean, if there's nothing – "

"That would be lovely, Mr Travers."

The little man beamed.

"Mr Travers." Harriet turned back in the doorway. She paused, as if for thought. "There's one thing you could tell me now. Why did they call the house Shadow Black?"

Her new friend gazed at her fondly. "Oh, tradition, my dear – a silly legend. It was Lord Edmund who had the house built, in the 1560s – 'Edmund the Buccaneer', they called him. Built it for his new wife, a girl much younger than himself (not much older than you, my dear) – died young, too..."

"Mr Travers?"

The little man seemed to have slipped into reverie.

"Oh! Sorry, my dear... Well, young Maria was installed in the house already when Edmund came here for the first time, in the summer of 1564. It was a brilliant July day. The household gathered on the steps to welcome the master. But as Edmund stepped over the threshold, the sky was plunged into darkness. A total eclipse of the sun, no doubt – a total eclipse of the sun."

"My dear!"

Mrs Van Voyd's bedchamber lay behind one of two sets of matching double doors at the top of a high landing. The lady, in a nightgown like a jester's motley, was propped on pillows and multicoloured cushions, and reared up massively over an amply-filled tray. Her morning face was a mask of stale makeup and her brow was banded with a tartan tam o' shanter. Beside her, Aldous, half-buried in the bed, nuzzled greedily into a bowl of poached eggs. Mrs Van Voyd clutched Harriet's hand and pulled down the girl's cheek to hers.

"Help yourself, Ariette – bacon and eggs, sausages, heap your plate high!"

"Oh, I don't think – "

"Nonsense, Ariette. A girl on the *brink of wedlock* must keep up her strength!"

Knowingly, the old woman rolled her eyes, waving Harriet to a rococo chair. By the chair was an elaborate arrangement of warming pans and tea things. Gingerly the young guest raised a silver cover.

"One seldom *goes down* for breakfast," the old woman mused, then slapped herself. "Oh dear, the *entendre*! Most *double*, hm? Still, breakfast *is* such an intimate affair, don't you find?"

Harriet thought it best to agree. Balancing her newly-filled plate on her knees, she stifled the urge to eat – she must, she *must* look her best for the wedding – and gazed instead about the extraordinary room: at the luxurious rugs that lined the floor and walls, riotous with scrolls and swirling mandalas; at the lush canopy suspended from the ceiling, gathered to a pucker round a pendulous chandelier; at the cascading bedcovers with their strewn books and papers; at the velvet corrugations of the parted curtains. Fingers of sunlight caressed the bright colours, and danced like little mischievous imps on the frame of a photograph by the old woman's bed. Further photographs covered the mantelpiece; above it, in the mirror, the room was repeated, ablaze with scarlet and indigo and gold. A sparkle visible through an open doorway hinted at an arsenal of exotic dresses. A smell of sandalwood hovered on the air. With unexpected longing, Harriet thought of India.

"... I had hoped, of course, that *that* was the least of his talents," Mrs Van Voyd was saying.

"Of course – "

"But I'm afraid, my dear, it was his greatest skill. Many a woman has made a worse discovery."

The old woman had been remembering her sixth husband, and the elaborate fried breakfasts he had prepared for her at his ranch in Wyoming.

"Ariette, you haven't listened to a word I've said!"

"Oh no!" Harriet started at the mock sternness. "But I was rather – admiring you room, Mrs Van Voyd."

"Room? I prefer to call it my *sanctum*."

"Your *sanctum*, of course."

Mrs Van Voyd held out her plate. "A few rashers more, my dear, if you please. And another two or three sausages, hm?"

As Harriet busied herself with the warming pans the old woman, leaning forward, delved among the papers scattered around her on the bedcovers. From beneath a dishevelled copy of the *New Yorker*, she produced a small ancient-looking book in a battered vellum binding.

"Thank you, my dear. And an extra drop of tea, too, there's a good girl. And do eat up, Ariette – you haven't touched your breakfast! By the way, my dear – " She leafed through the little volume. " – I happened to come across the book I mentioned. I'd almost forgotten."

Harriet had forgotten – until now, when Mrs Van Voyd, with a decisive air, placed the book on the edge of the bed. When Harriet picked it up, she discovered it to be of a somewhat alarming nature: the title page, above the name of an American publisher and the date 1905, proclaimed it to be *Satisfaction in Wedlock*, by Rachel M. Fishbaum, M.D., Ph.D.

"Of course it's frightfully old," Mrs Van Voyd said cheerfully. "But I dare say nothing's changed. The *fundamentals*, I mean."

Harriet murmured an awkward thanks. Gingerly she peered into the musty pages: *When these preliminaries have aroused a mutual ardour, the tumescent organ is ready to be received into the now fully-moistened –*

"Little slut!" came a voice.

Startled, Harriet shut the book.

The voice belonged to Yardley, who wandered into the sanctum with a proprietorial air. Swishing forward in *déshabillé*, she held her cigarette holder poised in one hand; in the other was the rectangle of a folded *Daily Telescope*. Bending gracefully, with tumbling hair, she kissed first Mrs Van Voyd, then Harriet, with open, casual affection. In the brief contact Harriet was aware of a cool smoothness and a pungent, intoxicating perfume.

"Who's a little slut, Yarders?" Mrs Van Voyd had put her tray aside and was clipping the end of her first cigar of the day.

"This Liz Taylor. A whole page devoted to her squalid love life. Really, I must speak to Collidge."

"She was lovely in *National Velvet*," Mrs Van Voyd ventured.

"She's grown since then." Yardley threw down the newspaper. "Has Cora been telling you about her husbands?" she asked Harriet, gesturing towards the photographs. "Your favourite topic, I believe, Cora?"

"Don't listen, Ariette. The Yard likes to *rib*."

Harriet looked at the mantelpiece with a quickened interest. There were perhaps forty photographs, mounted in silver frames. "These aren't *all* your husbands, Mrs Van Voyd?" she asked awkwardly.

"Really, Ariette, I only had seven!"

"Not even Cora's been that busy!" Yardley laughed. "The great game, honey, is to pick out the husbands from the lovers. Have a try."

"Oh, Yarders – "

"Come on, honey – "

Harriet stepped forward, relieved at least to put aside the unwanted second breakfast. She studied the photographs with real fascination. The variety of types was extraordinary. There were Englishmen, foreigners, old men, young men, fair men, dark men, the handsome, the ugly; there were even, to Harriet's shock, several Negroes, a Chinaman, and a swarthy fellow in a turban. One gentleman even wore a clerical collar – of the Catholic sort, too! Alarmed, Harriet lighted on a photograph of an innocent English face.

"Got it in one, honey," Yardley smiled. "Randy Grainger, am I right, Cora?"

"Oh yes," said Mrs Van Voyd, "that was dear Randolph. Minor poet and member of the Bloomsbury group. What times we had! Of course, he was a little – little…"

It appeared that Mrs Van Voyd was not going to finish the sentence.

"What happened to Mr Grainger?" Harriet thought he looked very nice.

"Honey, it's best not to ask! You name it, it happened to them! Choose another."

Harriet proved to have a rare ability to pick the husbands. She was right on Teddy Smallwood, Bradford mill-owner; Sir Cuthbert Trease, MP; Roberto de Francesca, Italian count, and Andy Van Voyd, engineering tycoon; wrong on Leroy Washington, jazz musician, Father O'Riley from Connacht, and Sheik Ali-Ben Raqi Khan, though she had chosen these last more from curiosity than certainty.

Soon the three women were collapsing in laughter.

"Yard, you're determined to ridicule me!" Mrs Van Voyd protested, wiping her eyes.

"I tell Cora she should write a book," said Yardley. "But she won't hear of it."

"And I tell *you* to write one," said Mrs Van Voyd.

"Perhaps you should get together," said Harriet.

Yardley, misunderstanding, smoothed Harriet's hair. "We are

together, honey. Cora and I are a team."

Smiling, Harriet turned away. She asked brightly:

"Did you love them all, Mrs Van Voyd?"

There was silence. Then the old woman said:

"There was only one that I loved." Her voice was strained.

Yardley turned from the mantelpiece. Reaching in the pocket of her peignoir, she drew forth a fresh cigarette.

"That's impressive," she said after a moment, blowing out a stream of smoke. "That's a really impressive score, Cora."

The two women gazed at each other lingeringly.

"Is this one of your husbands, Mrs Van Voyd?" Harriet, returning to the rococo chair, gestured to the single photograph by the bed. It showed a young man – indeed a boy – in a cloth cap and knee britches, a hunting rifle cradled jauntily under his arm. His open immature face and little wispy moustache attested to the extremity of his youth. He was a naïve boy: and yet there was a quality of character in the face, in the eyes particularly, which arrested the attention.

The awkward moment passed.

"My husband?" Mrs Van Voyd gave out a loud guffaw. "That's old Bunger, my dear – when he was young."

"Lord Harrowblest?" Harriet returned her gaze sharply to the photograph.

"Yes, my dear – Bunger. When he was young."

"Dear Eddie," Yardley murmured. She had perched on the side of her friend's bed, and was looking idly under the covers of the dishes on the low marquetry table. A raised china rectangle exposed a cube of butter, melting in the heat. She concealed it with distaste and sprawled back on the bed. "Do you swim, honey?" she enquired, arching an eyebrow.

Harriet bit her lip. She would not venture into water beyond the depth of her waist. But she did not want to tell this to Yardley. She smiled innocently at her beautiful inquisitor.

"Oh," she said, "in a manner of speaking – "

Mrs Van Voyd burst out:

"I'm sure dear Ariette is an aquatic queen!"

"I thought Harry might join us this afternoon," smiled Yardley. "We often make our way down to our little beach, don't we, Cora?"

"Yarders more often than I," Mrs Van Voyd laughed.

"You'll join us?" Yardley leaned across Harriet to deposit her cigarette-end in the ash tray by the bed. Focusing on the elegant hand, Harriet noted for the first time the curious little catch on the side of the cigarette holder which slid forward to release the butts. She had not seen one like it before.

"Honey?"

"Oh," said Harriet, "I'm afraid I haven't a costume. Until my box – "

"Nonsense, Ariette! Yarders has costume upon costume, don't you dear? Enough to clothe the cast of a synchronised swimming sequence. Well, several."

"Sure," said Yardley. "We'll have you kitted out in no time." She sprang up off the bed, offering her hand to Harriet.

"Yarders, that's not fair!" Mrs Van Voyd protested. "You're taking dear Ariette from me. And here was I thinking I had her all to myself."

"Silly Cora. Come too. You can help Harry choose."

"I couldn't possibly rouse myself so early. You seem to forget, Yarders, that I am a woman stricken in years."

"Or a woman with the energy of a beached whale," Yardley laughed. She cast an amused glance at Harriet. "Come on, honey."

Harriet looked up at her, not without apprehension. As she left, she permitted *Satisfaction in Wedlock* to lie unregarded amongst the tea things.

"Beached whale!" cried Mrs Van Voyd. "Now that was unkind. Wasn't that unkind, Aldous, hm?" She wiped away the egg yolk from the little dog's muzzle.

Left alone, the old woman lay back on the pillows, drawing on her cigar. On impulse she picked up the photograph by the bed. The young Harrowblest stared out at her with dark, imperative eyes. Poor Bunger! The old woman remembered him this way. But her first memory was of an earlier Bunger still.

He had first come to consciousness in her – she recalled it vividly –

one dark afternoon in 1898, when she had visited Shadow Black for the first time. Cora Clasp had been eleven years old then, an insignificant member of a family-and-friends party gathered at the massive old mansion for Christmas. She was lonely, restless. Escaping her nurse, she wandered out into the frozen grounds when suddenly, at the back of the stables, she was ambushed by a group of boys. They looked like rough village lads, and carried catapults. She backed away. It was too late. "Get her, Bunger!" shouted one freckle-faced urchin, and a stone struck Cora Clasp on the side of her face. (Mrs Van Voyd still bore the scar, a small dark initiation-mark, covered for many years by makeup, covered now as much by the depredations of time.)

In her pain, as the blood ran from her cheek, Cora looked up at the boy they called Bunger, a dirty creature of perhaps fourteen in cloth cap and knee britches and ill-fitting coat. He looked like a stable boy. She brought up her hand to her face. On a pinnacle of bricks from a demolished outhouse, Bunger was laughing, his catapult still held aloft. Only as the little girl stared at him, blood spilling through her fingers, did he slowly let it drop. For a moment he seemed abashed, casting down his eyes. But he was only gathering his resources. When he looked up at her again Cora felt the force of his gaze pierce deep into her being.

Then he began to laugh again.

It was not until later that day that Cora Clasp realised the identity of the dirty boy. The shock had been curiously exhilarating.

Six years later, when she was seventeen, Bunger – as she always thought of him – would be the first boy she permitted to kiss her, against a yew tree in the decayed cemetery which adjoined her mother's garden (a gate in the ivied wall led to this wilder region; that they should pass through it that day had been inevitable; oh, inevitable...) He swore that day that he would marry Cora Clasp, if ever he were to marry. But he said he never would.

Mrs Van Voyd sighed deeply. She ground out her cigar.

"I call it my shrine," Yardley said wryly, leading Harriet across the landing.

Harriet drew in her breath as a dim anteroom, its panelled walls painted black, opened onto a vast chamber flooded with light.

Beneath a high gold-banded ceiling inset with circular paintings – Philomela and Tereus, Echo and Narcissus – the room was dominated by an enormous regal bed, its covers and hangings of a luxurious milky white, as if drenched in cream.

The white pattern was continued in the walls and the deep carpet, even in the ornaments on the huge mantelpiece. Innumerable little animals carved in ivory – elephants and antelopes, zebras and tigers – milled as if in worship about the gleaming Oscars that towered in their midst. White cabinets housed inferior awards, and against the radiant walls, between the framed reviews and the honorary degrees, was a vast display of photographs and carefully-preserved posters. The photographs showed stills from Yardley's greatest roles, the black and white blur of her beautiful face abandoned in sorrow or terror or rapture; in the posters she appeared as a gaudy illustration, a painted statue with crimson lips and monstrous swollen breasts. Luminous titles and frantic exclamations were seared above or below her.

Softly, from no visible source, the sound of mingling strings and horns lilted on the air (it was the *Allegro moderato* of Mozart's Horn Concerto No. 4 in E flat major, K.495).

Swishing silently through the massive chamber, Yardley opened a pair of gold-handled doors. Lingering for a moment in the doorway, Harriet looked back at the splendours of the shrine. A mirror which filled the far wall reflected in ghostly shimmers the streaming morning sun, the pictures, the memorabilia, the cream-coloured bed – and Harriet herself, watching.

Mrs Van Voyd's dressing rooms, from Harriet's brief glimpse, had looked like the chaos of a theatrical costumier's. Yardley's were laid out like the departments of an exclusive store. As her companion led her through the huge array of evening gowns, the furs, the shoes, the handbags, the lingerie, Harriet could not but express her astonishment, her delight. Yardley laughed and took her young guest by the arm. As if in paradise the two women wandered, the younger exclaiming, through the fragrant quiet of the dimly-lit rooms. Yardley spoke happily of Dior, of Chanel, of Edith Head. Silently, several servants tended the vast collection.

At the perfume counter the older woman paused, squeezing French fragrance at Harriet's neck.

The two women laughed.

An entire room was devoted to swimwear. Costumes ranged, as Yardley put it, from the classic to the contemporary; from the simplicities of sleek lines to the intricacies of frills and bows; from the exuberance of bright stripes to the starkness of black or white.

Yardley shunted Harriet to a mirror. Snatching a succession of costumes from the racks, she passed them before the young guest as a conjuror passes veils. It was then that Harriet felt her identity growing uncertain. Disoriented by the flickering images, intoxicated by the heady atmosphere, a cocktail of fabric and leather and perfume, she did not even stiffen, did not even mind, as she felt the long fingers working down her spine, undoing her blouse and her brassiere.

"You must try some things on, honey. I'm sure they'll fit you."

As Harriet dutifully continued to strip herself, Yardley stood by, receiving each item of the girl's clothing in turn, inspecting the fabric, inspecting the stitching, inspecting the labels with a horrified pity.

"You poor child. You shall have more than swimsuits. You shall – "

"When my box comes – " Harriet said.

But her voice was distant.

Yardley looked at her sadly. "Oh, honey – didn't Cora tell you? Frederick went to the station. It seems your box has been lost. It could be in Bristol, or Cardiff – or Carlisle, if it comes to that... all manner of dreadful places."

"Oh," said Harriet, "oh."

Yardley kissed her and said the matter was settled. "You shall make free with my collection. Dear Harry – I'll call you Harry, shall I?... We'll be like sisters and share – isn't that what sisters do?"

"I haven't got a sister."

"Neither have I."

They laughed again.

9
The Line

"Lady Anne Harrowblest. 'Bloody Anne' as she was known to her servants. Savage beatings were very much her forte."

Harriet looked enquiringly at the demure figure in a wimple. "Giving or receiving them?" it occurred to her to say.

Mr Travers smiled. "Do you know, my dear, I'm not quite sure? Fascinating, fascinating." And at once he snapped away his glance to the next in the line of portraits.

They were in the Long Gallery, which ran the length of the west wing. The bright glow through narrow windows illuminated against the dark panelling a collection of family portraits, stretching as if – so Mr Travers put it with a smile – to the crack of doom. Above them a low plasterwork ceiling writhed with twists and loops and burgeoning *fleurs-de-lis*.

"Sir George Harrowblest. Wrote for the stage in the time of Shakespeare. Oh, anonymously, of course. Well… not so much anonymously as *under another name*. You can't guess which one, my dear? Think of Bacon – I mean Sir Francis, not *and eggs*. Think of Oxford – the earl, I mean. Then think of Sir George – hm?"

The gallery was the climax of what Mr Travers had described as the 'Great Tour'. To the accompaniment of his unceasing commentary he had led his young companion upstairs and downstairs, indoors and out, through chains of dusty rooms with furniture under sheets, through a chill cobwebbed chapel, through a library with sunfaded shelf after shelf of musty volumes with cracking backs.

There had been times in the last hours when Harriet, growing weary, could have wished to escape this experience. She was restless, and neither servants' quarters nor apartments where kings had stayed could quell her agitation. Brave tales of the Armada, scandalous anecdotes of the Restoration washed over her ineffectually; in vain did the South Sea Bubble burst against her ears. She thought only of the agreement she had made to join Yardley on the beach that afternoon. The time was approaching rapidly.

Harriet struggled to conceal her nervous state. With affected fascination she followed Mr Travers past ancestral figures in silken robes and wigs, ermine and armour; past the Holbein, the Rubens, the Reynolds. The astronomer was posed with a telescope, the Lord High Treasurer held a white wand; the blue-coated admiral, his sword at his side, swelled up proudly before an anchored fleet. The general, on a rearing horse, played his heroic part in the Siege of Maastricht; the prime minister rested his fist on the *Journals* of the House of Commons. They passed the Landseer, the Lawrence.

"The crack of doom," said the little man.

"Pardon?"

They had reached the end of the long line of portraits. Succeeding the bewhiskered Victorian father of the present Lord Harrowblest was only an empty frame. "And here, Miss Locke, we await the work of Mr Vardell."

Harriet could not suppress a surge of pride.

"And there the line shall stop. The crack of doom, indeed."

"I'm sorry?"

Mr Travers looked at her wistfully. "You are very young, my dear." He took Harriet by the forearm and propelled her gently to the window. From high in the west wing they looked out at the rising dark mass of Shadow Black. "Think of all he has," said Mr Travers softly. "This house, yes: but others too, more magnificent than this. And papers. And more than papers. He is the most successful press lord who has ever lived. He is a genius..."

The voice trailed off. Harriet, turning to the little man, was startled by a strange new intensity in his gaze. He whispered, staring at her fixedly:

"Why did he do it?"

"I don't understand," Harriet murmured.

Mr Travers laughed, abruptly but kindly. His hand still holding his young friend by the forearm, he began to pace down the gallery floor, back and forth, back and forth.

"Quite a story. His father died early. Tragic. But not as tragic as what his older brother did then. Fifteen years Eddie's senior he was. Stephen: dashing Stephen, heir to the Harrowblest title."

Harriet thought of the story Mr Travers had told her that morning. Lord Stephen – he was the one who 'lost' the land where the holiday town was built, wasn't he? What sort of man had he been? Confusedly she scanned the line of portraits.

Mr Travers' eyes twinkled. "Oh my dear, you won't find him here!" There was triumph in his voice. Releasing Harriet's forearm, he circled around her, rather ludicrously, with little springs in his steps. For a treacherous moment Harriet thought, *He is like a malevolent imp*. Then she felt ashamed. But when the little man spoke again he spat out his words like venom:

"Stephen, the renegade! Stephen, the squanderer! Only ten years it took him. Threw away everything in his reckless rounds of vice – drinking, gambling, whoring. And did he ever pay? Did he pay?"

"I don't know," Harriet almost cried. She had no idea what Mr Travers meant.

Suddenly still, the little man stared up at her, glaring. "Dropped dead in a brothel in Wardour Street in 1902."

For a moment there was nothing more to be said.

"But I should not speak of this." Resuming, he was no longer strident. "My dear, I see you are shocked."

"No – please." For Harriet, who had barely listened to so many of his stories, it now seemed imperative that he continue this one. She felt as if a door were being opened to admit her, but opened with agonising slowness.

Her companion grimaced and wrung his hands. "Something in the brain, they said – Stephen, I mean. Just went, like that." He snapped his fingers. "It can happen. But no doubt his dissipations hardly helped." He sighed. "Of course there were claims."

"Claims?"

"Oh yes. Take a woman called 'Maisie T' – also known as 'The

Duchess', I believe. Employee, as it happened – one might go so far as to say a shareholder – in the very establishment in Wardour Street I mentioned. Well, you can believe old Maisie, Stephen's most regular consort, was hardly averse to making demands – for the maintenance of her *illegitimate child*, of course..."

Mr Travers, adjusting his waistcoat, pulled himself up short. "But that is hardly important, my dear. Of course young Master Eddie inherited all. But then Eddie found what poor Maisie T, left out in the cold – oh, deservedly, no doubt – did not have the chance to find: that *all*, after Stephen's reign, meant little. Very little."

"How dreadful," Harriet said respectfully.

"Not at all, my dear. To some, adversity is a spur. You know the story: decayed aristocrat saves fortune by going into newspapers?"

Harriet nodded; but she was not quite convincing. Briefly Mr Travers rehearsed the tale.

The young Lord Edward's rise had been swift. At twenty, with the remnants of his family fortunes, he launched a comic paper called *Halfpenny Half-Holiday*. Modelled closely on Harmsworth's early ventures, it exceeded them as much in the modernity of its layout as in the extremes of its mirth and mayhem. Its success was instant and massive. Within two years it was followed by a host of periodicals aimed similarly – so Mr Travers put it – at the lower orders. For children there were *Funny Pictures, Illustrated Funnies, Willie Wonder's Comic Paper*; for the housewife, *Fireside Friend, Chit-Chat, Woman's Place*; for the factory girl, *Pocketful o' Posies*, a sentimental story paper. The list grew longer and longer, and every title made money.

At the age of twenty-five Harrowblest launched his first daily newspaper. The notorious *Evening Empire* had one aim, and one aim alone: to maximise circulation, and hence advertising revenue. A relentless round of competitions and giveaways buttressed a farrago of sex, crime, astrology and sport.

But the *Empire* was a mere stepping stone. On the profits of the scandal-sheet Harrowblest launched the *Daily Telescope*, a morning paper designed to rival *The Times*. Harrowblest became respectable.

The war hastened the process, with Empire Press leading the way in patriotic fervour. In 1915, in a blaze of publicity, the handsome young proprietor joined the Royal Flying Corps. In 1918, when the war was almost over, he was shot down over Germany. He was horribly injured. His public career was over. Lord Harrowblest retreated into seclusion, but from behind the scenes, in the post-war years, he masterminded the expansion of his empire around the world.

"So, my dear, I ask you: why did he do it?"

Harriet was confused. "To save his fortune?"

Mr Travers, with an exclamation, pirouetted suddenly away from her. It was as if the little man were an ungainly bird, struggling absurdly to take flight.

"Not his fortune, my dear!" he cried. His gestures swept past the portraits. "Look around you – think what we have seen! The poet, the prime minister, the admiral, the astronomer! The architect, the explorer, the philosopher – the general, the tragic cavalier! Think, my dear, not least of the glorious ladies – what a pageant of superior beings has passed us by! I ask you, my dear, was it for gain alone, for sordid gain, that young Eddie Harrowblest, abandoned to fate, grasped so firmly the nettle of life? No, my dear, no – it was the line, the line!"

The little man's voice had risen to a shriek. Flinging out his arms he cried out again, as if with joy:

"The line!"

The words ricocheted wildly down the Long Gallery.

Then as they died away Harriet, with a growing horror, watched Mr Travers slowly collapse before her. His knees buckled beneath him and he drew up his hands, shielding his face.

She went to him.

"Mr Travers – " She reached uncertainly for his quaking shoulder. His temple throbbed like a beating tom-tom and as he shook he made a succession of strangled inhuman sounds.

The little man peeped guiltily from behind his hands. It was not until she looked into his face that Harriet realised the truth: his convulsions were those not of sorrow, but mirth. A strangled guffaw escaped him as he rose unsteadily to his feet.

"I'm sorry, my dear." He wiped his eyes. "It's the irony, you see."

"The irony?"

"Oh yes. After all – where is the line now?"

Harriet considered the question. "Lady Harrowblest has – "

"Borne him no heirs? Impossible, my dear."

Harriet flushed.

"But there *was* an heir." Mr Travers spoke calmly. "His father worshipped him. If you were not so *very* young, my dear, you might remember the story. The boy's name was Peter Harrowblest – the product of Eddie's first marriage. Date of birth, February 20th, 1919. Conceived – if you'll pardon me, my dear – in his father's last leave before his – hm – *debilitating* accident. It was a kind of miracle..."

"He lived?"

"Oh yes, my dear – lived to be a man. Look: I always keep it." From his waistcoat, the little man produced a crumpled photograph, giving it a transitory glance before he extended it to his new friend. "He was... he was like a god in human form," he added, his eyes downcast.

Carefully Harriet took the photograph. With a curious reverence she gazed at the image of a young man in uniform – a flight lieutenant in the RAF. His blond radiant beauty was almost overwhelming, and as his eyes – so it seemed – looked up into hers, she experienced a peculiar, unaccustomed stirring. She shuddered. Then in an instant of terrible certainty, Harriet imagined an aeroplane falling through the air, and the beautiful young man consumed in flames. Unbearable. Her hand was shaking as she handed back the photograph.

Mr Travers smiled at her kindly. He said simply:

"Thirteen years ago he disappeared."

"What?" The curt syllable escaped before Harriet could hold it back.

"It was the winter of 1942. On leave in London. Never reported back to base. A hero of the Battle of Britain, and he simply... vanished." Mr Travers held up the photograph as if he were about to tear it.

Harriet cried out.

There was a sharp crack-cracking noise. Hastily Mr Travers returned the photograph to his pocket, and Harriet twisted around to see a large heavy door opening unexpectedly in the far end of the gallery, which she had thought to be merely a blind, panelled wall. Standing in the doorway was a tall young man, painfully thin, with prematurely grey hair, combed harshly back. For so young a man his bearing was strangely stiff. Harriet supposed him to be one of the servants, although what position he might occupy, she could not say. Dressed in an immaculate dark suit, he bore more than a passing resemblance to an undertaker.

He pushed the heavy door back briskly behind him and strode towards them with a determined tread.

"Excuse me, my dear." Mr Travers drew Harriet back and stepped forward, colouring.

Turning to the window, as if in polite deference, a puzzled Harriet strained to hear the muttered conversation. A glimmering awareness of the geography of the house told her that the far end of the gallery must connect with the West Tower, the astronomer's tower. Mr Travers had said the tower was unsafe, but it was from there that the servant must have come, if servant he were. As it happened, both his words and the manner in which they were uttered – harshly, between clenched teeth – suggested otherwise.

"The Long Gallery is to be kept locked. *Only the painter*: you knew that."

"I thought our young guest – "

"You *thought*." Investing the words with an infinite contempt, the tall young man broke from Mr Travers and advanced, with a genial but ugly smile, towards Harriet. Struggling to conceal her alarm, she smiled in return.

"Miss... Locke, isn't it? Charmed to meet you, charmed. My name is Charles Collidge."

Harriet looked into the stranger's face. From a distance it had seemed a smooth mask, falsely suggesting youth; up close, it belonged clearly to a man of fifty, perhaps sixty. But if his skin was deeply lined, scattered with a thousand thin precise wrinkles, by a strange paradox it appeared also to be drawn too tightly, like the skin of a drum, over his bony forehead and jaw. The effect was to give him a disturbingly desiccated look, as one might find, perhaps, in the features of a corpse that was no longer quite fresh. Yet for all this there remained a quality of youth, even a fleeting handsomeness, which seemed as Harriet watched to play about Mr Collidge's face, clashing disturbingly with the suggestions of death.

Polite phrases clattered from his lips.

"You are the *fiancée* of our young painter, Miss Locke? His work shall soon, we hope, be joining this illustrious exhibition… I do hope you enjoy your stay."

Walking back down the gallery with Mr Travers, Harriet only asked:
"Mr Collidge – is he a servant?"
"Not quite, my dear – not quite."

10
A Positive Woman

The glories of *Bluefinch*!

Toby raked back his windswept hair. *Bluefinch* was his secret, he was sure of it. In *Bluefinch*, he could escape. Through screwed-up eyes he turned to look back over the dazzling stretch of water behind him. The ragged ascending curve of cliff, culminating in the grim edifice of Shadow Black, was far off. Could they see him from the house? Impossible. The angle was all wrong. His heart exulted.

Bluefinch rounded the promontory into Lightletter Bay. Under the brilliant sun the two Lightletters staggered down to the sea. To the east was the fishing village with its ancient leaning houses and lapping boats; to the west was the holiday town, a forlorn ruin. Blind and impassive, a tall hotel looked out over the silent bay. Boarding houses, white like skeletons, flanked it like a phalanx of affronted old maids, supporting the vicar in a hopeless campaign. The pier with its flashing silver dome sent out a stranger, more sinister signal.

The part of the pier which joined it to the promenade had collapsed, leaving only a collection of rusted girders, prodding up uselessly from the sand. Cut off from the shore, the great edifice hovered above the sea like a vast exotic creature, raised terribly from the depths. At close range the rusted pylons contrasted strangely with the silver of the dome; but then the dome itself lost much of its splendour. From a distance it looked like an alien vessel, bulging from the end of the pier like the unsunken half of a monstrous ball-bearing. The riveted sections of weathered iron Toby saw now came almost, absurdly, as a shock.

He cut the motor. Gliding towards the mysterious ruin, he felt as if he were slipping into a different world. A dream. He breathed deeply.

Once upon a time and a very good time it was – but it wasn't, not really – Harriet sat huddled under a black floppy hat, attempting half-heartedly to read a book called *A Portrait of the Artist as a Young Man*. The sun seared high in the late afternoon. Wrapped round her shoulders was a black kimono, slithery and silken, concealing the scanty swimming costume it embarrassed her to wear.

Yardley, in a white one-piece swimsuit, with a stylishly bullet-shaped matching cap, luxuriated on a long towel, leafing through a magazine propped upon the rise of her barely-covered breasts. Mark, resplendent in white trunks with a black band round the waist, lay at an angle to both women, his brown back upturned to the sun, his belly pressed directly into the grainy sand. His jaw rested on the muscle of his forearm and his sunglasses, pushed up from his closed eyelids, lay in the tangles of his salty steaming hair. A towel, an open sketchbook, a bottle of suntan lotion and a pair of espadrilles lay beside him in a jumbled heap. Piled in a hamper at the back of the little party were the remains of a picnic tea.

Earlier, returning to her room from the gallery, Harriet had found the little maid Milly once again putting away clothes. For a moment, Harriet had been relieved. Her box? But her box had not arrived. Milly held up lavish gowns and lingerie, expatiating excitedly on her Ladyship's goodness; Harriet, with a sigh, and to Milly's surprise, only sat heavily on the edge of the bed. What she felt was a sense of foreboding. Something strange had come over her in Yardley's rooms that morning. She felt as if she had been, in a manner of speaking, seduced.

Sweltering under the black kimono, Harriet leafed surreptitiously through her book. Was it ever going to become a proper story? She was not sure that it was. Baby talk, moocows and wetting the bed – it was all rather distasteful, but she had finished her Daphne du Maurier on the train. This strange book would have to suffice.

For some time Harriet had been attempting – after a long delay – to read the books Miss Padbury had urged upon her, in the days when Newnham College loomed. After all, Harriet reasoned, she must try to educate herself, if she were to talk to Mark's artistic friends. But really, she supposed she still felt guilty – guilty, or at least sad, to have disappointed Miss Padbury. But could she have forced herself to read books like this one – let alone write essays about them? Harriet would never have dared tell Miss Padbury, but in truth she almost always preferred books written by women – which proved, no doubt, that it was just as well she had never gone to Cambridge.

If only she had a copy of *Jane Eyre*, right now!

"Trash!" Yardley, with a contemptuous snort, discarded her magazine. "I'm going back in. Coming, kids?" She did not wait for them, running lightly down the twenty yards to the sea, her hands flapping girlishly, the white of her costume flashing against her sun-darkened flesh. Her delighted cries rang out across the beach as she splashed into the shallows.

Harriet shifted on her towel. Beneath the kimono, her swimming costume cut painfully into a figure just a little more ample, despite Yardley's assurances, than that for which it was designed. Enviously, Harriet thought of Yardley: the high cheekbones; the arching throat; the firm uplifted mound of the breasts. The long limbs were proportioned like the statue of a goddess.

"She's so beautiful," Harriet said aloud.

Absently, she twisted at her golden band.

"Dear Hattie!" Mark opened his eyes. "She's an old woman. Well, almost."

"Oh Mark, she isn't!"

Smiling, Mark rolled onto his side. He took her hand. As he lay relaxed beside her, sand crumbling slowly from his hard brown chest, Harriet thought how handsome he looked. Sometimes his presence almost overwhelmed her – his presence, and the clever, outrageous things he would say. Oh, he was so clever, so much cleverer than her! For some reason she remembered – she often remembered it – the day she had told him, in an indifferent tone, about Miss Padbury, and Newnham. How Mark had laughed – and when Harriet asked why, he had stroked her hand, kissed her, told her she had had a narrow escape, and made a joke about the Isle of Lesbos. For a moment Harriet had been shocked, deeply shocked; then she had laughed too – harder, it seemed, than she had ever laughed before.

And had loved Mark more.

Gazing upon him now, she struggled to frame some remark which would express, with appropriate indirection, the depth of her passion. But should she speak?

"Mark, I – "

"Look at this! How vain she is!" Mark, with satirical contempt, took up the discarded *Hollywood World*. The magazine lay open at the pages Yardley had been idly studying. One page was filled with Yardley, in glamorous monochrome, *circa* 1935. On the facing page, a headline cried:

Whatever Happened to… YARDLEY?

"Once she had the world at her feet," Mark read with mock sonorousness. "Then she gave it all away – gave it away for love. Feature writer Heidi Hoppelmeyer looks back on the career of Yardley Urban, and asks if one of Hollywood's brightest stars shall ever return to the screen."

Harriet struggled to suppress a smile. She glanced uneasily towards the sea, where Yardley's brown limbs could be seen cleaving smoothly through the glassy still water. The white bathing cap bobbed up and down.

"Here we are," said Mark. "Born Eunice Grubb in Stepney, East London, in 1907… there! She's nearly fifty!"

"*Mark!*" Harriet hissed. But hilarity overcame her. "Eunice Grubb!"

"Stepney!"

They laughed together.

"That's my girl. Let's see what else they say – "

"Mark," Harriet said suddenly, "you do love me, don't you?"

"Hattie!" Mark scrambled up onto his knees. His chest heaved with a deep, deliberate breath. "Of course I love you, darling. What's brought this on?"

Harriet looked down. Confused thoughts struggled in her mind. Already, more than once, the wedding had been delayed. First it had been planned for February. But Mark had been working towards a new exhibition, and it seemed sensible to wait. Then it was June, but things went wrong. The exhibition was a failure. Mark had been experimenting with a new style. The aim of his work, he had told Harriet, was to convey the strangeness of life. He had been driven to extremes to communicate his vision. Now he would essay a new subtlety. But the public was unimpressed. It wanted vomit and Princess Margaret in a brothel. Mark plunged into depression, and the wedding was planned for August. Then Mark was offered the Harrowblest commission, and could hardly turn it down. Now Harriet did not know when the wedding would be. Would it ever happen? But this was something she could not quite bring herself to ask.

She said only, "Mark, I worry I've... done *wrong*, coming here. I thought perhaps you weren't pleased. It was meant to be a surprise for you." Her face was shadowed by the broad brim of her hat and her words were barely audible. Mark's brow furrowed and he moved to embrace her. "It was a *nice* surprise, wasn't it, Mark?"

"Hattie, of course! My poor darling – "

Harriet rushed on, "I thought it was Lady Harrowblest who'd invited me, you see. Then I realised it wasn't, it was Mrs Van Voyd. It's almost as if they're playing some – *game*, and I thought..."

"Darling, who cares who invited you? You're here now, and I'm glad. Don't worry about silly old Mrs Van Voyd, or Yardley either. They're an eccentric pair, but they mean no harm."

The embrace was long, enveloping and warm. Harriet's heart pounded, but with fear as much as joy. When he released her, her face was still troubled.

"I can't help it, Mark," she murmured, looking into his eyes. "I *do* worry. There's something about this place. When I arrived I had the strangest dream... and then today..."

"Oh do come in, you two! It's wonderful!" Yardley, like a sea-nymph emerging from the waves, shouted and waved from waist-deep water.

Mark waved a casual hand in return. "Better keep Her Ladyship happy. Coming, darling? You haven't been in at all." He sprang up, pulling Harriet by the hand.

She resisted, shaking her head. "No, Mark – I don't feel up to it today. Really. You go in." She smiled broadly. "I've got my book."

Mark swooped down to kiss her the cheek. "No more silliness, do you hear? And darling – don't strain your eyes over that mouldy old book." He grinned. "You wouldn't want me to pack you off to Lesbos College now, would you?"

Harriet laughed, "Newnham. It's called Newnham!"

And running down the slope of the beach, Mark kicked a great clod of sand into the air. The clod exploded into a powdery cloud and he leapt up in triumph, like a footballer at a goal, and splashed into the water with a joyous whoop.

11
The Negative Man

"You are the last survivor of your race. Our ray has annihilated all life on this planet but your own – "

Toby's favourite astronomical story was 'The Vondrillon Invasion' by Chad Heavydale III. The Vondrillons were an infinitely advanced technological race. They were nine feet tall with faces shaped like hatchets and cold reptilian skin patterned in black and white stripes. They wore huge bat-like capes, had no emotions, and could adapt to any environment. Originally from Vondrillos, the sixth planet of the Aldebaran system, they had spread out to colonise the universe, destroying all life forms which stood in their way. In 'The Vondrillon Invasion' they attacked the Earth with the intention of annihilating the human race.

They succeeded.

Their method was intriguing. So advanced was Vondrillon weaponry that all that was needed was a single 'repeater ray' to be fired by one member of the small invasion party. Striking its human target, in microseconds the ray burnt out the cerebral cortex, then disintegrated the entire fabric of the body. This was impressive enough, but the ray – by no means exhausted by this simple task – was then able to 'jump' to the next available human. Seeking out all organic forms like the one at which it was first aimed, the ray would 'jump' endlessly until all such life forms were atomised. Only the Vondrillon commander, with a special 'jamming' signal, could halt its remorseless onward path.

The story began on the day on which all the dogs in the world were found dead (the Vondrillons had been doing a 'trial run'). It proceeded through charades of negotiation between the invaders and the

Earthmen; then at the climax the 'cleansing ray' swept the planet, impossible to escape. In the last scene, when the ray had done its work, the one man who had been made immune from it, the despicable Ira Finkelstein, grovelled before the commander, cringing and crying. The pacifist scientist had co-operated with the invaders, thinking they would bring about world peace. Instead he had seen his own wife and daughter fizzed into atoms as the ray zig-zagged through them. "Shut it off!" he screamed, "shut it off!" But the Vondrillons had no pity.

"This planet has been cleansed for superior beings – "

Toby affected a harsh metallic voice. He was the Vondrillon commander. Ira Finkelstein knelt before him, eyes upturned in terror.

Beneath the dome at the end of Lightletter Pier lay a great round empty room. It must have been a ballroom. Toby stood in the centre, the highest point of the dome above him. As he spoke, the hard inverted bowl of the ceiling returned the expected echo.

Then the echo died.

The calm was narcotic. Only the faintest breeze stole through the panes, cracked and salty, of equidistant windows. Perilous chandeliers chimed softly overhead. Cobwebs hung from them like diseased lungs, magnified enormously, breathing grotesquely in grey draping tatters. Clots of dust, thick choking whorls, shifted about the floor with an infinite languor. Beneath the floor, the lapping sea sucked at encrusted pylons.

Toby sighed. He turned about in a slow revolution, his espadrilles rasping on the ruined dance floor. Completing his shuffling circle he started a second, the murky walls swinging past his camera eyes. Then he began to turn faster. He was the Vondrillon space-corkscrew that could twist and twist into a planet's crust, sucking up vital core-energy, then – reversing instantaneously – spiral suddenly upwards into interstellar space.

He flung out his arms to their full stretch. The floor creaked under his rapid tread. He closed his eyes. Planetary energies flooded up through him, fuelling him for his impending upward surge.

Not yet.

Not yet.

Now.

He staggered, sprawling to the dusty floor.

"Ugh!"

Toby's arm twisted beneath him. Shards of pain burst in his wrist. He gripped it. The great dome wheeled above him; chandeliers swung impassively like pendulums. He rolled onto his side, drawing up his knees to his chest.

Toby breathed hard. The room was steadying slowly. He screwed his eyes up tightly, then opened them quickly: once, twice, three times. Four.

It was when he opened his eyes for the fourth time that he saw the pair of white shoes, gleaming with a pale phosphorescence in the gloom. Toby's heart thudded. His eyes travelled slowly upwards: he saw a pair of white trousers, a white jacket, a white shirt. Then there was the Panama hat. The figure stood some ten yards away. It remained silent and the features were masked in shadow.

Toby rose to his feet uncertainly, brushing thick dust from his clothes and limbs. His wrist throbbed with a new violence and he clutched it to his chest.

"A charming performance." There was a sharp report as the stranger clapped his hands: once, twice, three times. Four. The leaden applause rang out like shots. "But the pity of it! Your daring *pirouette* – "

The irony was cool and strangely impersonal, delivered in impeccable public-school tones. "How pleasant to ramble in these Gothic splendours! I'm pleased your – *tastes* so accord with my own. Some would avoid such desolation – in disgust, even in fear!"

As he spoke the stranger moved forward. Coming closer he assumed definition, like a subject being focused through a photographic lens.

"For us, such a place is food for the imaginative life. *I am certain of nothing but the holiness of the heart's affections and* – how does it go? – *the truth of the imagination.* So vital to live a *rich* imaginative life, to lift oneself above the herd: hm?"

Oddly, in so dim a place, the stranger wore dark glasses. For a moment Toby wondered if the man were blind. But no: he was aware of eyes, observing him from behind the glass. The face was an arrangement of ugly angles beneath the high dome of the forehead. The Panama hat was tilted far back: pale, almost colourless hair could be glimpsed beneath the brim. The man was not old: thirty-five, perhaps, or forty. But the visible skin had a battered, leathery look.

"Some are afraid of the imaginative life. They have debased it, made it something ugly." A fleeting bitterness came into the voice. The stranger surveyed the empty ballroom. He mused, "Do you think there might be *ghosts?* Oh, not the ghosts of real presences – here there were none. The ghosts of what might have been – a wafting faded waltz, a snatch of bright laughter? The glimpsed silhouettes of wheeling gowns? Perhaps some more malevolent spectre? Or perhaps there is only the ubiquity of decay: hm?"

Around his neck the stranger wore a black cravat, tucked into his white shirt. The detail disturbed Toby obscurely. Only later did he realise what the stranger resembled, all in white with his black-banded neck. Of course: he was like a priest, but a priest *in reverse*, as if – yes – in a photographic negative.

"You have hurt yourself." When the negative man stood close to him, Toby saw that the white costume, which from a distance had seemed immaculate, was deeply creased and soiled. There was a pungent sweet aroma, like sick. "Give me your wrist."

Tentatively, Toby lowered his crossed arms from his chest.

"It shall not hurt."

He snatched them back. His eyes darted from the stranger to the doors.

And yet there was something transfixing about the stranger.

"Who are you?" The question was the stranger's. "Tell me your name."

Toby said, "No."

"You can't?"

"No – " Toby was confused. The intense sick smell had become a heady incense, drugging him. Exotic fumes seemed to curl about him like cords, binding him inescapably to the negative man.

"Yours has been a difficult life. A confused life." The voice dropped to an easy intimacy. "But have there not been *intimations* that – at last – it is coming to a crisis?" A brown battered hand fingered Toby's forearm. "Give me your wrist." A wave of revulsion rose within Toby. There was something terrible in the negative man, a welling loathsomeness.

The negative man said again, firmly:

"Give me your wrist."

The wave broke. Toby darted forward. The negative man grabbed him by his twisted wrist. Toby cried out. His legs buckled. Agony shot up his arm like volts.

"Please – " Shock made his voice a dry whisper.

The negative man's grip was of startling force, and he retained it while, with his free hand, he gently helped Toby to his feet. "You have not quite recovered your balance," the stranger said kindly.

Toby staggered. His vision was blurring, blackening.

"Poor boy," the negative man was saying. "Ah, it is the fault of your own folly. But *a boy's will is the wind's will* – hm?" He adjusted his grip: for comfort, no doubt. Holding the wrist like a lead he walked three times around Toby in a ring, making Toby turn. Like a magic spell, but a magic spell soused deep in irony, the stranger recited:

> *Weave a circle round him thrice*
> *And close your eyes with holy dread:*
> *For he on honey-dew hath fed,*
> *And drunk the milk of –*

Toby felt sick.

The negative man stopped again where he had started. Smiling, he fanned the fingers of his free hand and gently pushed Toby in the chest. Toby staggered back, his agonised arm stretching to the full. Through their shielding glasses the negative man's eyes surveyed him, appraising him like a partner poised for the dance. "It shall not hurt," he repeated softly.

What happened next happened fast: the negative man twisted forward with a snapping jerk and jammed his back against Toby's chest, his foot on Toby's foot, and clamped the injured arm between his own arm and his side. First he wrung the wrist between burning hands; then he dug his nails deeply into the flesh. Toby cried out, clawed once at the black-banded neck...

It was over.

The negative man released his grip and stepped calmly aside, tucking his disturbed cravat back into place. Toby sprawled again to the floor.

"It does not hurt," said the negative man. "It does not hurt, does it?"

He adjusted his sunglasses; then he seemed to reconsider, and removed them. He slipped them into a pocket of his dirty jacket; from another pocket he produced a cigarette case. The gold lid blazed up as he clicked it open.

In a kind of shadow-vision Toby saw his arm still trapped in the crushing grip and twisting like putty, knotting, stretching; twisting impossibly, but the pain was gone, and he seemed to be watching, impassively, even as his hand was torn from his arm and rent into tattered fragments. There was no blood.

The negative man tapped his cigarette-end on the lid of the case, sharply, three times, before returning the case to his jacket. He delved again for a battered lighter and brought the cigarette to his lips to light.

There was no blood. Toby raised his wrist to his eyes. There was not even bruising, only the fading semicircles of the stranger's nails. He rose slowly to his feet, turning his back to the negative man. *The pain was gone.* He flexed his fingers: made a fist: rotated it. Gently, then decisively, he prodded the flesh. Horror fought in him with wonderment as he turned again slowly to the stranger.

"Who are you?" Toby said hoarsely.

"Who am I?" said the negative man. "I know exactly who I am. The question, surely, is – who are *you*?" Unshielded, the stranger's eyes glowed with a curious lambency. He flung aside his cigarette. "Toby – "

"You know my name?"

The negative man smiled wryly. "Toby. Tobias. Tobias Oliver. Tobias Oliver Chance." He pronounced the surname with a peculiar crushing of the syllable between his teeth.

"How do you know my name?"

The glowing of the eyes seemed to have become brighter. "My dear boy, that is not the question. The question, surely, is how do *you* know your name?"

Toby stared. The negative man stepped closer. Only the extraordinary thing which happened next – the *illusion*, as he would think of it – gave Toby the strength to break away. Later, when he tried to recall what had happened, he would put it to himself that it was as if the eyes which glowed so strangely, apparently with an inner luminescence, were not really human eyes at all. In the negative man's eyes, it was rather as if the pupils and irises of human eyes were simulacra only, tattooed on some curious membrane between the eyelids and the eyes. What happened now – the terrifying *illusion* – was that in each eye these membranes seemed to slide back like curtains, parting the pupils and irises to reveal beneath them the blank radiance of eyes which were without pattern, without colour: were of only a white, searing incandescence.

12
Hideous Thing

"Empire up fifteen cents when Wall Street closed... *FT* reports City boom in Empire shares... Empire still most solid investment, say top analysts – report from *Business Guide*... Message from New York – *sell WXBC Wisconsin?*... Northern Regions franchise set to go – network penetration proceeding on course... *Singapore Telescope* still doing well, but continuing format adjustment advised..."

Was the old man listening? Collidge, at the lectern, shuffled the sheaf of messages. The thick file contained only a number of those which had arrived since yesterday's Reading. Re-routed, after sifting, from New Telescope House – Miss Fenwick made the first selection – each day the messages flooded the communications room. Forced up through concealed cables that connected the tower to the world, noisily they vomited from the banks of telex machines – entreaties, statistics, felicitations, warnings. From Miss Fenwick's generous selection, Collidge chose a smaller selection. These formed the texts for the Reading.

That the Reading was the hollowest of rituals was as evident to Collidge as it was unimportant. It had been different when they first moved their headquarters to Shadow Black, thirteen years previously, after the bombing of the old Telescope House. That had been a delicious period. As Collidge read, sonorously like a Sunday minister, his master had circled the lectern in his chair, turning and turning like a man pacing, dictating his orders from his isolated eyrie. Like a poet possessed entirely by his muse, dutifully Collidge had transcribed the commands – to sell, to buy, to sue, to sack – that later he would cable back to London. But as the years passed the old man retreated into silence, and it was up to Collidge to supply his voice. The Readings had become a hollow shell, a form.

And yet Collidge knew it was not the end. With an ineffable slowness, the pellucid period was coming... it was coming.

Thirty years before

What he had noticed first was the silence. Alone, he had been standing by the window in the editor's office in the *Daily Telescope* building. Behind double doors, set almost invisibly amongst the panelling, the dissonance of inferior offices was inaudible; the rapid unending hammerings of typewriters, the raised voices and telephone bells had passed into oblivion. Double thicknesses of glass shut out the traffic sounds from Fleet Street, far below. Pressing his forehead to the cool glass, Collidge stared down at the strangely silenced scene. Thus it was on the day, thirty years before, when his life had first acquired meaning.

Charles Collidge had been twenty-five years old then, a pale bland young man in an ill-fitting brown suit. He was a solicitor. Three months earlier he had been made a junior partner in his uncle's City firm; the months since had been dispiriting. That he was not a success was clear; that he would never be one was clear too, at least to Charles. He wished he were dead. His life enfolded him like a grey, irremovable cloak.

And then his uncle, the previous evening – they had been dining at his uncle's club, of which Charles had recently become a member – asked him what he thought of *this Harrowblest fellow*.

"Harrowblest?" Charles hesitated over a mouthful of mutton. The matter was of no interest to him, none at all. But Uncle Matthew held firm views. It was important, Charles knew, to express the approved opinion; determining this opinion was the difficult part. *The fellow's a bounder*, it occurred to him to say – but was his uncle so predictable? Perhaps Uncle Matthew thought Harrowblest was admirable.

"An extraordinary success story," Charles suggested lamely.

"The fellow's a bounder," bristled Uncle Matthew. "If there's one thing I detest, it's the yellow press."

"Of course," Charles said glumly, and endeavoured to adjust his celluloid collar. All day the back stud had been digging into his neck like a malicious, burrowing insect. Uncle Matthew's words – his uncle had embarked on a lengthy disquisition – washed over him like silence.

Later Charles would think of this time as a sort of prehistory, a chrysalis phase of his life. Had he known that even then? Sitting in the club with Uncle Matthew, Charles had thought of his lodgings, his suits, his neatly ranged shoes, the brilliantine he combed each morning into his hair. He thought of his cigarette case, the hateful hideous thing, a present from his uncle on joining the firm. The old man's jaw had been set decisively as he informed his nephew, in a kindly tone, of the future that was planned for him. Charles, of course, had accepted; accepted even the leaden hints that he would marry Uncle Matthew's daughter. Was he to refuse? He thought of Cousin Cynthia. Her bland loveliness filled him with a vague unease.

"So what d'you think, m'boy? Would you consider it?"

Startled out of his lethargy, for an absurd moment Charles thought Uncle Matthew was referring to Cynthia. (A mournful waiter hovered; coffee and port had succeeded, at last, to dessert.)

"Strictly on a trial basis, you understand."

"Of course." Charles smiled tightly. What was his uncle talking about?

"Fellow's a bounder, as I say. Nasty libel work – unsavoury, I'll grant you that. But the account is not to be sneezed at."

"No," said Charles.

"Good lad!" Startlingly, his uncle patted his hand. "All settled then. You're to see this Bocks chap tomorrow morning."

Bocks?

"Bocks," Charles said aloud now, turning from the window, examining the editor's office. Large and light, it was panelled to the ceiling in varnished pine. There were no decorations; only matching unornate vases on a mantelpiece and a photograph on the wall above, framed in sleek silver. Placed around the walls were low-slung chairs made of chrome and leather, and low tables made of chrome and glass. The carpet was a patternless beige, as luxuriant in texture as in appearance it was bland. Before a sheer expanse of window, filling the external wall, the great wedge of the editor's desk jutted from a backdrop of dispassionate sky. Charles could have laughed. It was 1925; the modernity was exhilarating. How different, this, from the dingy Victorian chambers of Collidge Collidge and Crust!

One feature puzzled Charles. In a crescent shape surrounding the desk, a flat curve of hard blond wood cut through the carpet like a path. At each end of the path, flanking the desk like twin sentry-boxes, bulky square pylons ran between floor and ceiling. Set almost flush against the plate-glass windows, the pylons were the width of several men and panelled in the same pale timber as the walls. What purpose could they serve, these pylons, this path? Symbolically to cut off the editor from the room, to create around his desk a zone of unapproachability? Charles revolved the idea; then he had a better one. Of course: the path – as he thought of it – was a path in fact, lining the route where the editor paced the floor. The notion had about it a certain delightfulness, and Charles turned back towards the room. Surveying it afresh, his eyes lingered on the photograph above the mantelpiece. He had barely noticed it before; now he felt himself drawn to it, as if by a curious magnetism.

The subjects were a uniformed young man, and a young woman in a wedding dress. The woman was beautiful, but Charles studied the man. He was an officer in the Royal Flying Corps. Fair and gauntly handsome, undoubtedly a gentleman, he was one of the few persons Charles had seen who could be described legitimately as 'dashing' – the epithet rose embarrassingly to mind. But the compelling quality of the young bridegroom lay not in his general bearing; rather it was in his extraordinary eyes. Dark and deep, they drew the viewer irresistibly towards them – as now they drew Charles. He moved around the massive cluttered desk towards the picture.

Standing beneath the portrait, he felt himself impelled to stretch up his hand. The moment was one of strange significance; but the nature of the significance, Charles knew, was not yet clear to him. Absurdly he reached up to touch the frozen image, thrilling to the coldness of the dividing glass; absurdly the identity of the bridegroom had not yet come to him.

What happened next happened quickly.

"Damn, damn, damn!"

Charles snatched away his hand. He spun round. A burly man, his tie askew, strode towards the desk, the panelled doors of the office slamming behind him. The intruder – for so he seemed to Charles – was a massive mountain of fat, his cheeks bloated and purple, a huge cigar suspended from his lips.

"Who the hell – ?" The mountain of fat reared, glowering, on Charles; Charles swallowed, crimson with shame. He stared dumbly at the bloated purple cheeks, the heavy-hanging cigar, the thick roll of fat that bulged above the collar.

Then the strange thing happened. With a whirring suggestive of concealed machinery, the panelling of the left pylon slid upwards from the floor. In an instant Charles realised what the pylons were: of course, they were elevators, cleverly concealed.

There came a harsh metallic voice – "*Bocks!*" – and then, from the pylon, the owner of the voice emerged, advancing round the curve of the wooden arc in an elaborate wheeled chair. The chair appeared to glide automatically over the blond track; the sound it made suggested it was mechanical. The occupant's left hand was poised above a control panel on the side of the armrest. He pulled a lever and the moving chair stopped in the centre of the track.

"Sir – " Bocks hovered obsequiously over the cripple.

"This farrago," the cripple began, "has gone on long enough. Am I to have my good name besmirched by that woman? Let legal proceedings begin at once."

"Sir – "

There was a rapid round of orders, fired in a sort of staccato oral shorthand.

Fascinated, Charles studied the figure in the chair. The cripple was a man of perhaps forty, but so evidently damaged that it was difficult to tell. Stationary on his track, he stared ahead fixedly. The side of his face that was visible to Charles was an ugly mask of scar tissue. The flesh appeared to have been churned up with a plough; the socket of the eye was an arid pit. A strange longing fought in Charles with revulsion.

At the cripple's entrance the room had begun to darken. The grey sky grew greyer; rain began to slither down the doubled glass.

"Bocks." The voice, so close, seemed to echo from afar. "Who is with you?"

"This young man, sir – "

"What young man? Bring him to me, Bocks."

Charles's head throbbed violently; passively he allowed himself to be ushered towards the blind man.

But the man was not blind. Standing square before him, Charles saw the truth, the terrible division of the face. *These twain*, came the phrase, *these twain, these twain*. The right side was a ruin, from puckered forehead to twisted lip; the left was the smooth visage of a handsome man – the sort of man, of course, whom one might call 'dashing'.

"Do you know who I *am*, boy?"

Charles moistened his lips. He felt himself breaking down, crumbling within. "Yes, Lord Harrowblest."

And Harrowblest asked Bocks: "Who is this boy?"

Bocks stammered, "Sir, I – "

"Remove that foul cigar when you address me, Bocks. I profit from but do not admire your moral and spiritual loathsomeness. This boy I can see is of a different ilk – your name, boy, your name."

Charles told him. "From Collidge Collidge and Crust, sir. I had an appointment – "

Harrowblest attempted a wry laugh; the effort, evidently, caused him pain. "This latest absurd crisis has overturned all appointments. Boy, are you familiar with Lady Beatrix Bayes?"

Charles, who was not, said that he was.

There was a dark sparkling in Harrowblest's good eye. "You are *not* familiar with her Ladyship, boy. You could hardly speak of her impassively if you were. Lady Beatrix Bayes, I declare, is the most profligate whore in Britain."

"I meant, sir, that I had heard of her," said Charles, crimson; "that her reputation had – reached me."

"A glib tongue," Harrowblest said sardonically. "No matter. That woman in any case is about to be destroyed. Perhaps you, in your humble fashion, could assist me? Come."

And with that the cripple, ignoring Bocks, set his chair in motion again. The wheels slid soundlessly over the second half of the semicircle; the panelling of the second pylon slid upwards. Uncertainly, Charles looked back at Bocks. The editor pushed the wet end of his cigar between his lips, his fat neck swelling. The thought came to Collidge, apparently from nowhere: *Bocks is unreliable. He shall let Harrowblest down in time.*

Later that day, as he left Telescope House, Charles could barely suppress an urge to leap into the air. The destruction of Lady Beatrix Bayes would soon be in train; its reason was as obscure to him as its necessity was apparent. It was a case that Charles was to handle brilliantly. His rise would be swift – as swift, indeed, as the disgrace of Bocks. For of course, Charles had been right about Bocks. He would be right about everything.

On his last day at Collidge Collidge and Crust, his uncle took him aside.

"It's no good asking you to stay, Charles." It was not a question, it was a statement of fact.

"We've been through this, Uncle." Charles did not look up from the tea chest he was packing. Cast down carelessly on his desk behind him was the cigarette case, the hideous thing, which his uncle had given him on joining the firm.

"We must go through it again, Charles. Am I to assume that you are entirely irresponsible? To take on this Harrowblest work, a little of it – that was acceptable..."

"Your idea, Uncle. And a good one. Look at the income it has brought this firm."

"Don't, Charles. To take on some – *consultancy*, I say, is one thing... But to *join* that wretched company, to become a lackey of that – creature..."

"Instead of yours? I've been a lackey here, Uncle. At Telescope House I shall be chief legal adviser."

"You fool! You – you puppy! 'Legal adviser' in a cesspit, a brothel – "

"It's a view." Charles dropped a heavy legal dictionary into the tea chest with a thud.

"And Cynthia?"

"I've told you, Uncle, I don't intend to marry Cynthia, I never did.

And oh – " Charles shoved an arm absent-mindedly into his jacket, producing a crumpled envelope. "Could you drop this in at the club for me, Uncle? I'm terminating my membership."

Uncle Matthew struck the letter from his nephew's hand. The action was unexpected, so clumsily violent. Stiffening, Charles stared at his uncle. The old man was ludicrous, pathetic.

"I've heard things about Harrowblest – "

"I *know* things about Harrowblest. That he is the most successful newspaper proprietor in this country, for example. And he'll soon be more than that. The Empire is expanding. New worlds to conquer. We're pushing into America, the colonies – "

"*He shall weep at last.*"

"Pardon, Uncle? You're muttering."

But Charles had heard.

The old man, still muttering, retreated to his room. A little later, leaving chambers, Charles left behind on his desk the cigarette case, the hideous thing.

The years before the war had been the happiest of his life. He had lied, of course, about his status at Telescope House; his rôle was not so much legal adviser as personal assistant to Harrowblest. Constantly at his employer's side, indispensable, Charles witnessed the years of his master's greatest triumphs. From the *Rangoon Telescope* to the *Oregon Bugle*, the *Auckland Examiner* to the *Bombay Microscope*, the Empire grew at an astonishing rate. Rival companies capitulated to takeovers like maidens to Don Juan. Even the *Interrogator* – that venerable paper! – became under Harrowblest a thrusting tabloid, brimful of sex and crime. In 1928 the Glasgow magazine chain, F.C. McConnell's, yielded. Harrowblest soon controlled the British film industry; massive interests were purchased in American companies, too. Moves were made into American broadcasting – the field was wide open, as His Lordship said. While others scoffed, Harrowblest was the first man to realise the potential of television. His genius was unassailable. In his vast suite atop Telescope House, where the carpet was cut through repeatedly with tracks – curlicues and loopings and criss-crossings and spirals, rococo ellipses through carpet archipelagos – Harrowblest would circle repeatedly in his chair, dictating to Collidge his schemes for domination. Across the length of one wall was a massive world map. The countries His Lordship had 'conquered' were in yellow, dazzling yellow; those that had yet to yield were in black. Sometimes, contemplating these black spaces, Collidge felt himself filling slowly with a joyous, powerful certainty.

13
Fahrenheit 451

> Villa Santa Clara
> Thurs. 21st Jul., 1955

CHANCE

 would be a fine thing that YOU wd. write ME a decent letter, dear little Toe-by-Arse. You tell me Auntie Cora doesn't wear the flowerpot ALL the time (I had SO hoped) & you're stuck all summer in her FLAT IN CHELSEA, bored to distraction? I spit on your boredom! I spit on Chelsea (SOME FEAT from here!). SURELY Auntie Cora is a denizen of some FANTASTIC place??

 Chancer, you must write to ENTERTAIN. It is poor old EEL who is driven to DISTRACTION, & little Chance has no right to be. Hast THOU a Miriam? Hast thou a HOSEPIPE?

 Yesterday we ventured at last to dear FIRENZE, Miriam bleating about the HEAT all the way, Hosepipe INEPTLY veering the (MOST inappropriate) Bentley about the roads alarmingly; EEL TRYING to concentrate on LAST AND FIRST MEN (more later) & TRYING to ignore THEM (the SCENERY's no good, H&M spoil it).

 Alas EEL cd. not ignore the PARENTAL (HAH!) couple in dear FIRENZE, where Daddy 4 lumbered about the UFFIZI & the PITTI & the PALAZZO VECCHIO & the ACCADEMIA DI BELLE ARTI polluting the air with nasal-toned INANITIES which would have disgraced a party of blue-haired OMNIBUSSERS from Des Moines, Iowa. His CRITICAL COMMENTARIES on the works of BOTTICELLI, DONATELLO, DA VINCI, RAPHAEL, TITIAN & BELLINI, EEL cannot BRING himself to reproduce (ditto remarks on DAVID 'IL GIGANTE'); & is sure Toe-by can imagine for himself the hateful MIRIAM all the time flattering her beloved MANUFACTURER OF HOSEPIPES, when not of course BEMOANING the HEAT, her FEET, the TOURISTS, the ITALIANS, AND the EXCESSIVE complexities of her CAMERA.

Now WILY EEL of COURSE contrived to SLITHER away, but not without efforts DISTRESSINGLY excessive for so FIERY an afternoon – MIRIAM, in addition to aforesaid HEAT, FEET, &c., WOULD keep turning around & asking irritably, 'Where IS Eugene now?'... WHEN at last the EEL SLIPPED from the dim recesses of SANTA MARIA DEL FIORE, sacrificing the COOL interior for the GREATER relief of M&H-lessness, a STROLL along the historic ARNO (SLIPPED towards via blessed VIA CALZAIOLI) of course seemed in order – WESTWARD, preferably NOT stopping until the MEDITERRANEAN shore impeded FURTHER progress...

Suffice to say that the EEL, by the PONTE VECCHIO, seemed on the verge of a most INTERESTING adventure when – ALACK! ALACK! WHO should run SCREAMING across said PONTE but a RED-FACED Miriam, PATHETICALLY in pursuit of a ragged LOCAL YOUTH (OUTSTRIPPING her by far) who had taken a LIKING MORE ARDENT THAN HERS to the EXCESSIVELY complex camera?... Efforts at CONCEALMENT of EEL's length were in VAIN, & poor EEL cd. not SLITHER OFF from the terrible TABLEAU which SWIFTLY formed around him: a puffing HOSEPIPE (pulling UP THE REAR), a sympathetic CLUSTER of BLUE-HAIRED BUSSERS from Des Moines, Iowa, COMFORTING (all of them) a SOBBING

Miriam, BERATING (ALL!) a TARDY EUGENE, who for ALL his undoubted FLEET-FOOTED YOUTH had FAILED to SPRING AT ONCE into PURSUIT of the VILLAIN... Oh, MIRIAM! Oh, HOSEPIPE! Oh, BLUE-HAIRED BUSSERS!... Were EEL but LONG enough he would WRAP HIMSELF AROUND YOU – all! – & send searing through you his FATAL FIZZING CURRENT!

Miriam didn't even LIKE the wretched camera.

MADNESS is setting in. EEL's read nearly ALL the books he brought: FAHRENHEIT 451 (excellent – author CAN ACTUALLY WRITE!!), CHILDHOOD'S END (good, but), THE SPACE MERCHANTS (clever), THE ISLAND OF DR. MOREAU (4th time!!) have BITTEN THE DUST already. Now he's reading Last & 1st Men VERY slowly (boring in a way, but fascinating: same principle as SHAPE OF THINGS TO COME, but different)... he envies TOE-BY that stack of ASTRONOMICAL STORIES & expects PERSONALLY to inspect EVERY one!

So he supposes you DID tell him ONE interesting thing.

Eternally yours in shame & boredom,

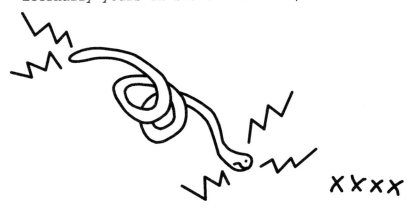

xxxx

Pee Ess. There has to be a TWIST in the Hugo story at the end. When the little RAT gets back to the

PRESENT, everything will be CHANGED. LASH will not exist. So how cd. LASH have built the time machine?? SHIT.

EMERGENCY PS.
 A NEW HORROR. MIRIAM has been BEFRIENDING the horrible AMERICANS - these from CHICAGO, not DES MOINES, IOWA - who have taken the next villa (this is SOME miles away, & takes EFFORT. They're no doubt RICH and USEFUL - a DADDY 5 amongst them, perhaps? he GROANED). Tonight we're DRIVING OVER FOR DINNER (which poor EEL will have difficulty not THROWING UP, he ASSURES his Toe-by)... INEVITABLY Chicago Dad & Mom have a LOVELY daughter, JUST EUGENE'S AGE, & wouldn't they all SO LIKE TO MEET EUGENE (her especially)???... Still, perhaps when Mr & Mrs Chicago MEET EUGENE they might JUST realise a CERTAIN SOMETHING about dear old MIRIAM she has no doubt tried PATHETICALLY to conceal, & DROP HER LIKE A ROCK. If they're refugee NAZIS it's ALL TO THE GOOD so far as poor EEL is concerned... His last message to the world - AAAAAAARGHHH!!

14
The Running-Back

"Really, Jelly!"

"Jell-O, honey!"

There were titters amongst the servants. Upside down, the white letters welled out of blackness, then faded to reveal the monstrous inverted figures of Yardley and Bret Cable, their lips drawing apart as their passion cooled.

"Oh dear me. Oh dear me." Blundering back to the projector, Mr Travers barked his shin against an unexpected little table. He gave out a cry; then there was a crash as he reached to steady himself, and knocked a decanter of wine to the floor. "Lights, lights!" he wailed in despair.

Mark's huge shadow darted past the screen where Yardley, dancing on the ceiling, had flung out her arms at the climax of the last big production number.

The flickering grey image faded suddenly, and the room was flooded with light.

"Poor Jelly's dreadful during this one." Mrs Van Voyd, her armchair close to the sofa, leaned confidentially towards Harriet. "The last great hit, you know. Before poor David was *minced* by the iron horse... And of course it's the *special day*, so close now."

"The special day?" asked Harriet.

But Mrs Van Voyd was raising her voice to Yardley:

"I don't know why we don't send him out of the room while this one's on, Yarders."

"He likes it," said Yardley. "Everyone said this was his finest hour."

"Hmph!" said Mrs Van Voyd. "I thought it was *Slopes of Andalusia* this week, anyway."

The old woman was disappointed. She had dressed for the evening in what she imagined to be the garb of a simple Spanish peasant girl: high leather boots; a ballooning black skirt; a white blouse, all ruffles and starch; a short blood-red jacket with padded shoulders; copious necklaces and bangles; and a black broad-brimmed hat. Her hair was a tangle of dark ringlets, and in her ears were huge hoop-like golden earrings. Aldous wore a little red cape like a bullfighter's.

"I think we all need another drink," said Yardley, springing up, wreathed in cigarette smoke. "No, go away, Staines. Pass round some more – *beer* for your friends, or something. *I* shall wait on the ladies and gentlemen."

On film evenings, Yardley always insisted, the lesser members of the household came to the Great Hall only to be entertained. Ranged on wooden forms behind the sofa and three armchairs of their superiors, the fifteen servants sat in attitudes ranging from awed to awkward reverence. A snuffling kitchen-maid, directed by the fat cook, grovelled by the projector, warily picking up pieces of the smashed decanter.

"Leave it, leave it," said Yardley, kicking forward the little table to cover the broken glass. "Tonight was made for pleasure." And she planted a quick kiss on the frightened girl's cheek.

Harriet, her mind cloudy with wine, looked on with bemusement. It was her fifth day at Shadow Black. The days had fallen into a routine. Mornings she spent in the sanctum with Mrs Van Voyd, attempting to divert the old woman from embarrassing topics; her afternoons she was obliged to spend on the beach, where her attempts were to avoid the sun, the sand and the sea. Evenings until now had been consecrated only to dinner; but now it was Sunday evening, and Sunday evening, Harriet had discovered, was Film Evening at Shadow Black.

She leaned back on the sofa. With a smile she smoothed the warm depression in the cushion next to hers. How handsome Mark was, how kind! Now he stood expectantly by the light switch. Harriet looked up at him, blinking back tears. A hand squeezed hers. It was Mrs Van Voyd's.

"You might as well sit down for the next half hour, dear," the old woman called to Mark. "Ariette's lonely."

"I don't mind," Mark smiled, misunderstanding.

A moth fluttered in through the open French windows.

"Just a technical hitch," muttered Mr Travers, floundering with the projector.

The thought came to Harriet that the little man was drunk.

"Harry. Claret, I'm afraid. Jell-O has smashed the Beaujolais."

"Oh, I shouldn't really – "

The moth fluttered about Harriet's head.

"Nonsense, honey." With a swift graceful movement Yardley plucked the moth from the air and flung it away from her, broken, towards the hearth. "What a pity young Toby hasn't come tonight. He might have enjoyed himself. Now where's Mark's glass?"

Harriet watched her, fascinated. Tonight's film must have been made over twenty years ago, but if anything Yardley was more beautiful here than she appeared on the screen.

Mrs Van Voyd was admonishing the projectionist. "You ought to be ashamed of yourself, letting the servants see the ending, Jelly. You've gone and spoilt it for them now, their one pleasure. Typical."

But surely, reflected Harriet, the servants had seen the film before. In her Hollywood career – so Mark had whispered over the titles – Yardley had appeared in fifty-nine films. (There had been early British silents, but these the actress dismissed as juvenilia.) Shown at the rate of one a week, her films therefore formed almost an annual cycle, repeated at Shadow Black again and again.

"Ready, Mr Vardell!" called Mr Travers at last.

The room returned to darkness, and the final reel of *Showbiz Ahoy!* It began at a famous point – the moment when Babydoll (Yardley) learns to her surprise that the comical ship's cook is her estranged beau, the infuriating Tad (Bret Cable) in disguise.

It was only in the wartime revival in London that Yardley had played Babydoll on stage. By then she had been too old for the rôle, but even in the film she was not quite believable as the star-struck teenage waitress from the Florida Keys, caught up with drug-runners. It hardly mattered. The story was the merest pretext for the Travers and Carp show-stoppers: *Showbiz Ahoy!*, *Times are Tough*, *When I Meet Mr Ziegfeld*, *They'll Be Singin' in Sing-Sing Soon*, and Yardley's celebrated solo, *A Boy to Call My Own*.

The last reel brings the plot to its euphoric conclusion: Tad proves to Babydoll that the smooth Cuban (Antonio Gomez in his inevitable part) who offered her the singing engagement on the luxury yacht, and romanced her through the middle reels (to the chagrin of the disguised Tad), is really the drugs boss who shot her highway patrolman brother. Though they can't stand each other, Tad and Babydoll unite to defeat the Cuban's vicious gang. There is a massive reward. Tough times are suddenly easy: the shot brother can have the operation to restore the use of his legs; fisherman Tad can buy his own boat at last; Babydoll can afford the fare to New York to audition for the Ziegfeld Follies. Only one thing is wrong: Tad and Babydoll aren't together. The last moments don't attempt logic: Babydoll belts out a thundering reprise of the theme –

> *That's my biz, the one biz*
> *That gives me joy*
> *That's showbiz -*
> *SHOW-BIZ AAA-HOOOOOYYY!!!*

– and Tad rushes forward and sweeps her into his arms. They kiss.

"And wind back the film this time, Jell-O," quipped Yardley, after she had received her standing ovation.

Mark, with a grin, offered his assistance to the stumbling projectionist. During the last reel the little man had procured a bottle of whisky, and had swigged from it wholeheartedly.

"You'd be too young to remember the *stage* version, Ariette," Mrs Van Voyd was remarking. "The Yard did it in London during the war. They changed the Cubans to Nazis... Well, they're all foreigners, aren't they?"

"That's a lovely song, the one about the bird," offered Harriet. "Did Mr Travers really write that?"

"Only the music, dear. The words were David's."

"What a talented man he must have been. Why did he – "

"Become a *felo de se*? He was on a promotional tour. With this picture actually. Yardley and Bret got the big cities, Jelly and David had the dregs. It was Saskatchewan that did it. It must have been *so* depressing."

By the doors, the servants took their leave of Yardley. They filed out one by one, paying their respects, like humble parishioners leaving church.

"It was just so... *beautiful*," snivelled a certain maid, refusing to relinquish her grip on Yardley's hand. "So very, very – "

"Come along now, Milly," rapped Staines, and the little maid broke off with a jerk. Yardley smiled benevolently on the girl's simple piety.

Meanwhile Mr Travers had lurched to the piano. He flung up the lid, breaking into a sudden tuneless caterwauling:

Craaa-aaazy,
Craaa-aaazy,
Those crazy Kar-a-maz-ov boys!

"Oh dear, he's far gone," said Mrs Van Voyd.

The film, rewound, flapped on a spinning spool. Mark looked for a switch.

The composer was engaged in a restless search of his own. At once he broke off and started another song:

> I think the future's rosy
> With this boy called Bosie...

"A musical version of the life of Mr Wilde," muttered Mrs Van Voyd. She puffed her cigar. "Pathetic, isn't it, Ariette? Ever since David died he's been trying to write a show on his own."

"Couldn't Mr Travers find a new partner?"

"My dear! Who could stand him?"

Yardley, between servants, called:

"Oh, *do something* with Jell-O, Cora!"

Mrs Van Voyd rolled her eyes.

> Mother,
>   Mother,
>   Mother!
> I didn't know it was you –

"*Oedipus!* With an exclamation mark, my dear. It'll be *The Ramsay MacDonald Story* next. Would you mind, Ariette?" The old woman thrust Aldous into Harriet's arms. She struggled up from her chair. "Jelly! Jelly!"

Harriet looked with dismay at the smelly little lapdog.

Yardley turned from the now-closed doors.

"I think it went *well* tonight," she said with a smile. "It's always been one of my most *popular* pictures. Did you enjoy it, Mark?"

"It was – " *Extraordinary*, Mark might have said. He retreated into his search for the spool-case instead.

"A lovely song, the one about the bird," said Harriet, quickly.

"You're so kind, honey. We must have a reprise of it, just for you." And sweeping past, Yardley cupped Harriet's face in her hand. "You haven't gone and got yourself one of those, too?" she remarked, noticing Aldous.

"Oh – no."

Yardley advanced on Mr Travers.

"What a load of tosh..." Mark flopped down on the sofa next to

Harriet.

"Shh – Mark!"

"You're right, Hattie. We shall be turned away without references."

Harriet giggled. How she loved him!

The little dog squirmed from her lap.

"Gather round, gather round!" called Yardley, from the piano. "A special treat for the *select few*. Jell-O, honey! Hands on keys."

Snuffling, Mr Travers extricated himself from Mrs Van Voyd's arms. Experimentally, resigned, he pressed the familiar chords.

"Ariette, where is he?" said Mrs Van Voyd, smiling.

"Oh," said Harriet, "I'm ever so sorry – "

There was a wail of despair.

"No harm done." Mark sprang up. Aldous was padding towards the open French windows. Quickly the young artist scooped up the runaway.

"He just – *squirmed...*"

"Ariette! Aldous does *not* squirm." Mrs Van Voyd, receiving her beloved, kissed his wine-stained muzzle wetly. "Because he loves you, Ariette, he shall forgive you. But you must promise *never* again to be so lax... I'm sure *Marcus* will agree with me, hm?" The old woman's eyes twinkled.

"A request," cried Yardley. "Lights down a little, Mark honey. Hm?"

The party gathered respectfully about the piano. With intense concentration, his nose almost pressed to the keyboard, Mr Travers essayed his most celebrated opening, all minors and diminished sevenths. In the dim light Yardley took on again the aspect of the *ingénue*. Her admirably adequate mezzo-soprano floated on the hot night air:

> *There was somethin' sad*
> *An' I guess a little bad*
> *'Bout my bird*
> *In a cage –*
>
> *But you came one day*
> *An' seemed to say*

> "Time to turn
> The page" –
> When friends ask me where he's gone
> I smile an' say, "I guess
> He's gone back where he came from
> An' I'm glad, I confess" –

(With perhaps a little too triumphant an emphasis, Mr Travers reached at last the C major chord which, in his glory days, he had cannily delayed for so long.)

> ... I had a bird called loneliness
> But now he's flown –
> Instead I got a boy
> To call my own...

"I must dance. Jell-O – the Babydoll Ballet."

The melody rippled into classical pastiche. Mr Travers played by instinct now – one might have said unconsciously. Boldly the little man threw back his head. Yardley kicked off her high silver shoes. Lightly, like a child, she dashed with little steps into an empty area of floor, one hand gathering up the train of her gown, the other stretching luxuriously towards the ceiling. She rocked from side to side. Her gown billowed back and forth, gently, like a curtain. Slowly she swivelled on silken feet. The music welled; she whirled... The music burst into sparkling runs. She started back and forth like a frighted gazelle. Daringly she sprang up onto a wooden form and skipped along its length, then back. She leapt off into the air. Her earrings flashed. But her eyes, when the light caught them, glistened more intensely...

"Cable. Cable." The dancer span towards the silent watchers, plucking Mark from Harriet's side. Unawkwardly, by instinct, he wheeled in Yardley's arms...

It was very bad, of course – dreadful. But in the dim light, on a hot summer evening, after too much wine, it was magic.

Harriet watched, entranced.

15
The Weight of the Head

The lines of the composition were well-established now, the marks of pencil sketching almost concealed beneath the first exploratory brush-strokes. Mark raised his eyes from the canvas to its subject. In the five days since the sittings began, Lord Harrowblest had uttered not a single word, nor had he once moved of his own volition, submitting passively to the many small adjustments of his limbs or the angle of his chair that Mark had seen fit to make. The old man's hands were heavy and cold as a corpse's – yet one sensed in them a sleeping power...

Sometimes, contemplating Harrowblest, Mark found himself filling with a deep, strange wonderment. How he had hated this man, this man who had married Yardley! But now his hatred had subsided like a curtain, as at the cessation of a breeze. There was only the painting, their mutual task.

The tower had become as familiar to Mark as his own thoughts, his own pulse. The high round room was perhaps fifty feet in diameter. Entirely undecorated and barely furnished, it was dominated by a bulky wooden lectern, standing inexplicably in the centre of the floor. By the largest of its several windows sat the silent cripple, half-turned towards the room, by a table covered with ancient astronomical instruments. The easel stood between the cripple and the lectern. Collidge sat by a mullioned window, watching. The silence was profound.

On the first day Mark had been unnerved by the eerie calm – how different, this, from his London studio, filled as it was always with banter, with high feminine laughter! Yet slowly he found himself relishing the silence. It was as if he were absorbed into a peculiar *concentration*, a profound meditative state he had never before experienced. His feelings about his work began to change. His flounderings towards a new style, which he had exhibited so disastrously, seemed to him now like the daubings of an infant. Each day as he left the tower he would gaze up, amazed, at the high midday sun above the courtyard. Absorbed in the picture, he had been lifted out of time, and was surprised to find it had proceeded on its way without him. Had he ever truly been an artist, until now? At the easel Mark worked slowly, only occasionally adding a stroke to the large canvas. Yet already along some shadowy mental gallery he seemed to approach the completed painting. He imagined it: it loomed out at him with a serene yet intense, enveloping splendour.

It was a masterpiece...

The focus of the composition was the head. Rendered almost as an exotic African mask, it hung massively forward, too weighty for the light body. The suit which hung from the hunched shoulders (each fold of fabric evoked exactly, in soft undulations of shade) hinted at the figure as an emblem of hubris, or rather its aftermath: the sitter as some broken Ozymandias, exhibiting not his works but himself as an object of despair.

But this impression could only be fleeting. Beneath the great bald dome, the angles of the face – the firm Roman nose, the line of the lips and jaw – suggested a magnificence which yet persisted in defiance of decay.

The figure was shown half in light, half in shadow, the left unravaged side turned towards the viewer (yet there was a hint of the terrible dark side). The gnarled hands, loosely clasping a golden astrolabe, appeared at once bony and bulky, at once possessed of and devoid of power. In the corner of the picture a spoked wheel was just visible, beneath the arm of the electronic chair.

The background fell into three parts – the wall, the window, and the table before the window, cluttered with the astronomer's devices and charts. By the corner of the frame bulged an ancient globe, depicting an America of inexact dimensions. A telescope protruded from a partially-opened casement. The wall behind the head was of massive raw stones, like a castle's, rugged porous blocks infused with ancient ghosts. From the crevices between them there oozed a cryptic darkness, while light shone brilliantly against the dark mullions of the window. Beyond the window the viewer could just glimpse the high gables of Shadow Black – then, beyond them, was a silver glitter of sea, fused imperceptibly into a dazzling sky.

If the weight of the head dominated the picture, the window was essential to its meaning, its effect: with the calm of a certain faith it suggested the existence, if at some far horizon, of a realm of endless light.

The room in which the old man sat was time; beyond time was eternity.

"The Hungerford Bridge?"

"Of course, he intended to destroy it," said Mrs Van Voyd, resting her cigar on the side of her plate. "But for some reason – he could never say why – he simply rolled it up and took it. It was the one inspired stroke of his life. He owed everything to the caprice of that moment."

Harriet, her plate balanced on her knees, peered at the photograph on the mantelpiece again. It showed Andy Van Voyd at the height of his glory, bursting from a tight dinner suit, swollen with the pride of fame. It was difficult to imagine the bald, florid gentleman as the wiry boy he must have been on the day when he passed through Ellis Island. He had escaped the dull routine of his father's engineering office in Rotterdam on a sudden impulse, one wintry afternoon in 1902. In a pocket of the boy's trousers was cash from his father's desk; rolled up under his jacket was the blueprint of Brunel's bridge which the senior Van Voyd, prefatory to an interminable lecture, had pinned above the benches in the drawing office as 'inspiration'.

Andy Van Voyd travelled steerage to New York.

"Poor Jan," mused Mrs Van Voyd. She had devoured the last of her six sausages, and took up her cigar again. Aldous sniffed at her greasy plate, his muzzle yellow with scrambled egg.

"I thought he was Andy," said Harriet.

"Andy in America, my dear. But inside he was always a little Dutch boy called Jan." The old woman's eyes twinkled beneath her elaborate headgear. This morning she wore a rainbow-coloured nightcap with multiple pompons which sprung from her head like exotic flowers. A sunburst-yellow negligee was visible beneath her paisley wrap. She tittered, "Not that I knew him when he was *little*, I have to say."

Harriet, sensing that *Satisfaction in Wedlock* might shortly be mentioned, offered quickly:

"But why was he so inspired? Taking the plan, I mean."

"Ariette, are you entirely ignorant of the career of my late husband?"

"I'm afraid so, Mrs Van Voyd."

"Ah, youth!" the old woman smiled; and leaning back against her multicoloured pillows, drawing back on her cigar, she embarked upon the story.

In New York the young Jan attempted without success a number of careers. Soon the impatience which had made him leave Rotterdam gnawed at him again. With only the money he had saved from his work by day as a baker's delivery boy, and by night as a bellhop in a hotel on the Lower East Side, he set out for California.

He never got there, at least not on that journey. It was in a small town in Iowa, broke and hungry, that Jan — but he was Andy by now — learnt of a contest to design a new bridge to replace the primitive structure that then spanned the town's slow, muddy river. For the first time in months he thought of the plan he had stolen from his father's office. For some superstitious reason he had kept it; crumpled in the bottom of his rucksack, it was somewhat the worse for wear. It did not matter. Andy produced it; the townspeople applauded.

The success of this first commission was soon repeated by Andy throughout the Midwest. Of course there is a specificity required in the building of bridges, but from the beginning Andy was happy to leave mere details to subordinates. It was the *creative* work that counted. In a few years he was head of the largest engineering firm in the United States; by this time he could leave not only the details to others but the broad outlines, too.

The fact of his success was a source to him of unceasing delight; he grew very pompous and very fat; and as the years passed his profession as a bridge-builder came to him to partake of a moral quality. In after-dinner speeches and graduation addresses he would speak with a declamatory air of 'building a bridge', of 'spanning the distance', with what struck many as a metaphysical intent. In time these pronouncements were gathered up and transmuted into a series of public lectures. The literal meanings of the metaphors dropped away, and it was seen that Andy Van Voyd (like his adoptive country) had been embarked upon a spiritual mission all the time. His lectures were a triumph in forty-eight states – which, in those days, were all the states there were.

Poor Andy! Alas, he was not quite spiritual enough, and could never stop eating, or drinking malt whisky; which made him ever more obese; which gave him trouble with his heart; which led to his demise, *aetat.* fifty-six years, during the course of an extensive lecture tour, on the bosom of one Marybeth Leibowitz, who described herself as a 'chorus girl', in a certain small city in Iowa in 1942.

Cora, the last of his several wives – she had married him for his wealth, his respectability, his reputation as a lover (false), and because she wanted to set up a *salon* in New York – had been curious to see the room in which her husband died. In elaborate mourning, involving seven black veils, she stood one bleak afternoon in the squalid little boarding house in Iowa; and, stooping, noted that from the window, when lying on the bed, one could just glimpse, from the corner of one's eye, Andy's first copy of Brunel's suspension bridge, the foundation of the Van Voyd empire. It gave her comfort. Gently, stretching forth her lacquered nails, she stroked the covers of the mean single bed, the last to have creaked beneath her husband's bulk; beside her, hands twisting in an agony of deserved shame, stood the room's tenant, the gawky, buck-toothed Marybeth Leibowitz, the last sentient thing to have groaned beneath that considerable burden, for three minutes before – and some twenty-three-and-a-half despairing hours after – the fatal orgasm.

As Mrs Van Voyd left she pressed two dollars fifty into Marybeth's hand, for after all the poor girl had never been paid.

There were tears in the old woman's eyes when the story was over.

"Andy," Harriet said gently, "... was he the one you *really loved?*"

Mrs Van Voyd blinked away her tears. "Goodness me, Ariette, not at all – "

Before she could continue they were interrupted by Yardley. Floating into the sanctum, the beautiful creature fluttered down to kiss her friends before alighting, a silken wraith, on the foot of the bed. "Cora, it's tomorrow. What have you – *got* for me?"

"Oh, you'll find you've excelled yourself this year, Yarders."

Harriet had no idea what they were talking about. She watched curiously as Mrs Van Voyd delved amongst the bedclothes, tossing aside a day-old *Evening Empire* and several *Telescopes,* a bound volume of *Night and Day,* an empty upturned teacup, three used lipsticks, a cracked powder compact, a frizzy orange wig, a signed first edition of *The Joyful Delaneys* by Hugh Walpole, and a crumpled blue Penguin called *Confessions of a Young Man.* At last, from beneath the fluffy recumbent ball of Aldous, the old woman produced the object of her search. Triumphantly she held up a pair of knitting needles, unfurling from the bent spikes what appeared to be a small, somewhat irregularly-shaped rug, coloured in alternating stripes of purple, green, orange and chocolate brown.

"I'm not sure what it is," said Yardley.

"Oh really, Yarders, it's a *vest*, can't you see? This is the back, and…" The old woman delved into the bedclothes again.

Yardley smiled at Harriet. "I'd say the stars and stripes for the 'big day', honey, hm?"

Harriet looked puzzled. The 'stars and stripes' was one of the more embarrassing of the bathing costumes she had reluctantly had to accept – but the 'big day'?

"Jell-O doesn't really like to celebrate it, of course – it's *also* the day poor David went under the train, you see. But we try to take his mind off it. Lessen the burden. A little get-together on the beach – "

"… And here is the front!" cried Mrs Van Voyd. "I'll just get Millicent to sew it up, and there we are." Experimentally, she held the sides together; the vest had a distinctly asymmetrical look.

Yardley said, doubtful, "Do you think he'll believe it's from *me*?"

"Why ever not, Yarders? I'm not giving up the toupee, so you can forget all thoughts of that!"

Yardley, with a wry look at Harriet, exhaled a long stream of smoke. "Well, what *else* is there, Cora?"

Mrs Van Voyd, leaning forward, opened a little cupboard by her bed. An avalanche of parcels tumbled to the floor.

"Oh dear. Ariette, you'll pick those up, won't you, dear?"

The parcels had been wrapped, with evident haste, in left-over Christmas paper; retrieving them, Harriet piled into a shaft of sunlight on the bed the crumpled images of red-cheeked Fathers Christmas, robins redbreast, fir trees, sleighs, bells, snow-covered cottages and Bethlehem stars, bearing the marks of previous strings and strips of adhesive tape. Knowledgeably, Mrs Van Voyd pointed to each package.

"A pair of tartan slippers – I thought they could be from you, Ariette; three handkerchiefs with a J-monogram, they'll be from Marcus; two pairs of fawn walking socks, they're from Tobias; a copy of *The Cruel Sea* by Mr Nicholas Monsarrat, I thought that'd be from Charles – oh, and a gramophone record by Miss Alma Cogan. That's from Bunger."

"Couldn't I give him that?" said Yardley.

Mrs Van Voyd sighed, "Really, Yarders, I *have* enclosed cards. Still, I suppose..." She moved to tear open the gramophone record. "But then the *hand-knitted vest* will be from Bunger. That doesn't seem *quite* right, does it? Ariette, what do you think?"

Harriet shifted on the rococo chair. She said uncertainly, "It's... Mr Travers' birthday?"

There was a pause. The two older women exchanged glances.

"Ariette, of course!" burst out Mrs Van Voyd. "Tomorrow! Really... have you been asleep?"

16
Punch and Judy

When Toby awoke it was not yet dawn and a spectral moonlight seeped through his window. For a period which seemed interminable he lay propped on his elbows, his gaze panning slowly about him, like a camera in a suspense film. The attic was alien in the icy light. His telescope in the window had become a meaningless form; the scattered clothes on the floor were grotesque shapes – rocky continents of a dead planet, lost from its orbit, chilling in space. He was puzzled by a queer heaviness in his limbs, which seemed to make rising from the bed impossible.

It was only through a gentle, almost imperceptible access of knowledge that Toby became aware of the stranger by his bed. The negative priest looked down at him with glowing eyes and a wry, twisted mouth. Then, without suddenness, without shock, the terror oozed over Toby in an icy, implacable lava.

When he really awoke the room was empty, and daylight glowed at the window.

After four nights of the dreams, Toby decided that the dreams must stop. He would go back to Lightletter.

He sat up, lit a cigarette, and crossed to the bright window. He spun his telescope about on its stand; sunlight danced on the spinning shaft.

Last term a boy in Toby's form had gone mad. At the time his behaviour was inexplicable; but Cramborne, whose aunt in Sevenoaks was a neighbour of the boy's family, had discovered the full story. Trevelyan had a chemical imbalance in the brain. His faculty of vision, refusing to remain a dutiful camera, had assumed instead the properties of a projector, casting out onto the world wholly fanciful images, which the hapless boy believed to be real. He might imagine, say, that he saw a cat walking through an empty room; he might open a dictionary to find a flower spouting from the pages.

As his illness proceeded his 'projections' became more alarming: he would look down at his plate at dinner and see coils of intestines, pulsing and bleeding; he would imagine that wounds had suddenly opened in his flesh. The climactic 'projections' were the huge jelly-like forms Trevelyan would see squirming towards him, monstrous transparent slugs which he believed to possess supernatural powers, and blamed for his previous delusions. He called them (he was not an imaginative boy) *the things*.

His insanity became manifest. When he was found convulsing naked on a bathroom floor, Matron insisted he merely needed a good rest (Trevelyan was a high-strung, studious boy, who practised the viola beyond the call of duty). Then he ran madly from chapel one morning, screaming *The things! The things!*, and struggled to impale himself on the spikes of the school gates. The boy was now in a sanatorium in Broadstairs, being treated with experimental drugs.

Every day since the day on the pier, Toby had thought of Trevelyan.

Later

The sun burnt high above, remote but searing. There were only the sounds of a light breeze, and the sea lapping at the little boat's side. Once or twice she knocked against the rusted iron pylon.

Toby drew back on his cigarette, slowly. *Bluefinch* was tethered to the pier; he had cut the motor some minutes before. Through straining eyes he looked ahead of him at the unheaving sea, then behind him at the white houses and the tall hotel, persisting impassively above the promenade. When his cigarette had burnt down he flung it into the sea. He climbed a brown-crusted, gritty ladder.

On the pier the sun-cracked decking creaked beneath his espadrilles. In the midday heat the empty aisles were unshadowed, pale and hard, against the dome's rising massiveness. Furtively, like a detective, Toby made his way past the untenanted booths. How strange to think they had always been empty; and yet the coconut shies that had never been, the shooting galleries, the fortune tellers, the stalls announcing sticks of rock, seemed nonetheless to possess some shadowy hints of life, as if in the desiccated surfaces of this pier were intimations of another, superior version, its bright atoms vibrating in a dimension just beyond this.

He pushed open the ballroom's rotting double doors. Inside the great dome, everything was as it had been before: the wind through the cracked panes; the huge hanging cobwebs; the muted sucking of the sea beneath his feet.

But there was no negative man; there had been no negative man. Standing again in the centre, Toby called through cupped hands: "*Hul-lo!*"

He called as one might call at the entrance of a cave, or leaning over a well: only for the echo. He turned and ran from the ballroom. Suddenly he was possessed by a surging joy. Running back along the pier he tore at his shirt, then his shorts and shoes.

He was not mad, he was not mad.

He plunged from the pier.

Afterwards he spread himself to dry on the hot decking, his bare chest offered up luxuriously to the sun.

When Toby woke, he felt a curious hot heaviness in his limbs. His eyes shifted painfully in their sockets as if all the moisture beneath the lids had dried away. He spat into his hands and rubbed his face. When he dressed, his clothes rasped painfully against his skin. How long had he slept? The sun, though still blazing, had begun its downward course.

But he could not go back to Shadow Black, not yet. Aunt Eunice and the others would still be on the beach. They might see *Bluefinch*.

He would explore the holiday town.

As he steered the little boat across the short distance to the shore, Toby began to feel a strange exhaustion. A dull throbbing had started in his forehead and the sun's glare was too bright for his eyes. Looking ahead at the sands he saw only a dazzling blur; the short distance became longer, and he found himself travelling further away from the pier than he had intended.

After dragging *Bluefinch* up through the moist wash of the tide, Toby sloshed out into the sea to waist-height and plunged his head beneath the water. When he broke the surface he expelled a great gust of breath and pushed back his hair with his hands, his neck arching upwards. His heart was hammering.

Then his heart stopped.

The promenade at Lightletter lay at a level of perhaps ten feet above the beach, supported by thick wooden columns sunk deep into the sand. By this stage of the afternoon the long strip of raised decking cast its shadow forward, dividing the sands in a dark line. Beneath the promenade was a series of darker spaces, and looming out against one of these spaces, hard by the overhang of the decking above, just visible round a curve of corner, was the unmistakable striped booth of a Punch and Judy man.

Toby screwed his eyes tightly shut, then opened them again.

The booth was still there. He had been unable to see it before, that was all.

Unless of course this was another delusion.

Approaching the booth, he felt the peculiar exhaustion, assailing him again. Arrayed before the booth were three deckchairs, their red and white canvas matching the canvas of the booth. Toby slumped into the middle chair. His wet clothes stuck uncomfortably to his skin.

He shut his eyes.

"Hul-*lo*, hullo!" came a high screeching voice.

His eyes snapped open and he sat up at once. Staring at him from the stage were the crazed wooden eyes of Mr Punch. The great hooked nose loomed forward enormously.

"I," said the little puppet, swanking back and forth, "can count up to five, and I am going to count the sides of this stage and find out how many there are. How many do *you* think?"

Toby, challenged, could not speak. But his eyes remained fixed on the stage. A compound of terror and fascination made any alternative unthinkable.

"Well, *you* wouldn't know because you're stupid," said Mr Punch. "Watch me. One, two – " The malevolent little creature pointed carefully first to the tasselled ledge beneath him, then to the right side, then to the frilly top, then to the left side of the stage. When he had reached the fourth side he did not stop but pointed again at the ledge.

"Five!" he exclaimed, triumphant.

Meanwhile the ugly figure of Judy had appeared behind him, her flushed cheeks a vivid index of her outrage.

"Mr Punch, don't be so silly! There are four sides, not five!"

A wrangle ensued. Delving beneath the ledge, Mr Punch re-emerged with his club clasped firmly in his little hands. After coshing Judy several times, to the accompaniment of violent execrations, he was left in possession of the stage. Proudly he declared himself to be the voice of reason. When the policeman emerged to challenge him, a dispute ensued on the difference between knowledge and belief.

Knowledge, declared the policeman confidently, consisted in the *agreement or disagreement of two ideas.*

If knowledge consisted in the agreement of ideas, returned Mr Punch, then the *enthusiast and the sober man were on a level.*

The play proceeded with more in this vein. The dialogue became more and more odd, until Toby understood little of it. If the play remained compelling, it was perhaps because at the end of each abstract discussion came an outburst of comic violence. After an incident in which Mr Punch gleefully battered the baby, the play climaxed in a scene of considerable mayhem involving the hangman and the crocodile.

During the course of the play Toby became aware that it was not only the dialogue but the way in which it was spoken that was odd: behind each affected voice was the hint of a foreign accent.

When the puppets took the stage for their curtain calls, Toby applauded loudly. His exhaustion was gone, replaced by a bizarre exhilaration.

What intuition made him glance down the beach, Toby could not say. But he ceased his applause at once and stood up awkwardly, a dark flush rising to his face. Approaching him over the sands was a girl. She was dressed in a simple striped shift, alarmingly short, and had long straight hair, dark as the plumage of a raven. She was beautiful. Only the showman, emerging from the booth, shifted Toby's attention from the extraordinary vision.

The showman was a podgy little man, very short and very hairy. His most striking features were a magnificent nose – which reminded one irresistibly of Mr Punch's – and a massive beard, which seemed to be made of wire. Waves of strong hair like unravelled electrical coils – some coloured copper, some silver – erupted from his lips and chin and jowls and crashed over his chest in great arrested cascades. The eyes beneath the thick brows sparkled darkly, with a quick intelligence.

The strange little man was dressed very shabbily, all in black but for a once-white shirt, visible beneath the waistcoat that stretched, a little too tightly, over his ample girth. His age was perhaps sixty or seventy. As he greeted Toby with a decayed yellow smile, barely visible amongst the formidable beard, his left hand squashed onto his head a black stovepipe hat; Mr Punch hung, upside down, from the showman's right hand.

The puppet looked a little affronted at this indignity, and the showman quickly turned him upright again.

"You have enjoyed Mr Punch, *mein Junge?*" the old man asked, gazing at the puppet affectionately.

Toby, clumsily, said that he had.

"*Ach*, but did Mr Punch enjoy you?" The showman dug into his waistcoat pocket and inserted into his mouth a small device, not unlike a whistle, which – as Toby was later to discover – is called a 'swazzle'. When the old man spoke again it was in the voice of Mr Punch, who expressed his unflattering opinion of Toby.

"For *Scham*, Mr Punch!" said the showman, removing the swazzle.

And looking up at Toby he laughed delightedly.

The girl joined them. Evidently she was no stranger to the showman. Toby looked at her, not without nervousness. At close range there was an admixture of ugliness in her beauty. The nose was a little too large, the mouth a little too hard; the raven-dark hair had a limp oily look, and there were open pores in the sleek olive skin. She might have been twenty-five, or thirty.

"Who is your young friend, papa?" There was a cold look in the hooded eyes.

The showman, declaring his mind to be a *tabula rasa*, said that he did not know. Dutifully Toby introduced himself.

"Toby? Ha!" The boy's name seemed to fill the showman with a peculiar delight. "Then I shall tell you, *mein Junge*, that you have the privilege to address Professor Gustav Becher, of the *Universitat* of Berlin. This is *mein* daughter, Heike. *Und* of course you know Mr Punch."

The Professor held up Mr Punch to Toby's face, making one of the little hands reach forward in greeting. Toby shook it; as he did so, the puppet's chipped wooden eyes appeared to stare at him with real intelligence.

The Professor laughed again.

"Our new friend must come with us to tea – you see, young Toby, we know your *Englander* customs. Come, Heike."

Reaching behind the booth the Professor took up a leather satchel which, Toby saw, contained the other puppets from the show. Laying Mr Punch carefully in amongst them, the old man shut the satchel and, clutching it against his chest, waddled off along the sand. Toby lingered uncertainly as Heike, with a practised efficiency, began to collapse the booth and the deckchairs.

She seemed to be angry.

"Let me help you," Toby insisted, and got himself into an embarrassing predicament with a deck chair.

"I need no help." The girl brushed him aside.

Waddling on ahead, the Professor was declaiming merrily to himself on the philosophy of art, his free hand gesticulating.

"We think the stage a mere vehicle of the *Illusion, ja*? This, *mein Freundes*, is not the case. The stage is an image of life, *nein*? But – let us examine this, *mein Freundes* – how can this be? The *Kunst* is the *Illusion* – but the *Kunst* is the life. With this paradox we contemplate the core of the *Kunst*..."

"Please." Toby, squirming, turned back to Heike. Reluctantly the sullen girl abandoned her attempt to carry three deckchairs under one arm, and the folded Punch and Judy booth under the other. Her face unchanging, she let the pile of deckchairs clatter to the sand.

Far ahead, the Professor, his old knees straining, climbed the stairs to the promenade.

The deckchairs were heavier than Toby had hoped. After some experimentation he endeavoured to hold them out horizontally before him, like a drawbridge let down from his torso. The frame of the lowest chair knocked against his hips.

"Does your father," he began, struggling to catch up with Heike, "does your father come here like this – regularly?"

"Every day," said the brisk girl. Her tone was matter-of-fact. "Every day – when he is well enough."

"And puts on his show?"

Toby knew he should not have asked this question. The girl rounded on him, her dark eyes flashing.

"So! You laugh at my father already!"

"No, I didn't mean – "

Heike strode forward, still faster. Trying to catch her up again, Toby stumbled, sprawling amongst the deckchairs.

The back of the Paradise Hotel was very different from the front: if on one side the hotel was a great plaster wedding cake, baked till it cracked and peeled, on the other it was only an expanse of dark red brick. The high wall had a raw, gaping look, like an open wound.

"Here." Heike indicated a shed in the yard, of the sort which might have held builder's materials. Inside the open door, she had already propped up the canvas booth. Toby cast down his own burden with relief.

The Bechers lived in a basement which led off the yard. A concrete staircase, without a banister, descended directly into a mean little room, illuminated only by two rectangles of frosted glass which let in light at ground level. The furniture consisted of a large number of tea chests, strewn about higgledy-piggledy, and three evil-looking old armchairs with bursting stuffing. In one of these sat the Professor.

"*Ach, mein Junge!* Come, sit by me." He indicated an armchair. "You will excuse me if I do not get up – *mein alt* joints, ha ha! Heike, tea!"

Weaving his way through the tea chests, Toby lowered himself gingerly into the armchair, shifting his haunches to avoid a jabbing spring. Heike, without words, disappeared through an open doorway on the far side of the room.

Toby looked about him. The room revealed little more to scrutiny than it had at first glance. In the corner, on top of one of the tea chests, was an unlit oil lamp and several shabby books. The Professor's satchel lay open by the hearth. Above, on the mantelpiece, were the unpacked puppets. Mr Punch had pride of place. Resting atop the crumpled empty glove of the body, the huge-nosed wooden head was still more grotesque.

"Well," said the professor, "this is nice, *ja?* I dare to say, Franz, you will read to me your *Essay* now." He smiled broadly, revealing stumps of teeth.

"I'm – sorry?"

"Franz?"

There was a pause.

The old man flared suddenly, staggering up from his chair. Spit flew from his decayed mouth and his dark eyes blazed with anger.

"You're – sorry?" he cried. "You're *sorry!* How long will this go on, Herr Schneider? You – you break *ein alt* man's heart! You come here, you sit here, you treat me with contempt – with detestation! What have you done? You spend your time in the beer halls, in the cabarets? *Verkehren mit das* – criminal? *Mit das schmutzig Prostituierte...*"

The remainder of the monologue was delivered in German.

Amazed, Toby cowered back in the armchair, the dangerous spring prodding at his thigh. Ranting above him, the old man seemed to have swollen in size and the wire beard vibrated fearsomely, as if charged with electrical current.

"*Papa!*" Heike, reappearing in the doorway, barked several jagged sentences in German. Twice Toby heard the name 'Franz Schneider'.

The old man's fit passed like a subsiding wave and he sank back into his chair. Heike made several ugly clucking noises, as if of comfort, as the fire died in her father's eyes.

After a moment she picked up the tray she had temporarily set down and threaded her way through the tea chests with experienced ease. Swiftly she unloaded two mugs of steaming tea, and two plates, on each of which was a slice of boiled fruit cake, roughly cut. She set down the items heavily: a brown spurt of tea leapt from Toby's mug, staining darkly the rough wood of the tea chest.

"Berlin," said Heike flatly. "My father remembers Berlin."

There was no reply Toby could make. He was thinking he should have sat in the other chair.

The old man was breathing deeply, head cast down.

"I suppose you think this is amusing," Heike went on. Her face had flushed and there was bitterness in her voice.

"I don't know what you mean," said Toby.

"*Ach!* You laugh at my father."

"No, please. He's a fascinating man – I'm so... *interested* in him."

Heike eyed Toby darkly. "I shan't let anyone harm him," she announced defiantly, "I shan't!"

Toby watched the backs of her bare thighs as she retreated through the maze of tea chests. *She's like a slatternly waitress,* he thought, and wondered how he could ever have considered her beautiful. Then, shifting uncomfortably in his dangerous chair, he realised suddenly that she was beautiful, even more beautiful than he had first thought. He turned to his tea, contemplating mournfully a chipped enamel mug of the sort he imagined might be used in a soup kitchen.

When he looked up again, the Professor was watching him. When the old man spoke, this time his voice was gentle:

"*Ach, mein* Toby, you have come... You must tell me everything about yourself, everything. Talk, *mein Junge,* talk, to a foolish *alt* man."

When he left, Toby promised to call again next day.

17
The Ice Bath

The next day was the day of Mr Travers' party.

"Oh Millicent," said Mrs Van Voyd that morning, as the maid was clearing the breakfast things, "have Master Tobias come down to me, will you? He does tend to *disappear* so... one must make sure he's *on hand* – if you'll pardon the expression, my dear," she added, for the benefit of Harriet – before continuing, similarly for Harriet's benefit, the story of her ill-starred marriage to Sir Cuthbert Trease MP, best remembered for his unsuccessful campaign for the reintroduction of public flogging. Mrs Van Voyd had just reached the point in the story at which she had discovered her husband *in flagrante delicto* with a club-footed scullery-maid (his tongue slithering over the sole of her orthopaedic shoe) when Milly, puffing from the stairs, reappeared in the doorway.

"It was an educational experience, Ariette. I have voted for the *Labour* gentlemen ever since, and should advise you to do the same... ah, but if only they weren't so *common*! Well, Millicent – and where is Master Tobias?"

"I don't think he's well, ma'am," the little maid panted. "All red and hot he was, and trembling something shocking."

"Goodness! What ever can the boy have been doing?" Mrs Van Voyd's eyes grew wide. "Come, Ariette – it behoves us to investigate."

Thirty minutes later

"Another one (*puff*) ma'am... Mrs Salloby (*puff puff*) says this is abso-(*puff*)-lutely the last (*puff*)..."

"Oh do stop panting, child. It's most undignified. Would I have been the toast of the *beau monde* on two continents, had I been unable to enter a room without my tongue *lolling* from my head like a dog's, and breathing in adenoidal gasps?"

The little maid, upending her heavy bucket, did not reply. The ice slid into the bath with an interminable, glassy crash.

"Mm, just about deep enough," mused Mrs Van Voyd, with an air of scientific deliberation. "Perhaps you could *plunge in* now, Tobias, while we await the next cascade?" She smiled, yesterday's makeup flaking from her face.

Toby did not move. Clad only in a towel, he hovered uneasily in a corner of the vast bathroom, his red arms crossed over his red chest. For all that Mrs Van Voyd had explained the virtues of the 'ice bath', he was by no means convinced. He eyed with alarm the heavy old tub, which stood expectantly on its tarnished iron paws; with as much alarm he glanced towards the awkward figure of Miss Locke, standing in an opposite corner, her eyes cast down in confusion.

"Off you go, Millicent," Mrs Van Voyd commanded. "One more *bucket*... Goodness, isn't that a vulgar word, Ariette? I suppose it *was* intended only for the lips of the lower orders."

"Ma'am – " Milly attempted, between puffs.

"What *is* it, child?" Mrs Van Voyd chewed her cigar-end. "Do you know, you look better with some *colour* in your cheeks, Millicent? Now if you lost some weight, and had your hair done, and pressed your uniform properly, and had a spot of plastic surgery on that hideous hare lip, and covered those incipient varicose veins, you might still stand a chance of marrying into the – hm – *lower* middle classes. How old are you now, dear?"

"Twenty-(*puff*)-six, ma'am."

"Well, perhaps not. Go, child!"

The bucket swung squeakily in Milly's hand. "Ma'am," she said quickly, "Mrs Salloby says – "

"Mrs Salloby does not run this household," snapped Mrs Van Voyd.

"But *ma'am*," Milly wailed, "Mrs Salloby says there's no *ice* for the party!"

"No ice! Why ever not?"

"You've used it all up, ma'am."

"Really, can't the wretched woman *make some more*? What does she want, a recipe? Tobias, don't you dare move!"

Seeing an opportunity to escape, Toby had shifted surreptitiously towards the door.

Harriet wondered if she could leave, too.

"But it's half-eleven already, ma'am," Milly was wailing.

Mrs Van Voyd sighed. "Well, we cannot upset Mrs Salloby. God knows, the wretched woman *runs* this household – Tobias," she announced with a martyred air, "it appears – and I, of course, am the last to be informed – that Mrs Salloby *requires* our ice..."

"Ah," said Toby. And made for the door again. Mrs Van Voyd grabbed his arm. "Ouch!"

"Millicent," she proceeded, "will therefore return in precisely twenty minutes, and *remove* it..." (A look of horror passed across the little maid's face.) "So whatever you do, don't melt it, there's a good boy."

"Really," said Toby, "I'm feeling *much* better..." He attempted a cheerful smile.

"In we hop." Oblivious, Mrs Van Voyd pushed him closer to the bath.

ASIDE: *No, don't go, Ariette. I may need your help. He's probably got 'heat stroke' or something – he may be dangerous.*

"I'm not going in."

"Tobias!" Mrs Van Voyd burst out. "After I've gone to all this effort!"

And the old woman whipped off Toby's towel. He leapt into the bath with an unmanly shriek. Harriet blundered from the room in horror, cannoning into Milly and her empty bucket; Milly, letting the bucket clatter to the floor, twisted her neck eagerly towards the freezing bath.

Mrs Van Voyd, who was closer, exclaimed:

"Really, Tobias, you're red *all over!* Whatever *have* you been doing?" And with a little laugh she added, *"Stirrings of adolescence!"*

As she left, ushering out the unwilling Milly, the old woman locked the bathroom door behind her.

Toby, his teeth tapping out an agonised tattoo, delayed for several seconds until Mrs Van Voyd's footsteps died away. Then in rapid succession he scrambled out of the ice bath, hopped about first on one leg, then the other, span on the hot tap over the washstand, rinsed his hand desperately under the spurting water in the hope that it would come hot, found that it wouldn't, towelled himself as vigorously as his sunburn would allow, and sprinted for four or five laps about the large bathroom, several times slithering dangerously.

As it happened he did not slither, but on his last lap he crashed into the suddenly-opening door, and the massive Paisley-wrapped form of Mrs Van Voyd. The old woman gasped, staggering, and dropped her cigar. Toby sunk to the floor.

"Tobias," she panted, "what extraordinary behaviour! It's as well I thought to check on you. Into the bath at this moment!"

Imperiously the old woman strode to the washstand, shutting off the now-steaming water, as Toby slithered back sheepishly into the ice.

"I am a woman of a charitable, not to say *liberal* disposition," announced Mrs Van Voyd, "but the young must learn that their *elders know best*. I'm disappointed in you, Tobias. I shall send Millicent up to watch you."

A key turned in the lock once again as the old woman made her affronted exit.

This time, Toby thought clearly. The bathroom was on the ground floor. There was a large casement window, which even at this very moment was open, showing a gleaming vista of sea. There were numerous empty rooms in this wing. The solution was easy: exit by this window; enter by next window. It would hardly be difficult in so sparsely-inhabited a house to make his way back to his room unobserved. He would fling on his clothes and run to the beach. The party would not yet have converged there, and access to *Bluefinch* would be possible. There was still time! Milly, arriving to supervise his bath, would find only a tub full of melting ice.

Toby wrapped his towel around his waist.

The first difficulty occurred to him as he set his foot on the windowsill. To think of this room as on the 'ground floor' was not without irony, Toby had to acknowledge, when considering exits and entrances of the sort he was planning to make. The window was on the sea-facing side of the east wing, the side of the house built directly along the edge of the cliff. There was almost a sheer drop to the rocks below. Toby contemplated this for some seconds, with some chagrin, until he decided that after all there was sufficient ledge of rock – six inches at least – on which to edge his way safely to the next window. It was not far; there were abundant handholds in the old stonework, not to mention in the ivy which clung to it tenaciously...

It was only when he was standing on the ledge that Toby reflected, with a rush of self-disgust, that he was re-enacting an incident in one of Aunt Eunice's films. It was the one he had been made to watch on his first night, where Bret Cable, escaping his creditors, made a similar exit – similarly clad – from the bathroom of his luxury New York apartment. There had been the inevitable vertiginous shots of a New York street, as seen from the height of fifty storeys; Bret of course had got stuck on a ledge... How had the scene ended? The film was called *It's Different with Dames*.

Toby sighed. How dreadful to be doing something like this: it was so embarrassing. He could never tell EEL.

At least it was easy. Toby proceeded swiftly from one handhold to the next. The rocky ledge did not crumble beneath him; his feet did not slip alarmingly; he did not look down and suffer giddy attacks; he did not cry '*Whoa-oah!*' once; even his towel did not fall off. Really, it was all rather pleasant. The sea breeze cooled his burnt skin; the air, as they say, was bracing. He was almost sorry that, after a minute or so, he had only to clamber into the next window – and it would all be over.

The window was locked.

Toby peered through the cobwebbed glass at the empty room beyond. After a burst of ineffectual rattling, he considered trying to smash one of the panes. He did not want to cut himself, but the window was old; the wood weathered. Perhaps if he simply hit one of the glass diamonds rather hard with the back of his hand it would fall out, and he could reach through the casement to the catch.

His first attempt convinced him that the window was more sturdy than it looked. On his second, as he swung back his arm, he almost overbalanced – and almost fell. If he did not exactly cry '*Whoa-oah!*', he cried out nonetheless.

Toby clung against the wall, his heart pounding. "I'm mad," he said aloud, "I really am mad."

Several minutes passed before he resolved what to do next. There was another window further along the wall; the odds were that it was resolutely shut. In any case the ledge became still narrower as it proceeded. It was impossible. With resignation Toby began edging his way back in the direction he had come.

"Master Toby! Master Toby!" Adenoidal tones floated from the bathroom window. Milly was evidently in deep perplexity.

Toby's heart sank – he had forgotten the maid. It was while he was casting his eyes towards the heavens, cursing this new horror, that he noticed the yawning casement on the floor directly above.

He revised his plan in an instant. The locked window would do him some service after all. With the jutting stonework which surrounded it, with the hanging ivy, there were holds enough. There was a thick lintel over the window. The distance to the sill of the window above did not look great. It was easy.

A minute or so into the climb he decided that perhaps it wasn't. A swathe of ivy tore away as he clambered towards the lintel. He gasped. His fingernails dug painfully into crumbling stone. His bare feet scrambled against the leaden ridges of the window. When he tried to lever himself up by pushing against the window there was an ominous cracking. "*Now* it's going to break," he muttered. He imagined his foot driving through slashing glass; his cry of agony as he fell… What would it be like?

He looked down. The sea washed impassively over glistening rocks. (Bret Cable had had a crowd, imploring him not to jump. But how *had* the scene ended?) Above the rocks, a shapeless white bird billowed through the air. It was not until Toby had watched it for several seconds that he recognised it as the towel, which until recently had been wrapped about his waist. He hadn't even noticed it fall.

I really am mad, he thought, clawing at the lintel. What was he to do? To go down again seemed as difficult as to keep going up. (In *It's*

Different with Dames, the fire department would have been called by now.) His arms ached and his hands were numb. He needed just one last surge, didn't he, to carry him onto the lintel?

"*Master Toby!*"

"Oh God," Toby said flatly.

Milly, doubtless after long ratiocinations, was craning her neck from the bathroom window, aghast.

"*Go away*," mouthed Toby. And with a painful heave he made it up to the lintel.

It seemed easier after that. It wasn't, but a sort of instinct had taken over. Carefully Toby reached up to the sill of the first-floor window; tested his footholds in the ancient stone; levered himself up into the open casement: and tumbled naked into Harriet's room.

Impossible. Impossible.

Her *most glamorous swimwear*, Mrs Van Voyd had advised; the stars and stripes, Yardley had recommended; *no kimono*, both had insisted.

Around three sides of the canopied bed Harriet had laid out a selection of bathing costumes. If she had chosen the least exotic and least revealing of those Yardley had given her ('bikini'-style costumes were firmly excluded), these were unexotic and unrevealing only by very relative standards. Harriet gazed with despair at the scraps of gaudy fabric – polka-dots and clashing stripes, riots of abstract shapes, swirling 'optical illusion' patterns – and wondered which might be considered the most innocuous. She decided on a haze of fuzzy-edged squares which Yardley had called the Rothko design, but even this was cut too low in the bodice.

Despondently Harriet turned to the black kimono hanging on the door; on the same hook was a large floppy sunhat. These were the two items of Yardley's wardrobe that Harriet had come to like most; they were the two items she needed if she were to appear on the beach.

In a rare moment of firmness, Harriet resolved to disappoint her elders. She *would* wear the kimono. Decisively she reached for the Rothko; she may as well have it underneath. She turned towards the mirror, holding the costume against her frock. Admiringly she thought that she really was a little less plump these days, a little less – babyish. Why, she was almost pretty! She slipped off her clothes.

Harriet was about to step into the Rothko when she heard the curious scuffling outside her window. Dropping the costume on the bed, she looked apprehensively at the open casement. Some days ago, a seagull had flown into her room. She had been terrified, and it had taken the combined efforts of Milly and Thomas to drive the bird out. Harriet hoped it would not happen again.

Cautiously the naked girl leaned towards the window ledge.

With a heaving cry the boy was upon her.

At last Toby remembered how the scene had ended in *It's Different with Dames*. Cable, naked (or so one was meant to think) had clambered into Yardley's apartment. *You might not believe this,* he had said, *but there is an explanation...*

It had been love, of course, at first sight.

"You might not believe this," Toby was saying, "but there *is* an explanation..."

The words tumbled out automatically. Toby cowered behind one pillar of the four-poster bed, closest to the window, Harriet behind another, closest to the door. The disentangling of their limbs had taken an eternity. Now it seemed that they would be in this new position for as long. Harriet had wrapped herself elaborately in the bed curtain.

Should I tell EEL about this? Toby wondered.

"I'm closest to the door," Harriet said at last. She spoke softly through pursed lips. "I'm going to dash over there and get my wrap. You'll... turn away?"

Toby mumbled assent. But as he heard the curtain swish back he glanced impulsively at the girl. Her pale body skipped lightly across the floor; he felt an alarming, unmistakable stirring...

"Now," said Harriet, safely in the kimono, "I'm going to get you something to wear." She flung open a cupboard door at random, grabbing the first garment that came to hand. She thrust it towards Toby.

"I can't wear this!" he wailed.

There was a knock at the door.

"Oh God," said Harriet, and for a moment Toby expected her to fall to her knees in prayer.

She did not have the chance. The door opened. Toby dropped down by the bedside, intending to slip beneath the bed.

"Ariette, my dear, we've come to collect you!"

Towing Aldous by a pink ribbon, Mrs Van Voyd sashayed forward, her bulk resplendent in multi-coloured polka-dots and barber's-pole leggings. A silver cape trailed from her shoulders and her headpiece was a display of tropical fruit, artfully represented in plastic. Each of her massive breasts was decorated in a swirling spiral; twin golden tassels hung from the tips.

"Oh Mrs Van Voyd, I'm not *quite* ready – "

"Of course you're not, my dear! Choosing your costume, a delicate undertaking. Now let's see, what would most *excite* Marcus, hm?"

"Really, Mrs Van Voyd, don't bother yourself, please – "

By the side of the bed next to the window Toby, having first discovered that the bed had wooden sides which extended to the floor; having then noted with alarm the consequences of certain recent stirrings; having then despaired for several valuable seconds; having then decided that action, in the last event, is better than inaction, was struggling into Aunt Eunice's pink chiffon negligee.

"So important for a girl to display herself *wantonly* – a woman of my years must of course be more modest... Now this is *most* attractive." Mrs Van Voyd held up a bright rag emblazoned with geometric shapes. "*Broadway Boogie-Woogie*," she read, examining the label.

Padding about on the end of his long lead, Aldous eyed Toby quizzically. Silently the boy attempted to shoo the dog away.

"But where are the *bikini-style* costumes?" Mrs Van Voyd was saying. "Surely the Yard gave you some of *those?*"

The old woman moved slowly about the bed; Harriet wondered if there were some natural-seeming reason why one might choose, quite suddenly, to fling all one's bedclothes onto the floor. She couldn't think of one. But she thought of something else.

"Oh, Mrs Van Voyd – the *bikini-style* costumes – I have them here..." Harriet gestured expansively towards the wardrobe. She clutched the old woman's arm.

"Yes, do show me, my dear... something more *provocative*." Mrs Van Voyd turned, smiling, from the bed. "Artemis and Hera," she remarked, gesturing towards the tapestry. "Goodness, it must be *years* since I've seen that old thing... I do believe I slept in this room as a girl – 1898, it must have been..."

Harriet exhaled deeply.

"Really, my dear, you shouldn't *pant*. It's something servants do – that dreadful Millicent, for example..."

Toby had got himself into rather a mess. His foot seemed to be caught in a tangle of chiffon. He pushed.

There was a loud sound of tearing, like a trumpeting fart, and Aldous began to bark.

"My goodness, whatever – " Mrs Van Voyd span round. "*Tobias!*"

The old woman was dumbstruck, staring back and forth between the two young people. Toby, scarlet, staggered to his feet, the torn chiffon clutched against his nakedness.

"Really, Ariette," Mrs Van Voyd finally blustered, "I am a woman of liberal – not to say *permissive* principles... but such *perversion* – and with a mere child!"

Harriet almost fainted with shame. "Mrs Van Voyd, you might not believe this, but – "

There was an anguished adenoidal cry and Milly staggered through the open doorway, clutching at a stitch in her side.

"Ma'am (*puff puff*), thank goodness I've found you – "

"Millicent, how many times have I told you – "

"But ma'am, it's Master (*puff puff*) – Master Toby!" The maid's deformed mouth hung open in shock.

Toby stood sheepishly before the three women. He tightened his grip on the concealing gown.

18
The Hidden Key

"I deserve it, don't I?"

"You might get it. But why do you deserve it?"

"Because you like me?"

"Coy." Mark, leaning against the mast of a colourful umbrella, held the sketchbook concealed against his chest. Beside him on the sand were an assortment of pencils, a cigarette case, a tarnished silver lighter, a crumpled *Telescope* (open to Pinker's column) and a glass of scotch in which the ice had long since melted. Yardley, returned from the sea, had dropped to her haunches beside him, and eyed the sketchbook expectantly. The rest of the party were many yards away.

"Come on, darling…" The whisper was deceptive. Her hand dived to his exposed ribs.

"Yeow! Cut it out!"

"The Yard is boisterous." Mrs Van Voyd, glancing wryly over her dark glasses, interrupted her monologue on her sixth husband, millionaire rancher Bowen Cartwright.

Harriet squinted miserably at the wrestling figures. Would the party soon be over? Dusk, at least, was beginning to fall.

Triumphantly, Yardley seized the sketchbook.

"Millicent. Millicent?" said Mrs Van Voyd. "Crank up the gramophone, there's a good girl." *Rhapsody in Blue* had run down. "They were lovely boys, George and Ira. Jews, of course." The old woman, elevated in her armchair, trailed a hand through Harriet's hair as Gershwin's sweet horns floated round them again. In a box beside the gramophone were discs by Al Jolson, Irving Kaufman, and the Paul

Whiteman Orchestra; there were copies of *The Varsity Drag* and *Doin' the Racoon*; there were the compositions of George M. Cohan, Jerome Kern, Rodgers and Hart, Cole Porter and Irving Berlin; there were – so Mrs Van Voyd put it – the *exotic rhythms of numerous Negroes*. There was all this, but there was no Travers and Carp: Mrs Van Voyd, a wise woman, operated a strict *no-Jelly* policy.

But how much worse could things be?

Mr Travers staggered along the shore, a whisky bottle in his hand. His new toupee was slipping from his head. Over his neck-to-knee bathing suit he wore an ill-fitting vest with unravelling seams; his tartan slippers and walking socks were sodden from the tide; a handkerchief hung crumpled from his pocket, its *J*-monogram webbed thick with mucus. Discarded somewhere on the beach behind him were the cheap edition of *The Cruel Sea* by Nicholas Monsarrat (its pages already experiencing that cruelty) and the gramophone record by Miss Alma Cogan, *I Can't Tell a Waltz from a Tango*, its grooves encrusted with sand.

I have done my best, thought Mrs Van Voyd. She closed her eyes. Her wrinkled fingers played in Harriet's hair, looping and twisting the silky strands.

"And then, my dear, came the twist in the tale." The cattle king Bowen Cartwright had purchased her, the old woman claimed, as he purchased the Somerset castle he had shipped in numbered pieces to Wyoming.

"And *then*" – she raised her voice just slightly – "came the twist in the tale."

"Yes?" Harriet jolted her attention from Mark. How dreadful she was feeling! It was all her own fault. Mortified after the discovery of Toby in her room, she had allowed Mrs Van Voyd to have her way. For her weakness Harriet had sat all afternoon *sans* sunglasses, *sans* hat, *sans* kimono, huddled in the remaining shade of the old woman's umbrella, wearing a bikini in the design of an American flag: one breast star-spangled, the other striped. With loathing she contemplated her exposed body. She was thin now; she knew she was thin; but somehow she still saw only a rolling, blanched lava of fat.

My dear, you look just like Miss Monroe! Mrs Van Voyd had assured her.

Again Harriet glanced resentfully at Toby. The boy lay some yards off, flat on his back, covered from feet to neck by a towel which a servant, directed by Mrs Van Voyd, would periodically take down to the sea and wet. It was another of the old woman's sagacious remedies, whether against sunburn or the *stirrings of adolescence* she would not say. Concealing the boy's face was an open magazine.

Jellicoe Travers longed for oblivion. He had reached the age of sixty; his life was almost over – but of course, of course, from the first it had been ruined. And today, nineteen years ago, David had died. The shallows washed round the little man's feet as he looked back at his companions. What a tableau they made, beneath the overpowering cliffs! He swigged his whisky. Should he break into song? Ah, if only he were a singer…

He kicked off his sodden slippers, clawed at the hideous, imprisoning vest. He had been drinking steadily for the last two days.

Toby, beneath *Astronomical Stories* (Nov. 1946), lay thinking about sea monsters. In that particular issue there was a story by Raymond Z. Rockline about a race of hideous squid-like creatures that lived at the bottom of the Pacific Ocean, down, down in the deepest trench. Disturbed by depth charges from a US Navy warship, the enraged monsters slithered up out of the ocean. First they devoured a beach full of bathers in Long Beach, California; then, trailing their lethal slime, they swarmed through downtown Los Angeles, annihilating humans, cars, buildings…

Toby would settle for the Long Beach scene, the location transferred to Shadow Black.

"Honey, they're marvellous!"

Toby could hear the voices faintly.

"You're dripping – "

"Don't worry, I'll be sizzling soon." Yardley smiled, pleased, when Mark laughed. Of course he remembered. *Everyone* did: the line was the most famous of her career (and had so nearly ended up on the cutting-room floor – how many times had she told that story?) "Am I really so beautiful?"

"Narcissist." Mark lit a cigarette. His banter was a pose: he was thinking of his painting. As the days passed he was drawn ineluctably – so he put it to himself – *into* the rich textures of his work, as if into a new and different world; and the world he had left, when he returned to it, was faded. He thought with contempt of his career until now, the 'society' portraits, the gimmickry, the obsession with fame. He had been a charlatan; the critics had been right. When he looked up at Yardley it was almost with pity.

The page at which she was gazing contained a succession of quick sketches. They could have been snapshots of the long afternoon: Mrs Van Voyd paddling in her barber's-pole leggings, Aldous splashing through the shallows beside her; Mrs Van Voyd and Jellicoe Travers tossing a medicine ball back and forth, Travers glum because he had dropped it again; huddled Harriet; a trestle table, laden with treats; harried maids struggling with a massive hamper, midway down the steps cut in the cliff-face.

The focus of Yardley's attention was an impression of herself, like some exotic amphibian, emerging erect from waist-deep water.

"Thank you, honey." Yardley plucked the cigarette from Mark's lips.

"Hey – "

"Answer my question."

"You're gorgeous, you know you are. That's why you're wearing *that*." Mark gazed again at Yardley's clinging costume, emblazoned with images of her own face. He lit another cigarette. "Do you want this too?" He offered her the warm scotch.

"Disgusting. Staines!"

The butler trudged forward. His suit was limp with sweat; his patent-leather shoes were filled with sand.

The sea monsters had gone.

How strange the pathways of thought, their tangled mazes, their mysterious connections! By what means he did not know, Toby had arrived again at a place to which, as he lay on the sand, he found himself perpetually returning: again he was erupting into Miss Locke's room, tumbling into the arms of the naked girl. The incident at the time had seemed barely real; in retrospect it was increasingly, excitingly vivid.

Carefully, beneath the towel, he turned onto his stomach.

"This one is the best." Mark turned the page.

Now it was Yardley's turn to laugh. "It's so elaborate!"

"A sitting target."

In scrupulous detail Mark had recorded the spectacle of Mrs Van Voyd in her present pose: resplendent in a sinking armchair, stately beneath the boughs of a crooked umbrella. Discs of dark glass concealed her eyes, suggesting a regal aloofness. A towel was spread before her like a carpet before a throne; her sceptre was a cigar; the huge melons of her breasts were twin orbs, complementing bizarrely her crown of fruit. To her left was a bookcase, filled with her favourite reading matter; to her right, on a round table, the ancient gramophone, its horn a lush, exotic efflorescence. Just beyond the edge of the shade basked Aldous, his pink ribbon pinned to the arm of the chair.

"But where's little Harry?"

"I excluded her," said Mark.

"Good idea," laughed Yardley.

"How terrible," said Harriet.

"Not terrible, Ariette – not in itself. I had quite enough to keep me... *busy*, I assure you! But why, I ask myself, did the wretched man get himself *caught*?"

It was the twist in the tale. Who would have thought that rugged Bowen Cartwright, Wyoming cattle king, was secretly – so Mrs Van Voyd put it – *a practitioner of Uranian love*? (Harriet assumed that *this* was not the husband Mrs Van Voyd had *really loved*.)

"By the way, where's Jelly? It must be time for the cake."

"I think he's gone behind that rock again," said Harriet.

"Really! The place must be awash with his excretions. Tobias, check on him, will you? Ariette, kick Tobias."

"I'll go – "

"Ariette – "

But Harriet was gone.

Mrs Van Voyd sighed. Idly she fingered the spines of her books. They were all there, in her special bookcase, the stalwarts of her maiden days: Ouida, Marie Corelli, Robert Hichens; more recent favourites too: *The Way of an Eagle, The Constant Nymph, Precious Bane, The Sheik.*

The old woman closed her eyes. Once – it must have been 1897 – Mummy, in the company of the Rector (ugh, the thick hairs that sprouted from his nostrils!) had declared that her daughter had the taste of a scullery maid. Cora had only laughed. Mummy, who read nothing but the Bible and the parish magazine, and had worn a widow's weeds permanently after Daddy died (when she was thirty-six), was the dullest woman who had ever lived.

Mrs Van Voyd lit a fresh cigar. Behind her, the darkening cliffs rose massively. Before her, the sea was a golden vastness.

"Mr Travers?"

Where was he?

The rising rock wall which banded the beach was like a curtain. The space behind it was deeper than Harriet expected; then the space began to narrow. In intense shadow Harriet walked down a corridor of rock. Seaweed was strewn on a carpet of sand. Then the way became rugged. Faintly, then strongly, she began to feel alarmed. She felt sick; she had drunk too much. She looked down, and the stars and stripes of her costume shot up from the gloom like fireworks. When she looked up again, she stared into a black abyss.

After some seconds she realised it was the mouth of a cave.

"Tobias! Dance with me."

Toby's reply had about it a mute eloquence. He rose up at once, the towel falling away from him, and sprinted into the sea.

"Like a young faun..." Mrs Van Voyd gazed after him wistfully.

Rhapsody in Blue was back in its sleeve. Yardley, who had joined her old friend, insisted on something more lively.

"You didn't bring Glenn Miller? I loved Glenn. Do you know, I cried for two days when he was lost?"

"I didn't know you were so sentimental," said Mark, approaching her from behind.

"Didn't you?"

His hands lingered for a moment on her hips.

"Mr Travers?"

The first cave had been but an antechamber to another; the chain of caves described an upright arc through the interior of the cliff, curving away from the beach to the east. Intermittently, holes in the outer wall illuminated the interior like jagged windows. Beyond them, the brightness of the sky was fading.

Harriet knew she should have gone back. But she scrambled on, mechanically. Her thigh was torn and blood flowed down her leg; she didn't feel it. How drunk she was! She hadn't realised it until now.

Stooping, she picked up a strange smooth-rough thing she felt beneath her foot. It was the striped vest; it trailed unravelled strands.

"Mr Travers?"

In *Astronomical Stories* No. 53 (July 1938) there is a story by Frederick Kroll called 'Wirelesses of Doom'. In a secret base on Titan in the year 1999, evil genius Vargo Ovale, expelled from earth by World Government, has plotted a devastating revenge. His agents are the Wireless Men – monstrous mechanical creatures with eyes like dials and loudspeaker mouths that broadcast lethal sound-beams. Dematerialised and beamed through space like wireless signals, the terrible monsters reassemble themselves suddenly in the offices of World Government leaders. The carnage is swift. But before emitting their lethal sound-beams, the Wireless Men – breaking into speech with clicks and whirs – relay to their trembling victims a vengeful broadcast from their creator. Ovale's voice, sucked through space, spat from harsh loudspeakers, is a shower of metal, alien and clanging.

The broadcast replayed in Toby's mind as he drifted on the cool salt water.

I could float here like this forever, he thought.

"Staines!" Mrs Van Voyd clutched the butler.

Awkwardly the old man attempted to oblige her. It was – oh, it must have been forty years since he had *tripped the light fantastic*. This *jitterbugging* was rather fun... He wished he could just remove his shoes... wished he could remove his *eyes*, too, from the bobbing tassels on his partner's breasts...

"Always the *ingénue*," Mark shouted to Yardley.

"Hm?"

"You're like a girl at the junior prom."

"Honey, I wouldn't be wearing this!"

They were jiving, too. Mrs Van Voyd had selected her most raucous record.

As in a dream, Harriet came upon the curious vision.

For some time the arc of the caves had been descending; then, ahead, she heard the soft lap-lap of water. At last she emerged from behind a screen of rock to see the little boat, tethered to its landing stage. Cross-legged inside it, the whisky bottle cradled in his arms like a child, sat Mr Travers, his toupee at his feet like a little dead animal.

"My dear." He turned to Harriet, welcoming her with a vacant smile. In his striped bathing suit he looked like a convict.

Toby had met Lord Harrowblest only once; the thought came to him that the old man's voice, in its harsh metallic clanging, was just like the voice of Vargo Ovale, projected through space. But Harrowblest was not so far away as Titan...

The thought of Harrowblest made Toby think of Vardell; the thought of Vardell made him think of Miss Locke. How absurd it was! Until today he had thought nothing of her, nothing at all. Now he thought:

Why is she marrying Vardell?

Yardley shouted:

"What *is* this music, Cora?"

"They call it *rhythm and blues*, I believe. It's for Negroes. Isn't it marvellous?"

"Excuse me, ma'am – " It was Milly. "Mrs Salloby's sent down the cake." The girl's face was flushed.

"Marvellous, Millicent! Dance with me..."

She cast off the butler. Staines, retiring, clutched at his heart.

"Ma'am, please (*puff puff*) – "

"You're young, child!" The old woman led Milly in a frenetic caper.

"Say, where's Jell-O?" called Yardley.

"Drowned, I expect," Mrs Van Voyd cried gaily. "I sent Ariette to find him."

"Hattie!" said Mark.

"You've remembered her, honey?"

"Goodness me, Millicent!" erupted Mrs Van Voyd. "Whatever is wrong with you? Staines!"

Milly, who had (*a*) hauled seven buckets of ice back and forth for Toby's bath; (*b*) climbed the steep steps on the cliff-face five times in each direction, once carrying one end of a heavily stocked bookcase; (*c*) waited on her mistress in the heat all afternoon; (*d*) endured Mrs Salloby's temper on this most difficult of days, and (*e*) much else besides, had found *jitterbugging* to Mrs Van Voyd's rhythm and blues record a little too much – and so had (*f*) fainted.

Harriet knelt gingerly in the boat with Mr Travers. He offered her a swig of his whisky; she accepted.

"I taught myself to play the piano," he said. "Did I ever tell you that, hm? There was one in the parlour of Mama's... establishment, when I was a child. That's what first got me going, you see. I used to flounder about on it... oh, no one minded, they were busy with other things. It amused Mama, I think – that was my rôle, to amuse her – but of course I wanted to play properly; she wouldn't let me have lessons. I became obsessed – haunted by an image of myself as a brilliant performer, holding a concert-hall spellbound... And I only knew about concert-halls from things I'd overheard the gentlemen saying, in the parlour... What rich, exciting lives those gentlemen lived!"

He laughed. "It troubled me much, this gap between my dream and the reality of my achievements... Then one day while I was hiding behind the velvet curtains I heard one of Mama's gentlemen reciting a poem, or a story perhaps – I remember nothing about it, except that it contained the phrase *the hidden key*. What it meant, I don't know. A metaphor, a literal door key? But the phrase resonated in my mind, and in my childish way I came to think of it as referring to a key in music... I knew there were things called keys; I didn't know much more than that. Now I thought the hidden key was the answer to my dilemma. I used to dream about it: one day, as I flailed about on the keyboard, suddenly I would blunder into the hidden key. All at once dramatic sonatas, wild mazurkas would ripple from beneath my fingers. It would be as if a door had been flung open, flooding a dark room with light... Of course, in time, I taught myself to play, adequately enough – oh, adequately."

Mr Travers took a swig of whisky. "She's called *Bluefinch*." He gestured at the little boat. "She belonged to Peter."

Harriet thought again of the photograph of Peter Harrowblest. Several times, since the day in the gallery, she had seen it – in her mind. She trailed a hand along the rough side of the boat. Everything about it was apparent to her at once.

"A secret," she mouthed, "a secret boat."

Mr Travers brought his face close to hers. His breath was a heady gust of whisky. "*Only I knew.*"

Harriet touched him. "You were very close?"

"He was like a... nephew." There were tears in his eyes. "I like to come here sometimes – it's all I have. I've kept her up over the years – just in case... I wanted to keep his room, too, exactly as it was – but Mr Collidge said no, it was morbid... he had everything destroyed. *Bluefinch* was the one thing he couldn't touch."

The little man laughed bitterly. "Collidge is a fool. We know Peter is alive somewhere, we all know it – "

"Mr Travers, how – ?"

"Oh, very easily. Shortly before he disappeared, three million pounds went missing from Empire funds – "

"Three million!"

"Yes, my dear. They never found out where it went, but... well..." He glugged back the last of the whisky, then threw the bottle over the side.

Harriet wondered: *How deep is the water?*

Then: *How much time has passed?*

"Mr Travers, there's... there's something I don't understand." She was finding it difficult to speak clearly. "You were a successful composer..."

He laughed. "The operative word, my dear, is... *were*."

"But you must have money, you can go anywhere! Why do you stay here, why do you...? Is it – is it Peter?"

"Oh, my dear!" The little man took Harriet's hand. "No, it's not Peter – it's me, it's me. I've left before, you know I have. After David came to stay in 1919, I left with him. I was away for sixteen years, that time. But what of it? I belong here – here or in Wardour Street, can't you see?"

"Wardour Street? I don't understand."

"Oh, I'm sure you do – don't you remember? The location of – hm – a *certain establishment* I've mentioned before. Very exclusive, very select. Presided over by a woman known as Maisie T..."

"Maisie T?"

Harriet recalled the afternoon in the gallery, and what Mr Travers had told her about Lord Stephen. *Dropped dead in a brothel in Wardour Street in 1902.*

"Her full name – you mean you didn't guess? – was Maisie Travers. A common prostitute. You see before you the product of her *miscegenation* with Lord Harrowblest, him that was..."

"You're his son!"

"Oh no, my dear, his bastard – there's all the difference in the world, you'll agree. Lord Stephen had no son – that's why his brother is Lord Harrowblest today... and why I must count myself lucky indeed that Lord Edward, good old Eddie took me in, after dear Mama's syphilitic demise... Do I *disgust* you, my dear? You have every right to be, every right in the world. Do I make you want to throw up?"

The little man's hands gripped the sides of the boat. Violently he began to rock it from side to side.

"Mr Travers, stop!"

"But why, my dear? If you want to vomit, you're in the right place!"

Harriet lurched forward. Her hair tumbled between the little man's knees. But she was not vomiting – she was crying. Her choking sobs rasped out painfully and echoed in the chill, watery cave.

With a start, Mr Travers ceased his rocking. Bending towards Harriet, he raised up her head. He took her hand. "Oh my dear, my dear, I'm sorry." He reached for the handkerchief with the *J*-monogram; it appeared that he had lost it, so Harriet had to wipe her eyes with her hands.

"We must go back," she said after a moment. "They'll be wondering where we've gone."

"Where *have* they gone? Tobias!"

Mrs Van Voyd's imperious call floated over the sea.

Toby, floating too, had been thinking about destiny. Did he have one? Or was he wholly free?

Surely not.

"Tobias!"

Mrs Van Voyd sighed. Two servants were removing the cake from a hamper; a third attended the reviving Milly; the butler appeared – but only appeared – to have died.

Not that anyone noticed.

MARK: *How long does it take to light sixty candles?*

YARDLEY: *Ages. Let's have it again.*

What picture was that from?

Mark cranked the gramophone.

"Oh, where are they?" Mrs Van Voyd – suddenly, as is the way with the elderly – was weary, weary. The rhythm and blues, she supposed. Too much. Languidly she thought of her last lover, the boy in New York. His name was Leroy – or was it Elroy? In any case she had given him seven thousand dollars. The old woman sighed.

Yardley tossed back her highball.

Yardley flicked the ash from her cigarette.

Yardley moved into Mark's arms; the music began again.

"Toby!"

As Toby sloshed back to shore, the figure blazed up from the shadows, seeming to emerge from the cliff itself. He stumbled back. The words escaped him before he could check himself:

"*Why are you marrying him?*"

Harriet stared.

"My dear boy, you are a little fanciful – " Behind her, Mr Travers lurched into view. "Miss Locke would hardly throw herself away on *me*."

Sagging, he clung to the boy's shoulder.

"It's a masterpiece!"

The sky had grown darker. With the candles lit, the cake blazed like a beacon.

"Ah, my dears – " Mrs Van Voyd, with outstretched arms, turned to Ariette, Tobias, the staggering Jelly.

Then she *screamed*.

"Swing me in your arms, honey!" Yardley cried gaily. The Negroes had launched into their final chorus.

Mark and Yardley collapsed onto the sand.

Mrs Van Voyd collapsed across the trestle table. Champagne bottles fell; the top tier of the masterpiece shifted, as in an earthquake – then it collapsed, too.

Mrs Van Voyd was oblivious. "My poor darling is drowned!"

The pink ribbon – the ribbon that had been attached to the armchair – had torn away.

Toby shrugged off Travers. The little man went sprawling. "Aldous! Aldous!" the boy called hilariously. He ran back and forth along the sands. In imagination he saw a massive Slime Creature, rearing up from the ocean.

Harriet's fingers twisted at her engagement ring. Mark and Yardley rolled across the sand. Their laughter, a sparkling counterpoint, rang above the music, rang above the sobbing.

Jellicoe Travers crawled on all fours.

"He's thirteen years old!" cried Mrs Van Voyd. "That's ninety-one in dog years!"

A deeper darkness swung across the sky like a scythe.

The water was colder than Harriet had expected.

And yet it was welcoming.

Jellicoe Travers wished the beach were not so clean. Had it been awash with filth, with sewage – oh, how his tongue would have darted to it eagerly, as had Mama's to her lovers' secret places!

"Aldous! Aldous!"

Should I answer? wondered Travers.

Mark Vardell gasped. His erection hammered in his bathing trunks, intolerably. The desire he felt was inevitable, inevitable. Yet what an idle thing it was, a *bagatelle*! Even now his spirit could float beyond it – even in his arms she was becoming unreal...

Harriet was floating. It was easy. She kicked lightly at the sandy floor; she moved her arms. She was free of gravity... she felt like laughing...

"Aldous! Aldous!" The cry was automatic.

Toby thought of EEL, of Miss Locke (naked), of *Bluefinch*, of Lightletter, of the Professor, of Heike; but every thought seemed only to lead him into tangles that twisted ever tighter like unbreakable cutting strings; and the more he struggled to free himself, the more ensnared he became.

"Aldous! Aldous!"

A scratchy heartbeat was dying away. The needle of the gramophone skidded across the label.

It wasn't until she realised she couldn't touch bottom that Harriet's pleasure was replaced by panic. As if from above she suddenly saw herself: adrift, alone, in a terrible vastness.

She cried out. Her arms were flailing.

Jellicoe Travers sniffed at seaweed.

"My God!" cried Mark.

"No – " gulped Harriet, "please, no – "

An arm gripped her. A creature of the sea, some terrible dark acolyte, had risen up beneath her and was pulling her down. For a second her struggles became more frantic. But her strength had gone.

As Harriet began to die she thought of the day she had first arrived, of the first appalling, exhilarating glimpse of Shadow Black – how darkly it had reared up above her, how darkly!

There was no struggle – the house was too strong…

In a strange way death was comforting after all, drawing her after him as to a place of safety. His wiry arm was clutched beneath her. How strong he was, how youthful!

"She's all right – she's all right – "

The voice was barely audible, a strangled gasp.

Death lay beside her, wrecked on the shore.

"She can't swim. I never knew." Mark's face was white.

"Get some towels or something," said Yardley. "Harry – Harry, honey – "

"It's all my fault," wailed Jellicoe Travers. "I told her, I told her about the hidden key!"

"Ariette, Ariette – did you see him out there, bobbing on the waves?… Ariette – speak to me! *Did you see him?*"

"Cora, you'll strangle her… Staines! Brandy!"

"Oh Hattie, Hattie…"

"Master Toby's a hero!" Little Milly, her revival complete, was lost in admiration.

Harriet was shivering.

She opened her eyes to the looming faces.

Toby lay beside her, his breathing laboured, a chill arm flung across her icy breasts.

19
The Catcher in the Rye

Sat. 23rd Jul., 1955
12.30 am

Hulloo the CHANCE!

   EEL has MADE UP HIS MIND about a QUESTION that has LONG been vexing him: WHICH IS THE WORST? Daddy ONE he didn't know – a SWIFT EXIT after ACT OF PLANTING. (Does this EXCULPATE D1? a MOOT POINT.) D2, the WILD-HAIRED PIANIST – a MASTER, indeed, but MORE, EEL fears, of metaphoric (& perhaps real) MASTURBATION than of MOZART. Currents of HATE... (Ah, if little EEL had not been so SLITHERY, how he would have RELISHED toppling a massive BLOCK OF GRANITE from a GREAT HEIGHT onto those HATED HANDS!) Decidedly EXCREMENT in human form... D3, not so much EXCREMENT as SHIT. But D4, D4! YES, he is the WORST!... Every night for the last WEEK we have taken dinner with the GOLDBERGS (American, Chicago, have daughter, v. RICH). The GOLDBERGS (EEL repents, America) are not the EXPECTED members of the SPIRITUAL PROLETARIAT... The GOLDBERGS are what is known as CULTURED – music, art & LITTER-ATURE... Also POLITE to a PRETERNATURAL degree, which they NEED to be to tolerate the WITLESS BOOMINGS of D4 on EVERY possible subject he DOESN'T understand... (NOT that he's better on the ONE he does: MIRIAM – it must be said – CAN – v.

occasionally SHUT HER MOUTH, but D4's policy of when-in-doubt-discourse-on-the-MANUFACTURE-OF-HOSEPIPES would cause even the ALBERT SCHWEITZERS of this world to QUESTION the concept of 'REVERENCE FOR LIFE' (UUURRGGGHHH, this page has ALMOST been SPATTERED WITH VOMIT)... How poor EEL looks forward to that DISTANT FUTURE TIME (FOUR yrs. away, FIVE?) when he is a REVERED writer of INTERNATIONAL fame. Shall he merely LAUGH at the HOSEPIPE HORROR then?)

CAN'T write any more now. Miriam COOKED tonight (to IMPRESS Mrs Goldberg - UNSUCCESSFULLY). Poor EEL, he REALLY feels like THROWING UP!!... He shall put himself GINGERLY to bed, NODDING to sleep over LAST AND FIRST MEN.

(Under same cover)

Sun. 24th Jul., 7 am

MIRÁCLE! - the GOLDBERGS are GOING AWAY. A three day CAMPING excursion to inspect sites of the ancient ETRUSCAN civilisation. But GUESS who's GOING TOO?... YYYYYYYESS!! - They asked us ALL (EEL

TOLD the Chancer they WERE polite), BUT as Chancer MIGHT expect the horrendous MIRIAM reacted with HORROR at the thought of being OUTDOORS AT NIGHT, & HOSEPIPE is FAR too FAT to CRAWL in & out of TENTS... OF COURSE Miriam – how she GROVELS to Mrs Goldberg – INSISTED that the sainted Goldbergs couldn't POSSIBLY be BURDENED with EUGENE, but Mrs Goldberg – EEL, come to think of it, could GROVEL to her himself – INSISTED they HAD TO HAVE EUGENE!!... So H&M can be left to INDULGE their GRUNTING PASSION (I've HEARD them, EEL has HEARD them) by themselves, while the happy EEL SLITHERS AWAY to SPORT amongst the ETRU-SSS-CANS (did EEL not always HISS that the ETRUSCANS were his FAVOURITE DEAD CIVILISATION??)!!... three cheers for the ETRUSCANS, FOUR for the GOLDBERGS!!!

EEL had better stop. They'll be here soon to PICK HIM UP.

Your supercharged

PS. Got sick of LAST & FIRST MEN (IDEA more exciting than ACTUAL BOOK – like a LOT of SF stuff, actually) but found something better. Has Chancer heard of a book called 'CATCHER IN THE RYE'?? Not SF, but AMAZING. Rachel Goldberg (the daughter) lent it to me.

20
Golden Band

The half-moon hung in the clear summer sky, its beams an alien chillness in the warm enfolding air. Alone on the terrace, Mark Vardell leaned over the balustrade, drawing back slowly on a cigarette. He had exchanged his bathing costume for a pair of white ducks and a white linen shirt. His sleeves were rolled back and his feet were still bare. Behind him, through the French windows, the Great Hall was in darkness.

It was long after midnight and the house was silent. Harriet and her rescuer were long ago in their beds, restored by brandy and baths; Jellicoe Travers, sobered by shock, had ceased his anxious flutterings. The servants had retired – all but the wretched Milly, compelled as she was to accompany Mrs Van Voyd in her desperate search for Aldous. When Mark had last seen the pair they made a crazy tableau in the moonlight, Milly breast-deep in water, straining the sea with a colander, while Mrs Van Voyd, slumped on the shore, alternately sobbed and execrated the heavens like a ham actor auditioning for *King Lear*.

Mark thought about Harriet. With a movement of horror he recalled her cold form spreadeagled in the wash of the tide, shuddering as if with the last spasms of life. Why had she done it? *An accident*, the others had called it. *A drunken impulse*. Harriet had offered no explanations.

Mark flung away his cigarette. He buried his face in his hands. There was no need tonight to check if the courtyard was illuminated with a square of yellow. As he stood in the group about Harriet's bed, beaming at the apologetic girl, Mark had felt Yardley's index finger working down his spine. The sharp surreptitious nail was an unmistakable command.

Making his way through the shadows of the great hall, Mark thought with a sudden influx of power:

This is the last time.

The last time: the phrase hammered at his heart as he passed the glimmering gong, opening the door beneath the overhang of the gallery. The dining room was in a deeper darkness, muffled in heat behind the heavy curtains. Mark groped his way towards the spiral stairs; at the top of the stairs he parted the curtains and again was in the great hall, high above head height. From the minstrel's gallery the vast room stretched eerily below him, the ancient furniture, the high-panelled walls, the pendulous stags' heads grey in the moonlight. Mark passed through the door in the corner of the gallery, climbing the dark stairs to the narrow passageway. He stumbled a little.

In the shrine the lights were low. The gaudy colours of the posters had dimmed; the mirror was a dark arrested swirl; on the bed lay Yardley, in a supine stillness. A breeze through the window stirred her wrap. The white fabric was of the finest silk, delicate as gossamer, and billowed over her sleek unstirring limbs like a wraith, an uncertain soul shimmering up, then subsiding, again and again.

"You've come." Her hand reached out instinctively, pressing a switch by the side of the bed. Soft music filled the room and the lights faded further; it was as if the surrounding room were disappearing and only Yardley remained, waiting, on the creamy bed. Mark padded slowly over the thick white carpet.

"It's over," he murmured, "over..." But the words could barely leave his lips; they hung suspended in the air, then dissolved as if they had never been, evaporating like tiny unmenacing clouds. Mark felt unreal, as if he were floating; the music was a sustaining medium, buoying him up. Its shimmering textures surrounded him in a slow but insistent eddy.

What was it? Elgar?

"My love..." The goddess was rising on the bed, her arms reaching towards him. Through the wrap, her breasts could be clearly seen; then the wrap fell away, vanishing like a clearing mist.

"Over..." Her hands ran over his back, her nails rasping through the white linen shirt. Their lips smeared together; his hands, unwilled, massaged the marvellous soft hardness of her breasts. When he closed his eyes he seemed to be falling, falling inexorably through an endless darkness...

Then came the cry.

"Oh help, help!" The voice was distorted, echoing through the barrier of the anteroom by the stairs. Beneath it beat a tom-tom of insistent fists.

Yardley reached for the light switch. "Cora?"

"No, it's Travers. Listen."

"You're right. Go into the dressing rooms, honey." Quickly Yardley covered herself in a less revealing wrap. When she opened the outer doors, Jellicoe Travers fell into her arms.

"It's Miss Locke," he sobbed. "I went to check on her and she's – she's gone!"

It was Mark who found her. As he ran along the cliff path she came into view, a pale ghost in the moonlight, grovelling in her nightdress on the chill beach below. Her hair was a wild, twisted mass; the tide washed round her searching hands. Desperately Mark flung himself on the weeping girl, dragging her back from the water.

"My ring," was all she would say, "my ring!"

And he promised he would buy her a new golden band.

Dawn broke with a grey lifelessness; there was an unexpected coldness in the air.

That morning in the tower Mark did almost no work on the portrait. A heaviness hung on his heart like lead and the colours of his palette seemed to fade perpetually. He stood staring at the cripple – so powerless, so powerful, the great carved head hanging like a mask. Sometimes as he looked into its impassive hardness Mark found himself wanting to speak, to reveal, as if at a confessional, all his secrets.

When he left the tower he went to see Harriet. The door of her room was open and as he approached he heard a jaunty, familiar caterwauling from within:

Voh-de-oh-de-oh
Voh-de-oh-de-oh
She's the gal for meee
Voh-de-oh-de-oh
Voh-de-oh-de-oh
Raise a li'l fammer-leee
With Bill
An' Sam
An' Sarah like we pla-a-anned
Our own li'l flock
On our own li'l block
In Lo-o-ove-laaand, Tenn-err-sseeee!!

Mr Travers, on a stool by the canopied bed, was dressed in a straw boater and a candystripe suit, strumming merrily on a battered banjo. Harriet, propped on many pillows, sat surrounded by wildflowers, bowls of fruit and the debris of a massive breakfast.

"That was marvellous, Mr Travers!" she cried, when the song was finished. The little man flushed with pleasure.

"Our first hit. From *Follies of 1921*," he said happily, sadly.

Mark stood in the doorway, watching.

21
Strange Heartbeat

It was a colander, washed up by the tide. Seawater drained through the holes as Toby held it aloft, leaving behind in the grey punctured bowl a strand of seaweed, a brown pebble, a cake mix of wet sand, some encrusted salt, and a small, golden band. He held it aloft; it glimmered. Then he slipped it onto his finger and sloshed out into the water.

The sun was swathed in a cloudy haze and a chill breeze ruffled Toby's hair as *Bluefinch* rounded the promontory. In the bottom of the little boat, crumpled in the prow, besides a pair of oars, a coil of rope and some rusted tools, was an old tarpaulin of the sort one might use to cover the lifeboat in rainy weather. Toby had not thought to remove it and it lay in arid corrugations, a torrid topography of jagged hills and valleys.

It was as he dragged *Bluefinch* up onto the beach that he noticed the movement under the tarpaulin. The stiff fabric throbbed as if with life. For a moment the boy stood wonderingly in the shallows, transfixed. It was not until he heard a familiar whimpering, rising in counterpoint to the strange heartbeat, that he boldly pulled back the concealing skin.

"Aldous!"

The little dog's fur was matted with sand and he yapped weakly at his benefactor. For a moment Toby felt only astonishment.

"Shut *up!*" it occurred to him to say.

Aldous, to Toby's surprise, shut up.

Toby began to wonder what to do.

If there was some appeal in the fantasy of drowning Aldous – then, perhaps, bringing home the body to Mrs Van Voyd – there was yet a more compelling argument for a benevolent course. If Mrs Van Voyd was insufferable with Aldous, she was still more insufferable without him. When would the lamentations cease, the sobbed prayers, the keenings – to what horrors would the accusations lead? Three times already she had burst in on Toby, insisting that he *knew* what had happened to Aldous. His knowledge, she imagined, was somehow bound up with his saving of Harriet, as if Aldous had been in the water too, and Toby had known it, and in an act of unimaginable treachery had chosen to save not the dog but the girl. There was no reasoning with the wild-eyed old woman.

There was no reasoning with Aldous either.

Had he really been concerned to restore Aldous to his owner, Toby afterwards had to admit, he would doubtless have turned *Bluefinch* around at once and made his way back to Shadow Black. Instead he reached for the coil of rope in the bottom of the boat; with his other arm he gingerly levered up Aldous.

Setting down the little dog on the sand, Toby strode towards the promenade, the thick coil slung across his shoulders. Halfway there, he looked back.

Some boys have what is called a *natural affinity* with dogs; Toby was not one of them.

"Aldous! Here, boy!"

He felt ridiculous.

A whistle did not work either. Aldous sat stupidly by the side of the boat. Toby, who had never owned a dog, had assumed that dogs simply *would* follow one about, as a matter of course. But then, reflected Toby, how adequate a dog was Aldous, after all?

With some disgust he trudged back, scooping up the little creature. It was an unpleasant experience. The dog not only began his imbecile yapping again but began to struggle too, and as he made his way back over the sand Toby had to squeeze the smelly little ball of fur ever tighter against his side.

"Shut up, shut up," he repeated automatically.

He was glad there was no sign of the Bechers yet. It was too early.

"Sit."

Aldous stood.

But at least he was likely to stay there.

The rope was long, and Toby wrapped much of it around the pylon. Doubling over what remained, he contemplated the business of knots: one around the pylon, one around Aldous? What would be suitable – overhand, figure-of-eight, sheet bend, reef, quick release, surgeon's, fisherman's, clove hitch, round-turn-and-two-half-hitches, rolling hitch, sheepshank, bowling, running bowline, carrick bend? Not that he could *do* any of these. Toby was good at many things, but he was no good at knots. He had left the Cub Scouts after his first meeting (all that Kipling, and the embarrassing chanting!).

The Scouts, as well as initiating him into the esoterica of knotting, might also have taught Toby a vigilance he failed to observe when absorbed in the intricacies of *something loose but firm*, encircling the pylon. By the time he turned back to Aldous he had begun to think how absurd it was to tie up a dog who seemed incapable of movement. He was forgetting, of course, that this was quite untrue; as Aldous, it so happened, had again demonstrated.

He was gone.

"Little bastard!" burst out Toby, and flung down the rope. His eyes roved around the dim recesses beneath the promenade.

No Aldous.

But surely the little creature could not have gone far.

When he realised just how far Aldous had gone, Toby was surprised. The glimpse came some minutes later, as he stalked exasperated up the sands, a horizontal hand shading his eyes. Yards away, nestling beneath the overhang of the promenade, was the crumbling brick structure of an ancient public lavatory. Now surely that was Aldous, that moving scrap, clambering a sunny concrete step into the shade of the lavatory door?

The little bastard was cornered now. Toby did not even run.

In all public lavatories there is a quality of horror: a suggestion of the chasms beneath communal life, of weakness, of failure, of the squalors of the body, of the vanity of our pretensions, of the imminence of death. If abandoned, like an abandoned graveyard a lavatory retains its power. The power clutched its tentacles around Toby as he crossed the threshold marked with a sunfaded sign:

GENTLEMEN

"Aldous?" His voice was a whisper.

A dim corridor led into the dimmer recess of the central chamber. Lit only by three high slits in the wall, it was a dark place of sagging washbasins and dry, cracked urinals. There was no sound of dripping. When Toby twisted at the handle of a tap, rust came away on his hands. There was no water. When he fingered the wall, it was unutterably dry; the paint had become powder and crumbled at his touch. And yet there was a spiritual dankness in the place: the very air seemed to ooze, to suppurate.

Around the corner from the corridor were three water closets. The door of each cubicle hung some six inches above the floor.

"Aldous?" Toby pushed at the first door; agonisingly, the rusted hinges creaked. From the darkness an ancient lavatory bowl loomed up defiantly, its wooden lid decorously shut. Above, an ancient cistern brooded forlornly.

No Aldous.

"Aldous?" In the second cubicle the lid was raised, exposing a stained dry porcelain gullet. Empty of water, it looked alarmingly deep, the hole an entrance to a terrible blackness.

No Aldous.

As he was about to open the third cubicle, Toby was compelled to pause. The shadows in the old lavatory were so deep, and nowhere deeper than in the line of water closets; and yet there appeared to be a dim light shining through the gap beneath the third door.

Toby swallowed hard. Absurdly the idea came to him that *Aldous was making the light.* How else could the light be explained?

An anger, an outrage against the little dog welled in him.

"Aldous!" he cried out, and kicked in the door.

Toby could have laughed. Blazing up in the open doorway was a rusted chain severed from the cistern, coiled on the floor like a dry, burnt snake; a dead seagull crawling with maggots; a lavatory bowl of unimaginable vileness, crusted with primeval filth; and, in the corner of the back wall, a two-foot hole where the bricks had crumbled or been smashed in.

With a wild cry, Toby kicked the seagull out of the cubicle and it skidded, a smear of decomposition, into the centre of the floor. Tensing himself, he plunged through the hole in the wall, rolling out onto the sand. Gasping, on his back, he stared up at the underside of the promenade above him. The brightness of the beach was only yards away; he lay close to the line where the sun cut into the shadow, or the shadow into the sun.

As he rolled, luxuriating, in the cool sand, there was a sudden crash of bricks. More of the lavatory wall had fallen.

Tight on his finger was the golden band.

22
The Sultan's Slave Boy

"You're sure you're up to it, my dear?" Mr Travers held out the kimono.

"Oh yes." Harriet pushed back the sheets, aware that she was allowing Mr Travers to treat her too tenderly. She had perfectly recovered, of course she had: she had had a bad shock, that was all. Yet it was impossible not to feel touched by the little man's attentions. Avuncular, his eyes bright with concern, he could have been a different man from the woebegone drunkard of the day before!

Harriet drew the kimono over her nightdress.

"Only one flight of stairs. Just above us." The afternoon's expedition was the first Mr Travers had allowed her. She had confided in him her difficulties with *A Portrait of the Artist as a Young Man* and he had suggested a visit to the library.

The little man offered his arm.

"I'm quite all right, really – "

It was then that something alarming happened. But it was not unexpected.

The door burst open.

"Ariette!"

As always, Harriet jumped.

"Oh dear." Mr Travers fingered his bow tie nervously.

"You're sure, you're absolutely *sure* – ?" The voice was an agonised wail. Wild-eyed, Mrs Van Voyd advanced on Harriet, her fingers crooked, ready to clutch.

Harriet slumped back on the bed. "I'm sorry, I – "

She had played this scene perhaps four times already that morning.

Uselessly the questions poured over her again: had Ariette seen, had Ariette heard, had Ariette felt, had Ariette *sensed*, ever so vaguely... ? Was there *no* sign: no struggling paws, no desperate piping bark, no *glimpse* of a bobbing sodden ball as it was *swept out to sea*? Then came the accusations: Ariette *had* seen him, she must have; Ariette was *holding something back* – Ariette was *ashamed of the truth* – she had *not* tried to save him... *Ariette had drowned him!*

"Cora, don't be absurd." Wearily Mr Travers attempted to restrain her. It was no good: one could only wait for the spasm to pass. Harriet sat passively as the spit showered in her face, borne on gales of reeking breath. The hands shook her shoulders and her head rocked.

"*Oh...*" At last Mrs Van Voyd broke down. She sank to her knees.

"There there, Cora..." Mr Travers helped the sobbing figure onto the bed. "She's tired herself out," he observed kindly.

Stepping back, Harriet looked on pityingly: since last night Mrs Van Voyd had been searching for Aldous, and since last night she had not changed her clothes. The elaborate bathing costume was a sordid ruin: the barber's-pole leggings were rumpled and stained; a breast had lost its golden tassel; the silver cape was torn; the crown of fruit had long been lost, exposing a mad penumbra of sparse white hair. In the grey daylight the face was a seamy foulness of dirt and smudged makeup, coursed afresh by the old woman's tears. She curled up her bulk on Harriet's bed. Slowly the whimpering died away, and the tired eyes closed.

"I think we ought to leave her," said Mr Travers softly. "She hasn't slept since it happened..." And he carefully removed the old woman's dentures, which had fallen askew.

"Oh, but – " Mr Travers looked alarmed. "You're still up to our little expedition, my dear?"

"Yes!" cried Harriet. "Oh, yes!"

Refracted through thick glass and cobwebs, the weakening sun disclosed the long room, its walls lined with musty, cracked-backed volumes. Wormy tables stood stiffly on faded Turkey carpets. Mr Travers crossed to a window, flinging open the casement. He turned, beaming, with a proprietorial air.

"I often come here."

Harriet joined him at the window. The silver glitter of the sea had become tarnished, the horizon blurred by clouds.

The library was in the east wing, stretched across the second floor. On the Great Tour the house had seemed to Harriet merely an impossible maze; she followed Mr Travers through its rooms as one might through locations in a dream, and the library like the other rooms had seemed as insubstantial. It acquired a new solidity as she surveyed it now.

"I didn't realise it was just above my room. Which window would be directly over mine?"

"Oh my dear, there are so many – I couldn't possibly tell."

Harriet moved to the shelves, gazing curiously at the faded leather spines: the sermons of Obadiah Harkness, D.D., collected in six volumes; Richardson's *New Vitruvius Britannicus* in two; a battered Jeremy Taylor; *Curiosities of Literature* by Isaac D'Israeli; a volume of Combe's *Microcosm of London*. The books lay at all angles and were obviously in no order. Harriet fingered an ancient volume.

"Mr Travers," she said suddenly, "there's something I've never told anyone."

"Oh my dear, are you sure you should tell *me*?"

Harriet turned from him, flushing.

"On my first day," she hurried on, "I was staring out at the sea from my room. I was dazzled. And then all of a sudden there was a cry from somewhere – a voice crying 'No!' – and a heavy old book, like one of these, came plunging past my window. As it fell it was falling apart and the pages fluttered up like birds... It was beautiful." She looked down sadly. "Then I caught one of the birds and it was a picture, from *Gulliver's Travels*... I thought it was a dream – I couldn't find the picture afterwards..."

"Goodness me," blinked Mr Travers. "How extraordinary."

"But don't you see? It wasn't a dream. The book was one of these. It must have been thrown – oh, from here, or here..." Harriet gestured towards the windows. "Yes. This is the one." She pointed with certainty at the open casement.

"Oh, I'm sure it wasn't this window," said Mr Travers. "This is *my* window" – and he indicated, as if in explanation, a capacious leather armchair.

Harriet felt she was being a fool. "I'm sorry, I – "

"Apologies, my dear, are hardly necessary." Mr Travers took her hand. "Now," he continued kindly, "what shall we select?"

"All these books!" Harriet shrugged helplessly. "I – I shouldn't know..."

They all look so dreadfully dull, she thought.

Mr Travers beamed. It was rather as if Harriet had especially pleased him.

She had.

"My dear, the solution is simple. You are incapable of making a choice. So why even try?"

"I don't understand."

Mr Travers reached into a pocket in his candystripe trousers. With the air of a magician he drew out a very large, very white, and surprisingly clean square of cloth. It was the last of the *J*-monogram handkerchiefs. He doubled it over diagonally, removed his straw boater, and motioned to Harriet to tie the handkerchief at the back of his bald head.

When he was blindfold he gave his next instruction. "Spin me about, my dear."

"Like this?" Harriet clutched the little man's shoulders, and as if with practised ease, she set him turning. During the first rotations he muttered that of course he must not tire her out, that really she must stop if she felt the slightest fatigue; then as his little feet trod faster and Harriet's hands, ever faster, slapped back and forth on his shoulders and chest he became excited, several times calling that she should go faster still; and Harriet was relieved when at last he cried "*Enough!*" Lurching, he blundered across the library floor.

"Oh, watch out for the... table," said Harriet, too late.

"One of the... hazards," gasped Mr Travers. He limped on decisively, zig-zagging wildly. "Am I close to the shelves, my dear?... I do believe I feel some books... It is *books* I'm feeling, my dear?"

Harriet said it was.

"Ah." After preliminary rumblings the little man gripped one of the spines. Grinning, he pushed up the blindfold and bore back the book in triumph to Harriet.

Harriet looked him uncertainly.

"Why ever not?" he asked. "Is there a better way? If you deliberated over these books, you should never make a choice – should you?"

Harriet inspected the volume in her hand. When she looked up again at her companion, his gaze was almost earnest. She could not help but laugh.

"No," she said, "no." And she thanked Mr Travers for her book. "Where shall I sit?"

She looked about her.

"But my dear – we're not ready yet." Mr Travers slipped down the blindfold. "You must spin me again."

Impulsively Harriet suggested that *she* be spun instead. As Mr Travers had chosen her book, so she should choose his. The little man agreed eagerly.

The handkerchief, Harriet realised, was symbolic in function. Had she kept her eyes open she could have seen through the white fabric, as through a mist, but virtuously she kept her eyes shut tight.

"Do you always choose like this?" she asked, as she whirled in darkness.

"Infallibly!" cried Mr Travers. He was in a kind of ecstasy, but not so excited as to forget Harriet's condition. Carefully he guided her past the obstructions in her path. As her hands groped along the shelves Harriet reflected on the curious texture of leather, at once dry yet sleek, infinitely dead yet possessing, it seemed, a residual life. The smell was like a palpable thing, smearing off on her hands.

She loved that smell.

The chair that Mr Travers drew up for her by the window was also of leather, like his own, the seat bulging like the black hardness of a beetle's back. Uncomfortable, but unwilling to admit it, Harriet sat in the dim sunshine, turning the pages of her musty book. Mr Travers' was called *The Sultan's Slave-Boy*; it sounded rather dubious. Her own was a volume of poetry – seventeenth-century poetry. Oh dear. She had hoped for a novel – and one rather more interesting than *A Portrait of the Artist as a Young Man*!

A pang of guilt assailed her. Really, whatever would Miss Padbury say? It was just as well, thought Harriet with a sigh, that she had never gone to Newnham College.

She turned to her poetry.

> THE WORLD
> *I saw Eternity the other night*
> *Like a great Ring of pure and endless light,*
>   *All calm as it was bright;*
> *And round beneath it, Time, in hours, days, years,*
>   *Driven by the spheres,*
> *Like a vast shadow moved, in which the world*
>   *And all her train were hurled...*

Harriet, sleepy in the sun, found her mind beginning to wander. She thought back to the climax of the party, and felt a profound shame. But why? And why had she gone into the water? She had drunk too much; she had been hot, confused...

"No, no, no!"

The cry cut through Harriet's reverie like a knife, and her eyes snapped open in time to see Mr Travers leaping up from his chair, flinging *The Sultan's Slave-Boy* from the window.

"Mr Travers!" Harriet could only gasp.

There was an awkward silence. Dust descended perpetually in the slanting sunlight.

"Oh dear," said the little man at last. "I seem to have done it again."

"But why ever – ?"

"I know I shouldn't." He wrung his hands. "I should restrain myself. But you see I get so dreadfully frustrated. None of these books is the book I'm looking for – *that* one certainly wasn't suitable."

"But I thought you weren't looking for a particular book. You don't know the title? The author?"

"None of that, my dear. I only feel when I come in here, there is one book which is the *key* I'm looking for – the hidden key." He turned a shame-crimsoned face to Harriet. "To my inspiration."

"Oh, Mr Travers!"

"It could be any book, you see. But when I find it, I shall know – I shall hear melodies begin to play, a stage shall come to life before my eyes..." He grimaced hopelessly. "You do understand me, my dear?"

Harriet said she did – although she made Mr Travers promise to throw no more of Lord Harrowblest's books from the window. "It really *won't do*, Mr Travers."

Then she laughed. She sounded like the Colonel!

"You're right, my dear. You're absolutely right." The little man sighed. "You're enjoying your book, my dear?" he asked after a moment.

Harriet bit her lip. "I had rather hoped for a novel," she admitted.

"Then you shall have one, my dear." And gently her companion picked up the poetry book from Harriet's lap and held it out past the window-sill. "Oh dear," he said guiltily, as he let it fall. "Oh dear, dear me."

Harriet had to laugh.

There was a rumble of thunder, far out to sea.

Later, when she returned to her room, Harriet discovered that the pages must have fluttered out from the seventeenth-century poets, as earlier they had fluttered from *Gulliver's Travels*. A sheet perched, stirring, on the sill of the open window. Harriet, as if to atone for her rejection of the poets, snapped it up.

> CORRUPTION
> *Sure, it was so. Man in those early days*
> *   Was not all stone, and Earth,*
> *He shin'd a little, and by those weak Rays*
> *   Had some glimpses of his birth.*
> *He saw Heaven o'r his head...*

For a moment Harriet felt her spirits sinking; then she rallied. Behind her, on the bed, the great sad mountain of Mrs Van Voyd was snoring. Harriet laid the poem carefully beside the old woman's dentures, and contemplated the question of evening dress.

She had decided that she was recovered.

23
The Door to Dimension X

The story 'The Door to Dimension X' by P. Monkton Wildgrove, Ph.D *(Astronomical Stories,* March 1950) was *not* one of Toby's favourites. In fact he thought it a particularly wet story: all about a man who bought a new house, and found in the back garden a door that led into 'another dimension', which he would visit every night. One of the silliest things about the story was the author's idea of what another dimension was like – all elves and gnomes and wizards and castles! One hardly had to *go* to another dimension to know it wouldn't be like *that*. Who did the author think he was fooling?

The point of the story seemed to be that the hero's life was totally different in one dimension from what it was in the other. In his drab real life in Pittsburgh, Harold Schwartz was weak and cowardly, bullied by his boss and nagged at by his mother; in Dimension X 'Harold the Red' was a hero, a bold knight in love with a damsel he'd saved from a wicked necromancer. Of course Harold wanted to leave Pittsburgh for good and live in Dimension X all the time; but the damsel's uncle, a white wizard, warned him he couldn't: Harold could visit Dimension X only at night, and if he tried to stay longer he'd soon regret it.

Did the hero take the advice? At first he said he would. But a bad day in Pittsburgh was enough to change his mind, and he overstayed his time in Dimension X; and he stayed; and stayed…

He was going to marry the damsel. Arrangements were made for a huge wedding; nobles came from all over the kingdom; the ceremony took place; but as the hero turned at the altar to clutch his bride she vanished suddenly into the air, and all of the guests and the great castle vanished too; and it was mid-afternoon in downtown

Pittsburgh, and Harold Schwartz had been sleeping at his desk, and his hateful boss Mr Smedley was shouting at him, "Schwartz, *you're fired!*"

Had it all been a dream? That night the garden door led only into a back street filled with trash cans, and Harold Schwartz could never go back to Dimension X again.

Toby thought about this story as he lay beneath the promenade. Thinking about the story did not make him admire it; in fact, the more he thought about it, the more he hated it. Why *couldn't* the hero stay in Dimension X? There was no reason at all, certainly not a scientific one – only the author's unresisted itch to tear down whatever image of happiness he had created. Seeming to indulge the imagination, the 'fantasy' author P. Monkton Wildgrove in the end revealed his contempt for it, dousing the reader in the cold water of his awful, sour morality.

It wasn't worthy of *Astronomical Stories*, it really wasn't.

How much time had passed?

Toby, emerging from beneath the promenade, glanced up at the hazy sun. It must have been almost four o'clock; he was far down the beach from where the Professor's booth had been. He was worried that he was late. In the Professor's presence he felt a sense of approaching revelation; the thought of missing the performance was terrible.

He ran down the beach to the Professor's corner, possessed by a vague foreboding. The holiday town, rising above him, was a dirty off-white; in the cooler sun the pier had ceased its flashing signals, and the great dome was grey. The faded sea, its horizon blurred, was not diminished but had become on this hazy day a still more ominous vastness.

When Toby reached the corner there was a stitch in his side. His breathing came in gasps.

"No," he exhaled.

The corner was empty.

A loneliness, like tears, welled up in Toby.

Does your father come here every day? he had asked Heike.

Every day when he is well enough, Heike had said.

Toby clutched his side and sprinted up the promenade steps. As he lunged towards the hotel there was a rumble of thunder, far out to sea. Entering the basement he stumbled on the stairs.

"*Ach!*" came a cry. "He has come, he has come! *Hereinkommen, mein Junge!*"

The voice was alarmingly loud and booming, and had in it a wildness Toby had not heard, even in the old man's most excited declamations. Amid the gloom of the squalid basement the Professor was in his usual armchair, but sprawled at a crazy angle, his waistcoat open and the silver-copper beard bent up at odd angles. Heike was nowhere to be seen. Grazing his legs in the dim light the boy blundered between the tea chests towards his friend.

"Professor! Are you all right?"

When he realised the truth, Toby was shocked.

"*All right*? Hah – everything, it is marvellous!"

Toby felt foolish. The old man was laughing at him, one hand swinging up from beneath the arm of the chair, an enamel mug clutched in the fingers like a tankard, the other hand reaching for a tall glinting bottle.

"Schnapps!" cried the Professor, with a lunatic grin. "Schnapps! You will drink with me, *mein klein Schuler*?" And at once he reached for the second enamel mug that seemed to be waiting, as if for this moment, amongst the several already emptied and the several unemptied bottles that cluttered the top of the nearest tea chest. He poured out a generous measure.

Toby, standing awkwardly by the old man's chair, inspected the clear, yet strangely viscous liquid. It was a type of gin, wasn't it? He braced himself and sipped it gingerly. His mouth was filled with a sudden acrid taste. It was horrible – so horrible he couldn't imagine how anyone could ever drink it. On his second try he gulped back the liquid faster, as if to bypass the taste; but a diffused heat crept back up his throat from his heart with a terrible corrosive burning. He coughed and water sprang from his eyes.

"*Feuer!*" The Professor's eyes twinkled.

"Fire!" gasped Toby.

The Professor laughed and waved the boy to a chair. "Drink, *mein Junge*, drink!"

Toby drank.

From behind a haze of alcohol, time becomes strange: it can be distended, it can be compressed, it can be tossed about like a ball. Our sense of its reality is blunted, as our awareness of objects, of spaces, is blurred. In like manner our feelings are altered, or not so much altered as extended in range, as a pianist, chording decorously in the centre of the keyboard, might under the influence of some sudden passion soar wildly towards the highest treble, or plunge to the lowest bass. Ephemerally – but in our madness we imagine for eternity – we are lifted from the round of everyday reality, as if into another dimension. It is exhilarating, rapturous, ultimately disappointing – an utterly inferior mode of transcendence.

How much time had passed?

The rumbles of thunder far out to sea had come closer, and closer, and at last the clouds had burst; long ago, stumbling and laughing, the Professor had lit the oil lamp; rain tumbled into the hotel yard and spattered ceaselessly against the black windows, high in the wall of the basement room, and slithered darkly down the concrete stairs.

In the flickering light, sunk deep in schnapps, the Professor was transformed, magicked into a companion of sparkling *bonhomie*. The wire beard coursed with a warm current, the little eyes sparkled gaily, the head and hands jigged back and forth as if worked from below by a merry master. Toby had never laughed so much; sometimes he cried. Into the swirling grim lake of philosophical discourses the Professor seemed to have opened floodgates of joy, and though free will and necessity and equilateral triangles and the perceptive apparatus would bob to the surface they were soon dragged under on a wash of happiness. It was the happiness of memory – of Berlin before the Great War, of the hilarities of boyhood, of the wonder, when we are young, of the future opening before us.

How splendid the old man was! How Toby loved him! Deluged in the surge of the old man's voice, the boy felt still more strongly the intimations of an approaching destiny: as if another voice, from some far edge of his mind (but creeping closer), were whispering: *something further will come of this...*

When he spoke of philosophy the Professor did not explain things; rather, he whirled up facts and images and jokes and stories and fragments of quotations into a heady vortex of language, sometimes English, sometimes German, incomprehensible but exhilarating. If Toby had told the Professor about the door to Dimension X (did he?), the Professor might have begun by asking (had he?) what were the meanings of 'door' and of 'dimension', as if he had never heard of such things, dissolving words as if in some chemical solution until their traces were gathered up and overwhelmed in the swirl of *space is an a priori intuition* and *the absolute is becoming*.

Then in imagination he returned to the University, in the days of the Weimar Republic...

Mr Punch, slumped on the mantelpiece, watched the drunken pair; his staring wooden eyes appeared to register his contempt. But tonight the little puppet was unregarded; even Heike seemed to have slipped out of existence. Once – it must have been many hours ago – Toby had asked what had become of the girl; the Professor had only laughed and said *Heike was upstairs. Heike was upstairs*. He could have been saying she would be down in a moment; he could have been saying she had left him; in any case it did not matter.

Time wore on.

How much time had passed?

At the height of drunkenness one imagines oneself to be carried along, exhilaratingly, as on a wave; at last the wave begins to subside.

"Soon it shall be winter." The old man set his cup down heavily on the tea chest.

Toby struggled to speak. "Oh, not – s-soon, surely? There's – *months* yet." It seemed important to emphasise the word.

"Heike *und* I – we shall move on."

"Where shall you go?" Toby struggled to say. Dimly he felt himself a fool. Had it never occurred to him that the summer would end? He was newly conscious of the rain, spattering at the black windows.

"Hm?" said the old man, after what might have been many minutes.

He was struggling to align the neck of the last bottle with the lip of his enamel mug. The liquid slopped into the mug, and onto the tea chest, and onto the floor. "*Ach*, we have travelled, *mein klein Puppe und ich* – we have had the engagements in the greatest courts in the land..." Leaning forward, he slopped some of the schnapps into Toby's mug, and over Toby. "In the court of the Black Pool – the Marred Gate – the Bourne Mouth..." The old man erupted into a wheezing laugh.

Spattered with schnapps the room, and Toby, seemed doused as if in petrol, slung about by an eager arsonist.

"Ach, I fear that the Light Letter – as *ihr Englander*, you say, leaves the 'much to be desired', *nein?*"

"Not much of an audience, I suppose," said Toby. He didn't mean it as a joke.

"*Ach – nein.*"

"I – " began Toby after a moment. He seemed flustered. "I've never paid you." With clumsy hands the boy searched his pockets, as if expecting to draw out money; he had none. Suddenly inspired, he tore instead at his ring-finger; eagerly he held up the golden band.

"*Mein Junge*, do not worry about the payment!" laughed the Professor. "Heike *und* I we have enough – *ach*, more, more!"

"I really don't need it..." The tiny circle flashed in the oil lamp's light.

"*Quatsch! Die Geld* it is needed in the whole of the universe – and the universe it is endless, *nein?*" Heaving himself up, the old man blundered between the tea chests to a corner of the basement beneath the high windows. With his shadow flung enormously about the walls in the lamplight, he reached down behind one of the bulky rough boxes to draw up, as if from a well, a smaller, smoother box. The light glittered on the gunmetal grey.

There was a fumbling as the old man opened the box; a key turned in a lock. When he turned back to Toby there was triumph in his eyes.

Even in his drunkenness, Toby had to gasp. The golden band slipped to the floor. The Professor held up a huge roll of banknotes, bound together in a tight spiral and secured with rubber bands. The roll was almost a foot in diameter. There must have been hundreds – thousands of pounds. The old man was rich.

"*Ja – ja, mein Junge*. It is you who will have the payment." He thumbed the roll, extracting a crisp note, and tossed it towards Toby.

"*No –* " Toby lurched up from his chair, scrambling after the fluttering note. To restore it to the violated roll was imperative.

"*There* is the payment you want!"

"I don't – "

"You would like more, *nein?* Becher can pay..."

Toby felt sick. Like a mad imp the old man was dancing between the tea chests, his thumb working at the roll, shaving off banknotes. As he went his merry way he cackled horribly, and in his cackles there seemed to be a mixture of hilarity and the blackest despair.

"Professor – please stop – " The joys of the evening had vanished. Through his surging sickness Toby felt a burden of responsibility, annihilating but inescapable. Desperate, the boy broke off his attempts to scoop up the banknotes, and staggered towards the Professor. "Stop, please – " He lunged towards the old man's wrist.

"Ha-ha!" The Professor danced away from him. Toby sprawled across the tea chests. A bottle fell to the floor and smashed.

"This is your inheritance, *mein Junge!*" the old man was crying. "Let us have it, *ja, die Geld, die Geld!*"

Banknotes fell like leaves over Toby's prostrate form. A sharp pain seared through his ribs and his forearm was gashed. In an agony compounded of physical throbbings, nausea and shame, he twisted up from the splintery tea chest and lurched back to his feet, just as the Professor crushed the ravished roll and threw it into the air.

It was almost like autumn in a speeded-up film. Banknotes rained around them. Man and boy staggered under the deluge.

Outside the falling of the rain was louder, pummelling into the yard with a drumbeat intensity.

"*Papa!*"

It was Heike. Her voice had the stern tone Toby knew well, but her appearance had changed bizarrely. Replacing the simple shift was a gaudy blood-red gown; her face was lurid with makeup; her dark hair was now a buttery gold. Teetering on spiky heels, she looked like a woman Toby had seen once in Soho, one Christmas with EEL; EEL, knowingly, had said the woman was a *lady of the night*.

"Heike, *mein Liebling* – "

Heike wove quickly towards the Professor through the tea chests, and decisively slapped his face. The old man's eyes closed and he stumbled back.

"Help me," the girl commanded, twisting on her high heels as she prevented her father from falling.

Toby's hands fumbled stupidly about the Professor.

"*Ach*, you are useless!" Pushing the boy away, Heike impelled her father to the nearest chair. The old man groaned with a dreadful sick sound and his bulk crashed into the cushions.

"He shall be well in the morning. After a time of sickness…" No longer a lady of the night, Heike, it seemed, was suddenly a nurse, adjusting the position of her father's head, crossing his hands in his lap, loosening his shirt-collar and the tops of his trousers. Tottering briskly through the inner door, she returned with a blanket and threw it over the senseless form.

"Will you please help?" Heike indicated the money-strewn floor.

Toby, sinking awkwardly to his knees, scrambled about amongst what he saw, now, to be the discredited currency of the Weimar Republic.

"I have counted it. Many times," warned Heike.

"That's not fair!" Toby lurched up, bundling a pile of notes into her arms.

"Of course," muttered the girl as she clip-clopped between the tea chests, stuffing back the money into the open metal box. "You are the *reich* boy, *die Geld* it is nothing to you – "

"*I'm* not rich – "

"Reich!" said Heike sharply. She would brook no contradiction. "I hardly know why you should come to a poor old man like Papa. What is wrong with you, you are some crazy boy, *nein?*"

"I – " Toby had nothing to say. He attempted, "Is he often like this?"

Heike rounded on him. "Like what?"

"He's drunk."

"You're drunk! What do you mean, to talk about Papa in that way? *Is he often like this?*" She imitated him cruelly. "My God – you English, you make me sick!"

"Heike, please – " Toby swung towards her. He caught her wrist. She tried to struggle free but he gripped her tight. Her gown had no sleeves and as he held her arm extended towards him the soft inner flesh turned upright to his gaze. In his drunken madness he studied with a kind of rapture the spectacle it presented. *How strange,* he thought, *how strange –* strange that she had worn a sleeveless dress before, in the blazing sun, and he had not noticed it; strange that she did not even attempt to conceal it; strange that it was not until now, in the dim gold of the lamplight, that he should see the blue number, etched indelibly into the tender flesh.

"Oh Heike, Heike," he moaned, and with what seemed an instinctive movement the girl stepped into his arms. In her free hand she clutched a clump of redundant banknotes; now she let them fall again to the floor about their feet. Toby stared into her dark eyes, oblivious in his rapture to the grotesque makeup that circled them; she looked at him impassively, at his silly, drunken face. The boy's cheeks were flushed, his eyes dilated; there was soft down on his upper lip...

Suddenly she pressed her mouth hard against his. He did not resist; the action seemed ordained. Eagerly he returned the pressure of her kiss. His eyes shutting, he felt himself almost absorbed into the deep interior moistness. He ran his hands down her back and pressed her close to him; the blood pounded through his body, inflamed.

"You're drunk. It's disgusting." Heike pushed him away.

"I've never been drunk before," he said delightedly. He clutched at her again.

"You must... you must *go* – "

"Heike, it's raining, I have to *stay* – "

He began to laugh. It was a game they were playing, a marvellous new game. As the girl swivelled away from him he grabbed her round the waist. He pressed himself into her back, exulting.

In the armchair the Professor was sleeping fitfully, his breathing a succession of swinish grunts.

Heike burst from Toby's grip and turned on him, frenzied. "Don't touch me!" He gasped as the girl's spit spattered into his face. She pushed him in the chest and he staggered back.

"Franz!" called the Professor, jerking in his chair in a sudden spasm. "Franz – nein, nein... Franz, I was your Professor! Franz, don't you remember me?"

"Stupid boy – you stupid boy..." Heike was sobbing, her thick makeup oozing horribly down her face. Tearing at Toby's shirt she tried to drag him from the room, her high heels slipping as she hauled him behind her. The stairs were slick with rainwater that had run in under the door. There was a ripping as the shoulder tore from Toby's shirt.

For a moment he swayed perilously on the concrete steps; then he doubled over.

"Oh, God. I'm going to be sick." He clutched his hand towards his mouth and slithered up towards the door, pushing past Heike. She had turned her ruined face into the wall; her sobs had given way to a terrible moaning. In their struggle her blonde wig had fallen from her head and lay in a wet heap at the foot of the stairs; her real hair, lank and dark, slipped down her back like thick, entangling syrup.

As Toby battered through the door the rain assailed him, soaking his clothes at once, roaring into his ears like a relentless wild beast. The dusty yard had become a black sea of mud and as his bare feet slid from beneath him and he splattered to his hands and knees in the filth the lava of vomit burst from his lips, pouring and pouring in scalding cascades into the swirlings of the liquid earth.

When the last terrible upheaval had passed, Toby had energy only to roll onto his back. The mud soaked eagerly into his shirt and shorts; the vomit eddied beneath his neck and round his shoulders, and mingled with the sodden dirt in his hair.

In this aftermath, with his eyes closed, Toby felt with a peculiar intensity the sensation of the mud against his back, the rain against his face, his torso, his limbs. On every upturned surface of his body it pelted evenly; he was spreadeagled on the ground; beneath him was the surface of the earth, and beneath that the layers wrapped round and round its core; above him was the dark rain, and above the rain a sky that was still dark, and above that a sky that was always dark, and stretched forever into an endless blackness.

24
Galleons of Spain

The little lamp by the bed flickered as if it had been a flame; in the fireplace the real flames leapt and darted, flinging their warmth as if in anger at the shadows of the room. The storm was growing wilder. Sheets of rain battered at the casement as if the sea itself, in its churning fury, were breaking against the glass. At the dark window Harriet could imagine herself in the cabin of a creaking galleon, tossed on the violence of the Spanish Main. When she closed her eyes she felt the floor lurch beneath her; her hand, when it reached up absurdly in alarm, slithered over the coldness of a juddering diamond pane...

"Goodness gracious, miss, you must hop into bed at once!"

Harriet, smiling, turned to Milly. Dutifully she clambered between the turned-back sheets.

"You're looking like the cat that got the cream."

"Milly, you sound disapproving!"

"Not at all, Miss." But then Milly turned to Harriet and giggled, "Oh Miss, he's a lovely gentleman, lovely!"

"I know. I know."

It had been a wonderful evening: Mrs Van Voyd was sedated in bed; Toby had not appeared; Yardley had retired early, declaring her fatigue. Only a merry trio had remained, dreamy and laughing in the great hall until midnight. Mark spoke excitedly of the progress of his painting; Mr Travers reminisced on his musical career, and performed with commendable softness a rendition of *Come into My Arms* (Mark stole an arm round Harriet's shoulder); flames crackled in the great ornate fireplace...

"Miss, I know I shouldn't ask, but – "

"Milly?"

"When you're married, you and Mr Vardell will live in London?"

Harriet said she supposed they would.

Milly sniffed and looked down at her shoes. The hare lip trembled nervously.

All at once she plunged towards the bed. She clasped the startled Harriet in her arms like a lover. "Oh miss, take me with you, please – I'll be ever so good, ever so faithful…"

"Milly, Milly, this is not how a maid behaves!"

"Forgive me, miss, forgive me – " The little maid's shoulders shook with sobs.

"Poor Milly. But whatever would Mrs Van Voyd say if I took you away?"

Milly looked up, wiping her eyes. "Mrs Van Voyd could find another one of me. But I could never find another one of – *you*."

Harriet squeezed the servant's hand.

"You'll arrange it, miss?" cried Milly.

"I'll speak to Mr Vardell."

"Oh, miss!" At once Milly began to bustle about the room, patting down the bed covers, closing a cupboard door, poking at the coals of the declining fire. Pausing as she was about to draw the curtains, she turned back eagerly to Harriet and cried delightedly, "Why, miss (*puff, puff*), this is just like being in a ship in a storm. I'm your faithful maid, and you're a beautiful English heiress, captured by the Spaniard cut-throats…"

"Oh, Milly!"

"It happened to Her Ladyship in *The Golden Galleon*. I've seen it seven times," said the little maid with pride.

"That will be all now, Milly," Harriet laughed.

"Ma'am." Milly essayed an elaborate curtsy. The galleon was gone; already in imagination she was in a luxurious London drawing room.

Alone, Harriet leaned back contentedly against the pillows. The fireplace was a golden, flickering pool; the tapestry on the wall shifted with a sigh.

She reached for her book, but her eyes were sleepy. With a smile she put the old volume aside again, pausing to run her finger over the binding. The title was stamped in gold on the pungent leather:

JANE EYRE
VOL. I

    The very title made Harriet happy. She thought of herself as a child of ten, curled in the window seat of the nursery in Highgate. She had been tearful, desperate, hating the new grey country, hating the new grey house... Then she read, with immediate interest: *There was no possibility of taking a walk that day...* Oh yes! This was better than that Irish moocow, coming down along the road!

    She switched off the little electric lamp. In the darkness the chaos of sound outside seemed louder, the clattering of the wind at the casement more insistent. Milly had forgotten to close the curtains.

    The old tapestry was breathing more heavily, bulging out recklessly from the panelled wall.

In Harriet's dream she was still awake, twisting and twisting between crisp new sheets. Rain flashed at the window like quicksilver; a terrible howling raged about the house. The tapestry billowed and flapped like a sail. Suddenly with a crash the casement flew open, and the storm was swirling about the bed.

    When the tapestry fell, it was as if the great ancient network had simply dissolved, the rotting fibres, the faded traces of Artemis and Hera crumbling unresisting at a too-eager touch.

    Harriet gasped. Where the tapestry had fallen, there was an open door. It led into what looked to be a vast room; from deep within the room glowed a burning light, but from where exactly she could not tell. With awkward reverence she entered the chamber. Inside, it was larger than she had thought, and more mysterious: a dim place of twisting corners, of gold coins glinting in open chests, of animal-skin rugs and armchairs covered with sheets set all awry about the polished floor. Against the dark panelling, darker paintings were suspended at odd angles and heads of boars and foxes hung upside down by heraldic shields, themselves set askew, and surrounded at random by axes and lances and swords in scabbards, or swords unsheathed. Suits of armour loomed out from corners like malevolent strangers; behind a chair a taxidermist's tiger crouched in frozen readiness to spring, his mouth set perpetually in an angry roar, his counterfeit eyes fixed hungrily. As Harriet walked on, curiously unafraid, the polished floor seemed to incline subtly downwards, and the unseen source of light always to be located behind the next of the many corners. She glanced behind her and the door through which she had entered was no longer to be seen.

When she turned and saw the stranger she betrayed no surprise.

Slowly the stranger smiled.

The Harriet of the dream would have reached out her hand; the real Harriet, who contained the dreamer, started awake instead.

The dream was real.

The casement yawned open and the storm swirled into the room. Harriet scrambled from her sodden bed. As she fought to shut out the inundating tide, her eyes gazed wildly at the terrible sea, churning beneath her like a vision of chaos. When she twisted back at last from the closed casement, a whiplash of lightning disclosed her ravaged room: the grey, quenched fireplace; the spreading slick of water; the bare impassive timber where the tapestry had hung.

Harriet flung herself towards the wall. Blundering in a sea of rotted fabric she clawed at the cracked panelling.

There was no secret labyrinth. The dream was *not* real.

It was only when a second flash of lightning, closer now, electrified the room in a stab of deathly light that Harriet, crashing back against the wall in fear, must have triggered some secret catch. The panelling yawned open and the startled girl was swallowed, screaming, in blackness.

Charles Collidge slept on a narrow couch beside his master's bed; or rather, he did not so much sleep as lie there at night, often not closing his eyes at all. Seldom, indeed, did he remove his clothes, but lay down as he was in his crisp formal suit, his waistcoat firmly buttoned and his tie knotted tight. He lay on his back, without blankets to cover him, gazing into the darkness with fixed staring eyes. His mission was to monitor his master's breathing.

The storm alarmed Collidge. On still summer evenings the rise and fall of the old man's breath almost filled the room; now, with the wildness outside, the breathing was obscured. A flash of lightning showed his master's chair standing empty by the bed; the sight of it made Collidge cry out.

The darkness was restored at once. When Collidge, a little later, brought his hand up to his face, he found that his cheeks were wet with tears.

Inside the wall, the violence of the storm was muffled into silence. The darkness was entire. Harriet had fallen, and stood slowly. Somehow the door had clicked shut again, and she was trapped. Beneath her bare feet the floor was of splintery timber. To her right was a wooden wall, the other side of the panelling; to her left, the wall was of stone. The space between was perhaps three feet wide. Behind her was only a further obstructing wall. She seemed to have fallen not into the labyrinth of her dreams but into a mean, dusty cupboard.

It was only when she stretched her hands in front of her and felt emptiness, and emptiness again as she advanced forward, that Harriet realised that this secret dark place was not the tiny prison she had feared, but a corridor.

There was no alternative but to discover where it led.

Mark rolled, gasping, onto his back.

The music was playing, but could not be heard. There was only the storm, driving at the window, rising in counterpoint to the rhythm of his heart. Yardley's fingers slid across his chest.

"I saw her."

There was a pause.

"Darling?"

"Just something I imagined. In the lightning." Mark pushed Yardley's head away and sprang up from the bed. Wonderingly Yardley raised herself on her elbows and gazed after him into the blackness. A flicker of lightning showed her his silhouette at the window, his hands raised and their spread fingers pressed against the glass.

"My love – what is it?" Yardley reached for the control panel by the bed, turning up the volume of the music. The sound of Mozart trilled through the loudspeakers. With a sudden twisting movement Mark flung open the casement. The storm's flailing tentacles burst in, lashing him.

"Mark!" Yardley was there at once. Urgently she reached to close the casement. Mark caught her wrists.

"I asked you once to come away with me, remember?" There was a brutality in his voice and his face was close to hers. Their naked bodies were wet with rain.

"It's impossible, you know it!"

"Tell me why! You left me for him, why?"

"Left you? You're crazy! You were just a boy – "

Mark slapped her face. Her hand, suddenly freed, clawed at his eyes. He grabbed her hand again and twisted it behind her back. Yardley cried out.

"Tell me why!"

"I love him!"

"You can't – "

"You know nothing – "

Thunder cracked over the wild sea. Yardley kicked at Mark's legs. He stumbled and she twisted away. For several seconds they slapped and beat at each other. At last Mark pushed her, sprawling, onto the bed. He fell on top of her, pinning her down. Her face gloated up at him through the dividing darkness. Her breasts pressed intolerably against his chest, her thighs against his thighs. She struggled again as his mouth sought hers. Their flailing bodies slid together inevitably, inevitably.

"I love you," Mark cried, "I love you!"

Yardley began to laugh.

He thrust himself into her again, savagely, as the storm washed in upon them.

Harriet's heartbeat grew strangely still.

In the blackness she might have expected to be struck by some unseen terror, some nameless dreadful thing; but when a curtain of cobweb fell draping over her face she neither gasped nor screamed, only brushing away the sticky, clinging fibres. She felt herself immersed in darkness as one might be in some transcendent state, of deep meditation, or desired dream.

Was she still dreaming?

After some time a staircase led to a higher level. The steps were of stone, chilling Harriet's bare feet with an Arctic coldness. When it proceeded the passage twisted and turned crazily, like a black maze of stone buried within the walls of the ancient house. Once there was a creaking door which Harriet pushed open; it opened only into a wider dark passage.

The labyrinth wound on.

Then a flash of light, as of lightning, fluoresced suddenly from the level of the floor. Harriet reached out to touch smooth wood. She pushed against it; it yielded.

The new place was a soft cave, fragrant with perfume. When she stretched back her hand to the door through which she had come she felt a cold sheen of glass. She turned to it. It was a mirror. Through barely-parted curtains a strip of stormlight revealed her pale reflection, shimmering before her in the gloom like a ghost's. Behind her stretched lines of hanging garments.

She was in Yardley's dressing rooms.

It was the swell of music, rising above the storm, that guided her easily to the gold-handled doors.

As Harriet stepped into the shrine there was a burst of thunder. Through open windows the sky's searing electricity flashed savagely, a sudden searchlight: over the gleaming whiteness of the carpet; over the paintings set in the ceiling; over the icons of the goddess fixed about the walls; over the ivory wild creatures worshipping the Oscars; over the mirror, ablaze with the tableau of passion: and on the bed, the passion itself.

Collidge had lain awake easily through many hot, still nights. How absurd that he should lapse into sleep tonight, as the storm clamoured at the window! He jerked awake with a start. How long had he slept? He gouged at his sleeve, clawing back his watch-face. He sprang up from the couch. Wind and rain and crackings of thunder assailed his ears. He wanted to scream. A metal band seemed to be tightening round his skull. He plunged towards the light switch.

The bed was empty; the chair was missing too. Collidge uttered a terrible cry.

He found his master in the astronomer's room. At the top of the tower the storm's violence was shocking, pounding with a savagery that might shatter the ancient stones. The lightning showed the lectern shuddering in the wind, the painting on its easel swaying; the telescope span round and round. To his horror Collidge saw that the window was open, and before it was his master, drenched by the rain. Rocking back and forth wildly in his chair, the old man clawed the air as if desperate to catch the telescope; his head lolled back as if half-severed from his neck.

"My lord!"

Then came the shattering flash. Harrowblest swung suddenly towards Collidge, the ruined mouth parted in a cackling laugh, the eyes a vortex that could suck in the lightning. Collidge slithered to the wet floor, clutching at the paralysed knees.

"My lord," he moaned, "my love..."

"Collidge!" The terrible voice was a screech of disgust. Collidge's body jerked. The old man's palm met the side of Collidge's head and pushed him contemptuously away. As his head struck the floor and a wheel of the chair ran agonisingly over his hand, Collidge's lean frame erupted in convulsions. Wave after wave of ecstasy swept through him.

"No. No..."

"Yes. It was meant to be..."

Yardley's whisper was warm, was soft; was sibilant as the hissing of a snake. Harriet's nightdress slipped to the floor. Unresisting, the dazed girl slid back onto the bed, her hand brushing a slickness on the crumpled slithery sheets.

The music was a massive promise of harmony, sounding emphatically on the violated air.

"We love you..."

Harriet felt Yardley's hands on her flesh, Yardley's tongue pushing between her parted lips.

And Mark was beside her.

Then she was rolling in Yardley's arms, then Mark's, then Yardley's again. Yardley's nails and teeth pierced her flesh; then it was Mark's nails, Mark's teeth.

Then he was moving above her – he was gentle now – as Yardley's hands still kneaded and pierced. The tears were running from his eyes (or was it sweat?), and Harriet, as the droplets splashed her face and neck, counted them:

One –

Two –

Afterwards Yardley took her beneath the covers and stroked her, tenderly; Harriet clung to her, clutched her, like a child.

The storm was subsiding.

But booming in the air about them, impossibly loud, the Rondo (*Allegro vivace*) of Horn Concerto No. 4 in E flat major, K.495, played for the fourth time.

The morning was a wet gleam, silent and still. Harriet's feet squelched through the muddy yard. Her eyes were blank discs, ringed with dark circles; her arms hung unswinging at her sides as she walked. She was naked. Blue bruises patterned her neck and breasts and dark dried blood caked her white thighs.

Quietly she pushed open a door of the old stables, and the shabby, familiar form of Ottoline loomed up in the light. With slow movements like a sleepwalker's, the naked girl climbed into the driver's seat. The key waited in the dashboard. She turned it. She knew enough; she had watched Mrs Van Voyd.

Again the lightning seemed to explode across Harriet's mind, shattering everything.

The Silver Ghost rolled from the stable; rolled from the yard; rolled onto the path that led to the cliff road.

Harriet held the wheel stiffly. She swung out onto the precipitous road with too swift a jerk. The wheels skidded on the slimy surface. When she accelerated, she thought, showers of mud would splatter magnificently from beneath the churning tyres.

Her foot poised on the accelerator. The sun's early light, intense through parting clouds, spread its molten slickness over the unstirring sea.

The storm would not return.

"But where, where are the galleons of Spain?"

The stranger was suddenly there. Perhaps he had stepped, ghost-like, through the rocky curtains that hung down one side of the ribbon of road. He stood in front of Ottoline, a hand resting lightly on her battered radiator.

"Good morning." He doffed his Panama hat. "So, it seems someone was to meet me after all. I could have saved myself a walk. Still, not to worry – saved you a drive instead, hm?" He spoke in a clipped Etonian voice, his mouth twisting into a wry smile.

Harriet only stared.

Briskly the stranger strode towards the driver's door. He opened it and Harriet, unresisting, shifted into the passenger's seat. In one hand the stranger had been carrying a small wicker box, which he slung now onto the back seat. The idling engine throbbed.

"I was expecting a Mrs Van Voyd," the stranger said cheerfully. "You must be... Miss Locke? And a more charming spectacle a man has seldom seen – if I may be so bold, my dear."

Harriet said nothing. The stranger slid towards her.

"My, but you are a cold girl! You are almost chilled through." He had placed a hand on her stomach. Slowly, the hand moved upwards, to massage an icy breast. He brought his lips close to her ear. "Oh, my darling girl... you have been a sleepwalker," he whispered. "Now you shall wake."

Harriet turned to him, her lips parting. But the stranger broke off suddenly. With practised ease he seized the gear lever and put the car into reverse.

As Ottoline trundled back towards the house Harriet heard a curious muffled whining. At first she thought she was making the sound herself. But its source was the wicker box on the back seat of the car.

When they returned to Shadow Black Harriet felt faint, her consciousness slipping as if she had been drugged. The stranger looked at her kindly, and reached to stroke her hair. He gathered her in his arms and, needing no directions, carried her effortlessly up the stairs to her room.

25
The Charnel-House of Love

The darkness was stained with a blood-red glow. For many hours (it seemed for many hours) Toby had hovered between sleep and waking. Dimly, the thought *I am awake* would loom into view, wriggling through his oblivion like a slow, strange fish; then the fish would disappear, dissolving back into the heavy medium through which it had swum, and Toby would dissolve again, too. Dreams clung to him like wet clothes, or shame: he was in a room, deep beneath the ground, laughing and laughing at a mad party. Then the party was gone; the room disappeared; in an oozing blackness, Toby and Miss Locke were clutched together, terribly, and as they rolled in the wet slush the gold radiance of her blonde hair turned to black.

At last he realised that he had been staring interminably at the deep twilit flatness of a ceiling. A rich crimson light had seeped into the room, bathing the white plaster and the circumambient air.

"EEL," Toby whispered.

There was no reply.

He closed his eyes. Of course, he had forgotten; he was in the infirmary. From somewhere he heard a sound of clinking, as of a spoon stirring in a glass. Matron?

Toby wondered: *How long have I been sick*? His body was aching and in his mouth was a bitter taste. Swallowing, he reached up a hand to his throat. As his fingers travelled across his chest, he realised he was not wearing his pyjama jacket. Tentatively he felt lower beneath the sheets. He was wholly naked.

The sheets were cool and strangely slithery to the touch; Toby realised they were made of silk.

As he scrambled upright in the unfamiliar bed, the dull ache that crouched in wait behind his eyes unfurled all at once to its full savage strength; he lurched forward, moaning, holding his head.

When the first pain had passed, Toby peered forward carefully into the obscurity. He was in a large room, furnished with heavy ornate chairs. The wallpaper was patterned with dark oppressive stripes; a ponderous chandelier impended from the ceiling. The clinking he had heard was the sound of its crystals, urged back and forth by a breeze. He was aware of an intolerable dank smell. On the far side of the room, diagonally from the bed, were two doors: one stood open, leading into the darkness of another room.

Cautiously Toby swung his feet to the floor. The fibres of the carpet were rough and damp. Standing, he pulled the covers from the bed and wrapped them around him. He moved towards the red-glowing window, the bed-covers trailing over the mildewed floor. Brightness pressed in blindingly as he parted the velvet curtains. The great bowl of Lightletter Bay juddered into focus.

Toby groaned aloud. He was in the Paradise Hotel: of course. Images of the night before rushed back.

But how had he got to this upper floor?

He turned back to the musty room. With a lurch of fear he saw a strange face staring at him; then with a second lurch he saw that it was his own. In a streaked mirror above the mantelpiece his face shimmered at him like an image of death, his sunken cheeks and circled eyes tracing unmistakably the skull beneath the skin. He smoothed back the haystack chaos of his hair. In the light from the window, as if to mock him, the dirty sludge of carpet had flowered into life; the dark bars of the wallpaper were a warm maroon; and laid neatly across a gilt-backed sofa were Toby's shorts and shirt. They had been washed and ironed.

Then Toby realised that his body had been washed, too.

Heike?

Shame suffused him. Quickly he slipped into his uncrumpled clothes (the shoulder of his shirt, he noted, was repaired where it had been torn). Restlessly he glanced about him, this way and that. In a corner by the gilt-backed sofa was a trunk, open and trailing women's gowns; magazines and photographs lay on the floor; on a low table nearby was a glinting cigarette case and the remnants of a meal. The two plates were heaped with cages of bones and greased with still-slick gravy. A crust of red wine on the neck of a bottle was clammy to the touch.

Was this where Heike lived? Toby recalled again the Heike of last night, the lady of the night. In the staleness of her room a fresh nausea welled in his stomach. Struggling to quell it, his eyes lighted on a certain photograph, staring up at him from an open magazine – a woman's face, illuminated strangely in the shaft of light. With a curious dull shock Toby realised it was Aunt Eunice. He grabbed the magazine. The photograph was an old one, but the magazine was new. A headline read: *Whatever Happened to... YARDLEY?* With something that was almost anger Toby flung the thing away; as it thudded down, the curling rectangle of a studio photograph came flapping up like a startled bird from the debris on the floor. Toby clutched at the glossy print. He noted only that it depicted a young man; for no reason he could explain he did not study the picture in any detail, merely kept it hanging from his hand as he continued his circuit of the room.

He returned to the window.

Between the parted curtains, at the base of the column of light, was a pair of binoculars. When he brought them to his eyes he found them perfectly focused; with sharp clarity his magnified vision swept over the vista of the beach and bay. It was already afternoon; the sea had resumed its sparkling stillness. The dome of the pier was silver again, and flashed.

One thing surprised Toby. *Bluefinch* was gone from the sands. But she lay as if in wait for him a little out from the shore, tethered to one of the rusted iron columns of the pier.

Heike?

The chandelier chimed like the plucking of a string. It vibrated tautly, a rich low note.

It was then that Toby heard another sound, which came as if in answer. He turned. From within the open door in the corner came a low, pained moaning.

It was a voice.

Toby crushed the photograph distractedly in his hand.

The voice sounded again: a man's voice, and the sound it made was not merely a diffuse moaning but a specific syllable, repeated with hushed urgency:

Vox. Vox.

What could it mean? He moved ineluctably towards the yawning door – edged himself slowly into the darkness.

"Professor?" His voice was the faintest whisper

There was no reply. The stench was stronger here; laced with the decay and the viscous heat was the acrid charge of a sick room, its squalors undisguised. Toby swallowed hard. There was no column of light to guide him here, only the merest chink in the curtains. In the muffled blackness he made out only gradually the figure on the bed.

"Professor – " He stepped forward.

The terrible, anguished croak:

Vox.

Toby stepped still closer.

Then he realised: this was not the Professor. The figure lay on its back and where the mound of the old man's bulk should have risen was only an emaciated smoothness. From somewhere in the room came a sound of hissing. The curtains parted slightly; in the meagre access of light Toby saw to his astonishment the face of a young man, contorted in pain, turning towards him with a terrible pleading. Dirty-blond hair fell across his forehead and his death's-head face was dotted with stubble.

Vox.

The hand that reached to touch Toby's forearm was a terrible pincer, three fingers lost.

"I'm sorry," Toby whispered, "I'm sorry – "

The sound of hissing came sharper, from somewhere beyond the bed. All at once Toby felt another pair of eyes upon him, like a beam sweeping through his mind, and the rotted carpet was suddenly alive with what seemed to be the scurrying of an enormous rat.

He fled.

Running from the dark room, wrenching wildly at the second of the two doors, Toby found himself in a long corridor, thick with cobwebs, punctuated by equidistant doors. He ran towards the dim window at the end. He found the stairs. He flung himself down, stumbling in the gloom. His desperate breathing echoed crazily about him in the stairwell, swirling cacophonously with an amplified hissing:

Vox.

Vox.

He battered at an exit. It splintered open. He staggered into the still street by the side of the Paradise Hotel.

It was as if none of it had ever happened.

By the time Toby was climbing the cliff path to Shadow Black his clothes, if they showed no evidence of his muddy collapse, showed equally no evidence of Heike's recent attentions to them. Had a day passed? He might be returning from an afternoon walk. Only the clamminess of his shorts, not yet dried from his swim to the tethered *Bluefinch*, bore testimony to the truth. He pulled at them irritably as he shambled up to the house. The dust of the cliff path, damp from yesterday's rain, pressed up coolly through his toes.

"Master Toby!" There was a squeal in the girl's voice.

"Milly! Are you trying to frighten me?"

Milly only wheezed, waving at the air in front of her mouth. She had appeared very rapidly from behind a large rock. Scrambling up at Toby's approach she had flung the cigarette away and now, with her flailing arms, was pretending to be in the throes of some small attack, in order to dispel the smoke. Toby watched the performance, impressed.

"Master Toby," puffed the little maid, after a moment, "I've been looking for you everywhere. Mrs Van Voyd wants you – at once."

Toby groaned. The thought of the old woman and her ludicrous questions was too much, just too much. Especially as he had *really* lost Aldous now.

"Where is she?" he asked, resigned to his fate.

"In the drawing room," coughed Milly. "Oh, she was ever so anxious –"

Toby strode off.

"Milly?" He turned back. "Give me a fag, will you?"

The maid, blushing, obliged.

"Tobias!" Mrs Van Voyd was upon him at once.

Toby staggered back, dazzled by the change in her, dazzled by the light from the sea-facing windows. The Great Hall was a silver haze.

"My dear boy." The old woman stepped back to look at him. Her mouth, freshly lipsticked, broke open in a beaming smile. She was dressed in the costume of a Palestinian peasant woman; or rather, the costume of a Palestinian peasant woman who, having come into a fortune, emigrated to the West, discarded her native ways and moved for many years in advanced artistic circles (at once mascot and powerful patroness), found it now, in the twilight of her career, an amusing affectation, or perhaps a bitter irony, to flaunt self-parodically in her dress and manner the curious fact of her origins.

Crushed against the old woman's breast was Aldous, his fur fluffed up from a recent bath, a spotted bow tie neatly circling his neck.

"It's all thanks to you – dear Tobias!" Mrs Van Voyd slobbered over the little dog's muzzle, blowing little hisses of smoke into his nostrils. "With no Uncle Tobias, there'd be no Tutor-man – and then where would poor little Aldous be?"

"Tutor-man?" Toby repeated blandly.

Mrs Van Voyd took his arm. "Oh Tobias, your new tutor has arrived – and he arrived *with Aldous!*"

In the blinding splendour of the afternoon Toby had not noticed the silent figure who sat in an armchair by the unlit fireplace, his back to the affecting scene: the figure which, standing, seemed now to materialise against the brilliant windows like a ghost, or a mirage, shimmering into view.

Blond hair fell sharply over the dome of the forehead; the skin was burnished like sun-warmed teak. A hand extended for Toby to shake.

Toby did not shake the hand. He could not speak. His eyes travelled downwards from the stranger's face, down to the white shoes; then up again slowly over the white linen suit, the white shirt beneath it, and the black cravat, tucked in at the neck, which – as Toby had thought when he first met this man – suggested so disturbingly the image of a priest in a photographic negative.

"Tobias," Mrs Van Voyd smiled, "meet Mr *Vox.*"

26
Travellin' Man

"... *Lost to sight, to memory dear:* Burmese days, I remember them well!"

"I remember India," Harriet offered shyly, awkward in Yardley's sequinned black gown.

The tutor smiled. "Orchids hanging from the eaves of verandas, palm trees swaying in the ultramarine sky... pagodas tinkling with oriental chimes... the pungent labyrinth of a Mandalay bazaar..."

"Go on, Mr Vox," urged Mrs Van Voyd, imperious in an eighteenth-century aristocrat's gown.

"... Scorching nights beneath mosquito netting, the dripping dense jungle pressed close to the bungalow... opium dens, dim-lit, with curling pipes... dens of deeper sin where a mere few rupees might purchase any ecstasy..."

"Go *on*, Mr Vox!"

"But I'll embarrass Miss Locke." Mr Vox smirked and drew back on his cigarette.

"Nonsense!" Mrs Van Voyd fluttered her fan. "Ariette came to us a mere girl, but has blossomed into womanhood – hasn't she, Jelly?" the old woman demanded.

At the piano, the little man essayed variations on *The Road to Mandalay*. He had not changed for dinner and had neglected to shave.

"Yes." His reply was mechanical.

Harriet had flushed. But indeed she was transformed, remodelled as if to suit the sequinned black gown. An unaccustomed gauntness had overtaken her face, accentuating her cheekbones. Around her neck was a collar of diamonds; her hair was scraped back severely from her forehead; her lips were shaded a claret red. Between black-gloved fingers she held, a little ineptly, one of the tutor's cork-tipped cigarettes.

"Dear Ariette – how I should miss her! Tobias, don't fidget so."

Toby winced. He had been watching Miss Locke (*What had happened?* he wondered); as he watched her, he twirled the stem of a full glass of sherry. Dutifully he desisted.

"My dear Vardell!" Mr Vox sprang up.

The artist hesitated in the doorway. The stranger advanced, smiling.

"We've met?"

"My dear chap, of course not."

"Marcus, dear – Mr Vox." Mrs Van Voyd swept forward. Above her massive upholstered gown her face was puttied with fresh white paint and dotted generously with beauty spots. Heaped precariously on her head was an elaborate arrangement of powdered hair in which was inserted, a foot or so above the level of her eyes, a silver cage containing a little mechanical bird that trilled as the old woman moved about. On a silken sash she led Aldous, decked with rubies, amethysts and emeralds. "See, Marcus! Mr Vox brought him back!"

"You're a dog catcher?"

"Marcus! Mr Vox has come to *take Tobias in hand*."

"Education, dear Vardell," the tutor explained.

"Of course," trilled Mrs Van Voyd, "there is nothing a boy likes to avoid more."

"You are mistaken, Mrs Van Voyd. A boy is always hungry for education. It is only a question of the sort he prefers."

"Mr Vox, you are so wise."

Toby attempted to sip his sherry. The taste of last night rose again in his throat. He swallowed, but wanted to be sick.

"More sherry, Mr Vox? Marcus? Oh do *drink* it, Tobias – think of the starving children."

Toby gulped down the contents of his glass.

"Now, Mr Vox, those *ecstasies* you mentioned…"

Mark took his place in the little group. He reached for Harriet's hand. All day he had been possessed by a sense of foreboding. As if from outside himself the thought came to him: things would not be the same any more.

But why did Harriet seem so composed?

"Tobias, do stop that," said Mrs Van Voyd.

Toby, who had been writhing rather annoyingly in his chair, swallowed back a mouthful of vomit, decisively.

Mark was studying Mr Vox. The tutor, he thought, was the sort of man one expects to be an expert in irony – a skill he might have acquired because of the curious combination of attractive and repellent features he presented to the world. Mr Vox was at once an extraordinarily handsome and an extraordinarily ugly man, and as he smiled about the little group with apparent benevolence these two qualities were evident in equal proportions. His hair was at the same time radiantly blond yet lifeless, a cadaver's, and fell over the impressive but forbidding dome of his forehead with a sharpness that was alarming; in the angles of his nose and lips was a severity that his smile did nothing to dispel. His eyes were wide and seemed almost to shine, but also to possess a dark furtiveness; the burnished young-old skin glowed like sun-warmed teak; and like a carving's, placed in the sun, its warmth, one was certain, was not its own.

Staines sounded the gong. Of all the applause that greeted Yardley that evening, the tutor's was the loudest.

Yardley, majestic in ostrich plumes and ermine, lingered a little longer than usual on the gallery before descending to join the party. Introduced effusively to the saviour of Aldous, she received him with patrician coolness.

"Tell me, Mr Vox, how did you find him?"

"You might say he appeared before me, Lady Harrowblest. When I appeared."

"When was that?"

"Goodness me, I've lost all track of time. At tea-time, wasn't it, Miss Locke?"

"I wasn't at tea." Harriet flushed. Fleetingly a memory – but no, it was an image, only an image – came into her mind. What could it be? Could it be the tutor's hands, caressing her, as she lay like an invalid on her dark canopied bed? Could it be his lips meeting hers, his body moving on hers? Why, the very thought... it was absurd, obscene... and yet there was something else, it seemed, stirring in Harriet's mind... some other memory... some other image... darker, deeper...

But no, it was gone again. Had she been unwell?

"Mr Vox has been fascinating us," Mrs Van Voyd was saying, "with his time in Burma."

"It was a hell on earth and a heaven," said Mr Vox, "and I shall go back one day."

"You were there in the war?" said Mark. "I was in Egypt."

"Dear me, no. I only went out when it was all over."

"You tutored kids there?" asked Yardley, uninterested. Crossing her long thighs, she took up a position on the arm of Mark's chair. Gently she swirled her highball in her glass.

Mr Vox leaned forward. "To tell the truth, I was in the newspaper game. You might say I am – that is, I was – one of your husband's employees."

"You're not really a tutor at all, then?"

"Yarders, really! Mr Vox is an old Etonian."

The intimacy between Mrs Van Voyd and Mr Vox had grown at an astonishing rate. In returning Aldous, Mr Vox had become for the old woman a combination archangel, beloved son and beau. She hung onto his words with reverent eyes; she fluttered about him like a flighty girl; her urges to touch the tutor's hand or thigh were continual, and seldom resisted. She led him in to dinner like a queen displaying her consort.

What happened next shook Yardley visibly.

Taking her new friend to the furthest end of the table, Mrs Van Voyd indicated the huge ornate chair. In dumb-show the tutor declined the honour, but insisted that Mrs Van Voyd...

"No – " began Yardley.

Mrs Van Voyd's laughter tinkled down the table. She took her place in the king's chair. Resplendent against the golden scrolls, the vast bewigged monarch sat with consort on her right hand, familiar on her left.

There was one subject of conversation that evening; the subject was

Mr Vox.

"Mr Vox," Mrs Van Voyd said proudly, "almost became a don."

"Oh Mrs Van Voyd, you flatter me."

"Come, Mr Vox – you must reveal to us the beguiling narrative of which you intimated to me this afternoon. At the age of twenty-two" – the old woman's eyes widened – "Mr Vox underwent a *spiritual conversion*."

Mr Vox shook his head. "Oh, Mrs Van Voyd!"

But then, after a sip of wine, he took up the story. Its setting was Cambridge; its period his student days, just before the war.

Young Adam Vox:
A Cambridge Romance

As a young man, Mr Vox revealed, he had been of a temperament wholly different from that which he now displayed. Now, he liked to think of himself as an adventurer through life, a vagabond on the broad highway with happy-go-lucky heels (this was how he put it; Mr Travers' ears pricked up). But in the dark days of his youth, said Mr Vox, he had been a sober and godly boy, the only son of a bishop and his grimly devout wife. ("My goodness!" said Mrs Van Voyd.) Piety surrounded him like an enveloping cloak; the young Vox seemed destined for the ministry as surely as day would give way to night. When, at Eton, a charismatic master had turned the boy's thoughts to a scholarly life, this revolution could occur only because scholarship became endowed for the young Vox with the aura of a spiritual quest.

Reluctantly the elder Vox agreed to the change of plan. It was a brilliant change. When in due course the young Adam read English at Cambridge, his career climaxed in a First so spectacular it might have exploded over the Cam like fireworks. Of course he would stay and become a fellow of his college (which was Emmanuel). A subject for a dissertation must be found; Adam, eager to push back the frontiers of knowledge, elected to research the life and work of one Obadiah Harkness (1686-1739), himself a one-time inhabitant of Emmanuel, an eighteenth-century religious leader famous in his day for his fiery sermons and scathing moral tracts. To Adam's tutor, Harkness was a neglected great writer, an 'unsung classic of English prose'; for Adam, his attraction was his ardent austere piety, and the fact that he had been born – and later established a spiritual community – in a village near the bishop's Cotswolds home.

Eagerly Adam plunged into the dusty works: the six volumes of sermons; the controversial pamphlets (*On the Utter and Irredeemable Depravity of the Stage*; *On the Folly of Straying from the Path of Reason, or, Heresies of the Deist Sect Expos'd,* &c.), and of course the great moral treatise – reprinted twenty times in the eighteenth century – *An Injunction Most Earnest to Christian Dying*. With equal eagerness Adam sought out traces of the great teacher's life. In the library of Emmanuel he read crumbling records of Harkness' election to a fellowship, and of how his fellowship had been lost when he declined to take the oath of allegiance to George I, in what became known as the 'Bangorian Controversy'. On holidays at the bishop's house, Adam would cycle to the village of Melton Overreach, site of the once-famous 'Melton Community'. In an attic of the house where the community had lived (now a minor public school) he came across a cache of Harknessiana of inestimable value. Yellowing journals provided a portrait of life in the community; letters to Harkness suggested new dimensions of his character; an unpublished manuscript recorded vividly the prolonged religious crisis, at the age of twenty-two, which had driven Harkness into his rigid and already archaic Puritanism.

Adam's future as a scholar was made.

Yet it was shortly after this discovery – it was in the dying days of 1938 – that things began to go wrong. After some months deep in Harkness, Adam began to feel that he had made a mistake. A boredom, a restlessness crept over him. His subject began to repel him. Why this should be so he could not understand, much as he sought to do so. He scrutinised his conscience. He took to incessant prayer. Yet still his work became more intractable, and time ran on alarmingly. Returning to his rooms after each session of lying to his eager supervisor, Adam would fling himself down on his bed in anguish. To admit his difficulties was impossible for the proud young scholar; he concealed his barrenness as an addict of some vice conceals his cravings.

In the Easter term of 1939, when he was twenty-two, the desperate young man made one final effort to draw together the materials for his dissertation.

Chapter I
BIOGRAPHICAL

he wrote at the top of a sheet of blank foolscap. Locked in his room at Emmanuel, he began to read again through the documents he had discovered at Melton Overreach School. The rust-brown ink blurred before his eyes. Difficulties in the texts irritated him beyond reason. A series of letters from one 'Geo. Warlock' – evidently a clergyman – was particularly puzzling: several times, in what struck Adam as a joking tone – to *joke* with Harkness? – Warlock, in his disturbingly florid handwriting, referred to a book called the *New Arabian Nights*. Illegible marginalia by Harkness accompanied a number of these references. It made no sense: the *New Arabian Nights*, Adam knew, was a collection of stories by Robert Louis Stevenson, published in 1882. To what could Warlock be referring, in 1721? Research soon revealed that no book of that title had been published in the eighteenth century; the *Arabian Nights* itself had been first rendered into English only between 1705 and 1708. It made no sense.

It was only when he was flinging his Harkness papers angrily about his room, late one desolate evening, that Adam discovered the fragment of the further Warlock letter (the handwriting unmistakable) that explained precisely – or so Adam thought – the *New Arabian Nights*. The book, it appeared, had been written anonymously by Harkness, and circulated 'in disguise'. Only Warlock 'knew the truth' (his tone became particularly bantering here).

Adam's old excitement returned in a flash. A 'secret' book by Harkness! The title, no doubt, was a metaphor of some kind. Perhaps it was a political book; perhaps Harkness had taken his opposition to the Hanoverian succession rather further than refusing the oath of allegiance!

To procure a copy was imperative.
It was also impossible.
Despondent, Adam found himself slipping again.

Chapter I
BIOGRAPHICAL

seemed doomed to remain unwritten. To proceed without finding the *New Arabian Nights* was unthinkable. Adam prayed for guidance. Hopelessly, he began haunting second-hand book dealers. He visited London, Oxford, twenty other towns. Under a pseudonym he placed an advertisement in the *Times Literary Supplement*. Nothing worked. He told his supervisor nothing of his quest.

All that summer he stayed in Cambridge, claiming to be deep in research. At college he had become a legend – his industry admired in awed tones, his hollow-eyed shabbiness attributed to genius. Even his piety commanded respect, so ardent did it seem. But Adam knew, irredeemably, that he was a charlatan: only a pride so intense as to refuse reality made him desist from rushing to his supervisor, confessing his incapacity, ending his folly decisively at last.

On the evening of September 2nd, 1939, Adam visited for perhaps the hundredth time that summer a dingy little bookshop in an alley off King's Parade. The seedy proprietor glared at him with distaste. Sorting between a box of halfpenny bargains, between grimy copies of *Lady Audley's Secret* (Tauchnitz edition) and *The Dollar Princess* by Harold Simpson (London: Mills and Boon, 1913), Adam noted with bitter irony a ragged copy of Harkness' *Injunction Most Earnest*. And what had Harkness come to, but this? Contemptuously Adam picked up the book, as if to tear it; but the cover fell away of its own accord.

A second later, Adam understood why his quest had failed. He understood that the book said to be circulated 'in disguise' had been hidden not in any ordinary sense, but inside the very covers of other, different books. Beneath faded boards stamped with the name of the moral treatise was a title-page declaring the book's true identity:

THE SULTAN'S SLAVE-BOY:
Or, A New Arabian Nights.

BEING
An Investigation,
Physico-Logical, Moral
& SPIRITUAL,
into the *Nature*
& *Consequences*
of Certain
PRACTICES
Favoured by the
Potentates
of the
REGIONS *of the* ORIENT.

With Instructive Illustrations.
By *A Gentleman*.

His hands trembling, the pious young scholar rustled through the decomposing pages. The small print zig-zagged in his dazzled vision, but the 'instructive illustrations' leapt out clearly enough. A cry broke from the stricken boy's lips. He blundered from the shop, the book flung down on the floor behind him.

All that night he wandered along the Cam, roaming the Backs like a crazed ruined creature. In the darkness he knew a despair so acute that he wanted only *the blackness of darkness forever.*

He decided to drown himself.

But day was breaking. As the first glimmerings of the sun appeared over the ancient town, Adam knew sudden joy. Something inside him shivered and cracked. He sank to his knees on the banks of the river. All at once he knew himself an instrument of God.

It was Sunday. All over Cambridge the bells were ringing for early services. But Adam rushed back to college and burst into his supervisor's room. He confessed everything to the startled old man.

At 11.15 that morning the war with Germany was declared. Adam enlisted at once.

Three months later he was discharged on psychiatric grounds. After a period in hospital he became a master at Melton Overreach School, affecting a limp to explain his exemption from the services. On weekends he became an adventurer in dark London, where in an establishment in Wardour Street in 1943 he was initiated into certain mysteries of the Orient. In 1947 he embarked on his travels.

There was silence for some minutes when the story was over.

"What I should like to know, Mr Vox," trilled Mrs Van Voyd, at last, "is whether you possess a *copy* of that book."

"Alas, no, Mrs Van Voyd. I went back to the shop after seeing my supervisor, but the man said the book was gone. I've never been able to find another."

The tutor looked up sadly. But strangely, there was smiling all around the table; only Mr Travers seemed a little troubled. He was slightly flushed.

Later, in the Great Hall

Something has happened.

Jellicoe Travers' bald head bobs merrily (troubled, it seems, no longer):

> *With his happy-go-lucky heee-aaart*
> *And his happy-go-lucky heels,*
> *Out on the broad hiiigh-way*
> *Bound f' wherever-he-feels...*

"Jelly, do contain yourself!" calls Mrs Van Voyd. But her tone is kind. "Drink, Mr Vox," she explains helpfully (but Mr Travers has been drinking only tonic water). "Usually he gets maudlin. Go *on*, Yarders – "

It is long after midnight. Mrs Van Voyd sits with Mr Vox; Yardley, leaning toward them, regales them with Hollywood anecdotes; Harriet leans eagerly over the grand piano. She says:

"Mr Travers, it's a wonderful song. When did you write it?"

"When? But my dear, I've just made it up!"

"Mr Travers!"

"Oh my goodness – my inspiration! I knew it would come back, I knew it!"

Happiness envelops the party like a golden haze. What barrier have they crossed, that evening – what can have happened, and how?

"I can see it," murmurs Mark Vardell. His eyes are closed. Sack-like on the floor he slumps against a chaise-longue. His head lolls on Toby's oblivious thigh.

"Make up more," says Harriet to Mr Travers, a finger stirring at the wet ring her glass has left on the piano-top.

"If you sing for me, my dear."

"Mr Travers, that's not fair!"

Yardley, twisted forward in her chair, continues:

"But then, when Marion Davies and Hearst come in, and I mean Orson is – like, *shitting himself*, don't you believe different..."

Toby is travelling. His tie loosened, his cigarette burnt low, behind closed eyes he feels himself plunging through the blackness of space. It is exhilarating. From the edge of the universe comes Vardell's monotone, describing what sounds like an Indian totem-pole; from another dimension faint signals reach him, bearing other voices, music, a trilling bird. (Beside the chaise-longue, some inches from Vardell's hand, is a carrot-coloured pool of liquid. How satisfied Toby feels!)

Mrs Van Voyd and Mr Vox collapse into laughter.

"I *do* love you, Yarders," says Mrs Van Voyd.

Mark Vardell can see his painting. This vision of a masterpiece he has seen before; now he sees it with a painful new intensity. If only he can keep this vision, hold it still...

"Mark, you're falling asleep!" Yardley kicks him playfully; the vision vanishes.

She turns back to Mr Vox:

"Listen, honey, you think that's cra-azy?" She gulps back a swig of brandy. "Craziest of all was on *Slopes of Andalusia* – me and Cad Ranger trying to be these two Spanish kids in love, remember? Now we're like, six, seven days into the shooting schedule – behind as a dog's ass already..."

"Yarders, remember Aldous!"

"... When we get it from front office that Louis B. Mayer's gonna visit the goddam set – "

Mr Vox listens indulgently; Mrs Van Voyd, beside him on the sofa, rests her heavy head against his. Her hand strokes his white trousers just above the knee. In the old woman's ample lap lies the sleepy Aldous, a jumble of gems and fluffy white fur.

Mark is smiling. The vision has returned.

"Now, my dear, let's just run through that last bit again. You're remembering this?"

"Yes, but – "

"No buts!"

"I can't – "

It doesn't matter. The shy girl assumes an unaccustomed panache. All eyes open and turn towards her. On the last chorus Yardley leaps up to join her. The song is a jaunty jazz tune; suddenly the great hall is a sweaty dive in New Orleans, *circa* 1920. As if on the soundtrack of a film, the piano swells to become a full orchestra. Imagination supplies the saxophones, the trumpets, the trombones, the double bass, the skittering banjo, the clattering drums. Mrs Van Voyd begins to clap her hands; then Mr Vox, then Mark, then Toby. The mechanical bird trills. They rise to their feet, all of them. Harriet and Yardley link arms joyously:

> *So his happy-go-lucky heee-aaart*
> *And his happy-go-lucky heels*
> *Carry him along the hiiigh-way*
> *Faster than whirlin' wheels –*
> *He don't feel so bou-ou-ound*
> *By things that bind us rou-ou-ound*
> *Happy-go, happy-go-*
> *Lucky travellin' man!*

"One more time!" cries Yardley.

"One more time!" cries Mrs Van Voyd.

(Aldous, meanwhile, has found his own fulfilment. Unregarded by his mistress, he laps eagerly at a carrot-coloured pool he has found beside the chaise-longue.)

Happy-go, happy-go-
Lucky travellin' maaa-aaan!

The applause is rapturous. Laughing, Harriet and Yardley fall into each other's arms. But the entertainment is not yet over. With an inspired flourish Jellicoe Travers at once changes key, tempo and time signature, recasting the tune as a romantic waltz. The New Orleans dive is spirited away; the great hall is a ballroom in Vienna.

"Mr Vox?" says Mrs Van Voyd.
"Mark," says Yardley.
"May I, Miss Locke?" asks Toby shyly.
Three couples circle round the dim-lit floor.

Mrs Van Voyd insisted, of course, on seeing Mr Vox to his room.

"It is as well, Mr Vox" – her puttied face was flaking; strands were unwinding from her towering wig – "it is *as well* I have retired from the fray."

Mr Vox leaned in the doorway, an elbow on the frame. The expression in his eyes was half-smiling, half-sad. The old woman, the sleepy Aldous cradled in her arms, pressed close to the tutor, strangely expectant. The little bird, keeled against its cage, had stopped singing.

"*As well*, Mrs Van Voyd?"

"Since you are so evidently a gentleman" – There was a crack in her voice – "of the *Uranian* disposition..."

Mr Vox raised his eyebrows. Quickly he kissed the old woman goodnight; he swivelled away from the frame of the door; he swung the heavy door into the frame, airily letting fall, as he did so, the words:

"You are mistaken, Mrs Van Voyd – you are mistaken."

"Oh – " The door clicked shut. The old woman, left alone, swooned against the panelling. With a little clang the broken bird tumbled at last from its perch.

It was the first of Mr Vox's contradictions. As the days unfolded the tutor would divulge (would seem to divulge) ever more of himself, sometimes in fleeting asides, sometimes in elaborate narratives: tales of India and Burma in the aftermath of independence, of life among the colonists in Hong Kong and Singapore; he would trail back, too, over the trials of his youth, touching them afresh with new highlights, new emphases. With easy confidence he covered a great canvas – here a sweeping stroke; there – some *bagatelle*...

But as if in its perfect surface one were to detect first one tiny crack, and then (one's eyes becoming sharper) more and more, until at last one saw only a spider's web of crevices, so the tutor's grand design would seem fated soon enough – at the brush of a hand, a sharp knock – to float to the floor in a powdery susurrus.

It did not.

"At Charterhouse – "

"But Mr Vox, you were an Etonian."

"A Carthusian, Mrs Van Voyd."

"Oh – "

And so he was; so he was.

27
Prospero's Island

"When we are young, we are prey to illusions."

It was next morning; it was Friday; dust floated endlessly in a slant of early light. Toby – yawning, eyes circled darkly – had taken his place at a table in the library. Mr Vox, who had spoken, stood by the window, his hands clasped behind his back, his back turned to the boy. His remark hovered in the air like a tangible thing, a frail fluttering creature that might vanish in the brightness, that might separate through prismatic wings the colours of the sun.

Toby watched it silently. Seconds ticked by.

"We'll begin our play then, shall we?" Mr Vox turned kindly to his charge. Toby looked down at his open book. Mr Vox, who had no book, paced about the table. In his immaculate voice he set the scene: Toby was to imagine an old-fashioned sailing ship, tossed on a stormy sea...

Suddenly there was a crack of thunder and lightning.

"*Boatswain!*"

The sound of the storm seemed to fill the room.

"Aldous, really!"

It was that afternoon.

Mrs Van Voyd, in Arab sheikh costume, tugged earnestly at the little dog's sash. "Don't look back, Ariette, don't!"

Harriet, who did look back, only laughed. Aldous was answering a *call of nature*.

"It's windy up here," said Harriet to Mr Vox. "I'm almost cold."

"Darling girl." Mr Vox slipped an arm about her shoulders. They were walking on the cliffs. Tough clumps of grass flapped back and forth like pennants; wildflowers waved on frail stalks. Mr Vox had jammed down his Panama hat harder on his head. Behind them the great house rose darkly out of rock; before them the sea lay like afternoon glass. But it too was rippling; distantly the wind made its surface shimmer.

"What are you thinking?"

"I'm thinking about the autumn."

The first speaker was Mr Vox; the second, Harriet. Strange images stirred in her mind. Was she remembering a dream, some bad dream?

But no, it was only the cold. The autumn, creeping closer.

"*Season of mists and mellow fruitfulness –* "

Harriet said: "I'm not sure I want it to come."

And Mr Vox, removing his dark glasses, murmured some lines of a different poet's:

> *That time of year thou mayst in me behold*
> *When yellow leaves, or none, or few, do hang*
> *Upon those boughs which shake against the cold,*
> *Bare ruined choirs, where late the sweet birds sang –*

"Mr Vox!" Harriet gazed into the tutor's screwed-up eyes. And strangely, she found herself thinking again of dreams, bad dreams she could not quite remember. What silly nightmare had disturbed her rest, not so long ago?

Something about Yardley. Something about Mark.

It must have been before Mr Vox had come. There could be no reason to be upset now – and the tutor, as if in confirmation, laughed. Turning from Harriet, he waved to Mrs Van Voyd, who struggled up the slope towards them. Aldous, in his little turban, scampered ahead of her, almost youthful.

"All shall be well," said Mr Vox lightly. He stretched out his arm, reaching into the space over the edge of the cliff. Suddenly, as if from nowhere, a splendid white seagull swooped down towards them. Staggering back, Harriet gave a little cry. But the gleaming bird perched on the tutor's wrist.

"Darling girl." Carefully Mr Vox bore the bird towards her.

Amazed, Harriet studied the golden-tipped wings, the smooth arched hardness of the beak and claws, the staring, intelligent eyes.

"Your light has failed."
It was that evening.
"Things have changed, honey."
"What?"
"Oh, I don't know." Yardley twisted uselessly at the cap of a gin bottle.
"Let me. Are you in love with him, too?"
"You're funny. Dear Mark." She would have kissed him, but they were not concealed.
"I'm almost finished," said Mark, matter-of-factly.
"Finished?"
"I've got him. Caught him."
"I'm glad. Mark – "
"Really Yarders, where *are* those drinks? Poor Mr Vox and I are parched!"
"Dear Cora." Yardley shook back her long dark hair.
"You have thirty seconds!" called Jellicoe Travers. "The last reel is about to begin!"

The days passed; they revolved round Mr Vox.

Each morning Mrs Van Voyd would rise with eagerness, preparing herself elaborately to descend to the breakfast room. There, but for the already-busy painter, the party would gather: dear Ariette; the Yard; Jelly; Tobias; Mr Vox. Often the tutor would be a little late, entering the room only when the others were assembled. Every day he was the same: always vigorous with life and wit; always in his somewhat crumpled, somewhat soiled white suit. At once he commanded the attention of all.

After breakfast the women were left alone. Withdrawing to a long-unused morning room, with magazines and coffee, novels and tobacco, they would beguile themselves until luncheon while the men pursued their more earnest activities: the lessons in the library for the tutor and his charge; the portrait for Mark; for Jellicoe Travers, a new-found discipline – each morning, he had decided, was to be spent at the keyboard.

These spaces between pleasures became for the women a pleasure in themselves: Mrs Van Voyd read *The Garden of Allah* again; Ariette read *Jane Eyre*; the Yard flipped through *Vogue* and *Harper's Bazaar*. Over coffee they discussed Hollywood, and society, and Mrs Van Voyd's husbands, and clothes, and Ariette's wedding (which Mrs Van Voyd was eager to organise, conjuring in imagination spectacular bridal gowns).

Yet behind these subjects there always loomed the presence of Mr Vox: *If Mr Vox were here*, or *We must ask Mr Vox*, or *What would Mr Vox think*? were phrases seldom from the women's lips.

Only Ariette sometimes seemed a little disturbed – frowns, from time to time, would flicker across her forehead, and Mrs Van Voyd, with a smile, would ask her what was the matter. Whatever could be the matter?

But no, it was nothing.

A dream? What was a dream?

The afternoons were dedicated universally to pleasure. After a long luncheon the party split into small groups – bound for beach, for library, for cliff-top walks – and here Mrs Van Voyd's only concern was to ensure that she was of the group which contained Mr Vox. But Mr Vox would not let her down.

In the evenings, before music and singing, they would watch the Yard's films. In the past the fifty-nine films had been rationed to one a week; now, because Mr Vox so evidently took pleasure in them, the Yard had declared that *every* night was film night.

These nightly screenings took on a different character from the weekly screenings of the past. A quality of reverence, of sacred ritual, was abandoned. The films became occasions for hilarious revelry, in which the Yard herself would laugh uproariously at the antics of her celluloid incarnations.

The servants were not invited.

On many nights the party watched two films in a row. It was after such debauches that Mrs Van Voyd experienced, during this time, her few pangs of sadness. The cycle would soon be completed, she thought.

And soon the summer would end.

"Mr Vox is a literary man," said the old woman one morning. "I dare say he's *writing a book.*"

The remark was apropos of nothing. The women had been discussing – that is, Yardley had been holding forth upon – the subject of last night's film. (The situation was almost grave; they had come as far as *Ballet Shoes* (1941). But they were not worrying now.)

"What, Cora?"

Mrs Van Voyd drew dreamily on her cigar. *The Garden of Allah* lay on her lap, open at the final chapter.

"Mrs Van Voyd said Mr Vox might be writing a book," offered Harriet. Her voice was dreamy.

"Perhaps about his days in Burma," the old woman murmured.

"Perhaps about us," said Yardley with a laugh. She drew up her long legs beneath her in her chair.

Silence descended, bird-like, amongst the coffee-cups, the ash trays, the fallen dust-motes. Did only Harriet feel the throb of foreboding, pulsing beneath the surface of the strange idyllic days? Flutterings of a dream passed through her mind. A storm. Light. Music. Mozart. And something... something horrible. Last night she had woken from her sleep, crying out loud. But why? What could it mean? And what had it to do with Mr Vox?

They all knew – they had known from the start – that Mr Vox had come to them not merely as Toby's tutor. That he had some mysterious purpose of his own was as apparent as the sun, burning above them. How it involved them – if it involved them – they could not yet know.

It was only after he had been at Shadow Black for three weeks, and summer was ending, that Mr Vox at last revealed his purpose.

It was Friday 19th August, 1955.

"I think I'm going to be sick!" wailed Harriet.

"Mr Vox, you must have a charmed life!"

Mrs Van Voyd snatched back her three-cornered hat, just as it was about to blown away. Ottoline thundered down the cliff road, scattering dust beneath impatient wheels.

"One more time!" Mr Vox cried. His face beneath his dark glasses crumpling in glee, the tutor veered violently round a perilous bend.

Harriet screamed.

"Mr Vox, where are you taking us?"

"To heaven, dear lady – or hell!"

Juddering violently, Ottoline plunged into the cave road.

"Mr Vox, shame on you! I'm not sure I should let you drive poor Ottoline at all."

"Of course you should, darling lady." And the tutor's hand, darting across Harriet's lap, squeezed Mrs Van Voyd's soft thigh.

At once all was forgiven.

"Poor little Aldous," the old woman cooed. "His heart is thumping like a frighted sparrow's."

"Aldous, a sparrow? An eagle, Mrs Van Voyd!"

"I don't like this bit," said Harriet, between them. "There are *bats* in here." She shifted uncomfortably. Wedged against her hip was the hilt of Mrs Van Voyd's sword.

Ottoline's headlamps cut through the darkness. Then all at once brightness returned. The twisting road wound through the Lightletter hills.

"Our destination," cried Mr Vox, gesturing sweepingly as the holiday town flashed into view.

"It's the silence," said Harriet. "That's what's so extraordinary."

With a strange wonderment – a dreamy wonderment – the girl gazed around her. From the promenade the empty buildings towered above her – the boarding houses, the tall hotel – their facades cracked and peeling, their very fabric appearing as if imminently it would crumble.

Suddenly Harriet darted down the promenade steps.

But why? What had happened?

"Ariette?"

"Let her go, Mrs Van Voyd. She's young."

"Ah, youth!"

They watched the girl sprinting along the sands, her arms flapping, her zebra-striped shift shimmering like a mirage, on the point of disappearing. Mrs Van Voyd adjusted her three-cornered hat. She was dressed that afternoon in naval costume, suggestive of Lord Nelson, though she had made no attempt to hide one arm. Aldous she had restricted to the affectation of an eyepatch, a miniature version of her own.

"A splendid idea to come here, Mr Vox." Her fingers smoothed the tutor's hand, which rested loosely on a railing by her own.

"You've been here before, surely?"

"Many years ago. Then it just seemed – oh, squalid, absurd. Now it has acquired an aura of romance. It's changed."

"You've changed."

The old woman laughed. "Tobias will be going back to Melton in a few weeks," she said, after a pause.

It was her companion's turn to laugh. "Are you giving me my notice?"

Mrs Van Voyd gazed earnestly into the tutor's face. "You could stay with us, Mr Vox."

"I could?" His tone was wry.

"I love you, Adam."

"Oh Cora, Cora." He took her in his arms. When he released her, she was trembling violently.

"Oh stop, stop!" gasped Harriet.

It was no good. A force had taken hold of her; she was sprinting wildly. Why couldn't she stop? She flung up her hands, crumbling to the sand like a graceless dancer. She had run far, far down the beach. Her legs entangled beneath her, she gazed about vacantly at the gently lapping sea, at the wall of rock rising at the end of the beach, at the flashing stricken pier, at the mysterious shadowy spaces beneath the pylons of the promenade.

She breathed deeply. Reaching out an arm she drew herself towards a pylon. The old timber pole was cracked and dry, its texture suffused with the seashore smell. She pressed her face against its splitting surface. Why had Mr Vox brought them here? Harriet's eyes closed and she was plunged back suddenly into the dream: of a stranger waiting for her, deep within a labyrinth, of the shifting torch held aloft in his hand; of the labyrinth darkening, and darkening again, until the darkness inevitably was violated by light...

Then there were the hands, running over her flesh...

"*Who are you, who are you?*"

Her eyes snapped open. The striped booth stood before her, the deckchairs ranged before it; the crazed wooden eyes of the puppet fixed her in their gaze.

"Hey, what's the hurry?" Mr Vox called.

"Ariette, such indecorous haste – "

Mrs Van Voyd and Mr Vox, their hands joined, were paddling in the shallows when Harriet came running towards them.

"*Who are you, who are you?*" the girl burst out, the words wrenched from her like a seabird's cry, dispersing hollowly on the bright, empty air. For a moment it seemed there were things she remembered. Dark, terrible things.

But no, she had only dreamed again. Hadn't she?

"Now what can our young friend be about?" the tutor murmured, slipping an arm round Mrs Van Voyd's shoulders.

"What have you... done to us?" Harriet faltered.

A dream. A bad dream.

"My dear Miss Locke... Mrs Van Voyd." Smiling, the tutor looked back and forth between them. "I think it's time we visited the Paradise Hotel."

The beach was silent but for the soft wash of waves, the gentle stirring of the air.

"Should we really be doing this, Mr Vox?"

"Mrs Van Voyd, who's to prevent us?"

"I rather meant, is it safe?" the old woman said nervously, clutching little Aldous tight against her breast.

The rotted doors atop the marble steps had yielded at once to the tutor's shoulder. They stood in a slant of light that fell across a faded red carpet. Beyond the light, the dingy foyer composed itself into shapes: of a destitute reception-desk waiting, abandoned; of circular sofas on claw-footed legs, pungent with decay. Ancient gilding glinted uncertainly; a chandelier above was an ominous metronome.

"Oh!" Harriet, moving forward, brushed a potted palm. The brown plant crumbled to powder at her touch.

A dream. Only a dream.

"I don't think there's really anything to see," Mrs Van Voyd said hopefully, pushing up her eyepatch.

"Nonsense!" Mr Vox took her arm. "Come." He led her into the gloom; Harriet followed. Before them, garlanded with cobwebs, was the cage of an ancient lift-shaft, the door drawn back, the compartment in place.

"Haberdashery, ma'am? Lingerie?"

"Mr Vox, don't be silly – "

"Silly?"

There was a faint hum, as of a generator. The tutor clicked open the door of the compartment. An electric bulb burned in the ceiling, casting a dirty light. Taut-faced, his charges filed in before him. Wonderingly they gazed over the desiccated walls, the tarnished brass handrail, the dust-thick floor. To their left and right, two little mirrors faced each other in the panelling, creating in the mean space an illusion of infinity. Mr Vox drew shut the door. Casually he jabbed the button for the top floor.

There was a terrible groaning. The electric bulb flickered; then after a moment of stillness the lift shuddered upwards. The women gasped. All thought was suspended; barely breathing, they listened to the lift's grim music of subterranean heavings, of sudden sharp cracks.

The lift stopped with unexpected suddenness.

Only a dream. A dream.

"Ah." Mr Vox stepped out into the mildew-smelling murk. "I'm sure the view from up here is magnificent. All we need" – he laughed – "is a window."

Jauntily he made his way along the gloomy passage, his fingernails scraping along brittle blistered wallpaper. Like a confident proprietor he tried the doors: one appeared to be locked; one to have swollen and wedged in its frame; a third was obscurely jammed. One stood ajar. There was a peevish crack of hinges as Mr Vox, with seeming casualness, pushed it wider.

Clustering behind him his companions saw a column of light through barely-parted curtains; then the shabby magnificence of the room. The décor was a heady fantasy of resplendence, an imperial splendour left to die and rot. There was stale trapped heat in the air and the smell of decay here was stronger than elsewhere, as if this hot room high above Lightletter Bay were paradoxically a vault, a charnel-house, a grim nucleus of death discovered at last after a passage through many lesser, satellite graves.

The two women looked around them wildly; Mr Vox smiled. It occurred to Harriet only then that the tutor had not removed his dark glasses.

"Extraordinary." Mrs Van Voyd studied the room, revolving slowly round. Abstractedly she set Aldous down on the floor.

"Why?" whispered Harriet; but no one heard. She breathed deeply, as if in defiance of the deathly smell. Standing in this room she felt no fear, only a sense of impending significance. Had she been here before? Been here in her dream? Everything seemed familiar. And yet she felt a strange distance from the scene, as if she were not an actor in it at all. Dispassionately she watched the events unfold, inevitable as history from a long perspective: the tutor removing his dark glasses, smiling; the women's questions hovering in the air; the sudden sharp barking; then the terrible moaning, aching from the darkness of the connecting room.

A dream. Only a dream.

Aldous had made the discovery first.

"Whatever – ?" Mrs Van Voyd cried out. She blundered through the doorway with an unthinking courage. For an instant the stench made her stagger back. Then the billowing of the curtain revealed the scene to her, the terrible scene.

Calmly Harriet moved to the dark door.

"Who?" The old woman turned to Mr Vox. "*Who?*"

In seconds she was sobbing, sinking to her knees.

Mr Vox slid to the floor beside her, his arms encircling her stricken bulk. Like a loving father he kissed her wrinkled eyelids, her withered painted cheek.

"My dear, my darling," he whispered tenderly, "you mean you don't know? This is Peter Harrowblest."

28
Crime and Punishment

Villa Santa Clara
Sun. 14th Aug., 1955

CHANCE was the name, wasn't it??
 EEL shall be ACCUSATORY. He is aware that MORE than a LITTLE time has ELAPSED since CHANCE's last COMMUNICATION with his slippery friend. Has CHANCE (by chance?) fallen into a STATE OF CATATONIA (not to be confused with CATALONIA), HUNCHED over a back issue of ASTRONOMICAL STORIES in his SPARSE back bedroom in the CHELSEA HOUSE?? (I imagine it sparse – AUNT CORA's room of course is a RIOT of flowers.) TELL me something INTERESTING, Chance – I need DISTRACTION.
 I was GOING to tell you ALL about the ETRUSSSCAN trip – three days of BLISS with the SAINTED Goldbergs (REALLY sainted; MIRIAM thought they were sainted BECAUSE THEY'RE RICH. EEL can wrap himself round the REAL reason.) But things PROCEED APACE... To tell the truth old EEL's been caught up in a BIT OF A DRAMA about the Goldbergs. – Seems they aren't ALWAYS polite. They have their LIMITS (as well they MAY!!)... Two nights ago at dinner, D4 – you must imagine him in FULL DRUNKEN CONVERSATIONAL FLIGHT – HAPPENED to be telling some WITLESS anecdote about some old supplier of RUBBER stuff he used to deal

Shadow Black

with (in his early days in the HOSEPIPE BUSINESS, you understand, though to tell the truth I think there may have been more than HOSEPIPES involved)... Anyway, HAPPENING to talk about this PARTICULAR gentleman, how should D4 HAPPEN to describe him but with a word which HAPPENED to be OFFENSIVE to EVERY other person in the room! D4, Y'see, HAPPENED to use the word KIKE (!!)... MIRIAM laughed, as if he'd made a JOKE... Unfortunately the GOLDBERGS didn't HAPPEN to see the FUNNY side, with the UPSHOT that the hapless D4 'family' are now VERY much PERSONAE NON GRATA in the villa of the sainted GOLDBERGS (& you can be ASSURED the sainted GOLDBERGS will NEVER again be crossing the threshold of Santa Clara!!)... MIRIAM, you may WELL imagine, is FURIOUS (D5 on the way, definitely), & OF COURSE has conveniently forgotten that her own stupid snorting LAUGH contributed ALMOST as much to this débâcle as HOSEPIPE's god-awful CESSPIT of a mouth... What disgusts me MOST in all this is the HORRIBLE thought that HOSEPIPE, MIRIAM, & - fizzle fizzle - your Poor old EEL shd. ACTUALLY be considered - I flush with shame - A 'FAMILY'. That Rachel shd. be FORBIDDEN to speak to ME because of MY association with... THEM!!... What shd. poor EEL do?? - SLITHER to the senior GOLDBERG's feet, PROTESTING - it WOULD be true - the PURELY INVOLUNTARY nature of my 'relationship' to H/M?? Would he even understand me? He'd think I was mad!!

    I thought I HATED Hosepipe before.
    I DIDN'T KNOW WHAT THE WORD MEANT.

At LEAST there are still BOOKS. RUSH to yr. nearest place-where-you-can-get-books NOW for a copy of CRIME AND PUNISHMENT by DOSTOEVSKY. It's NOT some boring old classic, this is the best book EVER. Rachel made me read it. She's the ONLY one who's acting sensibly in all this.

29
Firmament

"... *FT* reports 'Wall Street Boom' on Empire shares... Market penetration of Bolivia, Colombia, Ecuador and Peru continues firmly on course... Lima bureau says acquisition of Sanchez group now certain to go ahead... Hong Kong banking interests acquired as instructed... Buyer found for WXBC Wisconsin..."

Collidge looked up expectantly from the lectern. The instruction he awaited was not forthcoming.

"The time has come," said the voice at last.

"The time, my lord?" Collidge's mouth was dry.

The old man had ceased his circuit of the lectern. Now he turned his chair decisively towards Collidge. His one good eye looked up at the assistant; with sad clear eyes the assistant stared back. There was no need – there was never the need – to ask what was meant.

Collidge looked down, shuffling his papers.

For three weeks he had lived in a state bordering on beatitude. The old man, like a traveller returned from afar, must needs know everything that had happened in his absence. Collidge narrated share prices, circulations, news policies; amalgamations, acquisitions, cessations, inceptions were paraded proudly or in shame before his master. Sometimes the old man would praise Collidge fulsomely; more often he cursed him as a fool and a blunderer. Violently he overturned his deputy's decisions. Collidge didn't care. To obey his master was his greatest pleasure.

Now the beatific period would end. In these weeks – Collidge thought of them already with nostalgia – the world beyond the tower had scarcely existed. That the names and numbers he quoted might refer to real things, entangled in actual life, was hardly of moment to Collidge; the joyous readings were a game he played, its sole object the delight of his master.

Collidge raised his eyes towards the blazing casement. With the bright sunlight behind him, the crippled old man was shrouded in shadow, a terrible dark thing, and the assistant's gaze turned irresistibly towards the portrait. There the great head loomed out, magnificent as God. Only some details of the background were incomplete.

"Tonight, my lord?" said Collidge, after a pause.

"Yes," said the old man, "tonight."

"You can't mean it, Madeleine – I won't let you mean it – "

"He's my husband, Chet. I made a vow – "

"You're really walking out on me? Madeleine – Maddy..."

"Oh Chet, Chet – don't you see? In another time – another place... Oh Chet, goodbye!"

The camera lingered on the tear-blurred face, massive in close-up, a cheesecloth and monochrome essay in emotion. Music swelled beneath the choking tears. There was one last kiss, savage and brief... At last with a little cry the distracted Madeleine (Yardley) broke from her lover's arms. Music surged unbearably as the stricken Chet (Cad Ranger) stood gazing after her; then gazing, as if forever, at the yawning empty doorway. Forever, it seemed, he would be a lonely man, abandoned for eternity in his opulent drawing room. He hung his head and his shoulders began to shake; then as the orchestra crashed into a crescendo the terminal white words spurted across the screen:

A Paramount Picture

There was silence among the watchers. From each pair of eyes, perhaps, tears flowed quietly. Perhaps for a moment each person was Madeleine, or Chet.

Yardley searched for a handkerchief. For night after night since Mr Vox had arrived she had laughed and joked at images of herself. Comedies, tragedies, musicals, thrillers: all had filled her with the same gay ridicule. But tonight's picture, she had known from the first, would be different... Oh, she had tried; reminiscing loudly over the first reel about the ludicrous career of the film's publicist, a pious little Scotsman handicapped by an inability to recognise a *double entendre*:

HE OFFERED HER THE WORLD – OFFERED IT TOO LATE

the banners had declared for *Boston Story*:

HE GAVE IT TO HER – GAVE IT TOO LATE

had been the little Scotsman's first inspired draft.

But somehow tonight it didn't seem funny; and then the picture had gripped her, gripped her as it always did. It had gripped the others, too.

The picture had been her last.

"Still the same."

Yardley started.

From the darkness behind her came a sound of clapping: leaden, slow reports from heavy cupped palms.

The lights flickered on.

But no one had moved.

"Still the same, my darling, still the same." The voice was suffused with an infinite weariness – the voice was unmistakable. Unsteadily – she had cried that night into too many highballs – Yardley rose to her feet, turning.

They had slipped in while it was dark: Eddie mutilated and terrible in his chair; the grey form of Collidge rising behind him, inevitably, inevitably. Yardley wanted to laugh.

A loose strip of celluloid flapped on the projector: an insect beating at a window in vain.

Mr Vox had risen too. He announced, blandly:

"The time, as I said it would, has come."

What was he talking about? Yardley stared as he strode towards her husband. She was aware of the risen forms of Harriet and Toby, rigid as if in some certain expectation. Mrs Van Voyd stifled a cry.

"I don't know you, sir – " Harrowblest's tone was harsh.

"The tutor, I believe, my lord," Collidge said disdainfully.

Mr Vox kneeled before the old man's chair. "My lord," he said quietly, "I have brought back your son."

Mrs Van Voyd's cry broke out.

"What is it? What is it?" Yardley almost shouted. She exchanged wild glances with Mark and Mr Travers.

The others seemed like zombies; she wanted to beat them, hurt them...

"I've found your son," Mr Vox repeated, rising. "He's coming home, my lord – I've come to bring him home."

Behind him there was a sound like scuffling. Then came a sound of breaking glass.

Harrowblest's eye was fixed on the stranger. A vein began to throb in the great dome of the head.

"It seems my wife has fainted," he said, after a silence.

This time Mr Vox had a simple story to tell.

The Mystery of Captain Haldane, Hero of the Burma Campaign

"In 1952, I arrived for the first time in Rangoon. Burma had become independent some four years before, and was – as one might expect – in chaos. The country's economy was on the brink of collapse; in the cities, crowds seemed to threaten at any moment to erupt in savage violence."

"Hmph! Typical of the colonies," muttered Harrowblest.

"Indeed, my Lord," said Mr Collidge.

"Charles – shhh!" said Mrs Van Voyd. It was a little later. The stricken Yardley had been put to bed, and the remainder of the party had gathered round Mr Vox in the Great Hall. "Staines, bring up more wine. Mr Vox, do go on."

Mr Vox appeared to contemplate his cork-tipped cigarette. The squalid vista of post-colonialism amused him, he explained; he was also seeking, in beautiful grotesque Burma, a new and rejuvenating scene of life. It had been six years since he had left England. For two of them he had lived a pleasantly dissolute existence (he was not ashamed to say) in Bombay, Lahore and Madras, where he had witnessed the advent of Indian independence (Harriet shifted uneasily), and later in the colonial clubs of Hong Kong; but on the attenuation of the small legacy he had been left on his father's death he realised he must find some alternative career. A journey through China resulted in a book-length essay which was accepted eagerly by a London publisher; but the advent of Mao Tse Tung's regime in 1949 made the essay obsolete before it had appeared. Mr Vox turned his attention instead to certain 'business interests' (here he grew circumspect). He travelled widely through South-East Asia. But when he landed in Rangoon, after hastily departing Bangkok, he had resolved on a new course. The *Rangoon Telescope* accepted him eagerly.

It was some months after his arrival, in a certain establishment in a backstreet of the pungent city, that the tutor – the reporter – first met Haldane. He had heard already of this curious young man, whose course of life had occasioned some comment in the English community in Rangoon. Captain Haldane – as he had been in the war – was a wounded ex-soldier, at one time a hero of the Burma Campaign. But a Japanese grenade had blown three fingers from his right hand, and though this was from one point of view a lucky escape, the incident had destroyed his nerves. Now, lingering redundantly in the country he had helped to liberate, the sometime hero buttressed his broken existence with only a meagre army pension. His sole desire seemed to be to kill himself, slowly, through a campaign of dissipation he made no effort to conceal. Between bouts of drunkenness – and worse – Haldane alternated periods of feverish illness, lying on a damp mattress in his seedy rented room, tended by a sullen Oriental mistress.

"My goodness." Mrs Van Voyd's eyes grew wide. Lord Harrowblest sat rigid, a massive carved icon; Mr Collidge's mouth was strangely pursed.

Mr Vox continued.

It was not, he remarked, an extraordinary story; the Orient, after all, is filled with ruined Englishmen. But if Haldane were an object of interest to an unusual degree, the reason lay not far to seek. His origins were so evidently exalted: in the lineaments of his wasted face an aristocratic heritage could plainly be traced; his voice, though coarsened by years away from England, betrayed unmistakably the quality of his background.

There were rumours about his past: Haldane was the younger son of a duke, banished for some unspeakable crime; the miscreant scion of a cabinet minister; a disgraced decadent kinsman of the Royal House itself. Nothing was known for certain; only that 'Haldane' was the merest alias.

"I confirmed this," said Mr Vox. "Illicitly" – he smiled – "I called on the resources of the London *Telescope*. No traces of a 'Matthew Aloysius Haldane' were to be found before the beginning of his army career. He might simply have *appeared* at a recruiting office in Brighton in the winter of 1942. He was shipped to South-East Asia later the following year, already a junior officer."

The story intrigued Mr Vox from the first; when he met the young man, the reporter was more than intrigued.

"I became obsessed with him," Mr Vox admitted frankly. "Perhaps I felt the tug of some – *affinity* between us; perhaps his story stirred my pity. In any case I determined to become his friend – if needs be, to batter down all his defences to do so.

"I became more than his friend; I became his inseparable companion. But still he told me nothing of his family, his early life. I determined – shall we say? – *to probe beneath the surface*. I pounced directly; I circled loquaciously; I led him through labyrinths of entangling pleasure to startle him at last with a floodlit mirror. But always he turned away."

Toby, feeling awkward, fumbled for a cigarette. Mr Travers, with a J-monogrammed handkerchief, was mopping his sweaty head.

"Ah," said Mr Vox, "the hours I spent, my heart aching, in his reeking vile room! All through one summer it went on and on, in the dripping moist heat, in the rising smells of ordure and rotting food from the streets, in the implacable wash of monsoonal rains.

"To no avail. Sometimes he would cry out at me, knowing what I wanted, what I needed – but refusing me..."

"My third husband – "

"Cora, shh!" said Mr Travers.

"I grew despairing; how could my Haldane be so unkind? Yet in time I saw things differently. The truth was not, as I had crudely begun to suspect, that the shattering of his nerves had shattered *all* his memories of his earlier life. He remembered his army career well; he could describe vividly his induction, his basic training, his selection as an officer cadet. His comrades, the battles he had fought, the things he had suffered were present to him with a steel-hard clarity. It was his life *before* the army that was lost to him. We came to this realisation – it was a climax for us both – late one night in his squalid room, after opium and too much wine. Outside the open window, rain tumbled through the steamy dark air. My Haldane began to cry – it was the first time I had seen him cry. I held him in my arms."

Mrs Van Voyd began to sob; Harriet could not stop trembling.

That rainy night, Mr Vox thought later, marked the end of his Burmese days. It was the end of his wanderings, too. He knew then he would return to England, accompanying his beloved Haldane, seeking Haldane's origins.

Three months later they landed in Southampton.

"So you were never a tutor at all, Mr Vox?"

"It was a necessary fiction. There were things I had to discover."

The story ended there. It was a story Mr Vox was to tell several times, each time with small but significant variations.

But tomorrow Peter would be coming home.

Tomorrow: A Tableau

The sun burns painfully in the brilliant sky; pours its molten gold on the assembled household.

Early afternoon. They are gathered at the ancient arched entrance of Shadow Black. Crumbling stonework, a faded family crest, clawing tangled ivy hang behind them, a backdrop. Great oak doors stand open, expectant.

Centrally before them, in a curious chair, is a man perhaps as ancient as the house itself. Is he alive? And how can he live? For half his face is a ruin of scars; where the eye should be, on that side, is only an empty socket. In its immaculate suit, is this object perhaps a shop dummy, salvaged from fire, pressed back grotesquely into service again?

But an eye, we detect, flickers in the other side of the face. Could that be feeling, evidence of sensation? (Look – closer! – the hands are trembling.)

Behind the hideous thing, standing stiffly to his right, is a tall man we might assume to be an undertaker, not unhandsome: perhaps, on a mellow evening, we might even think him young. But the sunlight, this soothing gold molasses, is unkind.

The others are arrayed to the old man's left. Upper ranks are clustered on the terrace; the lesser trail down the thirteen stone steps – describe a stiff arc against the crumbly banister, spill onto the drive.

Shall we review them, our troops – our troupe?

First, and most magnificent – queen to the old man's king? – is a mountainous woman dressed all in gold. (Woman? Is she some object of Aztec worship?) In any case, let us confess, she is the first thing we noticed: respect deflected us to the master of the house (and somehow, too, to his expectant undertaker). The huge woman has about her, on this golden day, the air of one who has surpassed herself: it flashes unmistakably from her gold-coloured lips and eyes, the golden tendrils of her filigree-work wig. A huge collar, rising behind her head, is shaped into a cartoon sunburst. In her arms she cradles – is it living, or some fetish? – a little white animal in a golden collar, its furry back covered in a glittering cape.

Catching every light of the sun's intense rays, the woman seems fuelled by a fusion of her own.

Beside her is an ugly little man in a bow tie, his bald head gleaming as if newly waxed; by contrast the young man beside him is tall and handsome, with dark luxuriant hair (he seems, perhaps, a little too aware of his own manly beauty; he reminds us of a model in an after-shave advertisement: a bit of a cad?). His hand toys idly with the fingers of the girl who stands on his left (fair, just a little plump: rather plain, beside him?). To the fair girl's left, a straw-headed boy grimaces, running a finger round the inside of his collar. It is not choking him, surely: evidently an ungainly boy. He has shifted position, we surmise, several times: we come across him with one leg on the terrace (his knee is bent), the other on the top step of the stairs.

After the boy comes a black-garbed butler, admirable in the art of standing at attention; a stout cook, her hair in a bun...

Our eyes pass quickly over these lesser personages, noting with satisfaction the scrubbed cheeks, the starched aprons, the hair slicked down with water; if we shudder a little at one regrettable girl, her face disfigured by a hare lip, our eyes pass swiftly on; impatiently we sweep our distaste aside. There is hardly time.

At the foot of the stairs we turn back to our troupe. Have we drilled them well? Are they ready at last?

But wait – we pause.

Something is wrong.

Could we have forgotten our leading lady?

Oh, but this is absurd, absurd! Our gossamer hands beat our aery head! Is she hiding? Has she disguised herself? (There is no *extra parlourmaid*, is there?)

Amateurs, we sob, *amateurs...*

But here comes the crunch of tyres against gravel! Like a startled insect we flit back up our staircase; hover at the shoulder of our crippled old man. Looking through his good eye we see rock, water, air, the drenching radiant fire of the sun... and swinging into the foreground a battered Silver Ghost.

Stately, it stops by the thronged staircase.

Our old man sees the driver alight, a white-garbed figure in a Panama hat; first – it is a preliminary – the white man helps from the back seat a slender, strange girl. (She too is dressed in white, a white somewhat more immaculate than his: a crisp white dress, a matching peaked cap, white worsted stockings, even shoes of blanched leather! And what is it that flashes on the slope of one breast? A *watch*, perhaps, hanging upside down on a chain? Only the hair somewhat spoils the effect. Raven-dark, it drapes freely over her shoulders...)

The nurse stands to one side; the man in white walks to the left of the motor-car, slowly, with proper dignity – the old man's eye is blurring! We leap to the lady in gold, the hairless little bow-tied man – oh, are they all overcome with emotion?

Tall-dark-and-handsome is a safer haven. His flawless eyes, clear as a camera, record the slow progress of the invalid up the stairs, leaning heavily – *so* heavily – on the arm of his mentor. Dispassionately we note the cadaverous, haunted face (the face once, surely, of a handsome man!). His yellow flesh hangs from his skull as his shabby brown suit hangs from his skeleton-frame. The hair is a lifeless disordered mass, a faded dirty blond.

And then the miracle: slowly – it seems our film is running down! – the old man rises from his curious chair. There are gasps of shock – the golden lady is sobbing! Tall-dark-handsome – even him! – draws in his toothpaste breath a little sharply.

For three faltering steps the old man shuffles forward. His arms are outstretched. He hovers at the head of the stairs, precariously.

"My son!" The words erupt from his lips. He falls into the arms of the brown-suited invalid.

Help is at hand, of course, at once – the undertaker, the little man, even the handsome one. Earnestly they assist the man in white.

The decrepit father, the decrepit son, are ushered through the portals of the ancient house.

Before the scene ends there is a lingering moment. The girl – the fair girl – has hung back timorously. She is left alone – she thinks she is alone. She turns in the great arched doorway, looking up at the sky. Ah, it is brilliant, too brilliant; how such light does not strike her dead at once, she will never comprehend. She thinks of the scene she has mutely witnessed; she thinks of an ancient story she has heard; and all at once – such a foolish illusion! – she imagines a dark veil is drawing across the sky. The sun's golden ball becomes a sable disc; a flaming corona encircles its absence.

She thinks of some lines the man in white whispered to her, one strange morning when he carried her to her room:

The splendours of the firmament of time
May be eclipsed...

How did it go on?

but are extinguished not –

She blinks. The sun returns. She is a silly girl.
Then she sees the nurse at the foot of the stairs. One new arrival, it appears, has been forgotten.
Awkwardly the two girls exchange glances.

30
The Pleasure Faces

"Mr Vox, they're marvellous! Where *ever* did you find them?"

"You don't recognise them, darling girl?"

Again Harriet studied the curious entertainers. The gentleman on the squeezebox was a portly old fellow with a glowing red nose and mutton-chop whiskers, magnificently white; his bowler hat was patterned like a Union Jack, and a fob-chain jiggled on his generous girth. Accompanying him was a comically scraggy old woman who sawed back and forth on a fiddle. Round her gawky limbs billowed a gleaming white gown; tissue-paper garlands of imitation flowers circled her head and her scrawny neck, and glittery powder spangled her wrinkled face and hands. Stamping in time, their old faces beaming, the peculiar pair lurched into yet another chorus of *Yes! We Have No Bananas*.

Some moments passed before Harriet saw beyond the merry tableau to the memory of gimlet eyes fixing her in outrage, a scarecrow hand clutching at her hat, and a dusty sash window crashing down. "They're from the station – Lightletter Station!"

"And quite famous in these parts, too." Mr Vox smiled. He stood with Harriet by a trestle table, his arm around her shoulders.

"And the Punch and Judy man? Who's he?" Harriet looked towards the other end of the beach, where the puppets bobbed in the striped booth.

Mr Vox tossed back his champagne. "Now *that* you must ask Nurse Becher."

Harriet gazed at him, wonderingly. Then she laughed. She was happy, so happy.

"I venture to – to assert there's not a single metaphysical problem which hasn't been solved, or – or for the solution of which the key hasn't *at least* been supplied," cried the hangman, struggling to fit the noose round Mr Punch's neck.

"Space is an *a priori* intuition," taunted the naughty little puppet, and dealt the hangman a fearsome blow with his stick.

Slowly the beaten antagonist subsided from the stage. "It is possible to imagine nothing in space," he gasped, "but impossible to – to imagine *no* space..."

With dispassionate curiosity, Mr Punch watched him disappear.

"The absolute is becoming," the victor observed smartly, dropping his stick.

He bowed.

"Bravo!" called Toby. But his voice was hollow.

"Fit audience, though few," laughed the Professor, when he emerged. The second show had been for Toby alone. Toby, smiling, struggled to show his appreciation, but he didn't succeed.

"*Ach, mein Junge* – something it is wrong, *nein*?" The kindly old face was overspread with concern.

"No – no."

When he arrived on the beach to find the Professor's striped booth, Toby had felt an overwhelming happiness. Mr Vox, he sensed obscurely, had promised him a gift, and here it was. It was as if two worlds he had thought separate had been magically united. But Toby's happiness faded quickly. In the pocket of the cricket shirt he wore over his trunks was a letter he had received that morning.

The party, for Toby, was spoilt.

"Mind if I join you?"

The question seemed necessary.

Yardley sat apart from the others. Smoking, she leaned against the trunk of a beach umbrella, staring absently through her dark glasses, the latest *Hollywood World* unopened on her knees. Her costume was concealed beneath a bright peignoir.

She shrugged; Mark shrugged too and dropped to his knees beside her, his brown body dripping from the sea. He towelled his hair, eyeing her.

"So it's all over," she said, after a moment. She did not look at him.

Yesterday Mark had put the finishing touches to the portrait. Now, under cloth, it waited in the Long Gallery, already fitted to the empty frame. The unveiling was to be the climax of the day's celebrations.

"You'll go back to London. You'll marry that silly girl."

An infinite weariness swept through Mark. He had just completed the greatest achievement of his career (the painting *was* a masterpiece, he knew it). His spirit was soaring, or would soar, and Yardley – Eunice Grubb – would lash him to the dirt. He had thought her a goddess; she was just a woman.

Turning, she smeared the glasses from her face. "You could've taken longer – "

He had motioned to leave, but dropped back down. Today was the first day Yardley had appeared to the others since she had fainted, the night before Peter arrived. Now, as she stared at him, Mark could not disguise his shock.

"You really are ill…"

Yardley only tossed her cigarette aside and swigged from a liberal measure of bourbon. Swilling the liquid round her teeth like mouthwash, she gazed with vacant eyes at the cover of her magazine. Marilyn Monroe stared up at her luxuriously, in a Technicolor still from *The Seven-Year Itch*.

"Christ, what a slut." Yardley tossed the magazine aside. She lit another cigarette, her hands shaking. "Do you love her?"

"Marilyn Monroe?"

Yardley didn't laugh. Mark looked across the beach at Harriet, smiling and laughing with Mr Vox. Her flaxen hair flashed gold in the sun. She was wearing her stars and stripes costume – or rather, Yardley's.

"Yes, I love her." He hadn't admitted it to Yardley before. Perhaps not even to himself, not really.

"You're a fool."

"No."

"You're all fools." Yardley's hand – and Mark saw that the flesh had withered – clawed at his arm. "Vox is playing you all for fools." She laughed, and jiggling at her throat was a suggestion of crepey skin.

"Paul Whiteman Orchestra?"
"Mm. No."
"They used to be your favourites, Cora."
"They did rather tire me out after a while."
"Irving Kaufman?"
"Not loud enough, Jelly. See if you can find a Mr *Joseph Turner*. Just the ticket, I think."

Jellicoe Travers squatted by the gramophone, inspecting the box of records; Mrs Van Voyd, humming a little tune, was engaged in the delicate operation of fitting a film into her Kodak box brownie, which she had found that morning after an extensive search. As she pondered the arcana of science she listened happily to the monologue that drifted from beneath the next umbrella.

"I'm glad to be done with those wretched sittings. I had a perfectly good portrait, of course. Collidge would remember it. Damned thing was bombed to bits with the old Telescope House… damned good portrait. Or perhaps it was a photograph… something wrong with it, anyway…"

Peter smiled. It was five days since his homecoming. From the moment of returning home the broken heir had kindled, slowly yet certainly, into new life. Yet still his shattered memory would not stir. When he had first entered Shadow Black he had cried, not because he remembered everything, but because he remembered nothing. Today, in the umbrella's shadow, he looked again almost as he had looked when he was young. Only the looseness with which his shirt hung from his shoulders suggested his long sufferings. In dark glasses, his hair brushed forward, he sat almost silent at the centre of his party, every so often drawing slowly on the cigarette he held in the pincer of his damaged hand.

"I wonder about these wireless waves," he said at last, "these waves in the air. Do you think they're doing things to us?"

Lord Harrowblest puffed his pipe. "Probably are," he said after a moment. "Damned right, probably are."

Dear Bunger, thought Mrs Van Voyd. An irrational happiness coursed through her, and all at once she solved her scientific dilemma. As her film snapped into place she looked up joyfully at the old man and his son. Lord Harrowblest sat in his scroll-backed chair. Peter, by his side, was in a chintz chair like her own. Father and son wore matching scarlet robes.

Harrowblest stared at her. "Goodness, Cora, what a ridiculous old woman you've become," he said, not unkindly. It was the first time since he came down from the tower that he had addressed her directly. Beneath her heavy makeup the old woman blushed. She was wearing a wig of long blonde hair, and a scantily-cut bikini. Beneath the bikini, skin-tight fleshings over her limbs and torso simulated the appearance of youthful tanned skin, while tight – and unfortunately somewhat visible – corseting beneath the fleshings constrained her bulk to a considerable degree. But Mrs Van Voyd showed no evidence of suffering.

She was young. She was beautiful.

"Dear Bunger," she murmured aloud, then attempted: "Bunger, what happened to Charles?"

"Charles? You mean Collidge?" the old man grunted. "Seems to have drowned himself," he chuckled, stuffing a pipe.

Lord Harrowblest had ordered Collidge to go swimming, declaring that it would do him good. The assistant, his dignity evidently affronted, sweeping up his balance sheets from beside his Lordship's chair, had trudged off ludicrously in his undertaker's suit.

"Those servants must have lunch ready soon," Mrs Van Voyd said brightly. But she was feeling a little breathless.

"Is this shade taken?"

It was Mr Vox, perching lightly on the side of her chair.

"Dear Adam – " Mrs Van Voyd began gratefully.

Harriet, hovering beside him, mused suddenly, "That girl is strange – "

"Nurse Becher?" asked Mrs Van Voyd.

"Hm. That costume – "

"I thought it rather attractive, Ariette."

"She should wear her uniform," Harriet said firmly.

It was a reasonable view: Nurse Becher had seen fit to attend their celebrations in a cheap evening dress, coloured a gaudy red; her dark hair was concealed beneath a buttery-gold wig; her face was lurid with makeup, and the effect was completed with imitation jewellery of the sort one might win at a fairground, or find spread in jumbled heaps on a fleamarket stall. The girl looked ridiculous, and other things besides, and to cap it all was drinking to excess. Harriet felt a surge of outrage.

"Where did you find her, Mr Vox?" she asked, with restraint.

"Oh, these agencies – "

"My goodness!" burst out Mrs Van Voyd.

They all looked up. Standing before them was Charles Collidge.

"They're a little moth-eaten, I'm afraid, my Lord, but…" He trailed off. He was referring to the bathing trunks he must have kept since his youth, and now wore. His body appeared to be entirely hairless and his rib-cage pushed painfully against his pallid flesh.

"… But they should suffice," he blundered on.

And turning, with attempted dignity, he trotted away.

Like a theme tune, the continuing refrain of *Yes! We Have No Bananas* followed him to the water's edge.

Meanwhile, Jellicoe Travers still sifted through the records. "*Shake, Rattle and Roll?*" he said doubtfully, holding up a disc.

"That's the one, Jelly," said Mrs Van Voyd. She leaned confidentially towards Harriet and Mr Vox. "We thought we might send a – a *signal* to our musicians."

"Oh, you two! They're splendid!" Harriet cried.

"One doesn't deny it, my dear," said Mr Travers. "But their repertoire, you must admit, is limited. I'm afraid even *Yes! We Have No Bananas* palls after the first hour or so."

Harriet laughed.

"Herr Vox." Heike had appeared, holding out a glass of champagne to her employer.

"For me? Shouldn't you be tending your charge?"

Heike made a strange, momentary wailing sound. "You said you – you said – " Her hand spasmed open. The glass fell onto Mr Vox's thigh, soaking into the trousers of his dirty white suit.

He leapt up.

Heike turned on her heel.

"She did that on purpose," said Harriet, rising.

"She's highly strung," Mr Vox muttered. He set off in pursuit of her.

"Really," said Mrs Van Voyd. "Doesn't seem the most suitable sort of girl for *service*... Help me up, Ariette. Come on, Aldous. We must catch silly old Charles in action." She flourished her box brownie.

"*Shall* I play this record?" said Mr Travers. He swigged his tonic water. Shrugging, he gave the gramophone-handle a brisk efficient winding and set the turntable spinning. He dropped the needle. "Miss Locke, the pleasure – oh dear, how *does* one dance to music like this?"

In the water, Mr Collidge contemplated his predicament. He had waded out far enough to be able to crouch and conceal himself entirely but for his head. Would it be possible, he wondered, to perfect a sort of *scurrying motion* along the bottom, and simultaneous circling movements of the arms, which, combined, might create *the effect* of the powers of natation? And would this be adequate? It was more difficult than he had hoped; the water did tend to *buoy one up* so...

"Charles – smile!" called Mrs Van Voyd.

His grimace was terrible. He only hoped he was amusing his Lordship. But Lord Harrowblest's eye was elsewhere.

"We used to call him 'Jellygo'," he observed tartly, shouting over the raucous music. "Great sense of his own importance. And what did he come to? A purveyor of minstrel tunes. This sort of trash, no doubt."

The trash – as Harrowblest called the rhythm and blues classic – was interrupted by a gong for luncheon. When the servants came to lift his Lordship's chair towards the table, Peter said blandly: "He promised me a surprise."

"Mm?"

"Jellygo. He said he had a special surprise for me. Later."

Later

She could have been floating. Mrs Van Voyd rose and subsided on gentle, soporiferous waves. The sun, descending in the sky, had crept beneath the angle of the umbrella, beneath its drooping impossible petals coloured, in turn, red, yellow, orange and gold. Basting her languor with its golden honey, it created behind the old woman's sky-blue eyelids a little universe of amaranth stars – darting, colliding, exploding perpetually.

Lunch had been filling. The old woman slumped in Peter's armchair. Beside her in his scroll-backed chair was the sleeping Bunger, snoring a little. Turning towards him, her eyes flickering open, she found herself filled with an impossible tenderness. Tentatively she fingered the flesh of his forearm, rumpling back the sleeve of his scarlet robe, feeling his leaden, resolute pulse. She breathed deeply, then roved daringly higher, exploring, with dazed wonderment, the immemorial contours of his jaw, his face. The ruined flesh caught beneath her trembling fingers.

In the distance Peter Harrowblest paddled in the shadows, and Harriet held his hand. Intermittently, from further up the beach, came the surprised *pock!* of a ball against a bat. Cries of glee or mock-despair were succeeded inevitably by laughter.

There was a closer laughter. Mrs Van Voyd felt a sudden coldness. The source of the shadow staggered back; a glass of bourbon swayed in its hand.

"A tender scene." The voice twisted with contempt. Yardley's hair fell across her eyes, a tousled mass. She had lost her sunglasses and her face, puckered against the light, was scored with deep lines.

Harrowblest was stirring.

"Yarder – " Mrs Van Voyd was worried. All through lunch her friend had been silent, only drinking recklessly.

Yardley swigged back a great gulp of bourbon. Swishing it in her mouth like a child collecting spit, she lurched forward wildly. The bitter liquid spurted in her husband's face.

There was a cry from the cricketers; Professor Becher had bowled out Collidge.

"Let her go," Lord Harrowblest said wearily, as Yardley rushed towards the cliff-face steps. "Let her go. She hates our happiness."

They did not see Yardley again that afternoon.

The strangest of all the *Astronomical Stories* was 'The Pleasure Faces' by

John Hatton Quincy (August 1948). The story was set on a planet called Xaxon in the galaxy of Andromeda, where there lived creatures whose faces changed, quite literally, according to the seasons. There were two seasons on Xaxon, a long winter lasting some five earth years, and – because of the strange shape of the planet's orbit – a short summer, merely a matter of weeks. In the frozen winter the faces of the Xaxonians were of a hard metallic sheen, appropriate (as it happened) to the hard metallic reasoning in which they engaged during this time. But in the summer, which came suddenly, their faces would all at once wholly alter in molecular structure, the flesh taking on the viscid impressible amorphous texture of thick runny toffee.

Then they could play; the greatest pleasure a Xaxonian could know was to plunge his hands into the glutinous glop of his summer face, twisting, contorting, teasing out great strings of malleable formless gum. But there was a danger to this pleasure, a danger so acute that to many it was imperative to desist from it entirely. Carried along on his tide of joy, the face-manipulator could easily forget how soon the summer would end; and if his face were not patted smoothly back into place when winter fell it would remain, for the next five years, frozen in disfigurement. Those who displayed in winter the evidence of their summer pleasures were shunned, cast out from the society of metallic reason. Called Pleasure Faces, they became objects of derision, even of horror. Many felt that such imprudent indulgence should even be punishable by death...

Toby shifted uneasily in the deckchair. Why was he thinking about 'The Pleasure Faces'? The laughter of the cricketers rippled towards him like blown paper over the sand.

He picked up the warm glass that lay beside his chair.

"I was a philosopher," came a voice. "I was writing a book – "

It was Mr Punch. Unexpectedly he had returned to the stage.

"You are a philosopher, Mr Punch!" cried Toby emotionally, absurdly.

The little puppet ignored the interruption. "I was writing a book," he resumed. "It was all about the existence of – things. Whether they are really there, or are all just illusory. Increasingly I became convinced that they *were* illusory, that we inhabit a world of mere appearances.

I did not believe that these appearances concealed anything of – oh, let us say, a *spiritual* nature; I did not believe that the world was a 'dream of God' – I merely believed it did not exist."

Toby found himself screwing up his forehead. He sat forward intently. Something seemed to have happened to Mr Punch; he had changed. And why was the little puppet speaking like this, in the past tense, so wistfully?

"Go on, Mr Punch," Toby urged.

Mr Punch went on.

"I decided I would not allow this illusory reality to impose upon me any longer. To live with the knowledge of the 'insubstantial pageant' would be to live with the knowledge that nothing was of consequence. If one's actions were illusions, so were the consequences of those actions. But merely to *assume* this was not enough. Could one perhaps, by rigorous mental training, forego the illusion entirely, be *actually confronted* with the true nature of the world? Imagine waking from rest so intense that its stillness had spread into the air around you, arresting the dancing particles – for visible things, I knew, were a chain of vibrating molecules, jigging before our eyes too rapidly for us to see their incessant imbecile jigging.

"But why could we not see it? *Because we ourselves were somehow in tune with it*, we ourselves in such constant inner agitation as to vibrate with the vibration. My efforts, I saw, must be to *slow myself down*; by deep meditation to still the imbecile jigging inside myself. Then, when I was *out of time* with the external world, I should *see* its vibrations clearly... And in time, I *could* see them. But where, I asked myself, did these *outer vibrations* come from? And I saw that they came from me. I had barely begun to still myself! For if I could still myself yet further, I saw, my stillness would seep out into the world around me, and the world around me – at last – would *stop*.

"*This is truth consciousness.* In the first stage we become able to see the vibrations; in the second stage, we stop them."

Mr Punch ceased.

"And what would there be then?" Toby asked earnestly.

"Nothing," said Mr Punch. "A deep and profound awareness of

nothing."

He vanished from the stage.

It was only then, as Toby applauded, that he glanced along the beach to where several servants of both sexes, the two old musicians, and Collidge, and Vardell, and Mr Travers, and – yes – Professor Gustav Becher were engaged in their comical cricket match.

When Toby looked back to the booth he saw, emerging above the puppet-stage, the lank colourless hair, the curiously lambent eyes, the sun-browned old-young cheeks, the strange sagacious grin of Mr Vox.

"Does any of it come back to you?"

He cast down his eyes. "I remember – oh, a certain shape of rock, and the sea, and – something about a boat. A blue boat. But I don't know what it means."

They were standing still, the shallows of the tide running round their feet. Harriet took Peter's hurt hand in hers, careful to hold it only lightly. As she looked up reassuringly at his hanging face, she saw again, deep beneath the debris of his beauty, the young man in the photograph Mr Travers had shown her. For an instant both faces seemed present to her equally. How cruel life was, how unutterably cruel!

She said gently:

"Peter, do you remember what Mr Travers said to you?"

He did not; it seemed, indeed, that he had forgotten who Mr Travers was. But a little later Peter said, suddenly:

"He promised me a surprise."

A rebellion took place on the planet Xaxon. Those who were disfigured for the five years of winter, the outcasts known as the Pleasure Faces, refused any longer to accept their abject status. They refused even to consider themselves disfigured. The purpose of summer, their manifesto declared, was to indulge pleasure to its utmost. In the long winter a face marked by pleasure was not evil but good, a reminder of rejuvenating joys to come.

For a time the rebellion bordered on success. Unpleasure Faces sided with the Pleasure Faces. The High Xaxonians retreated to a bunker, deep beneath their besieged capital. But the wiles of the High Xaxonians were profound.

There was a flaw in the position of the Pleasure Faces. Their faces, frozen in winter into strange uneven shapes, were vulnerable to attack as the smooth, hard, metallic features of Unpleasure Faces were not. The molecular structure of a Pleasure Face was unstable. And so at the moment of their triumph, as they declared the city of reason theirs, the rebel leaders met their shocking end.

A ray directed from the bunker beneath the city shattered quite literally the Pleasure Faces, as a singer's high note shatters glass.

It was almost evening.

In her gaudy costume, in the rays of the late sun, Heike would have looked like a painted doll. The impression would have been strengthened, for an observer, by the way she sat, sack-like in a deckchair over the wooden arms – her back against one arm, her legs over the other.

But no one observed her, not now. The party clustered further down the beach, around the armchairs where Lord Harrowblest held court; around the trestle tables where the old musicians, their art long abandoned, hovered like crows round the remnants of the food, and were shooed off uselessly by tired servants; around the gramophone where Peter and Harriet, Mrs Van Voyd and Mr Vox, Mark Vardell and – no, it wasn't Yardley! – danced in sticky clinches to a faded waltz.

Mark was reduced to dancing with Milly!

Heike shifted her position, but listlessly: her discomfort seemed barely to matter to her at all. She had pulled off her blonde wig and it lay in the sand; her hair beneath was a sweaty, compacted mass. Without urgency she sloshed back the remnants of her drink; she gazed at the empty stage of the puppet booth; then she looked contemptuously towards the party: at Mr Vox in that old woman's arms; at Toby slumped drunkenly at her father's feet. *Poor Toby*, she thought, *you're just a substitute now.* Her father had found a new friend. Heike knew the signs: for some hours that afternoon he had been deep in discussion with the little composer.

But now silly little Mr Travers had disappeared.

Draped across the back of Heike's chair was a crumpled white shirt. Idly the drunken girl fingered the fabric. She felt the edges of a folded piece of paper, and sliding it from the pocket, she opened and inspected it. It was a letter, typed with evident haste in grey uneven characters. There was no address, or date.

```
Dear Chance (it read),
    This will have to be short. You're the only
person I'm writing to and I trust you to BURN THIS
and say nothing about it to ANYONE. Thumbscrews
will be no excuse!!
    Perhaps I could try and explain everything, prop-
erly in detail & all that, but I just can't. All I
know is you're going to hear things about me next
term, so I want you to have SOME idea of the truth.
    Rachel & I are going away together. We're leaving
tonight. Her parents found out about us. I mean
they found out EVERYTHING - there was more than I
let on. Now they're going to tell Miriam & bloody
Hosepipe & make the most frightful fuss.
    We're getting out. That's all I can say.
    Chancer, I can imagine your elaborate sarcasm
about all this but you'd be WRONG. There are some
things you can't understand unless you're in
someone else's head. But I've got to stop now,
there are things to do.
    I'll remember you (the one thing that made Melton
tolerable!!).
    Remember me.
    Eugene Eric Lomax
```

With a disinterest that was almost entire, Heike began to peruse the epistle again, studying with a mindless fascination the black holes punched in the paper by the full stops, the broken ellipsis of the big C in *Chance*, the twin rigid stalks of the double exclamation marks. How meaningless it all was; its meaninglessness resounded like the emptiness of a drum.

"Heike." Toby swayed above her. "Mr Vox says to come – "

Heike looked up, the letter crumpling in her hand. "Tell Herr Vox – " She broke off. She plucked up her glass from the arm of the deckchair; finding it empty, she threw it along the sand.

"What's that in your hand?" said Toby, suddenly alarmed.

Heike, rising unsteadily to her feet, kicked the deckchair away with contempt. *"You're the only person I'm writing to – I'll remember you,"* she intoned vacuously, waving the crumpled letter in the air.

"Give me that!" Flushing, Toby lurched towards her.

Heike pirouetted off, her red gown swirling. "Poor little English schoolboy, lost his little *Liebling!*"

"Give it to me!" Toby shouted. He was chasing her over the sand. He grabbed her, ripping out the shoulder of her dress. Spinning towards him, with wild hands she rent apart the letter, flinging the tattered remnants in his face.

"You bitch!"

Later, when he recalled the incident, burning with shame and horror, Toby saw himself as if in slow motion subsiding to the wet sand with the screaming Heike, sloshing into the shallows, her luridly made-up face beneath him twisting and contorting. With preternatural slowness, his buttocks squelched deeply into her belly, his left hand pushed against her chest to hold her down, and he swung his right hand back and forth, back and forth, like a pendulum striking her face. How slowly, how very slowly, the blood welled in her mouth!

As if in a dream he was dragged from the girl.

It was Vardell who clutched him, holding his wrists. Toby broke away. But his passion was spent. He sunk back to the sand, where Heike lay gasping. He looked at her, astonished, then slowly raised his eyes. A circle of faces stared down at him. At once, the faces became a mere blur – his eyes had filled with tears – but forever, he thought afterwards, he would remember just one: the Professor's, hovering above his daughter in astonished terror, his wire beard trembling. As he gazed down at her the old man was muttering syllables that could have been a mantra, could have been some Jewish prayer – only Toby recognised them as the name, now muttered softly, which the Professor had in the past cried out in horror: *Franz Schneider. Franz Schneider.*

The sun swung lower in the evening sky.

"Look!"

It was Mrs Van Voyd who cried out.

"I don't believe it!" said Mark Vardell.

"Peter, this is it!" said Harriet, suddenly joyous, and Toby's strange behaviour was forgotten at once. Chugging towards the party was a little blue boat, piloted unsteadily by a waving Mr Travers.

"I don't understand," Mrs Van Voyd wailed. "Where *ever* did Jelly–?"

"It's *Bluefinch*, Peter." Harriet clutched his arm, leaping with excitement. "*Bluefinch, Bluefinch!*" And almost dragged by him, she sloshed into the water.

"Oh, *Bluefinch* – " Peter sobbed. His arms extended as if to embrace the little boat that swept rapidly towards him. Mr Travers, rocking wildly, was upright on his knees in the stern, whooping. The sun's shooting rays made the moment golden.

Toby staggered forward, his face pale with terror. He felt as if the fabric of the cosmos were splitting; he felt as if a dimension, separate and inviolate, had been crashed by some vicious God into another, shattering all to atoms...

This could not happen.

Only as Mr Travers ran *Bluefinch* into the shallows did the true significance of the moment become clear. For perhaps three seconds, as if that were all he needed, Peter ran his good hand in wonderment over the cracked prow, his head flung back like a blind man's, experiencing all through touch. When he turned back to the astonished party on the beach his eyes and hair seemed to glow. The onlookers parted as he ran back through the shallows, up on the sand to the scroll-backed throne where Lord Harrowblest had sat, like an unintervening God, mute witness to the joy and terror of this scene and the last.

Peter fell to his knees in the sand.

"Father?" he whispered.
"Oh – " Harrowblest clutched his son's mutilated hand.

31
The Unveiling

Scarlet curtains concealed the panel of the wall. Beside the curtains hung a braided rope, ending in a golden tassel.

Harriet, contemplating the arrangement, found herself thinking absurdly of a theatre, as if when the curtains parted they would reveal not the static aspect of Lord Harrowblest, rendered in oils, but instead the tempestuous vista of a stage.

She checked herself. Such a thought was disloyal to Mark, as if the portrait were not exciting enough. Dear Mark! She smiled at him, then shivered, for the evening had drawn in cold. Fires crackled in the ornate fireplaces, but a chill wind insinuated itself into the Long Gallery nonetheless. The gables of Shadow Black were darkening rapidly and the line of narrow windows was becoming a line of mirrors, reflecting the room, the party, the portraits.

The gallery had been transformed for the ceremonial occasion. Midway down its length, ready for the dinner that would follow the unveiling, was a great baronial table, laden with silver and gold; sofas and armchairs lined the walls by the windows; the grand piano had been imported from the Great Hall. From the ceiling, as for a parade, hung a line of flags, stretching the length of the gallery, in which Union Jacks alternated with pennants depicting an eagle against a blazing sun – heraldic emblem of the Harrowblest family, and corporate symbol of the Empire. Covering the empty wall at the end of the gallery was a huge map of the world. The countries of the Empire were shown in gold; unconquered territories – Antarctica, the Soviet Union, mainland China – were black.

Seven had gathered there for the evening's performance. A little apart from Harriet and Mark sat Mr Vox, listening with a smile to Mrs Van Voyd, who had marked the artistic occasion, not quite appropriately, with what she called her 'mistress of Paul Gauguin' costume. Lord Harrowblest, restored to his electronic chair, whirred slowly along the line of portraits, expatiating on his ancestry to the wondering Peter. Mr Collidge hovered behind them.

"How poor Bunger has dreamed of this day," Mrs Van Voyd was saying.

"Indeed," said Mr Vox, "indeed."

It was time for the unveiling. That Toby or Yardley should take their places in the party was inconceivable – both had retired, distraught, to their rooms. The others waited only for Mr Travers, who had insisted on supervising the putting-to-bed of the Professor and Nurse Becher.

"Shall we begin?" said Lord Harrowblest, impatient, when Mr Travers appeared at last.

They gathered about the concealed portrait, their glasses freshly charged. The ceremony had about it a mechanical air. Mark spoke first, his expression a little too animated, his hands twisting nervously. He said that though he was an artist of some renown (he would forego the vanity of false modesty) his work until now seemed to him the merest dust and ashes in the light (he was bold enough to say) of the new depth his painting had acquired at Shadow Black. Whether his portrait conveyed adequately the character and qualities of his Lordship was for others (of course) to decide, but the artist knew that even if what he had done was judged a failure by all the world he had yet (in his own estimation) achieved the greatest triumph of his career. His time at Shadow Black (moreover) had been the happiest he had known, made happier still by the presence of the young lady who was shortly to become his wife...

Polite applause. Harriet blushed; Mrs Van Voyd made delighted exclamations.

Lord Harrowblest, whirring forward, spoke of the tradition of the family portraits (here in this gallery for all to see), of the great line of which young Vardell's work was now a part. He spoke of his illustrious ancestors; of the glory of the family; of the glories it had known, of the glories yet to come. His voice rising, he spoke of the Empire. At last, rapturously, he reached for Peter's hand:

"... I believed, indeed, that the Empire would end with me. In my despair, I even imagined its greatest days had passed. I see now that we have scaled but the merest foothills – that ice-capped peaks yet rise before us in all their exhilarating splendour. Oh my son, what mountains we shall climb!"

The hollowness rang down the gallery like a bell. Standing beside his father, Peter's face was blank.

As the applause for Lord Harrowblest subsided, Mr Travers, skipping to the piano, crashed into a chorus of *Land of Hope and Glory* (something imperial seemed appropriate). Harriet clasped Mark's hand. Mrs Van Voyd seized a fresh bottle of champagne, prising at the cork with eager thumbs. Lord Harrowblest, reaching up, pulled the braided rope. There were shocked gasps as the curtains drew back.

Mark cried out.

Harriet screamed.

Land of Hope and Glory suddenly stopped.

Mrs Van Voyd dropped the champagne to the floor.

"Oh my Lord – " breathed Collidge. Harrowblest had slumped forward, as if in stabbing pain.

"No – " said Mr Vox.

"I don't understand – " said Peter.

The portrait had been slashed repeatedly with a knife.

Toby was running.

He sprinted freely, heedless of direction. Only on the cliff path, catching his breath, did he realise where he was going. The sky was the aching grey-blue of a bruise. In the dim light, descending to the beach was dangerous. Toby didn't care. Recklessly he slithered down the rocky steps.

Then it was easy: *Bluefinch* was there for him, drawn up the sand where Travers had left her.

As the others had waited for the unveiling, Toby had been waiting too, pressed back behind a suit of armour, in the corridor outside the Professor's room. For a time it seemed that Travers would never leave, but when the little man was gone at last, Toby slipped through the door. At once the curious sensation came to him that he had stepped onto a stage, stumbled out from the wings while a performance was in progress. He stood blinking, frightened.

In a white nightshirt, the Professor sat propped on many pillows in the soft glow of a reading lamp. On his drawn-up knees was a huge book, like a magician's book of spells, and on the end of his arm was Mr Punch, his wooden nose pressed voraciously into the pages. The leather satchel lay open by the hearth and Judy, the baby, the priest, the doctor, the policeman, the hangman, the crocodile and the Devil were arranged carefully on the mantelpiece, warmed by the crackling fire beneath.

The Professor looked up. His expression at first was kindly – then alarmed.

To Toby, what happened next was only a blur of horror. He ran to the bed; he blurted his apologies. The Professor cowered, whimpering, then crying out *"Franz Schneider! Franz Schneider!"* When Toby in desperation tried to plead with Mr Punch, the old man flung up his arm like a lash. His frantic hand knocked against the reading lamp. Suddenly the room went black, and Mr Punch was flying through the air.

As Toby wrenched open the door – desperate only to flee the stage – the last thing he saw, in the sudden light from the corridor, was the little puppet, empty on the floor, his huge nose snapped cleanly from his face.

How it ends

Laughter, off.

Laughter, wild and crazed.

For a moment the party exchange shocked glances. From where does the laughter come?

In mute terror, Mrs Van Voyd *points to the map. The huge map of the Empire – which covers the concealed door in the wall – seems almost to be pulsing, vibrating.* Harriet *swoons. A great vertical gash opens in the map, slashing relentlessly down the Greenwich meridian.*

With drunken aplomb, as if expecting applause, YARDLEY *lurches through the opening, her hair a dishevelled ugly mass, her haggard face a mask of hate. Still she wears the costume of the afternoon, but now the bright peignoir is soiled and hangs open, revealing the rumpled dark bathing suit beneath.*

MARK   (*helplessly, he gestures at the portrait*): Yardley – Yardley, why?

YARDLEY   (*flourishing knife towards her husband*): Why? To destroy him… destroy him, as he destroyed me – him, and his sickening son. You wanted to know why I married him, Mark? Oh, don't look at me like that, you stupid boy! (*Swings towards Harriet.*) He's asked me often enough, you know. Usually when we're in bed together.

HARRIET *cries out. As if a pendulum, suspended in space, has returned at last to strike, she sees again the terrible night of the storm – sees, too, that she has been under an enchantment.*

Now the enchantment is broken. With a cry, she flails towards MARK. *She beats him, scratches him. He slaps her; she screams again. Only* MRS VAN VOYD *can restrain her. Sobbing,* HARRIET *collapses into the old woman's arms.*

YARDLEY *studies her knife; then, turning, smiles at* MARK. *Dishevelled, he pushed back his hair, adjusts his collar; dabs with a handkerchief at his bloodied face.*

YARDLEY   (*after a pause*): Why did I marry him? I had to. Collidge, that viper who does his bidding, said –

MRS VAN VOYD: Yard, this is absurd. God help him, but Bunger loves you. You loved him too, you told me.

YARDLEY   (*horrified*): Could I love that – that hideous thing?

MRS VAN VOYD: He's a great man –

YARDLEY: Great man? He's a fool!

Shadow Black

There are intakes of breath as she swoops towards HARROWBLEST. *He jerks in his chair. Then suddenly she flicks the knife towards* PETER, *who stands, astonished, by his father's chair. He shambles back as the blade prods his chest.* YARDLEY's *voice drops.*

    The fool even believes that *this* is his son!

PETER *moans. Turning, he strikes his fist against the wall. Slowly he slithers to his knees, stricken.*

TRAVERS   (*going to him*): What – what does she mean?

YARDLEY: You're all fools! Vox has played you all for fools, can't you see?

Her eyes dart wildly from one face to another.

MR VOX *stands urbanely by the window, lighting a cork-tipped cigarette.*

MRS VAN VOYD (*quietly*): What do you mean, Yarder?

YARDLEY (*breaking down, knife clattering from her hand*): It can't be Peter – it can't be!

MRS VAN VOYD: What – what does she mean?

COLLIDGE (*stepping forward*): I think perhaps I can clarify matters.

Dressed again in his undertaker's suit, his hair slicked harshly back, the assistant has regained the dignity he had lost that afternoon. His pallid grotesque face is immaculately composed as he begins his narrative, pacing in a relaxed fashion before the ruined portrait.

COLLIDGE: The story begins, I suppose, in July, 1939, when we took over the Vainglory group. It was our greatest thrust yet into the American market. Suddenly we were as important in America as we were in the Empire, and to celebrate our triumph –

MRS VAN VOYD: Charles, I don't see –

COLLIDGE: Please, Mrs Van Voyd. (*He clears his throat.*) To celebrate our triumph, we held a glittering party at the Plaza Hotel in New York – in those days we were not averse to *glittering* parties, and this, you may be assured, was glittering enough. To be invited to our party was, as our American cousins like to say, to *be someone*. Guests included President Roosevelt, Vice-President Garner, William Randolph Hearst, Eugene O'Neill, Henry Ford, Shirley Temple, Louis B. Mayer, Sinclair Lewis, Pearl S. Buck... and a certain Miss Yardley Urban. Naturally it was a great success. I mingled with the guests; his Lordship watched – as was his wont on such occasions – from behind a two-way mirror in the ballroom... Unfortunately – I'm afraid I must say *unfortunately*, in the light of the present evening's events – that night his Lordship studied one guest a little *too* ardently. She was standing obliviously close to the mirror, in deep discussion with a rather ludicrous old woman who was, it appeared, her particular friend.

MRS VAN VOYD: Well, really – !

COLLIDGE (*overriding her*): Being the sort of man he was, his Lordship not surprisingly had taken little interest in the world of entertainment – for its own sake, that is. His knowledge of the motion picture industry was a knowledge of shares, of budgets, of profits and losses. But I'm afraid that from the moment he saw Miss Urban he realised, all at once, the beguiling glamour of the screen –

MRS VAN VOYD: Charles, I've heard this a hundred times –

COLLIDGE: Mrs Van Voyd, really – our guests, I'm sure, have not heard as much. (*And he almost smiles.*) His Lordship vowed that night that Miss Urban would be his wife. Of course he apprised me of his wish, and it was my duty to ensure it came true. But I'm afraid we had a little more difficulty with Miss Urban than we had experienced with the Vainglory group – didn't we, Mrs Van Voyd? I seem to remember it was you who introduced us – later I believe you even pleaded our case.

MRS VAN VOYD: To my shame –

COLLIDGE: Shame? Surely not, Mrs Van Voyd. We all did our best. We put our generous terms to her, but the woman remained recalcitrant. A meeting I arranged between Miss Urban and his Lordship was – regrettable, I'm afraid. (*Placing a hand on his employer's shoulder, which is shaking violently:*) I must admit I doubted his Lordship's wisdom in this affair. The only time I ever did – ever have. Still, I recognised too that it was not my place to doubt. I continued my efforts for some two years –

YARDLEY *moans, curling into foetal position on the floor.* Oh, what I suffered –

COLLIDGE *looks down at her with distaste*: At Christmas, 1941, Miss Urban came to London, as some of you may recall, to present her patronising contribution to our war morale. Now, what *was* that show called – ?

TRAVERS: *Showbiz –*

MARK (*bitterly*): *Showbiz Ahoy!*

COLLIDGE: In any case, it was the occasion for a further sally. As it happened young Peter was on leave from the RAF at this time, and we thought it might be suitable to send *him* to state our terms. Until now we had told him nothing of our campaign. But we had been grooming him, after all, as the heir to our Empire, and here was the young man's chance to gain experience of a particularly – *delicate* negotiation. He accepted the assignment eagerly –

MRS VAN VOYD: You – you monster –

COLLIDGE: Not monstrous, only factual –

MRS VAN VOYD: Monstrous! You must have known what Peter was going through. You *knew*, didn't you – ?

COLLIDGE *for the first time lets slip his composure:* What?

MRS VAN VOYD (*choking*): Peter and the Yard were lovers!

COLLIDGE: *What?*

YARDLEY: No! It isn't true –

PETER, *in the arms of* TRAVERS, *begins to whimper.* MRS VAN VOYD *has been clutching* HARRIET *tightly; now she sets the girl gently aside and staggers forward.* (*Hugging herself,* HARRIET *wipes her eyes; when* MARK *moves towards her, she shifts rapidly away, shuddering in disgust. She struggles to focus on the unfolding story.*)

MRS VAN VOYD (*murmurous*): I vowed never to speak of this again. But the truth has to come out. Even Bunger must know it, in the end. (*Gazing at Yardley:*) All these years I've struggled to forgive her. Only God can, now. (*The murmur rises to a pained declamation.*) Charles appears to have forgotten one important guest at the party in 1939. The most important guest, wasn't he, Bunger? – Just fresh from his first year at Oxford. (*She gestures to Peter.*) On the night Bunger fell in love with the Yard, Peter fell in love with her, too.

YARDLEY: No –

HARRIET (*alarmed*): *Peter* was in love with her?

MRS VAN VOYD (*simply*): Peter was in love with her. But of course Peter was a different proposition from poor Bunger – wasn't he, Yard, hm? You took the boy to bed, casually enough. It amused you – a sort of working off of nervous energy, why not? One can hardly condemn you. Unfortunately, for poor Peter, it was the greatest experience of his life. He became obsessed with you, pleaded that you marry him. You refused.

YARDLEY: It was too much. It was all too much –

MRS VAN VOYD: Peter was a sensitive boy, too sensitive. Whether or not we're fools about him now, we certainly were then. From the beginning we cast him as the golden young heir; then he was the hero of the Battle of Britain. Perhaps we expected too much of him – even loved him too much, I don't know. But inside he was cracking apart. I've always thought (*she snuffles back tears*) – I've always thought he could have got over the Yard somehow, if it had all ended simply with their affair. But when he found out she had *given away their child* –

COLLIDGE: What – what *child?* The crone is mad!

By now, servants have appeared, expecting to serve dinner. Looking up, makeup streaming, MRS VAN VOYD *instructs* STAINES *to find* TOBY. *Reluctantly the butler turns from the scene.*

MRS VAN VOYD: It's time he knew the truth – time we all did. Tobias is the Yard's son. Peter is his father.

A stunned silence.

Peter discovered that the Yard was pregnant. He offered her money – several millions, I believe – not to have an abortion, which she threatened to do. She accepted, of course –

TRAVERS: The missing three million -

MRS VAN VOYD: Yes, a large sum did go missing from Empire funds, a little before Peter himself disappeared. I'm sure it will gratify you, Charles (*she looks at him disdainfully*) at least to be able to *account* for it now –

YARDLEY (*wearily*): Oh, Cora, Cora, why are you doing this?

MRS VAN VOYD: Because it's *true*, Yard. You kept your word, didn't you? You had the child, but you'd made no promise to keep it once it was born. Oh, you were a clever concealer, I must say. It wasn't until much later that I discovered the child had been sent to England, to live with your long-suffering sister Bertha and her husband, Albert Chance. I dare say if that hapless couple hadn't been killed in an air raid you need never have seen Tobias again... Peter only knew that the child had gone.

YARDLEY: Oh Cora, you are more of an actress than me. All that time I let you take an interest in my nephew – just indulging some whim of yours, I thought – and there you were, thinking...

MRS VAN VOYD: I didn't think, I *knew*.

TRAVERS: Cora, how *could* you know all this?

MRS VAN VOYD: Because Peter told me – only the day before he disappeared. It must have been shortly after he saw me that you gave him your disgusting *assignment*, Charles. It's your fault that he disappeared. Peter revered his father. He would never have hurt him. But the discovery that his father loved the Yard was too much for him. He snapped. That's why he disappeared and took another name. (*Turning to him:*) It's true, isn't it, Peter? Oh, tell me it's true!

She holds out her arms, but he does not go to her. COLLIDGE *paces restlessly, face cracked in agitation. With shaking hands he fixes himself a scotch. As he does so, he begins to speak, this time in a wild manner, quite different from his earlier cool control.*

COLLIDGE: Have you finished now, Van Voyd – done all the damage you can do? (*Gesturing to* PETER:) Oh, he doesn't recognise you, you stupid bitch, how could he? (*Laughs.*) You think you know the whole story, but you don't, you don't. Only I know it all! Peter accepted my mission – oh, yes he did. He went to see her, backstage at the show. She'd cleared her dressing room, ready for a *scene*... Oh, she should have run out into the street rather than stayed. It wasn't Peter who cracked, it was *her* –

YARDLEY (*suddenly, in agony*): I killed him, I killed him!

MRS VAN VOYD: Yarder, no –

COLLIDGE: Yes! Yes, you killed him!

YARDLEY's *voice is hollow:* He was pleading with me. He wanted me to marry him in secret, or be his lover – oh, he wasn't as faithful to Eddie as you think, Cora. He would have killed his father and given me the Empire if I'd asked it, I know he would –

MRS VAN VOYD: That's not true!

YARDLEY: Oh Cora, Cora, does it matter? I was frightened; he became violent. I struck him; he fell; he hit his head –

COLLIDGE: Yes. Yes. Then you were *really* frightened, weren't you? Peter was dead and *you* had killed him. You telephoned me in desperation – who else could you turn to? I said I'd arrange everything. And the price? That was easy to guess at, wasn't it?

YARDLEY: Yes, yes –

HARROWBLEST (*moaning*): Collidge, is this true – ?

COLLIDGE *kneels by the old man's chair:* Oh my Lord, can you forgive me? To tell you what this vile woman had done, when I knew you loved her so much – I couldn't. Could I destroy all your happiness, all of it? I couldn't do that, could I? I told you your son had disappeared, that was all. But I told you on the same day that if we *said* he was dead, *then* we could make Miss Urban marry you –

HARROWBLEST *cups his ruined head in his hands:* She telephoned you, you said... You went to the theatre... It was long after midnight, everyone was gone... She let you in; you told her to go – she couldn't bear to look at her bloody work again... But when you went to the dressing room, you told me, the body was *gone*... You realised that she had *not* killed him – that my son was wandering somewhere – dazed perhaps, confused... But we would not tell *her* that, no – we would search and search... But in the meantime, I should – I should marry her... She made him go – and until he came back, she would pay and pay... Now you tell me he could *never* come back – now you tell me my son is dead...

COLLIDGE: He *is* dead, my Lord. Oh, forgive me –

HARROWBLEST (*thrusting him away*): Oh – ! Oh – !

HARRIET (*falteringly, staring at the supposed* PETER): But if Peter Harrowblest is dead, then – who is this?

MR VOX, *during all this, has stood by the window, gazing at the reflections of the drama in the panes. He turns now, a long ash crumbling from his cigarette*: This *is* Peter Harrowblest.

There is fear in MRS VAN VOYD'*s voice*. Mr Vox, what do you mean?

MR VOX *moves to her reassuringly*.

MR VOX : Mrs Van Voyd, our friend Mr Collidge has left out part of the story. Understandably, no doubt, but I'm afraid I can hardly protect him in his lies.

COLLIDGE: What are you talking about?

MR VOX: You know very well what I'm talking about, Mr Collidge. You have succeeded until now in an elaborate double bluff. You deceived Yardley, and you deceived his Lordship. What Yardley was too distressed to realise was that Peter was not dead – only stunned.

YARDLEY (*gasping*): Can it be – ?

MR VOX'*s eyes, with their curious lambency, seem to burn into* COLLIDGE'*s*: I repeat, Peter was *not* dead, only stunned. But his head had taken a terrible blow. Gambling that his brain might be damaged, you decided at once to play your desperate hand. You removed him from the dressing room – then some time later you dumped him, in a coma, by a roadside on the Sussex coast. In due course, Peter was found and taken to hospital in Brighton. When, after some days, he awoke, you had already made sure he would be confused about his identity. After all, the doctors and nurses called him 'Mr Haldane' – they would hardly assume the enlistment papers they had found in his jacket were forged. Oh, you were clever – very clever indeed...

COLLIDGE *laughs woodenly*: And you, Mr Vox, are very amusing. (*He slams down his glass.*) This tissue of absurdities is beyond belief!

MR VOX (*stepping close to him*): Is it, Mr Collidge? I don't think so. I don't think so at all. I've been watching you, Mr Collidge. I think there's nothing you'd have wanted more than to get rid of Peter Harrowblest. He'd usurped your place, hadn't he? You were envious of the son and heir – you were then, and you are now!

COLLIDGE: No!

He looks about him wildly. He clutches at his forehead, claws at his hair. Staggering back, he sets YARDLEY's *discarded knife spinning beneath his foot. He seizes it, lunging at* MR VOX.

COLLIDGE: I'll kill you!

There is a struggle. The knife clatters from COLLIDGE's *hand. He sinks to the floor. He grovels to* HARROWBLEST, *clawing at the blanket on the old man's knees.*

COLLIDGE: I love you, my Lord, I love you, I love you –

For brief seconds HARROWBLEST *clutches* COLLIDGE's *throat.*

The old man's hands sustain a savage grip. A great vein pounds in his temple and the hideous scarrings of his face flame up. COLLIDGE *cries out; his lips foam; his strangling face is awash with ecstasy.*

Suddenly HARROWBLEST *slumps back, inert.*

COLLIDGE *gasps as the hands fall away. For an instant it seems he would snatch them back, grinding them again into his purpled flesh.*

MRS VAN VOYD *wails, sinking to her knees.*

But all is not yet over.

PETER *grabs at the spinning knife.*

A cry comes – "Haldane!" – and there is a searing light, seeming all at once to fill the gallery, setting every atom of the air ablaze. Later, those who are there shall say – though only to each other – that the light seemed to burst from MR VOX's *eyes.*

But when the light vanishes, MR VOX *is gone.*

For it is too late – too late. Knife in hand, PETER *has sprung at* COLLIDGE. *For perhaps a second, lurid in the strange light, they roll on the floor.*

Then PETER *is stabbing at* COLLIDGE*'s chest, plunging the knife in again and again, again and again as –*

The curtain falls

32
Aftermath

Snow fell softly over Shaftesbury Avenue as Harriet alighted from the taxi. She was late. Her lecture had run on longer than she expected, and the train from Cambridge had been slow. Her heels clicked rapidly over the slushy pavement.

In the doorway of the theatre she paused, ostensibly to slip out her invitation card from her glove. But her heart was pounding in fear – why, it was almost as bad as her first day at Newnham! She gazed through the glass of the lighted doorway. The foyer was empty; the performance had begun. Harriet thought she would turn and leave. Then, from behind a pillar in the red-carpeted expanse, an anxious pacing figure came into view.

Harriet had to smile. It was Mrs Van Voyd. Her cigar smoke clouding the air, the old woman was dressed in what Harriet took to be a suit of mourning, a monstrous arrangement of black feathers and furs surmounted by a top hat which sprouted what appeared to be a bonsai yew tree, its branches painted black. A vast length of veil was thrust back over the brim.

Behind the old woman on a black leash trotted not the fluffy white familiar form of Aldous, but a strange little black dog of similar size and breed.

Harriet's fears were almost stilled. When the invitation had reached her, earlier that week, she had reacted at first with horror. It was outrageous, impossible. But the next day a letter had come from Mrs Van Voyd, and Harriet had seen things differently. *I shall wait for you there*, the old woman had written. *Afterwards we shall go to the party together.* She had reminded Harriet that shortly they most both appear at Peter's trial, and must not do so unprepared. Besides, they must try to forgive.

Harriet steadied her breathing. Adjusting her own modest headpiece, she pushed decisively through the swinging door.

"My dear!" Mrs Van Voyd turned, arms outstretched.

The two women embraced.

"Ariette, I knew you'd come."

"Sorry I'm late. Have we missed much?"

"Don't worry, my dear. We've both *seen it before*, haven't we?"

Harriet laughed, then checked herself as Mrs Van Voyd bent down to gather up her new black dog.

"Is Aldous – ?" Harriet began.

"Died," murmured Mrs Van Voyd sadly, "died."

"Oh – "

There were irritable hisses as the latecomers took their seats, but Mrs Van Voyd only smiled as her yew-tree hat obliterated the view for perhaps fifteen rows behind her. She squeezed Harriet's hand as they stared towards the stage.

The lighting was dim, intended to suggest moonlight on the Florida Keys. On the wharf before the darkened seafood restaurant, Babydoll was alone. She hugged herself with joy. She span a little on her toes, whirling out the hem of her gingham dress. At any moment Tad would come to meet her; to an invisible orchestra they would dance in the moonlight. Then she would tell him about the Cuban's offer – a singing engagement on a luxury yacht! It seemed her dreams were about to be fulfilled. She could not know now that Tad's reaction would be very different from what she might hope. She could not know of the dangers her future held, up against drug-runners on the high seas... Now she was only filled with love, and a familiar prelude played. She stretched out her arms, her fingers brushing the edges of the spotlight that grew ever more intense around her.

A sigh rippled through the theatre as Babydoll led the way – lingeringly, caressingly – to the famous refrain:

> *... I had a bird called loneliness*
> *But now he's flown*
> *Instead I got a boy*
> *To call my own...*

Listening in the darkness, Harriet closed her eyes, and it seemed all at once that the summer had returned. She thought of the film evenings at Shadow Black, and the night in the Great Hall when Yardley had sung this song. She thought of her mornings with Mrs Van Voyd, and the awkward afternoons on the beach with Mark and Yardley. She thought of silly mad little Mr Travers, and Milly, and that dreadful boy Toby (whom she'd decided, in the end, was a little in love with her). She thought of Mark, and what a fool she had been. She thought of the terrible night of the storm.

When she opened her eyes they were blurred with tears.

"She's gorgeous!"
"*Mar*vellous to see her back – "
"I *grew up with her*, of course – "
"... Yes, in the war – the very same theatre!"
"I *can't* believe everything they're saying in the papers – "
"I never knew she could *really* sing!"
"... No! Really? She was born in the East End?"
"*Boston Story*, that was the best – "
"A whole floor of the house just for shoes – "
"*Dar*ling, hel*lo* – "
"She's *still* beautiful – "
"I'm in *love* – "
"*Lovely* – "

It was the interval. Mrs Van Voyd handed Harriet a gin and tonic. "Perhaps, my dear, we might move out of this *crush?*"

The crowd parted for the formidable old woman. "Such a *smoky* atmosphere," she brayed, waving at the air with her freshly-lit cigar.

Someone said: "Who's that old lady in the funny black hat?"

Eyes turned.

"Oh!" cried Harriet. She felt a stab of pain. A camera had flashed in Mrs Van Voyd's eyes; the old woman, stepping back, had crushed Harriet's foot.

"Ma'am – ma'am," an American voice barked. "*Cora Van Voyd*, right?" The thrusting young man grabbed a notebook from his jacket. "Now what our readers Stateside wanna know – "

Mrs Van Voyd thrust him aside. "Really, I have no idea who *Cora Van Voyd* is – "

"Lady, don'cha read the papers?"

"And it's *Mrs Van Voyd* to you, young man!"

They had reached the far wall. "I *am* sorry about this, Ariette," said Mrs Van Voyd, setting down her little black dog on the ledge. "But I thought perhaps you wouldn't be ready for *backstage* yet."

They sipped their drinks.

"You have a meditative look, my dear. Perhaps you're thinking you *don't* hate her, after all?"

Harriet was thinking about her throbbing foot. But she looked up and said:

"I admired her, I really did – I *do*. She doesn't mean to hurt people, does she?"

Now Mrs Van Voyd appeared to meditate.

"There's a ruthless streak in her, Ariette," she said, after a moment. "But think where she came from. She was born in Stepney – Stepney!" The old woman shuddered. "Everything she's got, she's had to fight for. She escaped the prison of poverty – then, when she was free, along came poor Bunger and dear Peter, wanting to put her in different prisons of their own. They meant well, of course, but – "

A camera flashed again. The little black dog began to bark.

"I have to say, my dear," said Mrs Van Voyd, gently crushing the camera against the photographer's spectacles, "that if there's one person I really *can't* forgive in all this, it's Millicent."

Harriet had to smile. Of course the tragedy at Shadow Black had been impossible to keep from the press. The death of Lord Harrowblest, and the simultaneous murder committed by his long-lost son, had caused a sensation. Reporters descended on the ancient house like locusts. In the anarchy at New Telescope House following the death of Mr Collidge, even the Empire Press showed no restraint. But the worst was to come when the little maid Milly, throwing up her position, rushed to London to offer her services to the Empire's main rival. Her ghost-written reminiscences, *Shadow Black: I Was There*, had enthralled the readers of the *Sunday Watch* for week after week with their lurid 'revelations'. The unscrupulous little maid had even purloined Mrs Van Voyd's box brownie, illustrating the series with the old woman's photographs. Film rights to the series had now been sold.

Already a rich woman, Millicent Untermeyer was now herself the quarry of reporters. Rumour had it that she was presently in Los Angeles, where a leading plastic surgeon was correcting her defective lip.

"Of course, she'll never be accepted in *decent* society," said Mrs Van Voyd. "Crooners and trollopy actresses, that's about her level... But come, Ariette, you must tell me about your studies. You've turned into quite the bluestocking, I believe?"

"Oh, I wouldn't say – "

"What a pity we have votes for women! I can just see you with dear Emmy Pankhurst, shoulder to shoulder and backs to the wall!"

Harriet had to smile again.

"Mrs Van Voyd, there's one thing I don't understand," she said, a little later. "I remember once I asked Mr Travers this question, but it seems even more a question I should ask you. You've lived such a *rich* life. Why did you stay at Shadow Black? Did you love Yardley so much?"

For a moment there was surprise in the old woman's eyes. Then the surprise died away, and she patted her young friend's hand.

"Oh Ariette, I thought you realised. I love the Yard, even now. But I didn't stay for *her*. Do you remember, I told you once there was only *one* of my husbands I really loved?"

Comprehension spread slowly over Harriet's face.

"Yes, my dear – I was Bunger's first wife. He fell out of love with me, but I always loved *him*."

"Oh – " Harriet looked down sadly. "And Peter – ?"

"Peter is my son."

The bell shrilled for the second act.

"Drink up, my dear." And Mrs Van Voyd tossed back her drink, gathered up her black dog, and imperiously began to clear their way back though the crowd.

Harriet gazed after her, numb with astonishment.

"Smell?"

"I don't know – "

"Number?"

"I don't – "

"*Primary* is extension, solidity, number; *secondary* is colour, smell, sound. Stupid!"

It was Locke's theory of the primary and secondary qualities. Convinced that Miss Locke was a descendant of the philosopher, Mr Punch found her sadly wanting. He said that her mind was a *tabula rasa*. Well, really! Harriet had a good mind to tell the nasty little fellow that she was, if he didn't mind, a Cambridge undergraduate. It wasn't every girl who got into Newnham!

"*Ach*, Mr Punch, so rude to our friend." The Professor grimaced at Harriet in apology. A string of spit swung down from his swazzle.

"He's too clever for me," Harriet laughed, but added archly: "In philosophy, at least."

"Of course I am," said Mr Punch, and throwing back his huge nose he strutted off haughtily, his crazed wooden eyes in search of new victims. The Professor, trying in vain to restrain him, had no choice but to follow.

Nurse Becher followed too, silent in her white uniform.

"Such an amusing gentleman," said Mrs Van Voyd. "He and Jelly are inseparable." She winked at Harriet.

Harriet smiled. If perhaps she found the Professor more wearing than amusing, nevertheless she could not help but admire his spirit. He had known experiences of unimaginable horror – and yet, in the end, he could begin a new life. With the help of Mr Travers, the Professor had already presented his unorthodox Punch and Judy show at a festival of 'absurdist' theatre in Paris. In time he would become a cult figure among undergraduates, and later (in the 1960s) a noted performer on satirical television programmes.

For a moment Harriet's eyes followed the old gentleman, whose magnificent beard gleamed like copper wire. Homing for the kill, the jigging puppet on the end of his arm began assailing a society photographer and the beauty columnist of the *Evening Empire* on (perhaps) Kant's antimonies, or Hegel's Absolute, or Bishop Berkeley on the existence of matter.

Except when one looked very closely, one could no longer discern the glue-lined crack around the base of the little puppet's nose.

Mr Travers rippled out a melody.

Yardley's new flat occupied the entire top floor of a massive Georgian edifice in Piccadilly, overlooking the Green Park. It was a happy chaos. Guests milled amongst pots of paint, ladders, tarpaulins, rolls of carpet, tea chests disgorging streamers of packing paper, sofas wrapped in plastic like avant-garde sculptures. Framed photographs of Yardley and framed film posters leaned against walls still pitted and streaked from the removal of old wallpaper. Gleaming statuettes were strewn about with abandon.

"Goodness, who's the Yard holding court to now?" Mrs Van Voyd craned her neck.

"A television executive, a film mogul and an advertising agent," said Mr Travers, not looking up from the white grand piano. "An unholy triumvirate for you, Miss Locke. Oh, and that's a New York publisher sharking up on the starboard side. Offer for the memoirs coming, I should expect." With the fringe of his new toupee flopping over his head, he brought to an end what Harriet recognised already as the love theme from *Mr Punch!,* his work-in-progress.

It was dreadful, truly dreadful.

Harriet gazed through the crowd with a strange, mixed emotion. Earlier that evening, far too briefly, Yardley had pressed the pale girl's hand. *So good of you to come,* the words had floated, wraith-like; *my dear, my darling, so good of you to come.* And away Yardley had wafted, her hair heaped high (coloured golden for the show), a dazzling fur clinging to her shoulders and trailing behind her on the floor. Now, white-gloved, radiant under a streaming chandelier, she stood in the centre of the huge unfinished drawing room, tossing back her head in a throaty laugh, a long cigarette holder poised in her hand.

She had resumed her divinity: the performance had been a triumph, climaxing in a thunderous standing ovation and a stage strewn with flowers. Advance bookings had ensured full houses for three months, but now the revival of *Showbiz Ahoy!* looked set to run for years. Yardley's long absence from her public had made her a bigger star than ever.

"Ariette!" hissed Mrs Van Voyd.

Harriet turned from the dazzling vision.

"Ariette, would you judge me a – *conspicuous* woman?"

"Mrs Van Voyd, what do you mean?"

"Only that I've just seen *Ariette Comber*. God knows why the Yard invited *her* – most frightful bitch in London; has been for four decades."

Harriet glanced furtively towards a vulturous white-haired old lady who scrutinised the guests as if for prey, twirling a champagne flute viciously in her talons.

"Dreadful that she should have the same name as you, Ariette – a kind of outrage. Still, I'd better do my duty. You wouldn't mind holding Aldous, my dear? Baroness Comber is *allergic* to animals – a sure sign of moral and spiritual corruption."

The old woman departed.

"So this one's called Aldous too," said Harriet to Mr Travers. She thought now that the little dog *did* look remarkably like the old Aldous, only black where his predecessor had been white... And did he not *smell* remarkably similar?

There was a moment of misunderstanding. "My dear Miss Locke, I'm not sure what you mean."

"Mrs Van Voyd told me Aldous had died."

"Oh no, Miss Locke – Aldous is dyed. *Dyed*. There's quite a difference, I'm sure you'll agree."

Aldous sniffed eagerly at Harriet's champagne.

"The Professor has rather taken to him." Mr Travers chorded softly. "But he will insist on calling him *Toby*."

"Toby?"

"I wondered myself, my dear – then I remembered. Traditionally, the Punch and Judy man always had a dog – a little terrier that sat on the side of the stage with a ruff around its neck. After the performance it went among the audience, collecting pennies in a bag it held in its mouth... Well, you see, this little dog was always called *Toby*."

He paused, looking contemplatively at the keys.

"Toby must come back, mustn't he?" said Harriet.

It was a question that many were asking. In the lull before Peter's trial the story of his crime had fallen into temporary abeyance. In the meantime the papers seethed instead with the mystery of the 'missing heir'. There were rumours, theories, there were false trails. The abandoned *Bluefinch*, found many miles down the coast from Lightletter, was the only real clue that had come to light.

"Another boy from Toby's school went missing last summer, curiously enough," mused Mr Travers. "Ran off with a young American heiress, on holiday in Tuscany. They were caught within a few days."

Harriet plucked a fresh drink from a passing servant's tray.

"Mr Travers," she said suddenly, "what *will* happen to Peter? He won't – ?"

The little man looked at her kindly. "He won't be *hanged*, my dear, we're sure of that. His *mental condition*, as they say, will be important – and of course we shall all do our best for him on the witness stand. Then... I suppose we shall just have to wait for him."

"Yes," Harriet murmured. "Yes, I suppose we shall."

A hand clasped her shoulder from behind. "Hattie, you look lovely."

Harriet turned, affecting a naturalness she did not feel. She had known this moment would come.

"Mark." There was a catch in her throat.

"Thought I ought to say hello." He attempted a winning smile. Harriet had seen him earlier, in Yardley's dressing room after the performance. But they could not talk there. A crowd had separated them. Harriet had only seen him embrace Yardley eagerly, ardently, for some minutes, crushing an offering of roses against her breasts.

There was an awkward silence.

"So," said Mark, "you went off to Lesbos College after all?"

"Newnham," said Harriet. "It's called Newnham."

"Can't say I see the point – for you, I mean. You're a pretty girl, Hattie." The winning smile again.

Harriet was astonished. Did Mark really think the compliment would please her? Could the man be such a fool? How she longed to scream at him! Couldn't she at least throw her drink in his face?

But no – no. Control, control.

Now, earnest: "But you're happy, aren't you, Hattie?"

Don't call me Hattie. "Oh yes, Mark." Harriet's face was stiff as a mask. "Happier – *much* happier – than I've ever been before."

"Er – I ought to see to the Professor," said Mr Travers, flushed, swivelling off the piano stool. "Nurse Becher isn't always reliable. You'll be all right, my dear?" he whispered.

Harriet reassured him. Turning back to Mark, she eyed him sceptically. He had grown his long dark hair still longer, she noted, and was dressed in a caddishly 'sharp' Italian suit. The fingers clutching his drink and cigarette were circled by several rings and a heavy gold bracelet hung from his wrist. He leaned a hand on Harriet's shoulder, directing her eyes to a willowy man in a gold smoking jacket who held court in a corner, laughing uproariously with a gaggle of theatrical fops.

"That's Pinker Major – Bertrand Pinker," Mark said confidentially. His tone suggested that Harriet should be fascinated.

"The critic who's always been so kind to you?"

"Yes. Would you believe, he made a *pass* at me just now? Said it was time to *call in his debts* – well..." Mark made a rude gesture in Pinker's direction; Pinker, whose back had turned, would not, of course, have seen it.

Harriet set down her drink on the piano; she had begun to worry that her hands were trembling. "You're working on a new exhibition," she offered, her voice flatter than she had intended.

Mark nodded. Harriet realised that he was rather drunk.

"They said in the paper you'd gone back to the old style."

"Old style!" Mark blew out a long stream of smoke. "It's *modern*, my love, you must admit that. *And* it's mine. *Virgin Queen in a Vat of Vomit... Hollywood Actress Smeared in Porridge...*" He laughed; then his lips swooped close to her ear and his hand clasped her shoulder again, harder this time. "To tell the truth, Cousin Hattie, I learned one thing last summer," he murmured. *"Don't change a winning formula."*

Straightening, he stretched up a hand in greeting to Yardley, as she floated through the adoring assembly.

"And you haven't," Harriet said coldly.

"Hm?"

It was too much. Harriet realised she was weaker than she had thought. Grabbing her drink again, she dashed it in Mark's face, smashed the glass to the floor, then slapped him, hard. "You fraud! You pathetic, talentless fraud!"

She blundered away.

"Hattie – " Mark, staggering, gazed after her in surprise. What had got into her? Really... women! And they'd been having such a pleasant conversation, too! He was going to follow her, but was waylaid at that moment by Bertrand Pinker, who had appeared suddenly behind him.

Mark knew where his priorities lay. Smoothing back his long dark hair, he blinked the stinging drink from his eyes, and grinned broadly:

"My little cousin – a bluestocking, you know."

The crowd sucked Harriet back like a tide. At last she pushed her way into a darkened room, and was alone.

She shut the door behind her and lowered the black Aldous to the floor with relief. The window was uncurtained, and in the eerie light from the falling snow she saw that the room was filled with rack after rack of Yardley's gowns. All appeared grey; how strange to think that a flick of a switch should set them ablaze with colour. Of course they would all be magnificent then.

For the first time it occurred to Harriet that Yardley's rooms at Shadow Black would now be stripped and bare. It was a strange thought.

Her heels clicking on the bare floorboards, Harriet crossed to the window. The sash slid up easily. There was no view of Piccadilly or the Green Park here, only a narrow canyon between buildings, a mean place of parked cars and garbage bins and tradesman's entrances. She held out her hand into the darkness. The snow was falling more rapidly now, more thickly, blanketing black London with its white ironic blessing.

Harriet exhaled deeply, her breath condensing to clouds on the icy air. How strange, the way the seasons change! How strange, the way a summer ends! The summer had been filled with mysteries, but in the end, it seemed, all had been explained. It was over, all over. There had been darkness – black shadows – and light had flooded in. But this, Harriet knew, was the merest illusion. Beneath it all there was a secret history. Beneath it all was a hidden key.

The face of Mr Vox filled her mind. Bizarrely, absurdly, the tutor – the supposed tutor – was the one person in the 'Shadow Black affair' who had, as they say, escaped publicity. Even in Milly's series in the *Sunday Watch* he figured only in the most minor role, as the 'journalist based in Rangoon' who had discovered Peter's identity. There was nothing to indicate how extraordinary Mr Vox had been. Perhaps no one would believe it. Perhaps Milly didn't know. But Harriet knew. And what troubled her was not that he had vanished so strangely, not even that he was gone, but that in the end she hadn't understood him, hadn't known what he *meant*, when he was here.

Had he been a devil, or an angel?

Sometimes, alone, in her room at Newnham, Harriet had imagined she could hear his voice, whispering in her ear as he had whispered, so softly, on the day he carried her up the stairs to her room. Had he made love to her, there on the big bed?

She hoped so. Oh yes, she hoped so.

In any case she thought she heard him now, and the words floated around her like her own cloudy breath:

> *As imperceptibly as grief,*

he said,

> *The Summer lapsed away, –*
> *Too imperceptible, at last,*
> *To seem like perfidy...*

Harriet let the tears fall freely from her eyes.

"Ariette, it's you." Mrs Van Voyd clicked the door shut behind her. "I'm in hiding. I'm afraid I threw a full glass of champagne in Baroness Comber's face."

She joined Harriet at the window.

"My dear, you'll catch your death."

"I've been thinking – "

"Hm?" The old woman slid an arm round Harriet's shoulders.

Harriet didn't go on. She leaned back against the ample black breast.

"Dear Ariette – oh Ariette, we shall always be friends, shan't we?"

"Yes – oh yes."

The two women stood silently in the darkness, embracing. Then, after a moment, the old woman said:

"Ariette, where is – ?"

There was a high-pitched growling and a rustle of silk. Aldous had wrestled one of Yardley's gowns to the floor.

Mrs Van Voyd turned to him, relieved.

"Aldous? Goodness me – how *surprising* you are, now you're black."

Appendix: The Films of Yardley Urban

Note
Dame Yardley Urban appeared, often uncredited, in at least forty-four British silents between 1923 and 1929, principally for Famous Players-Lasky (UK operation of the American studio which later became Paramount) and latterly for Gainsborough, Gaumont-British and British International. Many of these films have now been lost, and Dame Yardley's roles were in any case derisory; however, of the extant canon, her supporting roles in the following are of particular note: *Alibi* (Gainsborough-Emelka, 1925), *Jen of the Abbey School* (Gainsborough, 1927) and *Good Queen Bess* (Gaumont-British, 1928). Dame Yardley's leads in *The Young Enchanted* and *Scarlet Woman* (both British International, 1928) led directly to her MGM contract in 1929. After moving to Hollywood, Dame Yardley made no further UK pictures until 1975.

She appeared in only one US silent – a supporting role in *Our Modern Maidens* with Douglas Fairbanks, Jr. and Joan Crawford (MGM, 1929); but Dame Yardley's role ended up on the cutting-room floor and her official US debut was therefore in the early musical *The Dollar Princess*.

The Classic Period: US films, 1930-1942
The Dollar Princess (MGM, 1930)
D'Arcy of the Guards (MGM, 1930)
Hoosier Sweetheart [UK *Gal o' Mine*] (MGM, 1930)
Showbiz Ahoy! (MGM, 1930)

Shadow Black

Ziegfeld Baby (MGM, 1931)
Make Mine Manhattan (MGM, 1931)
Meet Me in Manhattan (MGM, 1931)
Babydoll on Broadway (MGM, 1931)
Baby, Let's Dance! (MGM, 1931)
Boy, Oh Boy! (MGM, 1931)
The Girl is Mine (Paramount, 1931)
Baby, Let's Dance Again! (MGM, 1932)
Broadway's for Me (MGM, 1932)
The Gal for Me (MGM, 1932)
Goodbye Wisconsin (United Artists, 1932)
Maggie My Darling [UK *The Mill on the Floss*] (MGM, 1932)
Lady Audley's Secret (MGM, 1933)
The Heir of Redclyffe (MGM, 1933)
Sweetheart of the Tumbleweed (United Artists, 1933)
The Eternal Triangle (United Artists, 1933)
Slopes of Andalusia (MGM, 1933)
It's Different with Dames (MGM, 1933)
The Golden Galleon (MGM, 1934)
Bel-Ami [alt *Gay Paree*] (MGM, 1934)
Lady in the Limelight (Paramount, 1934)
Mysteries of Udolpho (MGM, 1935)
Virgin of England [alt *Young Queen of England*) (MGM, 1935)
Mother-in-Law (MGM, 1935)
Tell it to the Marines [remake] (MGM, 1935)
Follow That Cab! (MGM, 1935)
That's No Lady – That's My Wife! (MGM, 1936)
Like Sister, Like Brother [UK *The Wordsworths*] (MGM, 1936)
Flowers for the Lady (MGM, 1936)
Ann Veronica (MGM, 1936)
Helen of Troy (MGM, 1936)
Vixen of the Spanish Main (MGM, 1937)
The Queen Was in the Parlour (MGM, 1937)
Beau Monde [alt *The Lady is a Lady*] (MGM, 1937)
Scarlet Woman [remake] (MGM, 1937)

The Revenge for Love (United Artists, 1938)
The Other Woman (Warner Bros., 1938)
Female of the Species (Warner Bros., 1938)
Damascus Road (Warner Bros., 1938)
Sally of the Sawdust [remake] (Paramount, 1938)
Gold Rush Hotel (Paramount, 1938)
That Bovary Woman! (United Artists, 1939)
The Joyful Delaneys (MGM, 1939)
Evil Woman (Paramount, 1939)
Joan of Orleans (MGM, 1939)
Keep the Aspidistra Flying [alt *Let's Fall in Love Again*] (MGM, 1940)
A Family and a Fortune (MGM, 1940)
Tender is the Night (United Artists, 1940)
Love o' the Legion (MGM, 1940)
Ballet Shoes (MGM, 1941)
Worrals of the WAAF (Paramount, 1941)
Brave Little Belgium (MGM, 1941)
Soldier, Soldier (Paramount, 1941)
Our Boys Over There (Paramount, 1942)
Boston Story (Paramount, 1942)

The Later Years: from 1955

During this period, Dame Yardley's activities were principally in stage musicals, cabaret and – most notably – television. In the UK, she appeared in the highly successful variety series *The Yardley Urban Show* for the BBC (1957-1962) and Rediffusion's *Yardley!* (1963-1965). The later *Yardley Urban Show* for the US NBC network was a situation comedy series which ran for three seasons (1968-71). In the 70s and 80s, Dame Yardley made numerous talk-show appearances, most famously with Michael Parkinson in 1977. Her films in this period, including those made for television, were as follows:

Around the World in Eighty Days (United Artists, 1956)
Shh, Sweet Baby, Shh! (Warner Bros., 1963)
That's Entertainment (MGM, 1974)

The Mysterious Affair at Styles (EMI/GW Films, 1975)
Susan Howatch's Cashelmara (ABC television, 1978)
Auschwitz: The Mini-Series (ABC television, 1980)
Airport '81 (Universal, 1981)
Agatha Christie's What Mrs McGillicuddy Saw! (NBC television, 1985)

Dame Yardley also released numerous recordings from 1956 onwards; the best of these may be heard on the compilation *Lady in the Limelight* (Columbia). Soundtrack recordings from the Hollywood years are most accessibly found on Gallerie's *A Portrait of Yardley Urban*, while Columbia's *An Evening with Yardley Urban* is a live recording of her one-woman stage show.

Of the many biographies, those by Alexander Walker (1979) and Donald Spoto (1988) are particularly recommended.

Sir Mark Vardell's many portraits of Dame Yardley are collected in his book *Urban/Goddess* (Phaidon, 1990); the most famous may also be found in *Essence and Quintessence* (Tate Gallery Publications, 1995), released in conjunction with the 'Vardell at Seventy' retrospective.

Dame Yardley's career has also been the subject of academic analysis; for a striking interpretation of *Showbiz Ahoy!* – and valuable bibliographical guide – readers are referred to Professor Harriet Harrowblest's *(Dis)placing the Goddess: The Feminine in Film and Fiction, 1900-1990* (Cambridge University Press, 1992).

Further information, regularly updated, is available on Yardleyworld, official website of the Yardley Urban Appreciation Society (www.yardleyworld.com).

About the author

Tom Arden, who grew up in Australia, has worked as a university lecturer in Northern Ireland and now lives in England. His first novel was *Moon Escape,* written when he was seven, but it was with The Orokon series that he hit the public eye when it began appearing in 1997: a five-volume fantasy epic set in a Ruritanian world halfway between Jane Austen and Mervyn Peake. Now a full-time writer, he reviews regularly for *Interzone,* and is a columnist for the sf, fantasy and horror website *At the World's End.*

Other science fiction from

BIG ENGINE

THE LEAKY ESTABLISHMENT

David Langford   1 903468 00 0   £8.99

Langford's 1984 comedy classic, not at all based on the author's work at a nuclear establishment nowhere near Newbury, with a brand new introduction by Terry Pratchett. Black comedy overtakes the unfortunate defence-scientist hero Roy Tappen when a "harmless" theft of office furniture lands him with his very own doomsday nuclear stockpile at home. Chain reactions of insanely comic escapades follow, with disaster piled on disaster, leading the increasingly desperate Tappen to the borders of science fiction as he seeks a way out of the mess.

   The Leaky Establishment was first published in 1984 to great reviews, and has lost none of its charm since. Terry Pratchett has written a new introduction to take it into a new century.

BAD TIMING & OTHER STORIES

Molly Brown   1 903468 06 X   £9.99

> *One of the most popular contributors to* Interzone, *Molly Brown's short stories are extremely crisp, clever and a joy to read... a collection is long overdue.*
> - SFX

That long overdue collection is here!
   An Earthman's stranded spaceship is besieged by thousands of cuddly aliens whose idea of war is to commit ritual suicide; a teenage princess is kidnapped by an army of undead skeletons; a Chinese demon rides through the streets of Soho; and Toni Fisher tells Joanna Krenski, "I'm

working on a calculation that will show density of shoulder pad to be in directly inverse proportion to level of intelligence. I'm drunk by the way."

From the satire of the award-winning "Bad Timing" to the horror of "Feeding Julie", via the mind twisting paradoxes of "Women On The Brink Of A Cataclysm" and the out-and-out comedy of "Agents of Darkness", these stories from the first 10 years of Molly Brown's writing career show her range and her versatility, and never fail to enthrall. Several of the stories have been specially updated for this collection.

THE ANT-MEN OF TIBET & OTHER STORIES

David Pringle (ed.)   1 903468 02 7   £9.99

Interzone is still Britain's best selling science fiction and fantasy short fiction magazine, and the only monthly one. *The Ant-Men of Tibet & Other Stories* is a brand new collection of ten of its most significant stories in recent years: flamboyant space opera, chilly thrillers, contemplation and comic fantasy. All are by authors who had their first or near-first sales to the magazine and every new story opens up a completely new world with new visions and ideas. This collection is a celebration of the diversity that is British science fiction.

The stories:

- Stephen Baxter: The Ant-Men of Tibet
- Alastair Reynolds: Byrd Land Six
- Chris Beckett: The Warrior Half-and-Half
- Keith Brooke: The People of the Sea
- Eugene Byrne: Alfred's Imaginary Pestilence
- Nicola Caines: Civilization
- Jayme Lynn Blaschke: The Dust
- Molly Brown: The Vengeance of Grandmother Wu
- Peter T. Garratt: The Collectivization of Transylvania
- Eric Brown: Vulpheous

Big Engine

doesn't just publish science fiction. See our web site at www.bigengine.co.uk for details of our novels and anthologies across the whole range of speculative and fantastic writing.

You can subscribe to Big Engine's titles at less than cover price.

Britain's newest science fiction magazine

3SF
**SCIENCE FICTION
SPECULATIVE FICTION
STRANGE FACTS**

Launching October 2002

Published six times a year

Columnists
Gwyneth Jones
Alex Stewart
Rich Horton
Christy Hardin Smith

A subscription for six issues costs £20/$36

See our web site www.3sfmag.co.uk for details